THE GENESIS PROJECT

PART I

TAYLOR STUTESMAN

This is a work of fiction. All of the characters, names, incidents, organizations, and dialogue in this novel are either the products of the author's imagination or are used fictitiously.

Armageddon Creativity LLC
PO Box #81 Howell MI 48844
8104941515
Taylor Stutesman

ISBN: 978-0-9977320-0-9 (sc)
ISBN: 978-0-9977320-1-6 (hc)
ISBN: 978-0-9977320-2-3 (e)

Library of Congress Control Number: 2017913807

Lulu Publishing Services rev. date: 10/19/2017

PROLOGUE

I didn't notice the bus approaching until it stopped right in front of me.

"John." The driver said, greeting me with a nod.

I nodded back as I slid a few coins in the box. "Hey, Andy."

We left it at that, and I took my usual seat in the back. I gazed out the window, looking at everything that passed without actually seeing it. My mind was working over some of the mathematical formulas I had learned about in the morning during my Advanced Mathematical Theories class. I wasn't really paying attention to my surroundings until I heard the news on the radio.

"Prophet Gates' speech today took many by surprise by his announcement that Miracle Children will take up a permanent residency in the cities around the world. He also specified that he plans for these Miracle Children to have a controlling interest in the politics and decisions of the cities. His speech was highly anticipated ever since the Republic of India formally accepted the ruling of the Church last week. With the inclusion of the Republic of India, the Holy Land now covers 80% of the world, marking a milestone for the Church. The presence of Miracle Children in the cities would mean an instant response if the Outside breaks through the Wall; however, the response to this announcement has been unease. While not every city would have a Miracle Child on standby, many of the ones in the Americas are scheduled to have a Miracle Child join them in the coming weeks. The exact cities were not specified. When asked about this decision later, Prophet Gates had this to say;"

The female voice that was coming over the speakers changed into a deeper, smoother voice.

"I have foreseen what is to unfold in the near future, and I'm afraid it isn't one that I hoped. I know this will come to pass, but I do not know when or where. Therefore, as a countermeasure, I will have Miracle Children in several major cities as needed. This is the wisdom granted to me by the Supreme and going forward from here will require dedication to the Supreme ..."

I let it fade back into background noise. Politics rarely interested me, and I wasn't sure I bought that whole fortune-telling act the Prophets put on anyway. The Prophets before Prophet Gates hadn't predicted much at all; yet Gates seemed to get these 'prophecies' all the time, even though he had only been in that position for two years. Prophets were always just regular humans, so why would they be able to prophesize anything?

I took a deep breath and moved my thoughts to the subject that had been the main reason behind my stress for the past few weeks; my future. I wasn't a pessimistic guy, but my future hadn't been looking good lately. I was currently halfway through my second year of community college. I lived alone in a small apartment that took two part-time jobs to afford after my college expenses. I had no girlfriend, only one good friend, and I almost never had any spare money. I had two more years of this stressful situation ahead—eight more at a university if I received a scholarship. The only career that seemed remotely interesting to me was researching ways to expand human's living situation. More specifically, taking steps toward making it possible to live on the bottom of the ocean or on the moon. Living under the constant oppression of the Outside wasn't acceptable to me. Yet, even if I managed to get through all the schooling required, would that career satisfy me? I shook my head and stood up as the bus slowed, approaching my stop. I hated thinking about it, but not thinking about it was worse.

"Thanks Andy," I said as I passed and got a grunt in response.

The district I lived in wasn't one to brag about. It was made up almost entirely out of three or four-story buildings, and a third of those buildings were run down or abandoned. The buildings that were still in decent condition were either used for office storage or cheap apartment housing. The street I was walking down was usually deserted, so I was surprised when I heard footsteps on pavement. I glanced up from the sidewalk, curiosity breaking through my distracted thoughts.

So ... here it was. The moment in a person's life that is pivotal. The moment that, years later, one would look back and say, "that's where it all started." This was it.

But the moment wasn't an experience, flash of insight, or wisdom. It was a person. A person who would make all my previous pessimistic thoughts about my life and future meaningless. A person who would drag me through hell, lift me through heaven, and walk with me in every place between.

When I first saw her, I felt myself immediately become motionless. I never had, and doubted I ever would again, see a woman who had as much natural beauty and grace as the woman before me. She had a pull on me—an almost physical effect as if she was wrapped in gravity itself.

The most predominate feature about her was her dark, deep red hair. No, not red. That's too plain of a description. It was crimson silk. The gentle breeze blew her beautifully long hair behind her as she walked. Her bright, brilliant green eyes made an exquisite contrast against her crimson hair.

She was wearing tennis shoes, which elevated her height by half an inch, but without them she couldn't have been taller than five-six. She wore black jeans, which formed around her legs attractively, and a thin brown belt around her waist was subtle enough that it didn't distract from the natural curve of her body. She wore a white blouse with the top couple of buttons undone; which hinted at her beautiful neckline while keeping her modesty intact. Her face was pale and flawless, with a small nose and full lips. Her eyebrows were drawn slightly together as if she was concentrating or in deep thought. Her body was fit, displaying slim muscle, but she still held a shapely appearance that my eyes found appealing. Her movements held grace and control, even with her walking at the brisk pace that she was, obviously in a hurry to get somewhere.

She was the type of woman that couldn't be ignored. The type of woman that drew the eyes of everyone around her without even trying. She was a woman that could charm anyone with a simple smile; yet her smile was absent from her features. Her eyes, which I couldn't help but attempt to meet, shocked me when I saw them. They were dedicated, emotionless, and fearless; a world of green ice that held very little life at all.

When I first saw her, she was on the opposite side of the street that I was, and was crossing the street towards me. She hadn't noticed me at first, but when she almost reached me, her brilliant green eyes glanced up at me and met my own. In an instant, that wall of ice melted into a variety of emotions that I had trouble deciphering. The emotions flickered from one to the other, too fast for me to accurately read. Her eyes slowly grew wide with surprise, and as soon as that wall of ice had melted she became something beyond merely beautiful. She was attractive. She had a pull on me, a desire to get close her. She came to an immediate halt at the edge of the road less than five feet from me, her eyes completely transfixed.

Time slowed, and seconds felt like minutes as her appearance made my heart beat faster. Her emerald eyes shimmered at me, as if something about me had shocked her. I felt the same, but I realized it was for an entirely different reason. This reason suddenly dominated my mind and consumed all thought; it bled panic and fear, and was dripping with the flight instinct.

Run.

I stared, completely frozen and momentarily surprised by my sudden thought.

She's dangerous.

I couldn't find a definite reason behind this conclusion. Perhaps it was the way she had moved before she noticed me. It was so controlled and precise that it made me think she had a lot of experience with handling her body. Or it could've been her stillness as she watched me. Her legs were tensed, ready to move at a moment's notice. Before I deduced the reason, the logical part of my mind started working again, and I dismissed my immediate impression. She couldn't be dangerous; she was someone who should be protected—I shouldn't be feeling as if I should flee from her.

I couldn't bring myself to look away from her, as if I was afraid that she'd disappear if I did so. Barely three seconds had passed since our eyes met, yet for some reason they had morphed into an almost watery shade of green, as if she was on the brink of tears. As soon as I had that thought, I saw a single tear had fallen from her left eye, slowly sliding down her cheek. Even her sadness had an unearthly beauty to me. It was like she was a painting—a moment frozen in time and perfectly preserved forever.

Her voice came out in a whisper, but her tone was completely sincere, "I'm sorry for your loss."

A cold chill ran down my spine as her words registered in my mind. My breath stopped and I felt my mind suddenly dip into suspicion. Was it a lucky guess or did she recognize me from somewhere?

I was good with faces, and I definitely would have remembered seeing a woman like her. No, there was no way for her to know my past. It was simply a lucky guess. That's all.

I started to reply to her, but I before I could even open my mouth, a deafening explosion sounded from the building across the street. My body tensed up completely, and my eyes jumped from her emerald eyes to the building. We were hit by the shock wave immediately and the woman collided into me. I felt her arms hit my chest as she brought them up in front of her defensively. We were thrown back several feet before landing on the sidewalk. I heard her cry out in pain before we even hit the ground and again after we landed. As soon as the she hit me, I felt pain all over my body. The back of my head slammed into the concrete, and for a moment I only felt intense pain and saw bright flashes in front of my eyes until it all went black. I fell into unconsciousness.

I knew I wasn't out very long, probably a minute or two at most, because the scene around me was still chaotic. I opened my eyes slowly, and clenched my teeth tightly as pain in my head flared. I sucked in air through my teeth and then coughed as I tasted smoke and fumes. I felt cloth behind my head, and sat up slowly to look back at what it was. It was my work shirt, now stained with dark blood, and looking down at my chest I saw that I was only wearing my thin, black undershirt. I knew I wasn't the one who put it there, so my eyes darted around the area, searching.

It wasn't pretty. It looked like no one else had been caught in the blast, but the office building was absolutely destroyed. The explosion had knocked out the front walls of the first two stories, and allowed me to see that the contents of the building had been incinerated. There was still a massive blaze burning inside the building, and there were chunks of the building lying around in the street with glass scattered everywhere. A chunk of the stone building collapsed in as I watched. If there was anyone inside, they were dead. There was no surviving that. I noticed the other buildings next to it were mostly untouched, even though it was such a large explosion. The bomb was well designed. I swallowed; my throat was dry from the smoke. It was difficult to think or focus, and the longer I stayed there the more nervous I became.

My eyes found the woman then. She was starting down a nearby alley, leaning heavily against the wall of a building. She had one arm behind her back, and with a groan of effort, she yanked out a large shard of glass that had been sticking into her. Blood started darkening her white blouse at a rapid rate. Grabbing my bloody work shirt and ignoring my throbbing head, I stood up and headed over to her.

My vision swam and became blurry before fading into darkness. I felt myself fall back down to my knees as pain rushed through my head. I gritted my teeth and waited for it to pass, or at least drop to tolerable levels. I heard the woman give another groan of pain, followed by the sound of glass shattering. I blinked rapidly, trying to get my vision back, and after what felt like ages, the blackness receded. I ignored the pain in my head and began to stand up.

"Hey!" I called out to the woman, trying to stop her from removing the shards of glass that kept her from bleeding out. She had already removed two of the three.

Whether she heard me or not, she didn't respond. She took a couple more steps down the alleyway and started to reach up behind her back again, attempting to get the last one out.

I tried again, this time louder as I approached her. "Stop! You're going to make it worse!"

I knew she heard me that time, but again she ignored me. Her fingers just barely managed to get a grip on the shard. I sped up my pace, trying to reach her before she managed to get it out. I hadn't made it very far before I heard her outcry of pain, and when the shard came free she collapsed.

I knelt next to her when I finally reached her.

"Are you crazy? You've made your bleeding worse by doing this," I scolded her and immediately pressed my already stained work shirt onto her bloody back. I couldn't believe she had the willpower to remove them.

"Get back, John," she muttered back, her tone serious.

I blinked, a little unnerved that she knew my name, but I was more concerned about her wounds. I put pressure on the shirt.

"I said get away from me! I'm not safe and I don't want to hurt you," she repeated. She lifted herself onto her hands and knees. Her voice was rough from all the smoke.

"What's unsafe is you moving around with these wounds," I shot back.

She stood up sharply and took a step away, forcing distance between us. "It's not safe! Stay back!"

She swayed into the wall next to her and started walking forward at a slow pace while using the wall as a guide.

"Where are you going?" I asked, standing up and starting to follow her.

"Anywhere but here," she muttered first before responding in a louder voice, "I need to heal in a safe place. Until then I'm vulnerable."

"You should wait here for medical help. I don't think these wounds are serious, but if you just let them bleed like that you could die," I said, worried.

She shook her head, "I won't die from something like this, and it's dangerous if they find me here."

"Who?" I asked her, taking a quick glance back at the burning building to see if there was anyone there I hadn't noticed. I didn't see anyone, as expected, and I looked back to her.

Her green eyes bore into mine for a short moment, "do not let anyone find me. Please."

I swallowed at her intensity, but didn't reply. She looked back down the alley, and continued her slow pace away from me. Her breathing was becoming more and more labored as she went. I started to wonder if she was being paranoid from the shock of her current situation.

I walked up next to her. My head still hurt, but my strength was returning steadily. "At least let me help you."

She flinched away from my outstretched hand, making me stop in my tracks.

"Don't touch me, John."

Her green eyes were serious and strong, even though her body seemed so frail.

"You're hurt. You shouldn't try to do this alone," I stated.

She shook her head, "you don't understand."

"What don't I understand?" I growled in annoyance.

Her panting was getting worse, and her face started to get flush, "This isn't from ... the wound ... I don't know ... what's happening."

She slowly slid down the wall to the ground, and sat with her legs tucked underneath her and her back against the wall. She rested there for a moment, breathing heavily with her eyes closed. Then she sucked in a rapid, deep breath and her green eyes opened again, showing determination.

"Get up, Miranda. Stand," she hissed, ordering herself to move.

She braced her hand against the wall behind her and started to push herself up.

I held out a hand in front of her, "you should stop pushing yourself like this with a wound like that. You'll only hurt yourself more."

Why wouldn't she just let me help her?

She shook her head sharply once as she panted through clenched teeth, "you don't understand. I ... I need to ...."

Then her eyes closed, and she fell forward into me. I caught her, and even though she was unconscious, she still panted heavily against my shoulder.

Well now what?

I thought about taking her back to the site of the explosion. The medical team should be arriving in a few minutes, and she could get treatment there. I remembered her emerald eyes, and how firmly they mirrored her belief that she was in danger. What should I do? Could I trust the pretty redhead, or did I have to go with an obvious, logical choice? Did one of these choices kill her, and the other save her? Or was my choice here completely unimportant?

My mind was starting to panic as my indecision held me in place. She should see a doctor. I knew this. She had three large cuts in her skin that needed to be cleaned and stitched. I looked at the blood stain on the alley wall as my thoughts whirled. From all the blood she's lost, she could probably use a blood transfusion too. Yes, I should take her to get medical attention.

But I felt one of her hands clenching my shirt in a fist, her body instinctively reaching for help and protection. I felt her rapid, hot breath on my shoulder.

I sighed. Who was I kidding?

I swept her legs over my left arm and wrapped my other arm around her back, gripping her upper arm for support, and pulled her against me. I managed to place my shirt between her back and my arm, attempting to slow the bleeding. I stood and turned my back on the explosion site.

Dammit. I couldn't go against what she had wanted. I wanted to trust her, but I wanted to save her too. So, I would do both to the best of my ability. I knew I was a sucker for a damsel in distress, but this was ridiculous even for my standards. No, that wasn't entirely true. I knew what choice I was going to make even before I had to make it. This was me. This was my choice, and I'd bear whatever followed.

The rest of the walk to my apartment building wasn't difficult. It was only a block away, but when I arrived I had to carry her up three flights of stairs. The landlord was either too cheap or too poor to repair the elevator that had been out of order for the past eight months. She was light, and it normally wouldn't have been difficult to climb the stairs like this, but my head wound started pounding painfully as my heart rate increased. I ignored it as best as I could, and managed to reach my apartment

The apartment I rented out was small and affordable. As soon as you enter the door, you stand in a short, narrow hallway that empties out into the largest of the two rooms that make up the apartment. The room was primarily a kitchen, but the other half of it doubled as a living room. The doorway on the left of the kitchen leads to my bedroom, and the bathroom is through there as well. The entire apartment has a thick, soft carpet in all the rooms except the kitchen, where the carpet was simply cut away, revealing a steel flooring. Since the building was so old, there had been a wood flooring beneath the carpet, but that had been replaced with steel when the price of natural wood went skyrocketing. The kitchen was almost always cold, but the rest of the apartment was bearable.

Because of how narrow that front hallway was, I had to turn sideways to fit through without hitting the woman's back against the wall. I carried her through the kitchen/living room and set her carefully on my bed before gently rolling her over onto her stomach.

Blood had drenched her shirt, staining the bright white with a dark red. I went to the bathroom and grabbed the first aid box I had under the sink. I set it down on the bed next to her then returned to the bathroom and got a bowl full of warm water and a rag. I returned to the woman and started to clean her wounds and stitch each of them up. I put gauze over the large wounds, and then started removing the numerous small shards of glass that had impacted her back. There were over a dozen of them total, but by God's grace they didn't penetrate too deeply into her skin, and I was able to pick them out easily with a pair of tweezers. Once that was done, I wrapped an additional large bandage completely around her waist and stomach to keep the thicker gauze on her wounds, and to cover her smaller cuts.

My own wound didn't stop bleeding until I was almost done. It wasn't bleeding very fast, but I kept feeling it drip down my neck and soaking into my shirt.

I couldn't help but wish that this didn't happen to her—that I could've prevented her from getting injured somehow. If I had known ….

I shook my head at the thought. No, there was no way for me to have prevented this. I knew that, but it didn't really make me feel better. I took a deep breath after my work was finished and shook off the exhaustion that was beginning to tug at the edges of my mind. My body wanted to rest and heal, but my mind wanted answers.

I set the first aid kit at the bottom of the bed, thinking I would require it to change her bandages tomorrow. Hopefully she'd be conscious by then. I tossed the bloody water down the bathroom sink and ran the tap water for a minute to thoroughly clean the rag, then rinsed off my bloodied hands and tended to my own wound. It had clotted up and I was able to wash the blood out of my messy brown hair. And yes, it hurt like hell to do it. I knew I needed a shower, but I was honestly too tired to even attempt it. I looked at myself in the bathroom mirror, my eyes glanced over my untidy brown hair and clean shaved face. I stared at my blue eyes in the mirror, noticing how much they stood out against my lightly tanned skin. Besides my head wound, I was in decent physical shape for surviving an explosion of that size. Of course, that was only because the woman had been in front of me.

She wasn't in danger of dying from those wounds anymore, but I wasn't a licensed doctor. My only medical training was what I had picked up from the Monastery, and that was barely passable. I shut off the water and left the bathroom to look at her again.

'I'm sorry for your loss,' she had said.

I sat down on the left side of the bed next to her, and gently swept her long red hair out of her face to get a better look at her. I definitely hadn't met this woman before; I was sure of that.

What the hell did it mean? Why did she seem so honest then? So sincere? I swallowed and stopped asking questions that I couldn't answer. Her breathing was quiet and peaceful next to me; slow and gentle. It was oddly relaxing, but I realized that I no longer felt the pull her beauty and femininity had on me earlier. Sure, even like this she was beautiful, but the feeling didn't have nearly as much depth as it had earlier. Now it was nothing more than physical attraction, and I could ignore that without much difficulty.

But I couldn't earlier. Not when I saw her for the first time—when her breathtaking eyes stared into my own. Back then, she had my interest in a way that was much deeper than any kind of lust or sexual instinct. I wanted to know this particular woman. I swallowed and shook my tired head. It must have been my wariness that had me thinking that way. Tomorrow would be different.

I stood up and turned to my left to face my small dresser that stood against the wall next to the door to the bathroom. I took off my bloody, black undershirt, and replaced it with a clean black one that had a grayish-white eagle on the front. I immediately tossed my undershirt in the trash, but I held my work shirt out in front of me, surveying it. I sighed as I looked at the blood stains that splattered it. Most of it was from me, but some of it was probably her blood as well since I had used it to try and limit her bleeding. It was beyond saving; I took off my name tag off and tossed the shirt into the trash on top of the other one. I'd have to spend money to replace it—money I wasn't sure I even had.

A jolt suddenly went through my sleepy mind and I looked down at the name tag in my hand. So *that's* how she knew my name.

I shook my head and felt a little stupid. I glanced at the woman one more time before I left, but what I saw made me pause. I noticed a small strip of leather sticking out of the back pocket of her jeans. I must've been too distracted by her wounds to notice it earlier. A wallet? Identification? This could give me a clue as to who the hell she really was. She owed me that at least, didn't she? Maybe there was even someone I could contact for her.

No. It wasn't right for me to go blundering in her personal business. I should wait for her to tell me herself.

I had my mind set on being a gentleman, but before I knew it I ended up gently tugging the leather out of her back pocket.

The leather was folded in half like a wallet, but its weight was much too heavy to be anything as simple as that. I hesitated for a moment, and then flipped it over with a flick of my thumb. Inside was a flat, silver circle with a single gold dot impression in the middle. It was three inches in diameter and a quarter of an inch thick. The gold seemed to have melted into the silver flawlessly, and the top was polished smooth. On the side was cursive writing that had been engraved elegantly into the silver.

"*To the one who can call down Heaven's wrath and wield the Supreme's personal judgment in her hands, I bestow upon Miranda Alexandria Peirce the Title of Skyfall.*"

I stared at it, completely fixated on it as my mind recognized it; a Seal.

I had never seen one personally, but only in pictures. I knew what it was immediately, and the gravity of my predicament fell over me.

God in Heaven. She's an Eve. She was of the kind known as Daughters of Destruction and Holy Demons. She was a warrior, a judge, and a hero—but yet a killer, a monster and a deceiver. She was one of the Chosen.

I stared at her and my heart beat doubled as panic flooded into my mind. An Eve with a Title? Dangerous was right …. People don't even like them brought up in conversations, yet here one was, asleep in my bed. My life was threatened. This woman would kill me.

My eyes jumped from her to the window for a split second, then back to her. The Church had tracked me down. That's why she wanted me to stay with her. I was going to be Judged and Damned. I felt myself take a step back, though I didn't ever tell my feet to move.

But what could I do? I didn't want to go to jail—even though I knew I deserved to. I wanted to avoid that place as much as possible, but that was the best-case scenario for me. The more likely one was my immediate death.

I felt my dark eyes look at her face as I ran through different ways to get out of my situation. She was unconscious and wounded. This would probably be my only chance to end her and save myself. If she awoke, I would have no chance at beating her if we came to a struggle, even with the wounds she had sustained. But I knew I didn't have it in me to kill her. She was a woman, and even if she was my enemy, I was sure I couldn't bring myself to do any harm to her. My guilt and sadness could be my downfall after all.

I swallowed, and after a moment of concentration, my body relaxed. No, I knew my identity was safe. Both the Family and the authorities believed me to be dead. I turned around and headed away from the unconscious Eve. I glanced at the large mirror I had shoved into the corner as I did.

I should've ran.

I shook my head at my reflection. "I regret nothing," I said aloud, arguing against my pessimistic thoughts.

But I might in the morning.

I gave up and walked back to the living room, collapsing into one of the two chairs. I tossed my name tag on the coffee table before I tiredly propped my feet up on it. I tightened my grip on the Eve's Seal in my hand, and stopped fighting off my exhaustion.

CHAPTER 1

Morning came too quickly. I hadn't fallen into a deep sleep and woke up several times during the night. This chair was barely tolerable when I was just sitting, and sleeping was only manageable because I was exhausted.

I felt her touch before I was fully awake, but I wasn't familiar with the sensation, or fully conscious, so I didn't react to it. Her fingers were pushing back the hair on the back of my head, examining my wound. When I moved my head slightly and grunted, I felt her fingers suddenly pull away.

I opened my eyes, then immediately closed them hard. I groaned and sat up straighter in my chair. I rubbed my eyes a few times, and then opened them again. She was sitting on the coffee table across from me with her elbows on her knees. She still wore her black jeans from earlier, but she had changed out of her bloody shirt and now wore one of my plain white tees. It was a little too big since I was broader than her. I knew that she was previously behind me, checking my wound, but I didn't hear her make a single sound when she moved to the coffee table.

I met her eyes, and the desire I felt yesterday came back immediately.

I wanted her to be mine.

I definitely didn't imagine this desire as I thought I had last night, but this time the desire was different. Her emerald eyes were guarded and cautious, making the desire merely a whisper in my mind.

She smiled, and I saw a brief glimpse of excitement in her eyes. "Hi."

Yesterday's events ran through my mind, and the Seal I was still holding suddenly felt like it weighed twenty pounds.

I remained silent and still. My only movement was blinking the fog out of my vision to focus directly on her green eyes. I tightened my jaw to suppress a yawn and took a steady breath through my nose. I didn't want to display how exhausted I still was, which I felt would be showing weakness. It must have been my pride acting out because it didn't matter whether I showed her weakness or not. Compared to a Holy Demon, I might as well be an insect.

Her eyes glanced at her Seal, which I was still holding. "You know, it's not polite to go through someone else's personal belongings."

I felt my fist tighten around the seal, bending the leather around the silver disk.

"Can I have it back please? It's important to me," she said, her green eyes glancing down at it before meeting mine again.

I returned it to her hesitantly. She took it, flipping it open to look at it once before slipping it into her back-left pocket.

"What do you want with me, Eve of the World?"

"What makes you assume I want anything at all?" she asked.

"You could've left the moment you woke up. Instead, you stopped to check my wounds, even before collecting your Seal. And …."

Her words from earlier replayed in my head. The sincerity in her voice is what troubled me the greatest. She had meant it when she said she was sorry for my loss.

"And?" she probed, with curiosity in her voice.

"And I feel like you know who I am," I finished.

Her lips gently curved into a small smile. "I know a lot about you. More than I should; less than I want to."

"Have we meet before?" I replied.

I knew we hadn't, but I was probing for answers. If the Church had a file on me there was no way I'd get out of this alive.

"The first time we ever met was yesterday evening. In fact, I didn't even know you existed until that moment before the explosion, after which you probably saved my life. A fact I'm very thankful for," she said, giving me another small smile at the end.

Manipulator. The thought was sharp and clear in my mind—an accusation made against her.

"I saved you without knowing your true identity. Don't assume I'd do the same now," I replied, my tone lacking warmth.

I was bluffing. After what happened with Rachel, there was no way I could let her come to harm. She knew it, too; I could tell from the way her guarded eyes became slightly softer.

"You're lying to me? Only our second conversation and you already dirty your words?"

I returned the stare she was giving me. "What makes you think I would lie?"

"I know you. Besides, I would never hurt you even if I was able to. You don't have to fear me." Her eyes changed then, becoming unguarded and warm.

"What do you want from me, Eve?"

Her emerald eyes jumped between my own. "You read my name on the seal, didn't you? You don't have to call me Eve."

"So?" I asked her coldly.

"Why are you bothered by my presence?" she asked.

Her tone held a gentle sadness to it, as if she wished I was comfortable with her instead of on edge. I didn't trust it, though. She was manipulating me. It was what Eves did. She didn't care how I thought or acted. It was all done so she could maneuver the conversation to her benefit.

"If you ask any person what you are, they'll call you a hero, but if I ask them what you are, they'll answer 'a monster.'"

She swallowed, and her gentle smile slid down into a neutral mask, but her voice had a small hint of worry in it. "Is that what you think of me?"

I suddenly realized I didn't like seeing the difference in those two personality states she had—the first one, which was excited, interested, but cautious, and the other one, which was unsure and worried. I preferred the first.

3

She's a manipulator. I thought again, but this time it was a reminder to myself.

"I don't know what to make of you. Your abilities keep the populace safe from the Outside, but at the same time you belong to an organization that's as dangerous as the monsters that roam beyond the Walls."

She raised an eyebrow. "You're not afraid to say what you think."

Her comment surprised me. I expected anger, or annoyance. I expected to be rebuked or maybe even Judged. In fact, it made me realize that I *was* being honest. I had originally intended to try and bluff my way out of this … when did I switch to honesty? I also noticed that her tone had changed again, the worry gone as I revealed to her that I hadn't thought she was a monster.

"Should I be?" I asked her.

"Maybe if I was a different Eve. Maybe if I didn't know who you really were."

Who I really was?

"Why do you have an interest in me, Eve?" I asked.

Her jaw set firmly as I saw annoyance quickly flash across her features. "It's Miranda."

I battled with myself in the silence that followed. It was rude to be silent, and part of me was very much against being rude to a woman whom I found beautiful. And intentionally or not, she did save my life. The glass would've impaled me had she not been standing in front of me.

"Are your wounds better?" I asked suddenly, and I regretted doing so immediately.

She smiled a little as the annoyance melted away, and I noticed how her smile seemed to make her eyes brighter. "Yes, thank you. We can recover quickly from physical wounds."

Damn it. I felt like I gave some control of the conversation over to her by showing her I cared about her health. I needed to get it back on track.

"Okay then, Miranda." I paused for a moment, realizing I liked the sound of her name on my tongue. Stupid hormones. "Why are you here?"

"John, I know something about you that will change your life completely," she said.

I replied in an unbelieving tone, "and what's that?"

She looked away from me for a moment, thinking, and then met my eyes again. "Eves have an ability known as the Eve's Gaze. Heard of it?"

I felt unease wash through me, and my eyes dropped to the floor. "I have. It's an ability to see every sin that a person has committed in an instant, all through simple eye contact."

What if she'd seen everything I'd done? My darkest moments and secret thoughts? If she did … I would be Damned. If not for being part of the Family, then for the path of revenge that I went down. I felt my hand gently tighten its grip on the arm rest.

I know you, she had said. What if she really did?

"That's exaggerated, but you're mostly correct. It's a rare ability among Eves, and even rarer for it to happen. And it's not sin that we see, just different memories—the ones that had an emotional impact on you. The 'important ones,' if you will." She held up her fingers and flexed them in quotations.

"And this happened to me …." I guessed.

I forced myself to meet her eyes and tried to keep the uneasy fear from showing in them.

Her eyes searched my own for a moment before she spoke. "I'm sorry. Although it was unintentional, I invaded a lot of your privacy. You don't have to worry about it happening again. It has never happened twice on the same person."

I couldn't say it was okay. It wasn't even a little bit okay. I couldn't forgive her so easily.

"What exactly did you see?" I said slowly, cautious of her.

"I don't need to tell you your own life story, but I saw the moment you learned of your parents' death, the moment a loved one died, and your revenge."

So, she really did see it. Except for the Family—unless she had learned something about my parents, but I had hardly known that much about them when they died. I doubted that she could've gained

5

that much about the Family from that memory, but it was still possible. It was also possible that she had seen much more and just hasn't told me. Regardless, I was going to be Judged soon. I had to escape before then, but how? She outmatched me in every physical way. Wait, something didn't make sense. Why would she check the damage of my wound if she was merely going to kill me soon? She did think I saved her life, right? Maybe this was her way of thanks.

No, that didn't make sense. Eves must stick to the laws, no matter what the circumstance. But instead of Damning me, she may have decided to lessen my sentence to merely imprisonment instead. Either way, I needed to escape.

"Why'd you cry when you saw me?" I asked, stalling for time.

"I have no control over the Eve's Gaze. It works on a select few, and so I'm never prepared for it. Even if I was, I doubt I'd be able to keep myself from feeling those emotions as strongly as I did. They may be your memories, but I still experienced them. During Eve's Gaze, I feel what you felt …. For that moment, I loved Rachel like you had."

I swallowed when I heard her name. Rachel …. What would she say if she knew what I had done? If she knew how dark my soul became? No. I was no longer worthy of her love. I was ashamed.

Yet part of me struggled against that shame.

They deserved it. I did nothing but give them justice. Surely justice isn't wrong? My thoughts argued back. Thoughts that were still infested with a dark fury at the thought of the human monsters that took Rachel from me.

It was wrong. I was merely human; did I have the right to decide who lived or died?

I shook my head and forced myself to stop thinking about it for the thousandth time. It would only depress me. I looked up and saw Miranda watching me, her eyes were focused and her interest captivated. I liked it, but wasn't sure I liked that I liked it. It made me uneasy that her focus was on me so intently.

I spoke up to relieve that steady, curious green gaze. "You said it in past tense, meaning you no longer feel emotions for my memories?"

She looked away thoughtfully, biting her top lip for a moment. "It's strange … I remember feeling those emotions, and as I think back about them I still see them and how you felt. But it's like they're covered in shadows, or I'm looking at them through a foggy window. I know what the memories were about; I can still picture several details about them, but I don't feel as strongly about it anymore. My emotional connection to those memories fades with time, but I'll still remember them."

I was hearing what she said but I wasn't really listening. My mind was running through different scenarios for my escape, but each one was resulting in a worse outcome than the last one. I gave up before she was even done speaking. I had no solution. I had no escape. She had me in checkmate as soon as she woke up before me. Might as well face it head on then.

"Can you do me a favor?" She asked, her eyes glanced away from me for a moment.

I raised an eyebrow. "Excuse me?"

She, the one who was going to kill me soon, was asking for a favor from me?

"I need my stitches out ..." she explained.

"Oh. Wait what?" I asked, momentarily dropping my guarded mental state in my surprise.

"We heal quickly," she stated again.

"Apparently. Hang on." I said.

I stood up and walked to the kitchen to grab the scissors I used to open packages of food. I began washing and sanitizing them when a thought ran through my mind that made me freeze. Why was I doing this for her in the first place? She was my enemy. I shouldn't be helping her when she could be taking my life later.

I glanced at her from the corner of my eye. She had her body turned to one side, subtly inviting me to sit behind her. She was looking down at her knees, momentarily not paying attention to me. Her crimson hair was tucked behind her right ear, and her hands were resting on her knees. She seemed oddly nervous. She was a Holy Demon—a woman so dangerous it was almost inhuman—but in this moment, right now, she was just a woman. I looked down at the scissors, watching the clear water wash over the silver steel. Woman or no woman, she was going to kill me. She was an enemy. I needed to survive.

There was a knife holder on the counter. I knew it was there without even looking at it. I would pass it on my way over back to Miranda. Arming myself wouldn't be a bad idea, but then again, it'd be pointless if I couldn't bring myself to hurt her. I could threaten her, though I doubted that it would work. After all, Miranda called my bluff before; she could just do so again. I swallowed and shut off the water. I had to try.

I dried the scissors off with a hand towel and started to make my way toward her. I felt nervous. My eyes glanced from her to the knives, and then back to her. I was preparing to grab one gently as I passed, but she looked up at me just as I was about to stretch out my arm. I stopped in my tracks, her attention immediately killing my plans.

"What's wrong?" she asked, curious of my reaction.

"Nothing," I said as I continued my walk toward her, leaving the knives untouched.

Damn.

I sat behind her on the coffee table, and shifted the scissors in my right hand into a comfortable position. Her crimson hair was long enough that it almost reached her waist. It had a little bit of dried blood on it from her wounds.

I cleared my throat gently. "Your hair is in the way."

"Oh. Right. Sorry," she said as she reached behind her neck and scooped her hair over her shoulder.

I grabbed the bottom of the white t-shirt she was borrowing from me and pulled it up to just below the middle of her back.

"Hold it there," I said.

She pulled on the shirt from the front, tightening it against her back and making it stay in place. Her three wounds really had been almost completely healed, and there wasn't even a mark where the small pieces of glass had hit her. It was hard to believe that these wounds could be healed like this in just one night. I placed my left forefinger and thumb on either side of her first wound, but when I did her back straightened up slightly. It wasn't very noticeable, but I felt her muscles tense under her smooth skin.

"What's wrong?" I asked.

"Nothing. Just .... Nothing," she muttered.

"Just...?" I asked, my curiosity getting the better of my cautious mental state.

She turned her head to the right to look at me from the corner of her eye. Her green eye never looked right at me, but at her shoulder. Her cheeks were slightly pink.

"Your fingers are cold," she muttered before looking forward again.

Whoa. That was cute.

I blinked a few times before shaking my head. She was an Eve; a Daughter of Destruction. She could kill me as easily as batting an eyelash. In fact, now that she knew a lot of my past, I was sure she was going to do. I can't let myself be manipulated into letting my guard down. I swallowed and looked back down at her wounds. She had goosebumps over her pale skin.

I frowned as her reaction disproved my suspicions. Can't fake goosebumps, can you?

Skin contact with her was ... odd. I couldn't say it was bad, and my pride refused to admit that it was good. Contact with her made the tips of my fingers tingle, but it may have been my imagination.

I tensed my jaw and forced my mind to focus, pushing the thoughts of how Miranda's skin felt out of my mind. I calmly lowered the scissors and cut the stitches, then pulled them out as gently as I could. Miranda didn't complain.

I did most of the work in silence, which was only broken by the sound of the scissors closing as I cut each of her stitches and the sound her calm, smooth breathing. I had just finished the last wound when I couldn't bring myself to avoid the topic that had me stressed any longer.

"So, you saw everything ..." I muttered.

"Not everything," she replied in a gentle voice.

"When are you going to Judge me?" I asked, calmly with a hint of impatience. I was faking it hard, because my stomach felt like a twisted, nervous wreck.

She let go of the shirt she was holding up, and it fell back down covering her back again. I saw her back tense up again, and she held very still.

"Who said I was going to?" she asked in a small voice.

I felt irritated. "Don't play games with me. This is my life we're talking about."

"I'm aware," she replied.

"So, answer my question. I can't beat you if it comes to a struggle."

"Would you do so even if you could?" she asked, looking at me with one eye over her shoulder.

Her stare was serious and calculating, but I got the impression from them that she was guarded, unsure of what my answer was going to be.

I swallowed. "Probably not."

Rachel may haunt me for the rest of my life.

She smiled, and her eyes morphed from that cautious gaze into an intriguing green sparkle. She twisted around so that she was sitting beside me instead of with her back to me. She seemed happy about my answer for some unknown reason.

"What?" I asked, curious and suspicious of the change.

"I made a guess on how you'd respond, and I was right," she replied, giving me a white smile.

I raised a cautious eyebrow. "Well you don't need be so happy about it."

She gave me another smile that faded slowly as silence spanned between us. I felt the need to break it.

"I'd like a straight answer to my earlier question. Are you going to Judge me or not?" I stated calmly.

Calmly? I suppose that's a word for it, but in truth I was just suppressing my fear and nervousness. I hadn't met a Miracle Child before, and if the stories I'd heard about them were true, then it wasn't out of the question to think that this Eve was merely playing with her food so-to-speak.

I know something that will change your life completely.

"No," she answered.

I blinked, a little surprised at how simple that answer was.

"No?" I repeated.

"Nope," she said, a small smile on her lips.

"I don't understand. You've seen what I've done," I said cautiously.

She threw her head back and laughed. It was a strong laugh, loud and sincere, and I found myself liking the sound. She slouched forward then, bringing her hand up to her mouth to try to suppress her laughter, but it didn't really help. As her laughter finally started to subside, her green eyes met mine. "Are you actually trying to convince me that you deserve to die?"

I looked at the floor. "Don't I? I personally killed two people, and I chased a third out of Chicago, probably resulting in his death."

"Do you want to die, John?" she asked. Her tone had turned serious.

I shook my head. "No, I don't."

"Then what's the problem?"

"The problem is I don't understand your reason for sparing my life. I am a murderer."

She hesitated. "I would've done the same if I was in your shoes."

Gee thanks. A monster understands how I feel.

"That cannot be your sole reason, or you couldn't properly judge anyone. And besides, you have the legal authority to kill anyone at any time. I don't."

I looked up at her when she didn't respond, and I saw a sad smile on her lips as her green eyes were locked onto her own patch of floor.

"You're quite intelligent, aren't you?" she stated.

I wasn't sure if she was mocking me or complimenting me.

"What are you hiding from me?" I asked.

"I'm not hiding it, I'm just unsure of how you'll react to hearing it … If you were more open minded, you probably would've already reached the theory that explains all my actions."

"Explain," I said, feeling irritated again.

"Think about it," she started, her voice low and somber, "what would explain all this? Why would I not only dismiss your crimes but also discuss so much with you? Why would my excuse be something as simple as 'I would have done the same?'"

11

"What are you getting at?" I asked, not bothering to keep irritation out of my voice anymore.

"The Eve's Gaze doesn't work on normal people. The person's brain has to function differently than the average guy on the street."

Work differently? How does one's brain function differently from another? Did she mean the way I thought? My thought processes? No that didn't make sense. Personality perhaps? How could that affect the Eve's Gaze? No, I couldn't see it having an effect. Wait, she said average guy ...

I shook my head.

"It's true."

I stared right into her eyes. "I'm not one of you."

I saw her swallow, then her mouth twitched in a nervous smile. "But you are, John. You're a Miracle Child, and my Adam."

I shook my head and looked down at the floor. I leaned forward, resting my elbows on my knees, and tensed my jaw. Me? An Adam? Impossible. I wasn't like them. I wasn't a cold, guiltless creature of absolute confidence in my judgment. I was human. I was me, nothing more than simply that.

"I don't know how you weren't found when you were tested on your twenty-first birthday, but you're definitely an Adam."

"... Impossible," I muttered as my mind started racing.

My body was tensed, and my vision was locked on the floor, though I wasn't really seeing it. I grasped my hands together tightly until my knuckles turned white. It's true that I hadn't tested positive on my twenty-first birthday, but that was because I wasn't tested at all. During that time, I was on the Outside, and when I re-entered the city I had a fake identity in place already. Only Vivian, my oldest friend, knew of my circumstances, and when I explained everything she agreed to keep that secret. Even so, I didn't feel anything like how the media describes Adams. Cold, fearless, unwavering, doubtless ....

Then again, the media wasn't exactly perfect on their descriptions of Eves either; unless Miranda really was putting on a show to manipulate me.

"What does this mean if you're correct?" I asked her, still staring at the floor.

"I am correct, John, and I have to take you with me to the Academy," she said, her voice calm and steady. "Your life here is over."

I shook my head once. This can't be real. "You can't be right."

"I am," she said, her voice ringing with a deep confidence.

I looked directly at her green eyes. "I cannot be one of you. It doesn't make sense—I don't have any abilities or Miracles."

"Only because you haven't used them yet. You're definitely an Adam."

I looked back down to the floor as my mind struggled to get a firm grasp on the situation I was in. I refused to believe it. Even if I didn't have a Miracle, I wasn't a perfect person that Miracle Children were.

"It's impossible, Miranda. You've seen my memories ... I'm not sinless. I'm not guiltless."

"Who said you had to be?" she asked.

"Adams and Eves are supposed to be sinless."

"No, we aren't. We are forgiven from them all as the Supreme's Chosen, but that doesn't mean we don't feel guilt for committing them. However, because you are a Chosen, you did have the right to place Judgment on those men you killed."

I hated this. I felt she was wrong, but a little part of me wanted her to be right. No, a huge part of me wanted that, and very badly. My internal moral struggle against my actions has been only a burden to me. It was incredibly tempting to agree with her merely so I didn't have to live with that burden any longer. But I resisted that feeling.

"Do you have any visible proof that I am an Adam?" I asked her.

"I need none. There's not a doubt in my mind that you are one."

"But I need proof. I can't completely change my identity based on your word alone," I said.

She didn't reply immediately, and from the corner of my eye I saw her hand slowly inch towards my arm. She hesitated above my forearm for just a moment, and then lowered it gently. Her touch was almost electric, making my entire arm tingle pleasantly. It was a supportive gesture, and a kind one. It surprised me, coming from an Eve.

Her voice was tender, and was the gentlest tone that I have heard from her yet, "I know that, and if you'd accompany me to the Academy, we can have you properly tested. You can see for yourself."

I swallowed, and then pulled my arm very slightly closer to me. She got the hint instantly, and her hand retreated out of my vision. I didn't pull my arm away because her touch was unpleasant to me, but because it was the exact opposite.

"I don't want to go there, Miranda," I said.

Her green eyes stared at me with a mix of emotions that was hard to identify before glancing down to the floor. Her crimson hair slid out from behind right ear as she leaned forward, resting her arms on her knees.

"Why, John? Why are you fighting so hard against me?" she asked.

"We've grown up in different worlds. You had the Church, where you've been raised with the understanding that Eves and Adams are solid, just, unwavering forces of good. I was raised by the rest of the world, and their opinions and views of you are completely different. They fear you, and mock you while your back is turned. I ... I'd be lying if I said I hadn't had those same thoughts. I don't want to go to the Academy because I'm afraid that you'll turn out to be right."

There was a moment of stillness in the room before Miranda spoke again. "Do you hate me and my kind?"

"No," I answered immediately. "It's just .... If you're right, that would mean that I am an Adam, and I don't want to become like the Adams I've heard about. Cold, ruthless, and emotionless ...."

"I see ... It's true to an extent that some Adams became that way. They have to carry a burden I have never fully appreciated until very recently."

She claimed the rumors are wrong. I had thought that it was a possibility.

I looked away thoughtfully for a moment before asking, "Are you going to take me to the Academy by force?"

"No. I won't. You can choose to stay here if you'd prefer, but I ask that you come with me."

"And what happens if, when I get there, I'm tested positive? My entire life gets reorganized. I'm shoved into doing whatever they want, my own goals and ambitions are completely ignored."

She looked to the floor again, "I know that.... Normally, you are given several freedoms that allow you to pursue your desires, but in your case, you've accidentally already made those choices."

"What choices?" I asked her.

There was a small hesitation before she answered, "I shouldn't say."

"Why?" I asked her, my voice slightly frustrated.

Her green eyes met mine again with confidence. "Because your guilt will influence your decision, and I would rather you come willingly, not because you think you should."

My eyes jumped back and forth between hers as my mind tried to figure out the mystery she was keeping from me.

"I think it's fair that I should know all the facts before I decide. Otherwise I may regret choosing one way or the other."

"But telling you may influence you in a direction that's against your desires," she replied.

I realized that I wasn't going to be able to convince her this way, so I switched tactics based on a hunch.

I spoke gently, and just loud enough to be heard. "Please, Miranda?"

Her eyes jumped back to my ugly, stiff carpet. "Don't ask me like that, John. Part of me already wants to tell you."

My voice turned serious. "I have to know, Miranda."

She raised her head up just enough for her to meet my eyes with a sideways gaze, looking through a small split in her curtain of hair. It was an odd look, coming from her. I actually found it damn cute, with the contrast of her bright green eye against her dark, almost blood red hair. The odd part was that it was a shy action, and I would never have assigned the word *shy* to a Daughter of Destruction.

She closed her eye after seeing my determination. She took a deep breath, then tucked her hair back behind her ear and straightened. I could tell that I convinced her.

Who's the manipulator now? I thought bitterly, but I had to know what she was keeping from me.

"Adams and Eves can pursue one of two types of careers; War

and Law. Those who choose the War career are the ones on the front lines, fighting the Outside whenever a Wall is breached or keeping the Outside restrained during a city expansion. They are also used to combat anarchy and threats to the Holy Land. They're specialty and advanced training revolves around survival and war tactics. Those who choose the Law career, however, are the investigators. They are the ones you'll see in the cities, and their jobs vary greatly. They can be assigned to solve crimes that the World Police couldn't, or do long stretches of undercover work to infiltrate and annihilate entire underground organizations. They may weed out political and corporate corruption or Judge in a courtroom case. A rare few in the Law careers even go down paths of researchers or scientists.

"These careers, although separate, can be interchanged if the need arises. For instance, even though an Eve of Law isn't as specialized or as experienced in combat as an Eve of War, she may need to assist the War groups in a city where a Wall has been breached. I am an Eve of Law, and I was investigating the surrounding crime structure in this district when I met you."

"Okay, that's a little confusing but why would you hide it from me?" I asked her.

"I'm getting to that. Eves and Adams are connected by more than just a simple emotional relationship. They are connected in a physical way, making them invulnerable to the other's abilities. This is done by the Adam giving some of his blood to the Eve, and the Eve adapts, linking them permanently together."

I looked away from her eyes, my mind starting to guess at where this was headed. Fan-flipping-tastic.

"Somehow, during the accident, your blood got in my wounds.... So now, if you test positive, you'll have to have me as your Eve, and become an Adam of Law."

I grabbed my fist and squeezed it. "Are you sure this happened?"

"I can feel it," she said, looking down at the hand she had set on my arm.

I thought back over the chaos of yesterday. When did it happen? When I was stitching her wounds maybe? I know my head wound was still bleeding then, so I suppose it may have been possible, but I thought I kept it clean …. Then again it could've happened any time yesterday. I was bleeding pretty bad, so bad that Miranda had put a shirt under my head before even taking care of her own wounds. Wait a minute ….

"The shirt," I said in my surprise.

Miranda's eyes looked at me questioningly.

"You used it to stop my head wound, and I used it again on your back," I said, realizing that this was all my fault.

Miranda made a hum noise in her throat, showing she understood, and nodded.

I spent a long moment in silence, thinking hard about what Miranda has told me. I didn't want to accept that I could be an Adam, but if I choose not to go it would always be a question in the back of mind, wondering if I was and Adam or not. Besides, I had unintentionally affected her life by getting my blood in her wounds. It sounded like a pretty serious connection, so if I refused to go with her, what would happen to her? On the other hand, if this connection was reversible in any way, the Academy would be the place to find that out.

"So, when do we leave?" I asked in a low voice.

Miranda's eyes jumped to mine, and a smile formed on her lips. "Soon, if that's okay with you. But I'd like to shower first."

She scooped her hair out from behind her and ran her fingers through it, feeling the area that had dried blood on it.

"Gross," she muttered under her breath.

My lips started to tug into a smile before I stopped them. She was an Eve. Remember that.

Her green eyes looked up at me again. "Do you mind if I use your shower really quick?"

I had opened my mouth to tell her that I didn't mind, but I didn't get a chance to before my door was suddenly smashed open. I looked up sharply towards the hallway that lead to the door of my apartment. Miranda reacted much faster than I had, doing way more than simply looking at the hallway in surprise.

First, her right hand shot out to my chest, grabbing a fist full of my shirt as she looked toward the hallway's entrance. She shifted her weight then, pushing down and sideways with her legs, and pushing me with the hand that was on my chest. She managed to slide us both off the coffee table and down to the floor, while twisting her body so that her back landed on top of me. While we fell, she released her grip on my shirt and held out her left hand in front of her. A quick, sudden burst of blue light erupted from the palm of her hand, and when it disappeared, she was grasping a semi-automatic pistol. We landed on the floor just as a tall, strongly built man came from the hallway, holding a shotgun. He had time to spin our way before Miranda fired a shot, which sounded long and loud in the small apartment. Blood immediately stained his black T-shirt on his chest as the impact forced him into the wall behind him, where he then collapsed to the floor. There was a second of silence, and then I heard footsteps running down the hallway outside my apartment.

Miranda cursed softly, switching the grip on her pistol from her left hand to her right. She grabbed the edge of the coffee table and effortlessly pulled herself to her feet. She jumped over the coffee table and raced out of the apartment, chasing down whoever was outside the apartment.

I blinked, and then sucked air down my throat as my heart went into overdrive. Although it was a delayed response, I had finally started to wonder what the hell was happening around me. The first thing I noticed was I no longer smelt Miranda's subtle perfume. The second thing I realized was I shouldn't be missing it. The last thing I realized was how to move my limbs again. I stood up slowly and swallowed, looking around the room once. My eyes fell to the now-dead man, and quickly surveyed him for any helpful details.

He was a large man far away, but as I got closer for a better look he only seemed to get more muscular. He had long, dirty blond hair that was kept out of his face by a bandanna tied on his head. He wore dark sunglasses, a black wife-beater that was stained with blood, jeans and black leather boots. Besides his massive muscles, the only threatening thing about him was the old shotgun that lay useless in his lap. It was well maintained, despite being an old model that was most assuredly outlawed. There was no question that he'd have been an old man by the time he got out of incarceration. If he felt confident walking around with that on him, then he was probably part of the Guards, which was the local crime syndicate in Chicago.

On his upper left shoulder, he wore a tattoo that I instantly recognized. It was a tattoo of an escutcheon—a decorative shield used as a coat of arms—only a handbreadth in size. It had a red outline and was filled with a pitch-black center. Coming out from the darkness in the center of the shield was a fox, who was hunched low and showed its small but sharp-looking white teeth, as if it was threatening the onlooker. It had one paw extended forward, protectively sweeping in eight flawless, blue jewels.

I reached up and gripped my left shoulder as I stared at it. He really was in the Guards, a gang that half of Chicago hated, but the other half loved. They were mobsters and caused trouble and mayhem in the Chicago Lowers, but claimed it was for the independence of Chicago—independence from the Church. Aggression and lawlessness may be their tools of trade, but they protected the cities from other organizations that were much worse. They don't deal in drugs, sex rings, slavery, or anything of the sort, but they insist on a fee from the businesses in Chicago to cover the cost of such protection. That was pretty much common knowledge around this area, and I had no idea what would possess them to break into my place. Unless they were after the Eve—I mean Miranda. If that was the case, then they were just plain stupid to think they were a match for her.

I glanced at his wound, and what I saw made me crouch down for a better look. Instead of there being one hole in his shirt, I found three, all in an almost perfect triangle near the center of his chest. She fired three shots? It had sounded like one, and she fired them that quickly with such accuracy. Hearing how dangerous Eves were was one thing, but seeing it was something else. Then again, from what's said about them, this wasn't the scary part yet.

Miranda returned then. I hadn't heard her, but when she spoke my name I looked up to find her entering my apartment.

"He made it to a vehicle before I caught up to him," she told me.

"Was there only one more?" I asked, curious.

"Yeah; two of them came up here, but they had a ride outside waiting for them."

She walked to the dead body as her green eyes flashed over him, taking in details rapidly.

"Guards, huh?" she muttered.

"Yeah," I replied as I stood up.

She pulled his torso forward and reached behind him. After a moment, I realized she was searching for a wallet or identification. She came up empty handed, and she leaned his torso back against the wall again. She then reached into her back pocket and pulled out her Seal. She pushed on the gold dot in the middle of the silver disk, and when she let go it made a small *beep* noise. The gold dot split apart, disappearing under the silver, and revealed a small sensor.

Miranda plucked a blond hair from his head, and dangled it just above the sensor. A blue light flared up from the sensor, highlighting the blond hair. After a short moment, it gave a *beep* noise and the light disappeared. Miranda flicked the hair back on the body as she continued to stare at the Seal. Another moment passed and the Seal *beeped* yet again, then the gold dot came together, closing off the sensor. She closed the Seal and slipped it back into her pocket.

"I just sent his DNA information to the Academy. It'll be there and already analyzed by the time we arrive," she said.

I looked down at the man. "What do we do about him?"

"Nothing. We've collected what we needed. Someone will call the authorities, having heard my gunshots, but we don't need to concern ourselves with that. The ballistics will come up registered as an Eve, and the case will be closed immediately. Anyway, it looks like I'll have to skip the shower. We should get out of this city as soon as possible."

"Oh, okay," I replied, allowing her to take the lead. I felt useless since I did nothing to help her, but then again, I was comparing myself to an Eve, which was hardly fair.

She shot me a smile. "Then let's go."

CHAPTER 2

As it turned out, Miranda wasn't comfortable in crowds. We had to take a bus to get to Transcontinental Express, which was the nearest airfield that had what we needed, according to Miranda. It took us an hour to reach it after all the stops the bus had to make on its way.

Neither of us talked much. There was only a comment now and then that didn't evolve into actual conversation. I had a hundred questions I wanted to ask her, but I also didn't want to discuss anything in public. Honestly, the entire Church subject made me nervous.

More people got on the bus with each stop, and it wasn't long before the bus was almost full. Miranda got more uncomfortable as we went, and I realized that it was the people around us that had the biggest effect on her. Whenever someone would sit down in the seats around us, she'd become slightly off, as if she was afraid of something happening. However, it was hardly noticeable. If I wasn't already watching her from the corner of my eye, I probably wouldn't be aware of it. Why would crowds bother an Eve? She could kill everyone here in about six seconds.

I leaned back in my seat into a more comfortable position, hoping that if I became more relaxed, she would follow suit. Hell, maybe she was noticing my sideways glances, and that's what was really bothering her. I closed my eyes as I thought about it, feeling relief as darkness covered my eyes. I drifted into a light sleep, dozing in and out of consciousness.

Miranda squeezed my arm gently, "John, we're almost there."

I opened my eyes, slightly disappointed. The trip felt almost instantaneous. I took a deep breath through my nose and sat up straighter. Miranda's composure hadn't improved in the slightest. She was breathing gently through her nose, and although I'm sure nobody else could've noticed, I could tell she was tense. I looked past her, out the window she was sitting next to.

I saw the bus approaching Transcontinental Express' main entrance. The entrance was large and inviting. There were three stone pillars on each side of the pathway leading to the doors, which were holding up a roof to give people shelter while they waited for transportation. The building was also stone, but almost all of the front part of the airport was glass—the reflective kind, making it impossible to see through. Two sets of automatic doors were at the entrance, one labeled "entrance" and the other "exit."

I followed Miranda out, passing by the crowd of people who were waiting to board the bus. She grabbed my hand and led me away from the entrance, weaving us out of the crowd. We ducked behind one of the stone pillars, giving us some small amount of privacy from everyone.

Miranda took a deep breath and let it out slowly, and she visibly relaxed and became more at ease. She swallowed, and I saw a small smile on her lips.

"Are you claustrophobic?" I asked her, curious.

She laughed. "No, I just don't feel comfortable in crowds like that. I like space around me."

"How come?"

"The type of Eve I am .... It's just not easy for me to be so close to people like that." She answered.

"You don't act that why with me," I replied, thinking of how close she was to me at the apartment.

She shook her head. "No, you're different. It doesn't matter if it's you."

I swallowed and looked up past her, no longer wishing to meet her green eyes. Undoubtedly, she was talking about us being linked together—at least, that's what we were from her prospective.

"Anyway, let's get going," she said, turning away from me and starting to walk away from the entrance.

I followed her, surprised that we weren't going inside the building.

We traced the edge of the building, and kept going even after that turned into a steel fence topped with razor wire. It was maybe a five-minute walk before we reached a break in the fence, where a single booth stood. Between the booth and the steel fence were three one-foot-thick steel rods that came out of the ground, preventing any kind of vehicle access.

Miranda approached the booth confidently. The man in the booth was young, maybe my age or possibly even younger. He had the military look down, with buzzed hair and the straight back. He eyed us cautiously as we approached. It made me uneasy to see his military posture show some discomfort. He suspected who she was.

Without saying a word, Miranda stepped up to the window, pulling out her Seal. The gold center spread apart in the same way as before, but this time it projected Miranda's own face. It spun in a circle, revealing all angles of her head. It was a perfect replica.

The soldier snapped to attention. "Ma'am!"

Miranda waved her hand at him lazily. "You don't need to be so formal. Are there any planes available for me?"

"Yes, Ma'am. A Blessed Pair took one yesterday, but we have another that's ready for use."

"We'll use that. Also, if you could please get us a pilot that would be willing to take us, I'd appreciate it. We have some matters that we need to discuss in private, and I don't want to be distracted."

"Understood. I'll have one ready for you as soon as possible, Ma'am."

"Thanks," she said, stepping past the booth and heading toward the two closest hangers.

They were isolated from the rest, and clearly better maintained. One of the hangers was open, revealing nothing but empty space, while the other was closed. There was a single soldier by the small door on the side of the building who eyed us just as cautiously as the man in the booth had. Miranda flashed the Seal at him, but didn't show her identity to him.

He stood at attention, maneuvering the rifle so it rested against his shoulder, freeing up his right hand so he could solute. Miranda moved past him, opening a small door to the hanger next to him. I followed her in, my eyes momentarily blind from the absence of light. They adjusted quickly, and after blinking a few times I could take in some details of the hanger.

It looked bigger inside than it did from the outside. The ceiling was much taller than necessary for the plane that was stored there and there was plenty of unused space.

The plane itself was small, but perhaps it looked that way merely because of the size of the hanger. It had four jet engines, two under each wing. It was the standard white, with "G730" painted in black on the back part of the tail.

Miranda approached the plane without hesitation, and stretched up to reach the handle for the door. It came down gently, stopping about six inches from the ground and creating a small staircase into the plane.

I followed Miranda in, taking note of the leather interior. Everything looked … expensive. Directly to the left was the door to the cockpit, and straight in front of us was the bathroom. Next to the bathroom was a short marble topped counter, which had a deep sink and a large microwave next to it. The marble counter sat atop a cabinet made of polished wood, which had only a single door directly under the sink. To my right was the seating area, which had three chairs, a couch and a love seat. Two of the chairs were stationed across from each other with a small table in the middle. The love seat was directly after the marble counter, facing the hallway with its back against the wall of the plane. The third chair was after the love seat, and was positioned the same as the love seat, with its back against the wall. The couch was at the very end of the hallway, facing towards the entrance. It spanned the entire hallway and behind it was a wall of polished wood. Each seat had chest straps on them, in case of emergencies. The straps were made of padded leather, and were the same cream color of the seats, making them merely a subtle reminder.

"Wow," I said, taking it all in while Miranda walked over to the love seat.

She gracefully took the seat farthest from the marble counter, crossing her legs as she did, "perks of working for the Church. This is considered standard for us. I don't like to talk about it much, but we are pretty spoiled for our services."

"Apparently," I muttered as I took a seat next to her.

I had just sat down when the soldier that was guarding the hanger stepped into the plane, "Ma'am."

"Yes?" Miranda replied, looking up at him.

"We have secured a pilot for you; however, he is rather green at transporting Miracle Children. If you'd prefer, we can get a more experienced pilot to fly you to the Academy, but that pilot isn't set to land for another hour."

"Does the pilot you have available have the training required to make the journey?" she asked.

"Yes, and he has been briefed about the landing procedures, but as I said before, this would be his first time actually flying to the Academy."

"It's fine. Someone's got to be with him for his first time, might as well be us. And it's important that we arrive as soon as we can. Please ask the pilot to join us."

"Ma'am," he replied, then exited the plane.

The door to the hanger closed with a subtle bang, marking the soldier's exit.

Miranda's emerald eyes met mine, "well now that we are all settled and have a moment of privacy, you can ask your questions, John."

For a moment, I didn't respond. It wasn't that I didn't have any questions, more like I had too many.

"Hmmm," I said thoughtfully, "where exactly is this Academy place that we're heading to?"

"Alexandria Academy. It's located on the south, center end of North America. Between Chicago and LA basically."

"Is it a coincidence that it shares your middle name?" I asked.

"Sort of. When I was born, I was tested positive for the genetic capabilities of an Eve. A Minister told my parents that I was going to receive my training at Alexandria Academy. My mother loved the name, so I became Miranda Alexandria Peirce."

"Interesting."

Miranda shrugged. "I guess. Actually, come to think of it I don't know your full name."

"Johnathon Abram Aster," I answered her implied question.

She smiled. "Good to meet you. Anyway, Alexandria Academy isn't exactly an Academy anymore. Its use was originally to train new Chosen, but it was adapted into a base of operations seven years ago, since it had such a central location."

"What should I expect when I get there?" I asked.

"They'll test you first, using your blood. After it's confirmed, they'll scan both of us, making sure that we really are linked together. Then, well, I'm not completely sure. I know you'll have to be trained both mentally and physically. You're intelligent already, and your previous education probably gives you enough to stand on, but they'll test you to be sure. On top of that you'll have your physical training, which is probably going to be the most grueling of your training. Adam's who were tested positive at birth have an advantage, since they can follow a strength program as they age and develop their abilities. You're far behind, and to get on their level it'll be rough. Plus ...."

I blinked, absorbing everything she was saying. "Plus, what?"

She met my eyes and smiled almost apologetically. "Nothing. You'll find out when you get there."

I eyed her suspiciously. "Thanks ...."

Her smile changed into a more natural one. It was almost contagious, and I smiled in return. I felt odd being with her, but mostly because I was holding myself in check when around her. I found her beautiful, and I couldn't let that interfere with my actions. I needed to distract myself. Luckily, a distraction appeared for me.

In our moment of silence, the door to the hanger opened and

closed, signaling someone's entry. We both looked toward the door expectantly, and after a few seconds a man entered the plane.

He was tall, with short blond hair. His short bangs were styled up, making his forehead seem just a little too big. He wore a pilot's uniform that looked new and well-kept; the light blue shirt was stain-free, and the dark black pants had no fading. The shirt was tucked into his black pants, and a black, leather belt was tight on his slim waist. His attire was wrinkle free and pressed, giving him a very sharp appearance. His sleeves were rolled up just past his elbows, and his shoes couldn't have been better polished. His face appeared long already, with a long and skinny nose, but seemed even longer when you combine his spiked hair and his partially open mouth. He seemed to be out of his element.

"M-Ma'am. Sorry to keep you waiting." His voice was stressed.

"It's quite alright. Can I trust you to deliver us to the Academy without incident, Clyde?"

"Oh God! It's true what they say about you! Miracle Children really are telepathic!" he said with a pale face.

Miranda raised an eyebrow. "I'm sorry?"

"My name ... you knew it ...." Clyde said, taking a moment to gulp loudly.

Miranda laughed. "I don't need Miracles to read your name tag."

He glanced down at his shirt, where a silver name tag said *Clyde* in black.

His face turned red, but relief was clear in his eyes and he gave a nervous laugh. "Oh, I should have known better ...."

I know how you feel. I thought, remembering how Miranda said my name when I first met her.

Miranda smiled at him kindly. "It's okay. I'd like us to take off as quickly as we are able to. I know the landing procedures at the Academy are both strict and complicated, so if you need any assistance don't hesitate to ask."

"I'll get us off the ground right away, Ma'am, and I feel confident about landing at the Academy. I will need your authorization at the appointed time though."

"Of course," she said, giving him a gentle smile.

"Ma'am. Sir." He met both of our eyes, and then entered the cockpit.

Even though his eyes did meet mine, I still saw fear and cautiousness in them. Was he afraid of us?

I voiced my question to Miranda.

"Weren't you also when you first met me? Superstitious rumors cause the biggest rift between us and the rest of humanity."

"I wouldn't say afraid ... more like ... cautious," I said, my pride feeling a little put out.

She raised an eyebrow and smiled gracefully. "I bet I could scare you if I tried."

I didn't doubt that.

"While we're on the subject, what exactly can you do?" I asked.

She hesitated, then lowered her voice, "I'd bet you're more afraid of what your own capabilities could be than you are of what mine are."

I stayed silent with my eyes glued to the floor. The more I thought about what she said, the more I agreed with her.

"I wish I could relieve some of that worry, but I truthfully have no idea what you are capable of doing. Miracles that Adams possess work differently than those of Eves. Adams can only use a single power, but that power is completely under their control. And it's genetic, meaning you don't get to choose what that power is. It can be as harmless as having a perfect sense of direction, or as dangerous as making things explode at will."

Damn. That wasn't very helpful at all. At least it meant I only had one problem to worry about and not a bunch of them. Still, the fact that it could be anything troubled me a great deal. If I was an Adam, I had a feeling my miracles wouldn't be the perfect-sense-of-direction kind.

I felt Miranda slide over the foot of space that separated us, and felt a hand run along my left shoulder. "John, it'll be fine."

Her voice was smooth, and somehow it was a comfort in my ear. I rebelled against that feeling. I didn't know her, and she didn't know it was going to be fine. I had a power in me that was unknown, and it was a dangerous combination. I killed people out of revenge for taking a loved one from me, and now I could have an incredibly dangerous power to control? It was a cruel joke. I couldn't control myself when I was just a regular human, but if I was an Adam and lost myself to that dark fury again … wouldn't the result be much worse?

If this was true, and I really did have an unknown and potentially dangerous power inside me, shouldn't I distance myself from everything and everyone that I might care about? I knew how easily it was to delve into my hatred, and I was afraid of what I might do to someone near me.

"John," Miranda said, gentle impatience laced in her voice.

No, that wasn't accurate. I was afraid of what I might do to *Miranda.* I might hurt a woman, albeit unintentionally. I might hear her scream the same way Rachel did.

"Johnathon," she said again.

I met her eyes this time, but my mind was still working hard on finding a solution other than simply hoping that I wasn't an Adam in the first place. I came up empty.

"I've seen your memories. I can guess what you're thinking now and how worried you are. I've seen how little you trust yourself, but I can tell you with certainty that it will be fine. Trust me. I'll be here with you, regardless if your power is gentle or frighteningly powerful. I have 25 years of experience with the Church. You couldn't ask for a better mentor."

But she couldn't know that it'd be fine. Memories or no memories, she hadn't truly seen me, had she? She'd only seen what I was through my own eyes and thoughts, and in those thoughts—in those moments, it didn't feel wrong to kill them. I didn't feel that I was in the right either; I had no sense of right and wrong. I had no just cause or righteous campaign. I didn't care about any of that. I burned with anger, and all I could feel was a desire to see Rachel's murderers destroyed. She hadn't seen me from the outside at that time. She hadn't seen what I saw in the mirror after it was all over had she? No. She didn't know me.

But what if she did? I searched her green eyes for an answer to my unspoken question. I needed to be more cautious around her. I needed to keep a tight control over my actions. I couldn't let people near me right now. Not anyone that might get close to me. If I become someone as dangerous as an Adam, and a person that was close to was taken from me again, I might not stop with a body count of only three.

A noise sounded outside the plane. It was electrical, and reminded me of a motor running. I looked out the window behind us and noticed sunlight creep into the hanger.

"It's the just hanger doors opening," Miranda said, answering my unasked question.

I needed a distraction, or I'd continue to think about all this and eventually be drowned by my thoughts. It always ended that way.

"Twenty-five years of experience, huh? Damn how old are you?" I joked.

She smiled and rolled her eyes as she removed her hand from my shoulder, "since I tested positive at birth, I was a part of the Church from the day I was born."

Huh, so she's a year older than me.

I looked back at her. "I have more questions to be answered."

"Ask away."

"Tell me more about this Academy."

"Like I said before, it used to be where newborn Adams and Eves were to start their intellectual education, as well as sharpening their moral compass. Basically, every Eve and Adam grew up there. But seven years ago, they adapted the Academy into a base of operations, but they never changed the name. What exactly do you want to know about it?"

"Hmm ... you lived your entire childhood at the Academy?" I asked.

"Yeah, but it wasn't as bad as you might think. They allow parents to be with their child for the first ten years, and since my father had a high rank in the Church, he could visit me often after that. And I was able to go home most holidays."

I heard the jet engines start up outside the plane, and shortly after we started moving forward, out of the hanger.

Miranda and I lived entirely different childhoods. I looked around the plane as I recalled that she had said this was standard for her. Her childhood was pampered, safe and instructive. It might've been tough without her parents being there all the time, but at least hers were alive. Mine ... well they weren't.

I was practically living on the streets since I was eleven. My parents died, and since they had no relatives, I was on my own. The Guards lent a helping hand now and then, but I learned early on that if I wanted to survive, I had to take what I needed. Only the lucky get what they ask for, and that seemed to include simply asking to work for what I needed. At least, that was my philosophy until I had met Rachel ....

"John?"

I snapped out of my daze, and met her eyes. "Hmm?"

"You've been quiet .... Are those all the questions you had?" she asked.

I took a deep breath. "You wish."

She smiled. "Keep going then."

"You said Eve and Adam's miracles work differently. If that's the case, what can Eves do?"

She sighed, "Of course you'd ask that question again .... While Adams have complete control over their Miracle, they only ever have a single ability, so their versatility totally depends on what they can do with that Miracle. On top of that, there hasn't ever been two Adams with identical Miracles. They could be similar, but not identical. Eves, however, all have the same basic Miracle, but some of them have an additional ability."

"I'm lost." I admitted.

She smiled gently, but it didn't meet her eyes. "This is what we can do."

She held out a hand in front of her, palm up. An electric blue light flashed for a mere moment, and when it disappeared she was grasping a long, silver dagger in a tight fist.

"What the hell ...?" I muttered, my eyes tracing along the perfectly smooth blade. It was polished so perfectly it looked like a silver mirror. She had used the same trick back at the apartment with the gun.

She flipped it in the air, and caught it by the flat of the blade between her thumb and fore finger. She held it out to me.

I moved to grab it hesitantly, my mind trying to make sense of her Miracle. It was made completely of silver except for the handle, which was of a black leather, making it more comfortable to hold. My hand brushed along the bottom of the handle, feeling the cool and smooth touch of the silver turn into the rough yet warm feel of the black leather. It was heavier than it looked, but well balanced.

As soon as I brushed the silver, I felt a rush of static go down my arm that made my hair stand on end.

"That's a neat trick." I met her eyes again, feeling impressed.

"That's only scratching the surface of what we can do. I can summon any weapon or tool that is at my disposal, be it swords, spears or even ballistic weaponry."

"How?" I asked, rubbing my finger along the edge of the blade carefully.

"It's complicated, but it has to do with our blood. We can teleport objects with it."

I whistled. "That could be useful."

I felt the plane start to move forward, exiting the hanger.

"It is. But there's a downside; I must picture what the item is perfectly. I have to know it's weight, what it looks like, how it makes me feel, how I use it—everything. The hard part is it's all relative to my own experience, which means I wouldn't be able to summon a sword I coated with my blood without getting to know that sword. Otherwise, when I teleport it to me, it would be misshaped or only half of it would arrive. Some Eves even name their weapons to help them keep it organized."

"Do you?" I asked, handing the dagger back to her.

"Some of the more complicated ones I do, or my favorites," she said, taking the dagger back.

"So where do you store these weapons?" I wondered.

"Alexandria Academy houses a couple hundred storages for Eves. Mine is stored there, completely secured and under protection. They're containers, each one linked to an Eve, and able to be transported if needed. However, I doubt I'll ever need to move mine."

"Why not?"

"If the location is destroyed, I couldn't summon any of those weapons, and it takes a great deal of time to replace a weapons storehouse like that. Really all it takes to prevent me from summoning one of my weapons is scraping some of my dried blood off the weapon."

"Oh, I see. So, it's your weakness."

"One of them, yes. The container itself can be moved, but there's risk involved with that as well."

I felt the plane start to pick up speed, and it wasn't long before the plane tilted upwards, leaving the earth behind. We stayed still until the plane stabilized.

"There's also something else you should know about our connection," Miranda stated.

"And what's—" I started to ask, but was cut off when Miranda suddenly stabbed me with the dagger.

I shouted out in surprise, leaning away from it as quickly as possible, but it was slow and sluggish compared to the grace and speed with which Miranda wielded the blade. The steel tip hit my shirt, piercing it effortlessly, and I felt the cold tip hit my skin with enough force to rip through my ribs—but it didn't. I could feel the pressure of it, and by all rights it should be halfway into my lung right now, but it was harmless against my skin.

Miranda leaned forward with a mischievous smile on her face. "We are immune to each other."

"And you couldn't just say that?" I asked, breathing deeply as my heart beat started to slow back down to normal levels.

She shook her head, "less fun. Here."

She flipped the dagger back around, and I took it once more. I poked my thumb a few times, each time going harder to see if it'd break my skin.

"I can sorta understand that we were immune to each other's power, because we, uh, exchanged DNA or whatever, but this is just a dagger. Why doesn't it pierce me like any other dagger?"

"Because I stored and summoned it. It's filled with my power and became a part of my Miracle the moment I stored it," she answered.

"Weapons that only ever hurt your enemies, huh? That's pretty neat," I said.

She made a single, humorless laugh. "As if our Miracle is that convenient."

I raised an eyebrow. "What do you mean?"

She pursed her lips together thoughtfully before responding. "You are immune to my Miracle and I am immune to whatever your Miracle will be. You will also be immune to your own Miracle, but I am not immune to my own Miracle."

"Meaning?"

She gave a nod at the dagger in my hands. "That can cut me."

I felt my eyebrows furrow together as I tried to understand that reasoning. If receiving my blood made her Miracle—and in affect, her weapons—unable to harm me, why couldn't it do the same for her?

"That's stupid." I replied.

She laughed. "It is what it is, John."

I twisted the dagger around and held it out for her to take.

She reached out and tapped the dagger's handle with her finger. The dagger instantly vanished from my hand, and it sent a gentle electric feeling down my fingers. I looked up at her in surprise. She smiled softly at me, then her gaze left my eyes and moved to the floor.

Silence settled between us. I knew it was intentional. She wanted me to process everything she'd told me so far. I had gotten a lot of answers, but I still had no idea what my future held in store. There were still a few things that I was curious about, but hearing how confident she was about me being an Adam and seeing how that dagger of hers couldn't hurt me at all added a bitter taste to my mouth. I let the silence pass by undisturbed, hoping that the taste would go away.

It didn't.

The fact that I was immune to that dagger was extremely convincing evidence that I was connected to Miranda, and regular humans cannot become linked to Miracle Children. Still, even with that demonstration, part of me refused to believe it, as if this was all just one elaborate joke.

The silence spanned on, and I started to get slightly uncomfortable, but it was then that Miranda moved. I felt her fingers gently touch my left forearm that was resting on my leg. I watched her hand trace my arm down to my wrist. She turned my hand so my palm was up before slowly threading her fingers between my own. I looked at her to see her already looking at me. Her eyes were steady and fearless, showing unwavering confidence. I watched her lips form into a small but graceful smile before I returned my gaze to her green eyes.

It was hard to think in this moment, but I still found myself asking, *why?* Why was she so comfortable acting this way? And, more importantly, why didn't I remove my hand from hers? The world labeled her as a monster. Yet—in this exact moment—the only thing I could see her as was beautiful. The plane shook as it hit some turbulence, and Miranda broke eye contact from me. She looked out the window behind me.

"Something wrong?" I asked, looking at her curiously.

"No …. It's nothing," she said, meeting my eyes again.

A moment of peace spanned, and I felt her thumb softly rub against my hand. Her presence was starting to affect me, slowly melting away the stress and tension I felt. It wasn't very long before another shock of turbulence went through the plane, this one more jolting than the last. Miranda's hand tightened in my own, and when it was over she looked back out the window again.

"First crowds, now airplanes. Anything else you are afraid of?" I asked.

Her eyes narrowed playfully. "Afraid? Hardly. They both merely make me uncomfortable."

"Uh-huh," I said in a disbelieving tone.

"It's true," she stated, "but to answer your question, yes. I'm terrified of fire."

"Really?" I asked, my curiosity peaked.

She nodded gently. "I received third degree burns all over my right arm when I was young during a training accident. As you can see, I completely healed myself to the point where it appears to have never happened, but ever since then when I'm around fire, it's usually all I can think about. I watch it from the corner of my eye, as if I'm afraid of it jumping out at me and hurting me again."

"Interesting. I didn't think Eve's would be so ..." I hesitated.

"Human?" she suggested.

"I suppose that's one word for it," I answered.

She shrugged gently. "It seems to be a common misconception about us. We may have a few more tricks up our sleeves, but at the end of the day we are still flesh and blood."

"Is that so?" I asked rhetorically.

'Still flesh and blood' ... I suppose. Yet I doubted that they earned the titles of Holy Demons and Daughters of Destruction with only a few more tricks. No matter what she may wish for, she will always be separated from the rest of humanity. It wasn't her fault. She was what she was, and after meeting her I could easily see myself being comfortable around her. But that was only after I spent time with her, and even having done so there's still a mental gap I've placed between us. Even with her hand in mine, I couldn't help but think that I was on one side of the fence, she was on the other. The only thing that's changed for me so far was how I viewed her side of the fence. But if I really was an Adam ....

I tensed when the plane shook yet again, this time much worse than the others. I got an odd feeling near the pit of my stomach, sort of like the feeling you get when a vehicle goes over a dip in the road too quickly.

I looked toward the cockpit without expecting to see anything useful, but was just following an instinct, "did you feel that?"

"Yeah ..." Miranda said with a cautious voice.

She reached past me, toward a small steel speaker that was built into the side of the counter that I hadn't noticed when I took my seat. She pressed the small white button on the bottom of the steel.

"Clyde, do you copy?" Miranda asked politely, then let go of the white button.

"Yes, Ma'am. Your timing is excellent." His voice was a little different than earlier, seeming even more nervous than when we first met him.

"I felt something odd with that last bit of turbulence. Is everything alright?"

"Um, I'm not exactly sure. It's odd, as you say. I haven't made any changes in our speed, but we seem to be both slowing down, as well as losing altitude. It's happening extremely slowly, and I think one of our engines is malfunctioning, but my diagnostics keep coming back fine. As far as my instruments are concerned the engines are in good condition, but the way the plane feels makes me think otherwise."

"What's the risk?"

"Minimal. I'll just have to keep a careful eye—"

The plane lurched downward, as if protesting to Clyde's assessment. Miranda's hand tightened against mine, and I grabbed onto the counter next to me for support. The plane stopped falling a few seconds after it started. Silence filled in the cabin, with both Miranda and I practically waiting for it to happen again. I heard my heart pounding in my ears.

The way the plane dropped felt incredible wrong. It wasn't as if the nose of the plane went down at all—we stayed perfectly level, in fact—but it was as if the entire plane was jerked straight down all at once.

Miranda took a few shallow breaths. "There's no way this is as simple as an engine problem."

I took several deep breaths as I battled the panic that had flared in my mind. I had a feeling that this plane was going down, and my mind was suddenly dominated by a single goal—protect her.

I reached around her and managed to pull the seat straps over her shoulders before she grabbed my left wrist, stopping me.

"I can do it myself, John. Get yourself strapped—" she was cut off when it happened again.

This time more aggressively, making us lose altitude even more rapidly than the first lurch. I flew out of the seat, hitting my head on the ceiling of the plane. Miranda pulled me back down to my seat by my wrist that she was still grasping. I grabbed the seat straps and rushed to put them on, fumbling with them for a few seconds before finally managing to get them tightened down.

The engines grew louder, and random items started flying around the cabin of the plane, no longer held in place by gravity. We were in free fall. The plane was shaking violently, and I could hear the metal straining to stay together.

"John!" Miranda shouted to me, trying to be heard over the chaos.

I met her green eyes, which were steady and matched her strong expression.

"We're going to crash," she stated.

I couldn't help but think, *no shit.* But I still managed to understand her meaning. I was panicky and flustered, but there wasn't anything I could do to fix this. The only thing left to do was to steady myself and brace for impact.

The metal *screeched* loudly, hurting my ears. With a final, deafening *bang*, the plane broke in half, separating us from the cockpit. Air rushed in, blowing violently in the cabin, and tossing Miranda's crimson hair in and out of my field of vision.

Miranda reached to me and grabbed my hand. Her grip on mine was tight, and even though she hadn't shown it, I got the impression she was as scared as I was. Or, at least, as half as scared as I was.

We started spinning, tumbling, and rotating. It was hard to concentrate on anything beyond holding on for my life. I saw bursts of green forest turn into glimpses of blue sky from the gaping hole where the cockpit used to be.

How ironic that I chose to go with Miranda in part out of fear for my life, and it was that choice that would kill me.

We collided with something. I felt the plane give a sharp jerk, and with a neck-wrenching impact we stopped falling downward, bouncing up in the air once before returning to the ground. We were going backward, with the tail end of the plane carving a path through the jungle. I closed my eyes out of reflex, waiting for us to come to a stop, and several rough jerks later, we did. Abruptly. My vision faded to black rapidly, and I was out cold before I knew what happened.

CHAPTER 3

When I first opened my eyes, I didn't know what had happened. It hurt like hell when I slowly lifted my head, and I suddenly felt dizzy. I closed them sharply, and I had to take a moment to make sure I didn't vomit. I breathed slowly and determinedly through my nose, calming myself as my memory inched its way back into my mind.

My head was throbbing, and it hurt to move my neck in any direction. I clenched my teeth in silence, the only noise was my breathing and the ringing in my ears. I waited for the pain to dull. It took a few moments, but eventually I could open my eyes again.

Oh, right. Airplane crashed. It felt like something was trying to burst its way out of my forehead, but I savagely pushed the pain back and forced myself to look around. The plane was on an angle. It wasn't completely upside down, but enough that if I undid my restraints I would fall to the other side of the plane. I could see green brush and forestry as I looked out of the gaping hole where the cockpit used to be attached. Some of the windows of the plane were cracked, but none of them shattered. There were bits of green leaves and plants scattered around the plane's interior, but as far as crashes go I thought the plane looked to be in pretty good shape.

I blinked as my memory suddenly gave me an important name. *Miranda.*

I looked to my left immediately, looking for her.

Miranda was clenching her teeth, and I didn't need her gentle outcry to tell me that she was in pain. My hearing still wasn't recovered completely, making the sound a lot quieter than it should have been.

"What's wrong?" I asked gently, getting concerned.

"Shoulder's dislocated," she hissed between her teeth, her face set with concentration as she battled with the pain.

I took a deep breath, starting to think about our situation. I regretted it a moment later as it seemed to make my mind yell with pain.

I swallowed and forced myself past the pain, slowly forming a plan. "Okay. I'm going to get down first, so I can catch you when you come down."

She nodded in response, but her jaw was tense with pain. I released the straps supporting me and slid off the love seat, falling about four feet before landing on the side of the chair across hallway. My legs were weak, and when I landed they gave out immediately. I had to grab the rim of the table to keep myself from collapsing completely.

"John?" she asked through her teeth, worry somehow making it through the cloud of pain in her voice.

"I'm fine," I replied, trying to sooth her.

I set my feet onto some sturdy footing and slowly stood. I steadied myself as I tried to ignore the jabs of pain that assaulted my head, and then looked up at Miranda.

Her green eyes met mine. I saw pain in them, and seeing that made my desire to help her flare.

"I'm ready," I said gently, holding out my arms ready to catch her.

She breathed deeply a few times, then unbuckled the middle strap that held the two shoulder restrains together. She used her left hand even though she was right handed which made me assume that her right shoulder was the one dislocated. She gave a sharp, quick cry of pain as her weight shifted fully upon her shoulder straps, which put pressure on her right shoulder. She used her left hand and shrugged awkwardly out of the right shoulder strap. Her body rotated to her left, having lost the support of the right strap. She kept herself in the seat by holding onto the seat strap with her left hand. She had her legs up, twisting her body sideways and in a perfect position for me to grab onto her. She was holding her entire body up with a single arm.

40

Her right arm continued to swing limply at her side, and she let out another cry of pain, this one longer and louder. I hated that sound, it twisted my gut and made irrationally furious. I gently grabbed her right arm and raised it so it rested on her stomach, putting her elbow on a 90-degree angle. It took a lot of the pressure off her shoulder, and her cries of pain ceased. I placed my hands under her back and under the back of her knees. I felt the tight slim muscle under her clothes, and I felt a wave of awe momentarily wash through me. Damn, she was a lot stronger than her slim muscle made her appear to be. It was a subtle reminder of how much more powerful she is compared to a normal human. I bet she could hold that position for an hour.

She slowly lowered herself down to me as far as she could, then prepared herself to let go. This was the hard part. I had my arms outstretched to reach her body, but as a result, I didn't have nearly the strength I would've if they were closer. She let go of the strap, and I couldn't support her weight with my arms fully outstretched. I jerked her towards my body to keep from dropping her. I managed to keep her in my arms, but her shoulder impacted with my chest, and she gave a cry of pain.

"Sorry, sorry," I said, furious at myself for a moment.

Her jaw was clenched tightly together, but she shook her head in forgiveness. I got off the chair I was standing on as smoothly as I could, and walked out of the hole in the plane. I glanced around swiftly, looking for any possible threats before I focused on treating Miranda.

The plane had slid along the forest floor until it smashed directly into the trunk of a huge tree. I could see the path it carved, stretching almost a half-mile long. I glanced at the plane behind me.

It was absolutely trashed. Both the wings were missing, only leaving the dented tube we rode here. There was no fire I could see, or any smoke rising from the debris. It just lay there, completely still and silent, as if the crash happened years ago—not minutes. The forest around us held the same stillness, as if it was watching us.

I walked over to the nearest tree, and lowered Miranda to the ground so she could lean against the trunk of the tree.

"We have to fix your shoulder," I spoke gently to her.

She nodded in response, still trying to keep her pain under control.

I grabbed her limp arm by the wrist with my right hand and her elbow with my left. Contact with her bare skin sent static through my hands and up into my arms, but it didn't hurt at all. I had only been shown how to set a dislocated shoulder once, and that was a few years ago at the Monastery. I knew the theory, but I hadn't done it personally.

I held her elbow against her ribs while I lifted her arm to a 90-degree angle. I bent her arm out away from her without moving her elbow until I felt pressure and heard Miranda suck in a sudden breath from the pain. Then, I moved her elbow forward, bending her arm and tensing her shoulder. Miranda gave a sharp cry of pain, and then she exhaled with relief. She leaned into my shoulder, breathing deeply.

"Thank you. That feels a lot better," she breathed.

I put my arm around her gently. "You're welcome."

She stayed that way for a minute, and then straightened. She stood up, rolled her right shoulder around, and then began stretching her arm gently.

"It'll be sore for a while. Maybe a couple of days." I said, standing too.

She shook her head. "No, I'll be fine in a couple of hours. You're a great doctor."

She winked a green eye at me as I rolled my eyes. It had more to do with her being an Eve than it did with how I set her arm. Still, I was surprised at how good her mood was, considering our plane just crashed in the middle of ... oh shit.

"We're Outside." I muttered, fear starting to cloud my mind.

"I know," she responded with a serious tone.

"What do we do?" I asked.

"We weren't in the air that long, but it was long enough that we won't be able to get back to a city before nightfall arrives. We're okay right now, because there are fewer predators during the day."

I already knew all of this, having surmised this myself. "But what do we do when night comes?"

She hesitated. "... Let's find a way out of here before that happens."

I took a deep breath and surveyed the silent forest around us. "So, what's the plan, then?"

"If we had the front of the plane, we probably could contact the Academy for assistance. If not them, then at least the city."

"Can we use your Seal? You said it sent information to the Academy," I suggested.

"My Seal isn't strong enough to reach the city, let alone Alexandria Academy. It normally reaches out to a tower in the city and then uses that to send the information to the Academy. Besides, even if it could reach the city, it could never penetrate the Wall. We need the equipment on the plane that's powerful enough to reach someone."

"But we have no idea where that part of the plane is. It could be a dozen miles away in any direction," I argued.

She started pacing, thinking. After a short minute, she nodded. "Okay."

"Okay what?"

"Okay, we have to know where the other half is. I need to get a good view of this place to be sure." She looked at the huge tree the plane crashed into.

The trunk was massive, easily thirty or forty feet in diameter. There were no branches for the first eighty to one hundred feet up.

"You can't be serious," I stated, looking back at her.

"It's the only way, John. Otherwise we're practically guessing."

"Still, you'd be crazy to attempt to climb that without any equipment. I don't think we should be so hasty to try that."

She took a step closer to me and looked up at my eyes. I felt myself tense as I mentally locked down; making sure that my attraction for her wouldn't affect any of my actions.

"It's sweet you're worried about me, but I'll be fine. It's not a hard thing for an Eve to manage. Here," her hand gave off a flash of blue light, and she held a pistol in her hand, "this place is dangerous, and you might need this. If I hear a shot go off, I'll come down as fast as I can, but it may take me a minute. You have fourteen bullets, so make them count."

I hesitated. I felt that I should to be the one going up, but that was impossible for me. Her logic was right, but that just made me feel more helpless.

"Fine," I agreed, taking the pistol she offered.

It was heavier than it appeared to be, and touching the steel sent up a current through my arm, just like the dagger did. It felt solid in my hand, and I felt less uneasy with it.

She turned and re-entered the plane we came out of, and began rummaging through the cabinet underneath the sink.

I looked up at the tree that towered above me, surveying it for possible dangers. Miranda returned to me, strapping on a small GPS to her wrist as she did so.

"Be right back," she said, shooting me a smile before turning toward the tree.

Her hands flashed blue, and in each of them she held twin, identical short swords, each one a polished steel with gold trim along the slim, silver hilt. They were elegant blades, which matched the graceful strides she took toward the tree perfectly. She took a deep breath, and then crouched down, bending her knees lithely. Her muscles tensed. Not just in her legs, but her entire body. Legs, arms, back—everything. She was as tense as a coiled spring, but grace still seemed to gently hum out from her skin. Then she jumped, letting out a small grunt of effort.

She passed the first ten feet in a blink of an eye, and didn't start slowing down until she was well over twenty-five feet high. It was just past thirty feet when she had reached the apex of her jump. There was a moment of stillness when she ceased going upward but hadn't started falling yet, and it was in that moment that she arched her back and slammed the small swords into the tree. They sank all the way to the thin hilt, catching her before she started to fall. After hanging there for a moment, she hoisted herself upward. It was a graceful movement, controlled and precise, and she maneuvered herself until she was standing on the blades instead of hanging off them. She leapt upward again, but because of her position she couldn't manage the height she could last time. She peaked at maybe fifteen feet—still an impossible jump for anyone normal—and with a flash of blue the twin short swords vanished from where she jumped and reappeared in her hands. She sunk them into the tree again, and repeated this process. I lost sight of her after she got around the first branch, and by then she was already only a dot on the tree.

So now I was alone.

I began pacing, waiting for Miranda to return with a plan. I wasn't afraid of my surroundings, merely cautious. I'd seen the dangers that lurked within the Outside with my own eyes. I was alone back then too. Alone and furious. I was just one predator among the others.

But it wasn't so this time. I wasn't hunting now. I was surviving. I was prey, and with the condition I was in, I felt like an easy target. My head pounded painfully with each step I took, but I tried not to think about it. This was not a place anyone wanted to be, pistol or no pistol. The animals that lived here were as mutated as the plant life. Thanks to us humans, nature now had much sharper—much deadlier teeth.

I heard nothing but the sound of my footsteps. Nothing echoed in this place. The silence radiating from the trees and plant life devoured any noise generated by me.

I waited, and time passed. Minutes slid by like hours, and it wasn't long before I took a seat against the same small tree Miranda and I had sat beneath earlier. I looked up to the canopy, hoping to see Miranda on her way down, but I saw nothing.

More minutes passed by, and I let my mind drift off into meaningless thoughts. The pain in my head was finally getting softer, at least.

Crack!

I was on my feet instantly, the steel of the pistol suddenly feeling heavy in my hands. It sounded like a branch snapped in half as something had stepped on it. I was barely breathing, and I tightened my grip on Miranda's pistol. I took a few steps forward into the small clearing. I didn't want to be near the edge of the forest for fear of getting flanked. I steadily surveyed the green forest around me, searching for any sign of something out of place. I kept looking in circles, being as quiet as I could while straining my ears for another sound. I heard nothing, but still … I knew something was here.

I could feel its gaze on me. It knew I was here, it knew where I was, and I got the feeling that it could kill me. I knew because I've been a predator myself. I've hunted and killed. I knew what it was like to stalk, and whatever was stalking me now gave me a deadly chill.

It growled then, but in the thick growth around me I couldn't tell where it originated. It was a throaty, rumbling sound that made the creature sound big—very big.

I had the pistol in front of me now, pointing at anything my eyes focused on. My pulse raced, making a *pound, pound, pound* sound in my ears. I was breathing through my nose, taking shallow but quick breaths. The pistol in my hand was steady—completely opposite of my nervous mind.

I didn't like being the prey. Not even slightly.

I walked backward until I was fewer than ten feet from the tree Miranda climbed. My eyes searching the area, but they found nothing.

I couldn't see it, I couldn't hear it, but I knew it was about to strike, and that I was about to die. My heartbeat was deafening as my body stayed completely still and tense, ready to react at any sign of danger.

I heard something hit the ground next to me on my left. It was gentle and subtle, but in my high tense state it sounded like a cannon blast. I dived into a roll away from the sound, and came out in a kneeling position. My mind recognized her crimson hair in time to keep myself from aiming the pistol at her.

She immediately noticed that something was wrong, and after only a mere glance at me, her eyes darted around the area, searching for a threat.

"What is it?" she asked quietly.

"Something is here … or at least it was. Sounded pretty big. And hungry."

Miranda's eyes swept our surroundings slowly, and then she lowered a hand to the ground.

"You couldn't tell if it was hungry or not from its sound," she argued.

I raised one of my eyebrows at her and retorted, "it was assumed."

"I don't sense anything. It's either very good at stalking, or it left.

Food as easy as us isn't exactly plentiful in the Outside, so I doubt it's the latter."

I muttered a curse under my breath, "... that's just fantastic."

"We have to reach the front of the plane before dark. It will have an even greater advantage then, since its senses are better than ours."

"Did you see where the plane was?"

"Yeah. The giant pillar of smoke helped. It's north of us. I marked it on the GPS so we should be able to find it."

A thought suddenly occurred to me. "Hey, couldn't the Church find us using the GPS?"

"Potentially, but I doubt they even know we crashed. Either way, we should see if the pilot survived."

I nodded in agreement. "How far away is it?"

"Not too far, but since we have to fight our way through the forest .... It's going to take a few hours," she said as she looked at the GPS.

I looked upward, trying to see the sky through the massive canopy. "Do we have that long?"

I heard her hesitate before answering, "we can reach the plane, yeah. But by the time any assistance would get here, I'm not sure. It'll be close to dusk when it arrives. Unless we hurry and keep up a good pace, we'll be in here during nightfall."

"Then let's go," I answered.

She glanced at the GPS, and then turned north. Or what I assumed was North. It was hard to tell without seeing the sun. A blue light flashed, and she held one of the twin swords she used to climb the tree. She started chopping her way through the thick brush, and I followed behind her, making sure I kept free of her swings. Even though they couldn't hurt me, it was just instinctive to stay clear from the blade.

The pace Miranda set was a good one. I never had to struggle to keep up, and it was fast enough that we were making good time. At the start of our hike my head pounded painfully, but it dulled down to where I could ignore it as time passed. It wasn't long before I was able to relax more, and I tucked the pistol that Miranda gave me in my jeans, having no other place to store it.

We traveled that way for almost an hour, stopping every few minutes to recheck our bearings. I kept my senses focused on the area around us, on the lookout for the beast that had stalked me earlier, but I hadn't sensed anything. I hoped that was a good sign, even though the realist in me knew that it probably wasn't.

Then things got weird.

We came to a sudden break in the brush and dense jungle to a very quiet section of bamboo. The weird part about these bamboo trees was that they stood straight up perfectly, without even the slightest lean. They also were spaced apart about 2 feet from each other without exception, with only soil in between the trees and no other growth. It was too neat in this messy place. It screamed unnatural. I looked to my right and left, seeing how far this patch stretched. I couldn't see terribly far, but it was far enough for me to realize that going around it wouldn't be a quick task. Miranda stayed still, surveying the forest of wood with careful eyes.

"I don't like it," I muttered to her.

"Me neither," she agreed.

"We should go around. It doesn't feel safe."

"No time, John. Look at it, it just goes on and on. It could be a mile wide for all we know. We have to try to cut straight through it."

"Miranda," I said hesitantly, not sure on this plan.

She met my eyes. "John, we don't know for sure if there's any danger in these trees, and if we don't get to the plane by nightfall, our survival rate decreases dramatically. This isn't like when you went Outside. You were still relatively close to the Wall, but we're miles away now. It was a miracle you survived out there, but that's a picnic compared to this."

She was right, and I knew it. But I couldn't shake that feeling …. *Something isn't right here.*

"Besides, you said that our stalker sounded big, and if that's the case it won't be able to follow us and stay hidden. We'd see it through the gaps in the trees. This is our best chance to lose it, or at least confirm that it's following us."

I sighed. "Fine. But I seriously don't like this. It's going against what my every instinct is telling me to do."

Miranda looked at the trees in front of us. She reached out and gently touched one of them.

Nothing happened.

She pulled away from it, then knocked on it one with a rap of her knuckles. Nothing happened to her, and as far as I could tell the tree didn't move a single inch, but the vibrations it made gave off a strange humming noise. It was similar to the sound that's made when a thick cord stretched tightly is suddenly pulled back and released. The sound from the bamboo didn't last longer than five seconds as it faded back into silence.

"… Well that was weird," I muttered.

"Yeah …" Miranda agreed thoughtfully.

"Are you sure about this Miranda? If we double our pace we might find a way around this."

"I know, John, but I doubt you could keep up of we go any faster. You don't know how to use any of your abilities yet, and with the thick terrain I just I don't think it's worth wasting our time. We're cutting through."

"Fine," I grumbled.

"Try avoiding touching the trees. I don't know what's causing their strange growth or their odd response to force, but I think it'd be best to avoid disturbing them just in case."

I took a deep breath. "Okay. If we're going to do this, we better get going."

She nodded, and stored her short sword with a flash. She started forward, weaving her way gracefully through the trees.

She didn't so much as brush one as we went deeper and deeper into the forest of bamboo. She moved with smooth grace and delicate control. I, on the other hand, would bump a plant in my rush to keep up with her. Nothing would ever happen to me, but Miranda heard every time I bumped one, making it appallingly obvious how clumsy

I was compared to her. We walked for a good thirty minutes. Every now and then we'd come across areas where the bamboo trees were snapped and trampled, as if something massive had fallen out of the sky and then trampled around on a rampage. We didn't stop to investigate, pressing onward to save time. My eyes had been drifting over Miranda a little too long, and I forgot to look where I was stepping. I tripped, almost falling over completely before I managed to regain my footing, but not before knocking into two or three bamboo trees.

Miranda looked over her shoulder and shot me a smirk. "Really?"

"Well we can't all be you, can we?" I shot back playfully.

Her smirk turned into a smile and she raised her chin a little. "I'll have you know that I worked hard to be this coordinated."

I raised an eyebrow. "'Coordinated'? I guess that's a word for it."

"Oh? And what would you say it is?"

"A gift from the Supreme himself," I muttered in an annoyed, yet teasing tone.

She snorted delicately. "Yeah, okay. We better keep moving."

I started to follow her, but was distracted when a tree behind me made that odd noise, as if someone had touched it. I whipped around, staring hard at the motionless tree. It was over three feet away, definitely out of my reach.

"Seriously, John. You have to be trying to do it this much," Miranda's tease reached my ears, but I didn't reply.

I could hear her soft footsteps continue to advance. She didn't stop, and I didn't blame her for it, but something was … off. Did I imagine it?

I looked forward again. "Mir—"

I cut myself off and froze as I found a big pair of yellow eyes staring directly at me. It was small, and at first glance I thought it was some kind of monkey, but after I took in more than a glance, it seemed less and less like the case.

The beast was clinging to the bamboo tree next to me, hanging upside down as its eyes met mine. They lacked any fear or aggression, and the only thing I could see in them resembled curiosity. Its basic shape was that of a lemur, with four legs and a long, slender tail. Its head was a little too small for the size of its eyes, making the creature appear wide-eyed at all times. Its face was completely flat, except for the small, pointing nose that was strutted out sharply from its face. Its mouth was small and tightly shut—in fact, if it wasn't for the small dark line, you wouldn't have been able to tell that it had a mouth at all. Honestly, the only thing that was seriously odd about this creature was its skin. While it's face was a light, fleshy-pink color, everything beyond that wasn't fur or skin at all, but pitch-black scales. I had never seen a creature like it, and at first glance it shocked my body with fear, which was immediately joined with caution.

It blinked at me, and I blinked back as I struggled to figure out what the *hell* this creature was.

"John …. What is *that?*" Miranda asked in a hushed voice. She must've turned around when I said her name, but I didn't dare to look away from the creature.

"I have no idea," I muttered back, staring at the creature curiously.

It blinked again.

"Most of these creatures haven't even seen a human. It's probably trying to decide if you're a threat," Miranda said.

"Yeah. Sure. Or maybe it's trying to figure out how edible I am," I muttered back to her, attempting to be humorous.

"Now that you mention it, that's more likely," she agreed.

"*What?!*" I hissed at her.

"Just stay calm. I'm within striking distance if it makes a move." I saw a gentle flash of blue from the corner of my eyes.

The creature reacted to the light, and its head flashed over to Miranda before turning its eyes back onto me again. It was a fast movement. Extraordinarily fast. So fast I wasn't sure I saw it move. Its body stayed still, and its head had moved a complete 180 degrees around to see Miranda, before turning back to look at me.

"… Well that was spooky," Miranda muttered.

"No shit," I agreed.

"Alright, John. Just edge around it, but don't hit any of the bamboo trees and don't break eye contact with it."

"Easier said than done," I muttered.

"Maybe for you," she joked.

I smiled, despite my current situation.

I started to circle him, keeping my body facing toward it. Its blinking eyes followed me as I continued to edge slowly past it. They never left mine, and only its head moved as it watched me, which was a full 180 degrees by the time I got near Miranda. I started to back up, putting distance between me and the creature.

"Wait, John—" Miranda started, but it was too late.

I felt my back hit a bamboo tree, which responded with that odd noise. I glanced over my shoulder at it out of instinct, and when my eyes returned to the creature, I realized something was very wrong.

It was angry.

Its nose was scrunched up and its glossy, yellow eyes held fury. Its mouth opened slowly, revealing long, dagger-like teeth, similar to that of an angler fish. I noticed something was moving under its scales. The creature's muscles shifted, moving around unnaturally and steadily growing. The way they moved made me imagine snakes slithering under the black scales.

The creature let out a howl at me, and its body began to grow. First it doubled in size, and then it tripled. Its weight started to bend the tree it was hanging on, slowly lowering it to the ground. Its muscle was a tremendous size, reaching a point where just one of its arms was larger than my torso. It was almost ten feet tall when it stopped growing, and that was on all fours. It resembled more of an ape-like creature now, instead of a lemur or monkey, but its yellow eyes stayed in the same, furious form. They were the only part of it that didn't grow, and when it was finished shifting they appeared small for the size of its head.

The creature lifted its massive arms above its head, and then slammed them back down to the earth. I felt the shock rush up my legs, making me feel unbalanced for a second. The trees around us started to play their unique song as the ape bellowed at me again, this time much deeper in pitch.

A single gunshot sounded from behind me, and a blue spark appeared on the creature's shoulder. It gave a grunt as the impact made its shoulder jerk backwards, but other than that it seemed completely unharmed.

"Move!" Miranda shouted.

I turned my back on the creature and ran.

Miranda was dashing backward while pointing two pistols at the creature, somehow still dodging the trees as she went. Shots rang out like thunder itself was crashing down on us. I glanced back at the creature, who was now gaining ground as it rushed toward us, crushing trees out of its path. As its front arms hit the ground, he picked his back legs up and moved them forward. Miranda's shots paused for a split second, and then two shots rang out together. They hit the creature's front arms as its back legs were off the ground. It was timed perfectly, and the arms of the creature were knocked backward out from under it. It tumbled, smashing down trees as it went.

Miranda turned around now, and started to dash forward. I had to double my speed to keep up with her.

Miranda came to a halt, and so I could catch up to her.

"We'll never out run it in this place. Even in the forest it'll have the advantage," she said, her green eyes meeting mine.

I looked back at the creature, which was starting to get to its feet.

"What choice do we have? Your bullets don't seem to do much."

"Of course not. It has black scales, one of the hardest hides a creature can have. It can only be penetrated with a very few weapons, one of them being a weapon made from other black scales."

I started to reach behind me to grab the pistol that was tucked into my jeans, but I stopped myself before I had even touched it. It was useless against that creature.

"Please tell me you have one," I said.

"Well ... kinda," She said, shrugging her right shoulder.

"Kinda?" I hissed.

She sighed and with a flash of blue her pistols were replaced with a single dagger. The black blade was maybe eight or nine inches long.

"Seriously? All you are going to do with that is piss him off," I complained.

"Oh shut up. Do you know how rare just a dagger of blackscale is? I just picked it up for emergencies. Most Law Eves don't even bother."

The beast had finally recovered, and was now looking around for its prey—us.

"We need a plan," I said.

"I have one. It involves you staying safely out the beast's reach while I handle him," her eyes were intense.

"Let me help. I could distract it while you wait for an opening."

"John, this creature could kill you in a single blow. I'm not letting you near it until your Miracle surfaces."

The beast finally saw us. It growled in a tone so low it vibrated the trees around it, making them play their own tune. Even though I hated it, I knew she was right. Logically, it was stupid for me to engage with it.

"We have no time, and going head to head against something so strong isn't a wise move. Are you confident that you can take him alone?" I asked.

She hesitated before answering. "No. I'm not. But either way, I cannot find a solution where you can both assist me and stay out of danger."

"What should I do then?" I asked.

"Just stay here out of the way. If it tries to attack you, run. If I fail to kill it, run. Even if I'm going to perish, you need to run," she said to me.

"Hell no," I shot back, meeting her eyes.

She lowered her voice as her eyes turned serious. "I know it's selfish of me to ask, but please John. Please survive."

I didn't have time to respond before she bolted away from me, sprinting through the trees with grace and precision. Her long, crimson hair whipped behind her as she ran. I looked away from her and back to the beast, wondering what it would do.

The beast's eyes followed her, and then jumped back to me, as if he was unsure which one to chase. He took a step toward me, seemingly not interested in Miranda at all, but as Miranda's pistol rang out, his mind quickly changed.

The beast bellowed at her as bullets assaulted him, and then charged. Her bullets didn't seem to even slow it down as it plowed its way through the trees, smashing them out of its way effortlessly. Miranda got a good distance between them in the beginning, but now the creature was gaining ground on her rapidly. She noticed this when she glanced over her shoulder as she dodged around the trees, and instead of increasing her speed like I expected, she came to a dead stop. She turned around, facing the creature head on.

It bellowed at her and charged faster, accepting her unspoken challenge.

"Just move," I commanded under my breath, terrified that the beast would trample her.

But she remained still, completely unmoving as the monster the size of a small building charged at her. She waited, fear completely absent from her eyes, until the beast was within ten feet of her, then she dived to her left.

The beast's momentum was too great to make that small hair-pin turn, but that didn't stop it from trying. It reached out for her as it passed. It grasped nothing but air, but that action made it lose its balance and it tumbled into a heap, knocking down the surrounding bamboo trees.

Miranda didn't hesitate to return to her feet and counter-attack. She ran toward the beast as it was still recovering, jumped off the ground and landed on the thing's chest. She stabbed the beast, sinking the dagger all the way to its hilt, and then yanked it out again. The beast howled in pain, and his arm thrashed toward Miranda out of reflex. She didn't have time to fully evade it, but managed jump and pull her feet up between her and the beast's arm. The blow wasn't nearly as bad because she was able to absorb some of the force with her legs, but she still went flying toward me, miraculously passing between two rows of trees for the first twenty feet before crashing into one of them. She let out a grunt of pain as her upper back collided with the solid bamboo tree, which played its strange noise but didn't budge at all. She fell the last five feet or so to the ground and didn't move immediately. The beast started to get up again, complaining with a loud bellow of anger. It's hateful, yellow eyes bore into Miranda's form on the ground. The beast gave a deep, aggressive growl in its throat as it crouched, ready to chase after her again.

I stared at the scene before me, wide-eyed and shocked. My body was tense, and my instinct to get to Miranda was on the verge of overwhelming me. I needed to shield her from this black scaled demon, but my mind was keeping it at bay.

I couldn't protect her from that. She told me to stay. I'd only get in her way if I went. She's an Eve. She can take care of herself. These excuses popped up in my mind, trying to keep my feet rooted in place. But a dark corner of my mind was shouting in fury, cursing the black demon for even existing in the same reality as the women that was struggling to get to her feet.

I felt my right foot move forward, taking me one-foot closer to the demon, but I quickly locked my legs still. *She said to stay. She's strong. She's an Eve. She can take care of herself. Trust her.*

But what if she's taken from me? What if this thing hurts her like the other demons hurt Rachel? What if I have to watch that happen again?

I felt my mental war start to lean towards a victor—I was going to do whatever I could to protect Miranda.

Miranda had begun to stand again, rolling her shoulders in pain. The black dagger, which must've vanished after she had gotten hit, re-appeared into her hand with a flash of electric blue light. She lowered herself into a fight-ready stance, prepared to confront the beast again.

I had taken three steps forward from my original spot when I saw her. I stared at her back, taking in the sight of her willpower and confidence, and the sight of her determination made me come to an immediate halt. If I went out now, it would mean that I wouldn't trust her strength, and I refused to accept that.

The beast charged again, running toward her. She shifted her weight very slightly to her left, preparing to dodge again, using the same tactic as last time. She waited until it was almost on top of her, then she dodged, rolling to her left.

She came up out of the roll smoothly, coming up in a crouch. But the beast didn't go for her like it did last time. It didn't falter in its steps a single bit, but its eyes shifted from Miranda as soon as she dodged and focused on me.

Oh shit.

It wasn't far from me. I had maybe four seconds before I was going to get trampled. My eyes flashed from the beast to Miranda's green eyes, and for the first time since I had met her, I saw fear on her features. I looked back at the beast. It was now slowing down, extending my life by an extra second, and began to reach for me. I stared, completely frozen in my surprise, at the beast that was reaching toward me. I was going to die.

Then, almost of thin air, Miranda appeared in front of me, standing upright and ready, as if she'd been there the whole time. Blue electricity arced from her right hand to her leg, and then disappeared immediately afterward. The beast caught her instead of me, wrapping its huge fingers around her chest. It trapped her left arm in its grasp, but she managed to keep her right arm free. The beast lifted her off the ground as it squeezed her, making her cry out in pain. The dagger appeared in her right hand as she brought it downward and sank into the beast's arm. The creature roared loudly and flailed around. The arm that still grasped Miranda flew toward me. I barely managed to get my arms up protectively in front of me before it made contact. Pain erupted in my arms and I felt myself go flying. I didn't go very far before my legs hit a bamboo tree, making my torso swing around. My head hit another bamboo tree painfully, and black dots appeared in my vision. I fell the ground and landed in a heap, completely immobilized by the pain that was flooding through me. I struggled to open my eyes—my vision faded in and out of focus before it eventually dimmed to darkness. I saw Miranda's fear filled eyes look at me before they morphed into fury and turned back to the beast. I drifted into unconsciousness, but I felt relief as it did, since the emptiness ate away the pain.

CHAPTER 4

"John?"

Her voice held fear and worry, but I recognized it immediately: Miranda.

I groaned as pain washed over my thoughts like water over rocks, drowning them completely. I slowly opened my eyes as I struggled to remember where I was, and what had happened to me. Oh yeah. Bamboo. Giant mutant monkey of death. Right.

"Hey," Miranda said, her voice gentle and unsteady.

My head was resting in her lap and she was looking down at me, her green eyes meeting my own with concern. Her bright crimson hair was tucked behind her ears, but a stubborn curl hung loose, dangling down between us.

"You're beautiful," I said softly.

She blinked, her eyes switching from worry to surprise as her cheeks turned to a gentle shade of pink. She made a barely audible high-pitched tone that sounded like "huh?"

Realizing what I had just said, I closed my eyes and groaned, "I didn't mean to say that."

I heard her laugh gently, clearly amused. After her laughter died, I looked up at her again, seeing only a small smile on her lips.

"Accident or no accident, was it an honest opinion?" she asked her tone curious.

"It was," I admitted.

She smiled softly, then, after a moment of silence, asked how I was.

That was when I started to realize how much pain I was feeling. My head was throbbing, even when I wasn't moving. My forearms were certainly bruised, and the bone in my left felt broken. The parts that hurt the least were my legs where I collided with the bamboo tree, but I knew that they'd feel a lot worse when I stood on them.

"My left forearm might be broken, but I think that's the worst of it," I stated, trying to be casual about it.

Damn it hurt.

"I checked it already. It's intact. It just took the hardest hit, and probably hurts like hell."

"You're right about that," I said, swallowing as I patiently waiting for the pain to die down.

My eyes drifted past Miranda and searched the canopy that stretched above us. Oddly, there was a hole in the canopy. It wasn't big, but it was perfectly round, and it seemed impossible for the canopy to grow that way. Then I noticed the orange sky past it and the odd circle was pushed from my mind.

"Wha—how long was I out?" I asked, my eyes flashing to Miranda.

"Don't worry," she said softly, "we can still make it to the plane before dark."

"What about help getting here?" I asked.

"It will definitely be nightfall by then. The cockpit of the plane could provide enough protection for the beginning of the night. I doubt it'll last until the end of it, but we might be able to last until someone gets here."

I lifted my left arm slowly, testing how much it would hurt. I could bear the pain without complaining, but it was still far from comfortable. I should've trusted Miranda more and moved back. Now, we're in a much worse situation than we were earlier. I lowered my arm, hiding my eyes in my elbow.

"How are you doing? I know you took some hits, even before you protected me," I asked.

"I'll be okay. The beast cracked my ribs when he grabbed me, but those are mostly healed by now. The others were nothing more than bad bruises and have already vanished."

"How long was I out?" I asked again.

"Just over three hours," she answered.

I swallowed. It was good to hear that she was going to be fine, but because of me, we were three hours behind. I took a deep breath and slowly sat up. The pistol that was tucked into my jeans bite into my back as I did so, but that was hardly noticeable compared to the pain in my arms.

"Easy, John. Don't worry about the time. Your health is more important," she said, placing a supporting hand on my shoulder.

I shook my head, but didn't say anything. I stood up, taking note how heavy my body felt.

"Take it slow," she cautioned as she stood up with me.

I grabbed a bamboo tree for support, ignoring the noise it made, and did my best to keep from showing how much pain was flooding through my body. I was right, the pain in my legs increased tenfold by standing.

"Careful. I think that's how the beast found us in the first place."

I took a deep breath, doing my best to ignore the pain that followed, and nodded. "That would make sense."

I took in my surroundings. In short, the area was completely trashed. There was a large clearing of bamboo trees which were either broken down and trampled upon, undoubtedly from the beast. There was several of them that were cleanly cut in half, and these I assumed were caused by Miranda.

The creature was … uh … a little bit of everywhere. Parts of its body lay in chunks around the clearing, with its torso laying in the middle and its head not much farther away.

"Damn, Miranda … what happened?" I asked, looking around.

The oddest thing about this area was the clearing a little way from the largest trampled area. This small clearing was perfectly circular and was about ten feet in diameter. There were no trees in this circle, nor was there plant growth of any kind, and the trees surrounding the circle were slightly burnt. This clearing looked like it lined up with the hole in the canopy I had noticed earlier.

She cleared her throat delicately, "well I sort of let my emotions get the better of me. I summoned my Core and vented."

"Your Core?" I asked, looking over at her.

She had some black blood on the lower-left side of her shirt. Or my shirt, I guess, since she was still wearing the one I lent her. She had a little on her jeans around her knees, but that was pretty much it. She tried to tuck that stubborn strand of hair behind her ear, but it didn't stay that way for very long.

"Yeah. Every Eve has one. It's a weapon we can summon that's more powerful than any man-made one. It also is naturally imbued with any Minor Miracle we have, making it easier for us to control it."

"What's the down side?"

She raised an eyebrow, "what makes you think there is one?"

"If there wasn't, I assume you would've opened with it instead of using that small dagger."

She smiled. "You're right. There is a downside. At birth, all discovered Eves receive a Limiter. Basically, it's a microchip surgically implanted in our brain to keep us from accessing our Cores. Through the process of joining with an Adam, the microchip is designed to automatically disintegrate."

"Oh …. Wait, what?" I responded, surprised, "they put a microchip into your brain and you're just okay with it?"

She gave me an annoyed look. "Well it's not like they gave me a choice, John. Besides, I understand their reasoning."

"What reason could they possibly have that makes it okay?" I asked.

She crossed her arms and took a deep breath. "Cores are, for the most part, incredibly powerful. I could waltz into Chicago, use my Core, and destroy everything without much difficulty. Only other Miracle Children could possibly stop me. That amount of power shouldn't go unchecked, so they prevent me from using it until I have a partner that can keep me accountable."

"Oh, so Adams get Limiters too?" I asked.

"No, Adams don't have Cores," she replied.

I sighed. "Why is it okay for Adams to go around unchecked but not Eves?"

Her tone had a slight impatience to it. "Because their Miracles function differently, John. Adams have Miracles that are defined, logical and precise. But Eves are the opposite; their Miracles are flexible, intuitive and temperamental."

"I don't follow. How does that explain why Adams don't need Limiters?"

"Adams have complete and utter control of their Miracle. They are masters of it and it obeys them completely. But because Eves' Miracles are tied in with their emotions ..." she sighed as she reached up and tucked the stubborn lock of hair behind her right ear again. "Look, John, it's complicated, but you'll get answers at the Academy, okay?

I sighed in response. "Alright. Anyway, I'm guessing you were able to use your Core this time because it was already part-way dissolved."

She nodded. "It usually takes a week to fully dissolve, so I didn't think it was an option in the beginning."

"Then how were you able to use it now?" I asked.

She hesitated, choosing her words, "Eves' Miracles are closely tied in with our emotions, so the Limiter isn't an exact science. Using it this time was on accident. I just saw you lying there and sort of ... I don't know, snapped, I guess."

I took another look around the gore covered ground. "You think?"

She shot me an annoyed look, and I responded to it with a smile.

"Can you walk?" Miranda asked, taking a few steps closer to me.

"Yeah," I answered instantly, but in my mind thought *hell no*.

"We should get going, then."

I looked up at the sky again. "How much time do you think we have left?"

"I'm not sure. Maybe an hour."

I nodded, thankful that we would at least have that.

"Are you ready?" she asked.

I tore my thoughtful gaze away from the sky to meet her eyes. "Yeah."

She gave me a soft smile before turning around and starting forward.

Since her eyes were no longer on me, I lessened the tough-front I was wearing. My neutral expression collapsed into a grimace of pain, but I managed to contain any verbal complaint.

I struggled momentarily with myself when it was time to move.

Just one step, just one step, I mentally chanted as I lifted my foot up and shifted my weight forward.

I thought the first step would be the hardest, but the second and third were equally difficult. I kept pace—barely—and that was only because Miranda was going much slower than she was earlier. At least this pace made it possible to dodge all the bamboo. We didn't touch a single one as we walked. It took us a couple minutes, but we managed to reach the stream of water.

It wasn't more than five feet wide, and I doubted it went deeper than a foot, but I was thankful none-the-less. The water was cool to the touch, and it felt fantastic to finally stop moving, even though I hadn't been moving very long. I stripped off my socks and shoes, then took a few steps out into the stream.

I handed my shoes to Miranda, who had already jumped across before me. Of course, she made it look completely effortless, but then again, it probably was for her.

I bent down and took several long drinks that satisfied my thirst. I cupped my hands and gathered some water. I splashed it over my face, then rubbed my cheeks to get the dirt and sweat off. I looked down in the water and watched my reflection get distorted as each water drop fell from my chin to the stream. I thought I was going to fall over when I straightened. I looked up at the sky and closed my eyes. I felt like I could just fall back into the stream and float away. No more effort, no more work. Just … rest.

I gave a sigh as I looked back to Miranda, then sloshed my way over to the shore. Her careful eyes were surveying me, but I didn't meet them. I was afraid she would see how much pain my body was going through. I hated being weak in front of her. Pathetic.

I sat down a little roughly next to her, then started to dry off my feet with my socks.

"Feel a little better?" she asked, her voice gentle and caring.

"Yeah," I answered honestly. The cool water did help me to some extent, but I doubted they would make it less painful to move.

"We won't make it at this pace."

I nodded. "I know."

"We'll have to speed it up a little. Will you be alright?"

I met her green gaze. "Sure. Just set the pace, and I'll be sure to keep up. It's getting better."

Her eyes grew sad. "You're terrible at lying."

I felt the smile I was putting on slide down a little, and I reached out my hand to her. I touched her arm with the back of my fingers and slid it down until I felt her fingers between my own. I knew it was an odd action for me to make, but I was in too much pain to guard my mind and emotions any longer. I didn't want to anyway. It seemed like a completely different world out here, and I couldn't deny the thought that if Miranda wasn't here, I wouldn't have lasted an hour.

"It wasn't all a lie. I know we have to do this to survive; so, if you set the pace, I will keep up."

"You are in pain, then?" She asked, her thumb running over my own.

I looked down at the stream running past us. "It's better now. The cool water helped immensely, but yes. My legs still hurt." Also my arms, head, and *everywhere else*.

"That's not saying much, John. You were in terrible shape before you passed out."

I was still in terrible shape. I shook my head. "Doesn't matter. We need to keep moving. Nightfall isn't going to wait for us."

"We could just get out of this bamboo field and try to manage on our own for the night," she said gently.

I didn't reply for a moment. It was tempting.

"We can't leave Clyde alone in this place. He definitely won't survive the night."

"We don't even know if Clyde survived the plane crash, let alone if he's healthy enough to stay alive till the chopper gets here. A creature found you within twenty minutes of our crash. I doubt he's fared much better, and I'm more worried about you."

There was a vein of truth to her words, and in my current condition we couldn't know if we'd even make it to him before nightfall. The best call for our survival could be to make our own shelter and then head toward the plane tomorrow. But ... I couldn't help picturing Clyde, his body torn and bloody in the cockpit. What if we arrive tomorrow only to find that he had survived the crash, but died during the night?

I shook my head again. "It's because we don't know those things that we must search for him. If he's alive and unharmed then we'd be giving him a death sentence by leaving him there overnight. He wouldn't be here if not for us, Miranda. We owe him this much at least."

She met my eyes for a long second, and then nodded. "I thought you would say something like that."

I stood up, suppressing a groan of pain as I did so. "I can do this. Let's get going."

She hesitated for a moment, and then stood up. "Fine. But don't push yourself too hard. If you need a break, or need me to slow down, let me know. Don't just try to tough it out. If you push yourself too hard—"

"I'll be sure to let you know," I interrupted her.

Part of me enjoyed how concerned she was, but the other part was anxious to get to the plane. I wasn't sure how much longer I could fight off the exhaustion that was creeping at the far edges of my mind. She looked at me with concerned eyes, then turned around and started walking. I followed her, staring at her feet. We walked in silence, which in all honesty was a relief to me. It took concentration to walk in my sorry state.

I don't know how much time had passed before we got out of the bamboo forest. Seconds felt like hours, so I had begun to keep track of my time and effort by my steps. It took two hundred and fourteen steps until we made it out of the bamboo trees. The dark earth we were walking on turned to long grass, but with the absence of the bamboo trees it was still much easier to traverse. I expected Miranda's pace to increase once we made it out, so I was surprised when it didn't.

I was tempted to play dumb to save myself some effort and pain, but ....

"Miranda, I can keep up. If we don't keep up a good pace we'll die, and if that happens saving me some pain will be pointless."

She stopped, but didn't turn to face me. She stood there for a moment, and I knew she was debating with herself.

"How fast can you go?" she asked.

Now it was my turn to hesitate. Honestly, I already felt like we were going too fast.

"I don't know. Just set a pace and I'll match it. If you go too fast, I'll tell you," I replied.

After spending another moment in thought, she consented. Her speed probably doubled, and I had to really push myself to keep pace with her. My breathing got heavy, and any uphill climbs made me pant. I started counting my steps again, but every time I reached one hundred I restarted.

Just one more hundred ... One more hundred ...

I don't know how many times I restarted my count, but I almost ran into Miranda when she stopped moving forward.

I looked up past her to see a steep, twenty-foot incline ahead of us.

"This forest sucks," I mumbled.

Miranda giggled a little as she held out a hand to me. "We'll make it."

I took it, and together we started upwards. I did my best not to lean on Miranda's strength, but she did help pull me up the last bit of the climb.

I was bent over, clutching my knees to support my upper body as I panted. That climb hurt like hell. My legs felt like they were on fire, and the pain in my head flared with each heartbeat.

"Your strength of will is impressive," Miranda commented, "a lesser man would've given up by now."

"I wish I felt impressive," I said, chuckling painfully.

She smiled half-heartedly as she started to pull her hair back, making me notice a faint trace of sweat on her forehead and neck. It was warm, but I'd thought it was only me feeling the effort it took to keep up with this pace. My legs started to shake from the effort of supporting me, so I immediately pushed off my knees to straighten up, trying to hide it from Miranda. The edges of my vision faded into black for a moment. Damn. I was getting physically weaker, and even if my willpower didn't break, my body's endurance would.

"How much farther?" I asked as I took a deep breath.

"We're almost there, but the sun is setting. We should make it there just as the night begins to wake up."

I swallowed. I was relieved to hear that we were close, but when we got there I'd be hardly any use to Miranda if we get attacked by the wildlife. No, more realistically, I'd be a burden.

"Let's get going then," I said.

"Okay," she answered, turning around and resuming her pace.

I had time to notice the fire-orange ribbon she wore in her hair, keeping it tied back and off her neck. The color complimented her crimson hair, and I found it charming. It was the little things that always made her seem more human than monster.

I resumed my count, letting the numbers consume my every thought. It had my complete focus, and it helped me ignore the agony that was pounding in my legs. I sensed it getting darker around us. Even though the sun hadn't set yet, it got shadows of the forest grew darker. I never saw any visible change in Miranda, but with each passing minute I found myself getting more nervous.

I had to trust her. If she said we'd make it at this pace, then I'd trust her. Thankfully, it wasn't long until we arrived, but what we found wasn't ideal.

Miranda was the one to notice it. "John, something isn't right here."

"What do you mean? Like what?" I asked, breathing heavily.

"I could just be paranoid, but I've been thinking a lot on the way here; the plane definitely wasn't a malfunction of some kind. It felt almost unnatural."

I paused, thinking it over, then I agreed with her. "The way the plane was acting, I don't think this was an accident. Could some creature be responsible for it?"

She shook her head. "I don't know. Let's be careful with our approach."

"If you feel that's best," I agreed.

We approached the crash site cautiously, moving from tree to tree. The area was transformed into a small clearing, most likely caused by the crash of the plane. Unlike how our half of the plane landed, this one looked like it crashed straight down and didn't move after the hard impact with the ground. It obviously burst through the trees above us, since the large hole in the canvas had several broken branches hanging down off the trees. The cockpit of the plane landed right side up, and debris was scattered around it. My eyes searched for Clyde immediately, but I found more than one person in the small clearing.

It was darker now, and I couldn't make out their faces without concentrating. There was five men near the plane altogether. I found Clyde first, who was the closest to the plane but was sitting on the ground. His clothes no longer held the crisp, clean appearance they once did, and were now dirty, ruffled and abused. His shirt was no longer tucked in, and his black pants had a large tear in them at the knee. There was a man standing near him, holding some type of rifle, but in the dark I couldn't make out any details. The other three men were standing a few feet off, grouped together. Two of them were conversing, and the other appeared to be surveying his surroundings. He was either unskilled at it or just too relaxed to notice us. Out of the four of them, him and the man guarding Clyde were the only ones armed. Even so, it was the two that were unarmed that made me nervous the most.

One of them seemed familiar to me from somewhere, but I couldn't recall where. He was tall with tanned skin like mine but a couple shades darker and with short blond hair. He had a young face but his posture was one of confidence and ruthlessness. It was obvious that he had experience being a leader, even though he was around my age. Although it was dark, I could see his cold, lifeless and calculating blue eyes. His presence made me nervous, but it was the other man who scared me.

The man was nearing middle aged. He was tall, at least six-four, and was thin, but I couldn't make out whether this was from slim muscle or lack of nutrition. His dark blond hair was a little long for a man, and the only part of his hair that was even touched was his bangs, which were cut roughly and unevenly. It was as if he had no care for physical appearance, and only cut his bangs to keep them out of his eyes. He had scruff, as if he hasn't shaved in a few days. His long brown leather coat had obviously seen a few years of wear. Underneath that he had on a dirty white button-up and a dark blue tie that was loose around his neck. He had on a black pair of pants with a belt, and his pants had a small hole in the knee. He had a deep set of eyes, as if he hadn't slept this week. His eyes held the look of boredom, yet they weren't unfocused. In all honesty, he didn't seem the least bit threatening, but the fact that he was so relaxed in such a dangerous place as the Outside was unnerving.

"He's strong," I whispered.

Miranda nodded once, "It's good you noticed. In my current state, I cannot fight them both at once, especially since I have no idea what either of them can do. We'll have to wait and see what happens."

Miranda started to back off away from the site, and I followed suit. After we got a little distance from the crash site, I followed her as she slightly circled around the site, and then approached the site again. I didn't realize what Miranda's plan was, but when we arrived at a fallen tree it became clear; she wanted more effective cover. She could peek over the top of the tree, allowing her to observe them while revealing the bare minimum required. I was impressed that she had deciphered her opponent's strength, assessed the situation, and had surveyed her surroundings all in the time it took me to figure a single man's strength.

She looked at me. "John, sit down and rest. Don't fall asleep, but recover as much of your energy as you can. I'll keep watch."

I nodded, and turned around to lean against the tree. I leaned my head back, and resisted the temptation to close my eyes. I concentrated on my breathing, letting the simple act of a slow and steady breath dominate my focus. I gradually relaxed each of my muscles until I was completely at ease. My thoughts slowly melted into silence as my mind began to rest along with my body, and it brought incredible relief to me.

Time passed slowly, and darkness seeped in around us. I doubted that Miranda would be able to make out any details at this point. I knew I wouldn't be able to. She probably could only see their rough outline.

Miranda spoke, "John."

My muscles tensed at her voice, and I looked up quickly at her. The lack of light made her crimson hair as dark as blood, but against her skin it only seemed to make her more alluring. I swallowed as my mind remembered how to think properly.

"We can turn this darkness into our ally. I want to move closer so I can hear what they are saying, but you need to stay close to me. Something might try and eat you while I'm gone. Can you move?" she asked me.

I nodded in reply.

It still hurt like hell to move, even with the rest, but I did feel an improvement. I shadowed her movements as we advanced undetected, stopping at the last circle of trees.

"—perhaps she died in the crash," said Ice-eyes, his voice precise.

"No. I've heard of Skyfall before. They claim her strength is immense. She would survive," Scruff-face answered. His voice was a direct contrast from ice-eyes. It was rough and deep.

"Then it appears you've miscalculated," said the man with the rifle.

Even through the darkness, it was plain that scruff-face's expression had immediately morphed into one of anger, and suddenly the rifleman was on the ground.

I blinked. What just happened? Scruff-face hadn't made a single move, but the rifleman was on struggling on the ground. He was groaning in effort and pain, as if a weight was pressed hard on his back.

"Who are you to talk down to me, insect? Perhaps I should crush your feet until the bones are nothing but fragments to serve as a lifelong reminder of your place. Or better yet, I'll just work my way up from your feet until you can properly apologize for your arrogance."

The man let out a groan of pain and started to sputter out an apology.

Scruff-face gave a cruel grin, "you call that an apology? Are you mocking me? Try *again*."

Ice-eyes glanced over at Scruff-face. "That's enough, James. We can't afford to lose a member every time you get bored."

"He insulted me. He deserves to die," James the scruff-face replied, venom coating his every word.

"You've proved your dominance. Anything further is pointless."

"It's not *pointless*. It's fun."

"It's also a waste of resources. Don't make me repeat myself again." Ice-eyes' voice turned from factual to challenging.

James hesitated for a moment, staring defiantly at Ice-eyes, but eventually relented. The force that was keeping the man down was evidently removed, because his cry of pain was replaced with gasps for air. He pushed himself up onto all fours, panting.

Ice-eyes looked down on him. "Stand up. The only reason you're still able to walk because you have some use to me. If I were you, I'd make sure it stays that way."

The man stood, but his legs were shaking.

He gave Ice-eyes a nod. "Yes sir."

"Let's head out, James. We're not spending the night Outside. She has either died, gotten lost, or isn't concerned about the pilot. Either way, we made the wrong gamble. Let's go."

"What about the pilot?" James said, a smile starting to form on his face as he eyed Clyde.

"He isn't necessary," Ice-eyes replied.

James stretched out a hand toward Clyde. "Music to my ears."

Ice-eyes spoke, making James freeze with a simple word, "Stop."

James gave him a questioning look mixed with annoyance.

"This forest will be his testing ground. If he survives, then he

Taylor Stutesman

deserves to live. If he dies, then it was his time. He is employed by the Church, so let their god decide his future, not us."

James snorted. "God, huh? When did you become such a believer?"

"I'm not, but leaving him here is a great way to test the Church's god."

"That habit of yours is rather annoying," James stated.

"So is your sadistic side. Let's get going."

"You sure you want me to use that? It's not something that I can do lightly, nor can I—" James began, but was interrupted by Ice-eyes.

"I am well aware of your limitations, James. Don't make me repeat my order a third time," he said in an annoyed tone, shooting a hard glare at James.

James exhaled sharply through his nose and looked away. Ice-eyes returned his gaze to his surroundings, content with his authority.

James turned around, putting his back to Ice-eyes and the plane wreckage. He lowered his stance and I saw his body tense with effort. A strange sensation filled the air around me, making my body feel momentarily lighter, as if James was lifting me off the ground. The feeling was so brief that I wondered if my exhausted mind had imagined it.

I looked over at Miranda, unsettled. "Did you feel that?"

She was looking down at her hands, her face set in concentration. Her hands tightened into fists as she tensed, then looked back up at James.

"Watch him, John. Take in every detail of what he does, and note anything that stands out to you. We might get a clue as to what his Miracle is." Her tone was serious, emphasizing how important this was.

Miracle? This guy was an Adam?

I blinked, shocked at this. Adam's were part of the Church. No exceptions. Why would the Church be trying to kill one of their own?

I calmed down and looked back at James, pushing this from the back of my mind. By now, the light was so dim that it was difficult to make much out, and it strained my eyes to try.

His hands were clenched and his body shook slightly as his face contorted into a snarl of effort—at least, it seemed that way to me

72

through the thick darkness. The strange sensation rolled over to us in waves, making my stomach uneasy, as if I was sea-sick. I ignored the feeling as best I could and continued to watch him. It wasn't long— maybe twenty or thirty seconds—but it felt like minutes had passed before he finally moved. He raised his right fist and held it straight out from him. The pose would've looked silly if it wasn't for the sensation I kept feeling. He held it for another few seconds with growl of effort, and then slowly opened his fist. It looked like it was extremely difficult to do so, and he made a final growl as his hand fully opened.

The effect was immediate. I felt like every part of my body had been suddenly yanked toward the air in front of him. It wasn't strong enough to move me, but it was impossible not to notice. The brush and small growth in the area all rippled toward a spot some ten to twelve feet in front of James. Ice-eyes body had swayed very slightly, and the soldier next to him was pulled a couple of feet in that direction before he could steady himself. The soldier near the pilot had to take a step forward to keep himself from falling over, and Clyde, since he was already on the ground, tumbled forward onto his stomach, but hadn't moved very far from his original position. The telekinetic pull was constant and steady, as if it was gravity itself. The surrounding vegetation made a constant sound, as if wind was blowing rapidly through them, and the air hummed gently.

Ice-eyes looked at the riflemen closest to him and jerked his chin toward the source of the telekinetic pull. The soldier hesitated, and then moved forward slowly. As he got closer to the source, it was obvious that the pull got stronger. He had to lean back away from it to keep his balance, and when he was a mere five steps away he was yanked off his feet. He was pulled into the source, and then immediately vanished from my sight. I took a moment to scan the area behind the source, thinking I just lost sight of him in the dim lighting, but he was just ... gone.

Ice-eyes walked forward as cautiously as the soldier had. He made it a little farther than the soldier had before he was lifted off his feet and pulled to the source. Ice-eyes' grace made it obvious that he was an Adam, since he kept his balance even after being pulled off the ground—a feat that most regular humans would find extremely difficult. The other soldier walked calmly and confidently away from Clyde, who was awkwardly returning to a sitting position. The soldier approached the telekinetic pull confidently, as if this wasn't his first time.

James took a step forward, and then hesitated.

He looked over at Clyde. "You may think me cruel, but what he just gave you is a fate crueler than anything I would have done to you. He may have let you live, but don't cling to hope. It'll only hurt more when you die in this hell of a forest."

He gave Clyde a final look, and then turned and walked calmly forward, completely unaffected by the telekinetic pull. When James vanished, so did the telekinetic effect.

As soon as they were gone, I looked at Miranda. "Why the hell would the Church be after us?"

"What?" she said, clearly confused, then it looked like she understood what I was thinking and corrected me. "Oh, no. He wasn't with the Church. He's a rogue Adam."

"Rogue Adam? I thought all Miracle Children were part of the Church."

"They're supposed to be. This was an anomaly. Let's go up." Miranda explained hastily, then carefully approached the clearing. Whether it was her intention or not, she walked forward almost soundlessly—a lithe predator stalking its prey.

In the atmosphere of the Outside, it made her seem dangerous, and I was reminded again that her true nature was not human. She was an Eve. I pushed that thought out of my mind as I thought of how she saved my life against the black-scaled monkey. She wouldn't hurt me.

I began to follow her, but in the darkness, I couldn't see my surrounds very clearly and ended up tripping over a root. I tried to save myself but the best I could manage was a fumbled roll. My muscles screamed at me as I picked myself off the ground again, but no complaint made it past my throat.

Clyde heard my stumble. "Who's there?"

It was obvious from his voice that he was afraid.

"It's Miranda. Remember? Miranda Peirce," she said, taking a few more careful steps closer to him.

"Thank God," he breathed, relaxing a little.

"Are you injured in anyway?" Miranda asked him, her voice smooth and calm.

"I think I have a few cracked ribs, but nothing life threatening," he replied, his voice still shaky.

"Good. Let me help you up." She approached him slowly and held out a hand.

I watched her, curious of her intentions. Clyde took her hand and groaned as she carefully pulled him to his feet. He mumbled thanks at her and she nodded.

"Lift up your shirt and let me look at those ribs. I want to make sure you aren't in any danger," she said to him, carefully. Her voice was again smooth and cautious, like she was trying to get a wounded dog to approach her.

I doubted that Clyde had noticed the tone of her voice. If I hadn't spent time with her, I wouldn't have.

"Oh, o-okay," he muttered again, obviously a little put-off. He grabbed the bottom of his shirt with both hands and lifted slowly. His face tightened in pain as he lifted his arms and stretched his ribcage slightly. Miranda gently traced each rib gently with her finger. I swallowed as jealousy swarmed into my mind, and I struggled to suppress it. I wasn't completely successful, but I was able to keep it from being seen. Watching the carefulness Miranda used and the delicacy of her touch bothered me.

She's not his. He shouldn't receive her compassion so easily.

I couldn't force this thought away from my mind, but I was able think up a counterargument.

She's not mine either.

Clyde's face turned a little red and his eyes jumped to mine. They didn't keep my gaze for longer than a second before he looked down at the ground. Apparently, he thought she was mine, and this made him uncomfortable. I didn't see any reason why I should correct him on that. A small smiled started to form on my lips before I could stop it.

The darkness of night had arrived, and each second that passed made it harder to fully see them. It wasn't long before Miranda was done, and when she did she took a step away from him.

"You're right. Two cracked ribs, but none broken. You are extremely blessed to live through that plane crash," she stated.

He swallowed and nodded to her, not meeting her eyes fully. "Thanks."

"Did those men say who they were or where they came from? We only arrived to see their departure," she asked, gently and calmly.

"The only one whose name was used was the scruffy businessman, James. The two people with weapons were soldiers, and their names weren't said. James referred to the other one as Boss. I'm not sure what to make of it myself. As to where they came from, I'm not sure. I was knocked unconscious when the place crashed, and I was woken when they dragged me out of the plane. I honestly thought that they were going to kill me."

"I wouldn't have let that happen," Miranda replied.

I didn't say anything, but part of me remembered how she suggested not coming here in the first place. I shook my head at myself. I could've easily thought the same thing. Wasn't I tempted to agree? I admit it's easier to turn your back on someone when you don't actually see them struggling. On top of that neither of us predicted that those men would be here.

I heard a gentle buzzing in the area around us, a reminder that the night had arrived.

"We should get in the cockpit," I suggested, looking at Miranda's dark form.

Only her hair could be seen clearly, but it was enough to tell that she nodded.

Clyde looked at the wreckage. "We can call for aid from there."

He walked toward the plane, but Miranda walked back to me. She grabbed my hand and gently pulled me to the plane, making me keep pace with her. My earlier jealousy seemed to be from an entirely different age, and my exhaustion reached a point where I felt like I was in another person's body. Movement was merely automatic now, almost like I was dreaming. I found myself mentally drooling over the idea of dreaming. Hell, at this point death had a certain appeal. Forever asleep. It felt like I needed that much sleep to recover.

I wasn't focusing on our surroundings until we were in the cockpit, and Clyde had turned on a flashlight. I flinched at the light, and squinted until my eyes adjusted. I was standing, barely, in the back of the cockpit near the door. Clyde was sitting in the pilot's chair with an open red bag in his lap, which is where he got the flashlight. Miranda was standing next to me on my left, still holding my hand. Clyde pushed the bag back under the dash of the cockpit, near where his legs were.

"Okay, let's see if we have power," Clyde muttered, and then felt along the edge of the computer monitor.

It was a decently sized screen, maybe twenty inches long, and was in the middle of the dash. I heard a small click as Clyde found and flipped a power switch. The monitor filled the room with light, putting the small beam the flashlight produced to shame. The light was so much brighter that it momentarily blinded me again, and I heard another click-click sound as Clyde shut off the flashlight he was holding.

After my eyes adjusted again, I was finally able to get a good look around the cockpit. As expected, I discovered that it was completely wrecked. Instruments were busted, parts were missing, one of the four windows was broken outward, and the monitor screen was cracked. It was a blessing from God that the thing still worked.

He fiddled with the monitor, touching the screen and shifting through the options that appeared. I was too out of it to see what he was doing in detail.

The buzzing insects outside grew louder, and then they started landing hard on the glass windshield. They were massive, easily the size of an orange, and made a loud *splat* sound when they landed. Their underbellies showed us their six legs moving as they crawled along the glass, drawn by the light inside. Every minute or so, the underbelly of the bugs would glow a bright green, then dim back down to darkness after a few seconds. They reminded me of beetles.

All three of us were staring at them, assessing them for any danger. My heart beat stronger from the small shock of seeing the bugs.

"They are no threat to us," Miranda said, looking back down at the monitor.

Maybe that was enough to satisfy her, but their presence made me nervous.

"Are you sure?" I asked, looking over to her.

She met my eyes calmly as she reached up with her free hand and tucked the stubborn lock of hair behind her right ear. I wondered how long it would last this time before coming free again. She gave me a reassuring but small smile, and then she nodded once.

Clyde swore softly, getting my immediate attention. "The distress systems seem to be in working condition, but we're missing a vital piece for a long-range beacon. It's a ... well for lack of better description, it's a high-tech antenna that's attached to the side of the plane, but I'm not getting any signal from it .... It must've been removed during the crash."

I closed my eyes for a moment, registering the bad news, and felt immediate relief. It felt so good to not have to use my eyes anymore. I wanted sleep.

"What are our options then? We need this back online," Miranda asked.

"Well we still have our short-range coms, so we can use that to send a single out from the plane to locate the antenna. The only issue is that we have so little power to work with that it could use up all of our reserves, in which case we wouldn't be able to contact anyone even if we did locate the antenna."

"What're the odds of that happening?" she asked him.

He hesitated. "Looking at how low the power levels are ... Honestly, I'm not sure if we'll have enough power."

Miranda hesitated, taking a moment to think before she responded. "We have no choice. If we can't send out a signal for help we'll probably die here."

I swallowed. She was right.

"Okay. We'll get an exact location up to a thousand yards in any direction, but after that we can only get a general direction. If it's farther than five miles away we won't get a returning signal," he explained as he shifted through the options on the computer.

"It'll take me a minute to set up," Clyde said as he shifted through some options on the screens display.

We all stood in silence, our attention on the computer screen.

Thunk!

Something impacted with the glass, making us flinch in surprise. We looked at the windshield in unison, but we found nothing but those strange bugs. It was impossible to see anything beyond a couple of inches past the glass because of the light from the computer monitor. None of us so much as breathed as we struggled to figure out what had caused that noise.

It was only a few seconds before it happened again, and although it was a brief glimpse, we got a look at the creature. The most disturbing thing about it was its mouth, which was made up of four parts, and each part—or lip—would open away from each other, like peeling a banana. Each lip had a dozen curved teeth, which made the loud noise as it hit against the glass. Its purple tongue wrapped around a beetle and pulled it into the deeper part of its mouth, where another set of teeth awaited. Over its lips could be seen a pair of yellow, beady eyes which were gleaming from the light in the cockpit. The creature wasn't much bigger than a cat, but it's leather-like wings made it appear larger.

Clyde whimpered.

"What was that?" I heard myself ask.

"Vyrms," Clyde whispered.

"'Vyrms?'" Miranda asked.

"Yes. I don't remember their Latin name, but in my studies, we referred to them as vyrms."

"Are they a threat to us?" Miranda asked.

"Their main food source is beetles and other insects, but they'll take out any large prey that ventures into their territory."

'Any large prey?'

"That sounds like us," I muttered.

The cockpit grew quiet as each of us considered how much danger we were in. A few more vyrms hit the windshield, but we didn't react like we did earlier. Tension was heavy in the small cockpit.

"Nothing we can do about it right now. Keep working, Clyde," Miranda said.

He gave an unsteady nod and resumed his work.

A black, fast blur shot soundlessly through the broken window next to me. It flew past me as if I didn't exist and headed straight for Clyde. I was stunned, surprised and confused. I hadn't even taken a breath. All I had time for was to think that Clyde was getting attacked.

A blue flash lit up the cockpit as Miranda summoned a silver sword, reacting with superhuman speed. She smacked the vyrm to the floor with the side of her blade. It hit the floor hard, but it recovered quickly. After bouncing off the floor, it spread its leathery wings, trying to take flight again. Miranda did a graceful, upward slice that severed its bizarre head from the rest of its body. Yellow-green blood splattered out from the creature in a narrow line that followed the arc of Miranda's swing. The lifeless creature dropped like a rock to the floor, landing with a sickening *splat*. More yellow-green blood slowly oozed from the corpse.

I was frozen. Not out of fear, but out of surprise. My body had tensed and my heart rate tripled, causing me to hear *pound, pound, pound* as my blood rushed through me. I realized I had taken a single backward step sometime during the commotion, but it never registered in my mind. It was only a reflex. The cockpit was quiet for a moment, the only sound being Clyde's panting, and then the vyrms started smacking into the windshield again. We all stared for a moment at the corpse, watching as its weird blood hardened into a solid in seconds on the cockpit floor.

"Is everyone alright?" Miranda asked, looking at me.

I nodded once, and she turned to Clyde, who also nodded, but a lot more shakily than I did.

I suddenly felt awake. My body wasn't in as much pain as before, and I could think clearly again. Adrenaline works wonders.

"We aren't safe here," I spoke softly, but I was plainly heard in the now-silent cockpit.

"We'll have to make do. We can't survive all night out there," Miranda replied.

"We can't survive all night in here either," I said.

"Would you suggest we seek out a different shelter?" Miranda's gaze reflected an internal conflict, but her expression was serious.

In an instant, I could guess what she was thinking. Clyde was a serious liability on us. I already slowed her down as it was, but Clyde didn't even have the experience I had. It was highly probable that if we dragged him along with us, he'd end up slowing us down and getting us killed. At the same time, we couldn't leave him. For a moment, I thought she was going to suggest leaving him to save ourselves. However, the look in her eyes was so brief that I couldn't be sure I had seen it at all. Either I imagined it, or she was doing very well at hiding her calculations.

"No. You're right. This is our best shot," I replied.

If we left this plane to try to survive the night, Clyde would die. I'd probably die too, given my current condition. Hell, even though this cockpit was a hundred times better than having no shelter, it wouldn't be safe without Miranda. Arriving at this conclusion, my mind suddenly made another one. One that I hadn't thought about before. One that Miranda had already arrived much earlier. The antenna was not in the plane, and with the obvious lack of safety this cockpit held, no one was safe in it without Miranda being there.

"It's done," Clyde's voice was like a hammer to my nail of reality.

Wherever its location, this isn't going to be easy. Whatever its location, we had to venture out into the forest, with only an Eve to protect us.

CHAPTER 5

There was an audible click noise from somewhere inside the console, and the backlight of the monitor suddenly dimmed. There was almost no delay between sending the signal and the receiving answer. The screen showed us a direction of two hundred and eighty-four degrees, and seventy-two feet. I felt momentarily relieved; seventy-two feet wasn't far.

"West, huh?" Miranda muttered, looking past me and through the broken window.

I suddenly noticed the absence of creatures. Bugs, vyrms—nothing was around the plane.

"It's too peaceful," I said as my eyes tried to peer through the windows in search of any threats.

Clyde spoke, "the creatures must've been able to detect the signal, but God knows how."

"What other tools do we have?" Miranda asked, her gaze returning from the windows to the cockpit.

Clyde reached down with a groan and picked up a small red bag. Opening it, he started to list off the few contents it contained.

"Two flares, four flashlights, four bottles of water, four meal packs, a notebook and pen, and a small survival guide."

"Okay. Give me the flares and a flashlight. Each of you take a flashlight as well," Miranda said, her eyes flashing back to the window.

Clyde started pulling out the gear, but Miranda turned around and walked up to one of the side windows before Clyde managed to hand her anything. He handed them to me instead, and I stepped up next to Miranda at the window.

The cockpit wasn't exactly spacious, and for us both to be at the window required me to be close to her. I wouldn't have called it a happy circumstance, but I didn't mind it either.

I passed her the flares and flashlight wordlessly as my gaze swept around the dark little clearing. She took them from me, holding all three in her left hand before slipping them into her back pocket. Her right hand was still grasping the silver sword she used to kill the vyrm.

Clyde had turned on his flashlight behind us, and was beaming it down into the pack. I heard the leftover supplies and the bag make a rustling sound as he fiddled through it. Even in the small space, he wouldn't be able to hear me if I whispered.

"This is going to be dangerous. And difficult." I said, my voice barely audible.

"I know. You'll be in danger," she replied, her voice calm but tense.

I swallowed. "We all will be. I don't like this stillness."

Miranda didn't reply, but out of the corner of my eye, I saw her move and felt her gaze on my face.

"You're tense …. Are you afraid?" she asked.

I hesitated before answering. "A little."

I knew how much of a burden this was going to be for her. She had to protect us, and I knew that won't be easy. I hated feeling helpless.

I felt the tips of her fingers just barely brush my forearm just below the elbow. It was as electric as the other times she'd touched me, but this was different. It didn't make my body tense and heart race with excitement. This time it gave warmth, and relaxed my muscles one at a time. My pain, already dulled by the adrenaline that had pulsed through my system, had faded down to almost nothing. My heart didn't change in speed, but instead it beat stronger, harder, as if it had more life in it. She very gently slid her fingers down to my hand and held it without threading her fingers between my own. She gently tensed her hand, squeezing mine once. I hesitated for a second, then my hand folded around hers and tensed back.

"We must survive. I will not allow you to be taken from me so easily," she stated.

Why am allowing myself to be this intimate with her? I didn't know her … but part of—well, a lot of me enjoyed that simple contact from her. Maybe it was my exhaustion that was preventing me from thinking clearly. Maybe it was my hormones mixed with a desire to connect with someone in this dangerous situation. Either way, I was no longer sure if being distant from her is what I wanted.

Miranda leaned into my shoulder, and for a moment I felt emotion come off her in waves. It was like a steady current pulsing around her, making the deep darkness of the cockpit dissolve and the room seemed to get lighter. It tore my attention from the silent Outside to her immediately. She had rested her head on my shoulder, but when I looked over to her she picked it up to meet my eyes. Her expression was a gentle one, but her eyes were almost excited as they stared into mine. She went up on her toes and kissed my cheek in one gracefully quick motion. And then she was gone.

The aura of warmth around her vanished as soon as she let go of my hand. Now she had her back to me, facing Clyde. It was strange how cold the air felt after brushing against that warmth, and how weak my eyesight suddenly became. My heartbeat immediately dulled, and I felt a hint of sadness wrap around me. It was as if some of my life went with her.

"Are you ready to go, Clyde?" she asked, her voice strong and confident.

I was trying to figure out where I was and how to use my lungs again while Clyde stammered out a shocked, questioning response. This woman stunned us both, but for completely different reasons.

Miranda's voice was smooth. "It's not safe in this cockpit. Both you and John must accompany me out to get the device, or you'll be defenseless while I'm gone."

I inhaled, finally remembering how, and then looked down at Clyde. He looked from her to me and back again. I shook my head, trying to clear it. I wasn't going to let my emotions control me. I hadn't a clue if those were my honest emotions anyway. She could possess a Miracle that could manipulate—

I stopped that train of thought and suppressed a sigh. She had no reason to manipulate me like that, and without any motivation, an accusation like that only makes an ass out of me.

"Is there no other option?" he asked, his voice tense and stressed.

"There isn't. We need that antenna or we will die here," Miranda stated.

He flinched at the idea of dying but nodded, gripping his flashlight tighter.

"Shut down the computer. We should conserve power," Miranda ordered as she stepped up to the door leading to the outside.

Clyde did so immediately, and the cockpit sank into sudden darkness. Silence spanned on for several longs seconds as we all stood still.

Clyde's whisper sounded almost loud in the darkness. "What are we waiting for?"

"Can you see anything?" I whispered back.

"Oh," he replied, understanding that we were waiting for our eyes to adjust.

Slowly, the cockpit became a little lighter, and it wasn't long before I could make out vague shapes. It was still very dark and hard to see, but it was an improvement.

Miranda opened the door, slowly, peering out the crack as she did so to look for threats. I took out the pistol Miranda had given me earlier, readying it. She opened it completely, and for a moment all three of us just stood there surveying the still, silent night, like we expected something to jump out at us in any moment. Miranda took a step down, exiting the plane. Her feet landed on the forest floor, making a small sound as she crushed the grass beneath her. She still stood motionless and tense, ready to react without hesitation. The area was noiseless, completely dark and motionless. It was eerie, and I felt like I was in an entirely foreign land, no longer on Earth.

The darkness was the biggest inhibitor. I could see maybe ten feet in front of me, and anything beyond that was just darkness. I was concentrating hard on trying to see farther, but all I was accomplishing was straining my eyes, making me want to blink often. Every few seconds I'd see a burst of movement in the shadows and focus my attention to go there only to find that it was my imagination. Miranda slowly moved her sword from her right hand to her left, then grabbed a flare from her back pocket with her now-free right hand. Miranda lifted her silver sword a little, ready to defend herself at a moment's notice. She held it out to me while still watching her surroundings.

"Help me light the flare, John," she whispered, but it was easily heard in the heavy silence around us.

I swallowed and took a step down from the plane. As soon as my foot hit the grassy earth, I felt a shiver run down my spine. It was like I was in a different world now, miles away from the safety the cockpit gave me. I felt fear, unease, helplessness, and terror all wash around me in an instant. I was going to die here.

Then I blinked, took a deep breath, and shook my head. I wasn't going to die here. I refused to. I had to be focused for Miranda, not off in a world controlled by my fear.

Clyde stayed back in the safety of the cockpit. I didn't tell him to do otherwise. If we needed to retreat after lighting the flare, he wouldn't be in our way.

I grabbed the tip of the flare with my left hand, and awkwardly pulled it apart. The flare made a small popping sound, followed by a constant fizzing noise as a dark red stream of fire shot out of the end. I squinted as the bright light assaulted my eyes, then immediately tensed up and focused on my surroundings.

Time passed as the silence around us devoured the sound of the flare. I swallowed, waiting patiently and following Miranda's lead.

"'Kay then ..." she muttered softly, then faced west, where the antenna was.

She held the flare up above her head, letting the light stretch as far as possible. The darkness was thick, but the flare cut through it all the way to the edge of the clearing, where the light was swallowed by the tree's shadows. Another dark blur of movement made my gaze snap to a patch of darkness near the edge of the clearing, but it vanished so swiftly that I thought it was merely my paranoia. I dropped the cap to the flare and gripped the pistol with two hands, ready to shoot the first threat I saw.

Miranda turned to look at me, her face illuminated in a red shade from the flare she was holding. Her hair was still tied up in an orange ribbon, and her face was set with a serious expression. She looked at me for a few long seconds before nodding to me once, giving me the all-clear.

"Okay, Clyde. You can come down," I said softly, not having to speak anything higher than a whisper.

The area was as silent as death itself. It was almost unreal how thick the air felt. I wanted to leave this place, or awake from this dark dream.

"Seventy-two feet…. Okay. John, you'll lead the way to the antenna and Clyde will follow five feet behind you. I'll walk between the two of you and slightly to the left. Clyde, be sure to match John's pace. If you go too fast I won't be able to protect you on the right side, and if you fall too far behind it'll be easier for a creature to pick you off before I can get to you."

I nodded.

Clyde gave a shaky, "O-Okay."

Miranda gave me the flare, which I took in my left hand and raised it up high like she had it, trying to see as far as I could.

"Can you count the distance, John?" she asked.

"Like in my paces?" I clarified.

"Yeah. I don't think it should be much farther than the clearing," she said.

"I'll keep track, but if we end up changing pace it's possible that I'll lose count," I replied, thinking of how long my stride was, and calculating how many it would take.

"Ready?" she asked as she held her silver sword in two hands.

I glanced at Clyde, who looked afraid, but determined. Then answered, "Yes."

"Go," she commanded.

I immediately moved, taking even strides and starting my count.

We weren't running, but it was faster than a walk. My legs throbbed with pain with each step I took, but I ignored them as I focused on counting.

Halfway there, I heard a high-pitched squeal-like sound to my left, and I looked over in time to see another vyrm racing toward me. It was much bigger than the last one, but with its speed it was hard to make out any details beyond that. Miranda took a step forward and placed herself between the vyrm and I. She swung her blade downward and severed one of the creature's wings. It cried out in a piercing screech that hurt my ears. As it fell, it passed through the space between Clyde and I, and then crashed into the ground. I looked down at it in shock, realizing that it wasn't a vyrm at all. This creature was similar in a lot of aspects, such as its head and its leathery wings, but the differences stood out clearly. It was at least twice the size of the vyrms, and this creature had a long, spike-tipped tail that was flailing about as the creature withered in pain. Not long after it hit the ground, the creature dried up and hardened like the vyrm had in the cockpit.

A short moment of silence passed, and then we heard similar high-pitched squeals from all around us. I heard something shifting through leaves and brush, and leathery wings could even be heard over the squeals.

Miranda's eyes flashed over to me. "Run!"

So, I did, hoping Clyde wouldn't hesitate either. I had to focus on the count, since it'd be very difficult to find the antenna in this darkness if I lost our progress. I heard Miranda move around us, and knew she was protecting us from the creatures, but I didn't move my eyes away from the ground in front of me. After a short moment of running, I halted my advance. I felt Clyde run into my back, but I managed to stay upright.

"It should be here somewhere!" I shouted, running my free hand through the brush as I searched the ground for anything resembling an antenna. I should have asked Clyde for a description before we set out. I heard Clyde fumble through the brush as well, and I prayed that one of us would find it quickly.

I felt a creature ram into my back and was pushed onto my stomach.

I flipped over and held the flare up, trying to see what hit me. One of the bigger vyrm-like creatures descended out of the darkness above me. I knew I didn't have time to pull up my pistol, but that didn't stop me from trying, and I barely made it halfway when Miranda appeared over me. She sliced the creature cleanly in half, causing small drops of blood spattered out from it. I saw the creature fall and I instinctively covered my face with my arm. The two pieces of its body had landed next to me, and the blood had already hardened before it hit me. I felt the small blood-pellets hit me painlessly. I moved my arm and glanced around at the darkness that stretched up in front of me, searching for any more threats. Miranda was already gone, having needed to deal with a different creature.

I lay there and panted before my willpower returned.

Move dammit. Just move.

I gritted my teeth and concentrated on what I was supposed to be doing. We needed that antenna and soon. If a creature could strike at me, that meant Miranda wouldn't be able to hold them at bay forever.

I rolled over on my stomach and pushed myself off the ground, coming to a crouch before standing up. Clyde was a short way off, fumbling through the brush. Miranda was next to him, finishing off another one of those creatures. I started moving toward them, knowing that the farther Clyde and I were from each other, the harder Miranda's job was. I made it halfway before my foot hit something hard, and I tripped, falling into the brush again.

"John?!" Miranda's called, her voice drenched in worry.

"I'm fine!" I yelled back, as I got to my feet and looked at what made me trip.

It was a small thing, but from how it felt when I tripped over it, I knew it was dense. It was a half-oval, roughly the size of a football, and coming out of the oval was a black, thick antenna that was about a foot long. It easily weighed twenty to thirty pounds, and since there wasn't a good way to pick up the antenna with one hand, I had to tuck my pistol back into my jeans to lift it. This had to be what we were looking for, and I looked over to Clyde to verify.

"I found it!" I yelled, heading closer to Clyde on my way toward the plane.

Clyde immediately looked over to me, trying to get a look at the thing I was carrying. The flare I was holding was burning brightly right next to the antenna, so he couldn't have gotten a clear look at it, but he nodded and followed me out of the brush. As soon as we made it to the clearing, I sprinted toward the plane as fast as I could. I trusted that Miranda could keep up, but her safety was still in the back of my mind. It was an urge I constantly had to suppress as it screamed at me: *Get to her. Protect her. Keep her safe.*

Clyde passed me on the way to the plane and I let him lead me to where the antenna was supposed to get attached. We came to a stop next to the plane, about the middle part right before the first set of windows.

He turned to face me as he reached for the antenna. I handed it to him, since he was probably the only one here that could install it.

"It's higher up than this. I'll need you to give me a boost while I install it," he said loudly, trying to be heard over the various squeals and the sound of wings.

"How high?" I asked, almost shouting in return as I made a foot hold with my hands and lowered my stance slightly.

"Three feet, but if I need to go—" he cut off sharply when a spiked tail shot through his chest, pierced through his body from behind.

In my shock, time seemed to momentarily freeze. I saw Clyde's face mix with surprise and pain. Fear clouded every part of his blue eyes as his mind registered what was happening to him. Then he was pulled into the darkness of the forest.

Clyde—and the antenna—were gone.

Miranda's arm stretched into my vision then, reaching past me toward Clyde, who had vanished just half a second earlier. I blinked and remembered how to move.

"CLYDE!" I screamed, stepping forward once toward the darkness.

Miranda moved, wrapping one of her arms under my chest and pulling me back. Her strength was much greater than mine, and I couldn't fight against it.

"Grab the door, John!" she ordered as she turned around the corner of the plane, dragging me effortlessly along with her.

My mind managed to figure out what she meant just as she jumped up into the cockpit, and I grasped the inside of the cockpit's door as she did so. It swung shut with a loud bang, signaling our momentary safety.

I heard two loud sounds from the door of the cockpit as the creatures tried to break inside.

"Clyde …" I muttered, still shocked by what had happened.

"He's gone. There's nothing we can do about that. All that's left is to focus on surviving the situation before us," Miranda said, releasing her grip on me after she had lowered me to the floor.

I was in the corner of the cockpit, and she had turned to face the windows. She pulled out a flashlight, and turned it on before dropping it at my feet. Another sword flashed into existence in her free hand, and she crouched protectively in front of me.

I swallowed and hardened my thoughts. She was right. I couldn't be thinking about Clyde right now. Miranda was here, and I needed to do my best to keep her safe. Not that I could do much.

I got up into a crouch, pulling the pistol out from my jeans and gripping it tightly. I grabbed the flashlight and held it next to the gun, aiming at the windows. It wasn't long before they started smashing into it, cracking the glass with each hit. A couple tried to fly in the window that was already opened, but they were too big with their wing span, and didn't manage to fit. That'd be a different story if they managed to break open the bigger, main front windows. It made me flinch each time they hit the glass. As soon as they made it through, we'd be in a conflict that we're unlikely to survive.

"Do you think we can live through this, Miranda?" I asked, speaking just loud enough to be heard.

Her voice was strained as she answered, "I want to say yes, but our situation is getting worse by the minute."

Another impact on the glass, and a couple cracks got bigger.

"If we don't …" I started, then didn't finish.

She turned her head slightly, peaking curiously at me with one eye.

"Thanks for keeping me alive this far," I finished.

Sure, if I never met her I'd probably not be facing my death, but that wasn't her fault. If she hadn't met me, she'd probably still be in Chicago. We were in the same place.

Another creature collided with the window, and this one knocked out a small chunk of the thick glass.

"Even with facing this …. Even if this is where we die, I'm grateful," she replied.

This time, when the creature hit the window, it broke in enough that it was halfway in the cockpit. Miranda didn't hesitate, and impaled the creature before it got any closer, killing it instantly. She retreated two steps, returning to her original position in front of me. Another creature stabbed its tail into the dead one, and yanked it out of the window, freeing up the entry point.

I tensed, waiting for them to rush in and overwhelm us. Waiting for them to kill us. I swallowed, ready for the first one to enter, but then I heard it.

A growl.

Loud, deep and powerful, I could feel it vibrate in my chest. The sound came from outside the plane, and as soon as it stopped silence followed. There were no squeals of the vyrm-like creatures, or even a single sound of their wings flapping. They had retreated immediately, fleeing from the sound of a more dangerous predator.

"That's it," I muttered softly to Miranda, "that's what I heard when we first crashed."

She looked at me and swallowed, "You're right. It does sound hungry."

CHAPTER 6

I don't know how much time had passed since the vyrms left, but the beast only attempted to break into the cockpit once. There were four gashes in the side of the plane now, each one parallel to the others and about a foot long. Only its four, pure-white claws could be seen as it pierced the metal and slid downward. After that, we only heard a few growls before it grew silent.

Miranda had taken a seat next to me, with about six inches separating us. She was wrapped in a survival blanket, the ones that are all silver and reflective. I had my own blanket, but it wasn't cold enough that I really needed it. Miranda, on the other hand, was shivering. The cold came with a thick, heavy fog that covered everything. It sat on the windows, completely blocking our view of the outside clearing. The fog made the windows damp, which in turn would slowly drip into the cockpit now and then, coming in from the holes and cracks in the windows. The only light source we had was a small flashlight, which lay on the floor and shined across the cockpit.

"What's the plan when morning comes?" I asked, looked over to Miranda.

"W-w-well, without the anten-n-na, we have no choice but to hike back to the c-c-city," she said, shivering.

I watched her for a moment. "If you're cold, take my blanket."

"N-n-no," she said between chattering teeth.

"I'm fine, just take it," I said as I started removing it.

She caught my wrist in mid-air as I started to pass it over to her. "but you're fine right now bec-c-cause of that bl-blanket. I'm n-not going to make you c-c-cold merely so that I'm more comf-fortable. That blanket isn't c-c-coming off you."

I noticed the fire-orange ribbon that she used to tie up her hair was now wrapped around her wrist. She had let her hair down not too long ago. It surprised me to feel just how ice cold her fingers were. Surely the temperature wasn't that low, was it?

I looked past her hand and met her stubborn green eyes. "Fine."

I grabbed her wrist with my free hand, and pulled.

"W-w-what are you doing?" she stuttered as her body was pulled next to mine.

"Obeying your stupid rule," I replied, spreading my blanket over both of us.

She didn't say anything as I swept my arm over her shoulders and pulled her over the last couple of inches. Her body was the same temperature as her hand—freezing. I evened out the blanket as I felt her settle into a more comfortable position against me.

"This is fine, right? Middle ground for both of us," I stated.

She didn't reply, but her head lowered a bit, resting on my shoulder.

"How c-c-come you're so w-warm?" she asked, rhetorically, "it's not fair."

I didn't reply, and as the minutes passed she slowly stopped shivering. I knew I couldn't keep pretending that nothing had happened. I felt like it was wrong to not talk about it.

"Clyde's death is my fault," I said simply.

Miranda looked up at me, but I didn't meet her eyes. After a short moment, she looked down again.

"Don't be stupid," she said, "it's definitely my fault and mine alone. Don't blame yourself for something that wasn't your responsibility in the first place."

"He was right in front of me, but I couldn't do anything. You couldn't protect us from everything. I knew that, and if I was more careful, Clyde would still be here."

She looked up at me again, but like before, I didn't meet her eyes.

She reached up and gently tilted my chin down to face her. Even though she had stopped shivering, her hand was still far from warm. Her green eyes almost glowed in the near-darkness, and I saw strength in them.

"Stop these thoughts. It's easy to think about how you could've saved him after the fact, but doing so only hurts your soul. He's gone. Thinking about how you could've done it differently doesn't change that, nor does it help you the next time a comrade gets put in danger. If you truly feel it's your fault, then pray, apologize, and move on. Anything past that is purely masochistic and pointless."

"Isn't that cold? Isn't regretting what I have done or obsessing over what I should have done different what makes me human?" I argued.

She held my eyes for a moment longer, then lowered her head back down to my shoulder as her hand fell away from my face. "We come from entirely different worlds, John. I've seen your world, so trust me when I say that between the two of us, I'm the one who's been more intimate with death. I know that what you're thinking doesn't help anything because I've had those same thoughts many times. It doesn't make you more human. It doesn't honor the person that died. It doesn't make you a better person. All it does it bring you pain, and slowly drive you into depression and loneliness. All that's needed is a simple prayer, fueled by belief and determination. Then you move forward again, and try harder to protect the next one."

I hesitated, thinking over her words. "Who did you lose?"

"Do you want the list alphabetical, or chronological?" she asked coldly, without any humor in her voice.

"Sorry. I shouldn't have asked." I replied, surprised at her cold tone.

She sighed. "It's okay. I'm just …."

I felt her shake her head, and her thought trailed off into the silence that followed.

A couple minutes passed before Miranda spoke. "John?"

"Yeah?" I answered her.

I had my head leaned back against the steel of the plane and my eyes closed. Sleep was subtly tugging at the edges of my mind, even in this deadly place. The pain in my arms and legs had returned, but it wasn't nearly as bad as it was earlier in the day.

"You know our chances of living through this are minuscule, right?" her voice was calm, but soft.

I opened my eyes, staring into the near darkness that surrounded us. "Yeah. They're not great."

I watched my breath as it escaped from my lips, swirling into the air. I hoped it didn't get any colder than this, or we'd be in trouble before daybreak even hit.

Miranda hesitated before continuing, "... Do you regret meeting me? If you hadn't, you wouldn't be here."

Her question surprised me, but I kept it hidden.

I answered almost immediately, "No."

Her head raised again, but I kept my head against the steel of the plane, looking up at the ceiling.

"Why not?" she asked, her warm breath brushing gently against my neck.

I hesitated thoughtfully. I truthfully didn't know. Maybe it was because I never really liked how my life was going or where it was headed. Maybe it was because I hated the pressure that school and the future had on me. Maybe it was because I was lonely. Hell, I didn't know, and right now I was too tired to think about it.

So, I answered her question with one of my own. "Do you?"

She looked down now. "No. Of course not."

"Why?" I asked her.

She paused again before answering. "I see your point."

Hm. I didn't even mean to make a point; I was just being curious. But now I was wondering what she was thinking. I knew that my reason for not regretting this revolved around some part of my distaste for the life I lived before Miranda, but why didn't she know?

Again, I stopped thinking about it. Thinking took effort, and I didn't want to put effort into anything right now. I felt my eyes slowly close as I gave into the gentle temptation of sleep

Time passed as I drifted in and out of consciousness, but I became alert again after Miranda whispered my name.

"Hm?" I asked, opening my eyes.

"Did you hear that?" she asked.

I paused, listening. I could hear Miranda's steady breathing next to me, quiet and gentle, and it was at a slightly faster rhythm than my own. Around us, the only thing that made a sound was the very subtle drip, drip of the fog-turned-water that slowly leaked into the plane from the windows. The electronics were dead and still, giving off no sound and making the cockpit a little eerie in the low light that the flashlight gave.

Beyond the cockpit lay a world completely different than when we went after the antenna. It was a world filled with a silence that was so thick it drowned out any sound that could be made in it. This silence was foreign to any that I had ever felt. The surrounding air when we'd gone after the antenna was one filled with uncertainty and patience as the creatures waited for us to leave the cockpit. Now, however, the silence was caused by terror. A type of silence that hangs in the air as you hide from the death that hunts you. The heavy and overbearing fog only amplified this sensation and made it impossible to see any farther than a couple of feet.

"I don't hear anything," I replied.

We both waited, tense and unsure, straining our ears for any hint of noise. I detected nothing at first, but soon I heard a gentle, rapidly repeating whumpa-whumpa noise.

"I hear it!" I announced, "is ... is that what I think it is?"

"Can't be. We never managed to call them," she answered.

She pulled her survival blanket tightly around her as she stood up, trying to keep warm in the still-cold air. I stood up and followed her over to the windows. We looked up, but couldn't see anything past the fog. The sound got louder, then the fog suddenly lit up in a flash of white light that quickly darted away. They were searching for us.

Miranda let the survival blanket fall away from her shoulders. "Get ready John. This is our last chance of escaping this place."

"Ready when you are," I answered her.

She nodded, her eyes focused on the fog. "The wind from the

helicopter will force the fog away so we'll be able to see, but stay on alert."

She bent down and grabbed a flare that was discarded on the floor after the failed expedition. She lit it and tossed it out the window, signaling the helicopter where we were.

A long moment passed, and with each second that passed I prayed that the helicopter pilot saw the flare and hadn't abandoned us. White light suddenly appeared again, bringing me incredible relief. Soon the fog cleared up and we could see outside of the plane. The fog hadn't completely disappeared, as it still clung to the ground, but it was enough to maneuver. It had been pushed back, forming a decent sized clearing, but the wind caused by the helicopter didn't reach the entire clearing. The fog that wasn't pushed back from the wind remained unaffected and looked like a tall, white wall. The helicopter didn't descend to the ground, and instead hovered some distance above us.

"What about the creature?" I asked, my eyes searching the edges of the clearing for it.

"If we're lucky, the sound of the helicopter drove him off," Miranda stated.

"And what are the chances of that?" I asked.

She didn't answer my question, but instead turned toward the door. "Let's go."

I took a deep breath and followed.

A flash of blue light signaled her summoning a blade as she opened the door and dropped down into the mist. I picked up my pistol from the corner, where we had been sitting, and jumped down next to her. We walked out toward the middle of the clearing together, cautious of our surroundings. The wind that was coming down whipped against my skin, and with the chill of the fog it made me immediately cold. I felt the fog seep into my clothes and make anything below my knees wet. I looked up, squinting at the bright white light that was shining on us and tried to see the helicopter. I couldn't see anything past the light, but I saw a rope ladder falling toward us, and after a moment it landed on the ground next to me.

A chill ran down my spine as a familiar sensation suddenly filled my body with fear. I had felt this way when we first crashed into this place. I was prey. I was food. I was being hunted.

"Miranda!" I said, loudly enough to be heard of the whumpa-whumpa sound of the helicopter.

"I know!" She replied, summoning a second sword to her free hand.

We waited, patient but tense. I could feel a pressure on me. It knew how to remain unseen and undetected, but it was purposely letting its presence known. I gripped my pistol with two hands and looked forward, straining my eyes to see past the mist.

I saw its yellow eyes first, shining reflectively in the light from the helicopter, but it was still too far into the fog to be seen. Slowly, confidently, it emerged and I felt my eyes grow wide and my legs tense as fear washed through my body.

My heart rate rapidly sped up as the flight instinct pounded through my veins. It told me to run until my legs gave out, and then, once I reached that point, to crawl. It was an urge so strong that I can't say I could've resisted if my legs weren't locked up.

It was huge, easily eight feet tall. It walked on all fours, and closely resembled a lion, except that it was the darkest shade of black I've ever seen. So dark it seemed to suck in the light around it, and the only light escaping was coming from its strong yellow gaze. The creature was broad and muscular, and every inch of it screamed a single word: powerful. Its black mane covered its shoulders and trailed down the front of its chest. The hair that coated the rest of its body was shorter and tougher. The back half of its body was still submerged in the mist, and I couldn't see any details. Not that it really mattered, since the front of it was plenty scary enough. It locked its gaze onto mine, and the frightful pressure I felt intensified. It opened its mouth slightly and let out a low, deep growl. It resonated so that I felt it in my chest and bones. It's gaze simultaneously held a proclamation of challenge, and the proud assurance of victory.

"John," Miranda said, her voice tense.

I looked over, meeting her cool, collected gaze with a wide-eyed, fearful one of my own. I sucked in a deep breath as the sight of her face broke me free from the paralyzing terror that had flooded my mind. I exhaled shakily and blinked several times. If I panicked now, how would that help Miranda? It wouldn't. It would only get us killed.

Miranda noticed the change, giving me a nod of understanding. "This isn't like the black-scaled monkey. This is completely out of our league. I'll distract it, but I need you to start climbing the ladder as fast as you can. I'll need at least ten feet of free space below you, but the higher you get the easier it'll be."

She was right. If I don't stay out of her way, I'd get us killed. I hated it, but she was right. I was helpless in this situation. I gave a single, stiff nod, then immediately turned and grabbed ahold of the ladder as I stuffed the pistol into the back of my jeans.

I didn't see it, but the black lion gave a deafening roar. My entire body tensed and my hands flew to cover my ears protectively. My ears started ringing after its roar came to an end, and the sound of the helicopter was suddenly softer as my hearing was weakened. I gritted my teeth and started climbing, forcing myself to move upward. I shook my head, trying to clear the unsettling sensation as I climbed, focusing on the one thing Miranda told me to do.

I felt the ladder start being pulled upward, but it didn't seem like the helicopter had begun to move yet, so I assumed that the ladder was being retracted. I looked down, feeling positive that Miranda was on the ladder by now, but all I saw below me was about thirty feet of loose ladder. My eyes darted around the clearing, suddenly noticing that Miranda wasn't there anymore. The black beast was gone too, and my eyes searched frantically over the fog for a flash of blue light. Anything to tell me that she was still fighting. My fearful heart pounded rapidly as I hung on the ladder, and my mind started to panic. What if she was dead? What if she lost because I was such a burden to her?

I suddenly noticed that the helicopter was much louder now than it was before, and I felt a gloved hand on my wrist. I didn't do more than glance at the man who was helping me into the copter before I returned my gaze back to search the fog. I stepped onto the landing skids and grabbed a loose handle that hung down in a loo from the helicopter's ceiling.

The ladder was still being retracted, and I held out a hand over it and yelled, "Stop!"

The ladder came to a halt, and I heard the man next to me ask me where Miranda was, but I ignored him. I felt like I didn't have time to explain everything to him.

Where the hell was she? I thought impatiently.

She said she'd follow. She said she'd—wait …. She didn't say that she'd follow. She only made it sound like that was what she planned.

I swallowed, unsure what to think, and even more unsure of what I should do. If I went down there I'd die. It'd be just like our fight with the black-scaled monkey, except I doubt we'd scrape by this time. Time seemed to stretch into infinity as I waited on a knife's edge. Finally, after much too long, I saw her dash out of the mist and into the clearing.

She crouched and jumped, skyrocketing toward the ladder. The dark lion lunged out of the mist after her, growling aggressively. The lion's outstretched claws missed her back by inches as Miranda jumped. She managed to grab on the very end of the rope ladder and then started to hoist herself up. The lion gave another deafening roar at her, then turned and dashed out of the clearing. Its speed was supernaturally fast for a creature of its size, but the main thing I noticed was the roar itself. It wasn't one of defeat, but of annoyance, and I got the feeling it wasn't done trying.

"Start reeling it in, and tell the pilot to take us up!" I shouted back behind me to whoever it was that helped me up earlier.

I watched Miranda as she pulled herself up far enough to put her legs on the ladder, and start to steadily climb.

"Come on, come on, come on …" I chanted as my eyes darted over our surroundings, looking for the dark lion.

Miranda was halfway to the helicopter when I saw movement from the corner of my eyes. It was barely noticeable, since it's black fur made it look like the darkness itself was moving, but I saw it rapidly clawing its way up a tree to our right.

I glanced down at Miranda and shouted at her, hoping to be heard over the noise of the helicopter. "Hurry!"

She only had ten feet left between her and the helicopter. If she hurried, she could make it. We could escape.

I looked back at the lion, finding it immediately as my eyes widened with surprise. It was running along a branch that extended out toward the helicopter, but there was still over twenty feet between the chopper and the end of the thick branch. Judging from its speed and potential strength, I didn't doubt that it would make the jump. She couldn't defend herself hanging like that, and I wasn't even sure if she'd noticed it yet. Miranda was out of time.

So, another person will be taken from me. Again, someone I wanted to protect and keep safe will be ripped away and destroyed. Again, I was stuck here, helpless and forced to watch as it unfolded in front of me. Another failure to burn in my mind and antagonize me over and over.

Hell no.

I felt rage, fury, and ferocity flood through my mind as my hand slipped out of the loop that hung from the ceiling of the helicopter. I wasn't going to be restrained this time. I wasn't going to let this world do whatever it wanted to what I deemed important. I refused to allow it, even if I had to burn the world to stop it.

I felt excitement flood through me. I didn't have to restrain myself anymore. I didn't have to be careful this time. I didn't have to hold back. I could let this anger and rage take control of my mind, after such a long time of making sure it stayed buried inside me.

I leaned and allowed myself to fall forward, away from the helicopter. I knew the lion must be making his leap toward her, but I focused on the ground, waiting for the beast to come into my vision.

I would change this. I would not let this continue its path. I didn't care what happened to me or what got in my way; I'd surpass it all. I'd crush this creature for even entertaining the idea of hurting her.

It came into view now; yellow eyes shining with victory as they fixed on Miranda. The creature looked up as it noticed me crashing down on him, and I felt my jaw tighten furiously. My entire mind, emotions, willpower, and heart were all intertwined around a single goal that burned within me.

I will kill you.

We collided right next to Miranda, but I couldn't see if she knew what had happened. The lion had much more mass than me, but I had momentum and gravity on my side. I landed on its neck, immediately forcing it downward and away from Miranda. My upper-torso hit first, and I wrapped my arms around its neck in an awkward, mid-air tackle. I noticed the black mane was soft to the touch, but also thick. I could easily grab fistfuls of it to keep from being thrown off as we twisted and spun around in the air.

In what seemed like an instant, we hit the ground. Through the grace of God, I landed on top of the lion, instead of the other way around. Although I had the cushion of the lion to soften my landing, the air was still knocked out of my lungs., Even so, the objective in my mind was so clear—so fierce, that it didn't matter. I pushed myself away from the lion's mane and stood up next to its head.

There was a very short moment of peace, then it suddenly sucked in a deep breath, signaling that it was still alive. It started lifting its head from the ground, but I felt strength pounding through my arms with every heartbeat; my system flooding with adrenaline. I grabbed its snout and gave a sharp, strong push. It snapped down to the ground immediately, as if the lion was no bigger than a cub. I'm not sure when I had grabbed the pistol that had been tucked in the back of my jeans, but it was suddenly in my hand. I didn't even pause before I pointed it directly a wide, staring yellow eye.

My finger tightened on the trigger, about to fire the pistol, but I saw a hint of something in its eye that made me hesitate. Did it know it was going to die? Did it know that I had it beat?

I felt my mouth twist into a smile as I glared down at the beast. For some reason, I was happy to imagine that it did. I enjoyed the idea of it knowing its mistake. I felt excitement at the possibility of the creature feeling despair.

"You deserve this."

The beast didn't move. It didn't breathe. It didn't even blink.

Before I could complete the shot, I heard something hit the ground hard next to me and a small grunt of pain. An arm immediately wrapped around my chest, and I was suddenly pulled up into the air and away from the animal. The dark lion got to its feet immediately and let out another deafening roar before it limped off into the tree line of the forest.

The injustice of the situation infuriated me. That thing deserved to end, to die and to rot. That creature was getting away with what it did—my prey was escaping. I wanted to fight against the hold on me and fall to the ground to finish what I started. It was an intense feeling, and one that took a long minute to bring under control. The only thing that kept me from doing so was the feeling of Miranda's body against my back and her tight hold on me. I kept reminding myself over and over that she was safe and that was all that mattered, trying to control my fury any way that I could. But until we were back inside the helicopter, it was all I could do to keep myself from going after it again.

The helicopter was already past the canopy when the ladder was finished being reeled in and we got on board. As soon as I was inside, I felt exhaustion hit me, and I lowered myself to the floor of the helicopter. My arms screamed in pain, and my lungs hurt with every breath I took. I didn't even have the energy to stay sitting, and I ended up collapsing onto my stomach.

Miranda sank to the floor next to me, asking me where I was injured as she quickly traced along my arms, feeling my bones. Then she turned me over onto my back. Her touch, normally pleasing, made my muscles burn with intense pain, and after I cried out she abruptly stopped.

"Where, John? Did the fall break something?" Worry and urgency coated her every word.

"My arms hurt like hell, but I don't think I broke any bones," I replied, opening my eyes and looking over at her.

She was sitting on her knees, half bent over me as her eyes searched my arms any damage. I saw blood trickle down her arm, and although it wasn't life threatening, there was still a lot of it.

"You're bleeding," I stated, trying to sit up.

She placed a firm hand on my shoulder to stop me. It was a good thing she did, since it would've probably been outrageously painful for me if I succeeded.

"I had a couple close calls, but it isn't anything that's worth you're concern. Close your eyes and rest ..." she was saying, but her voice got more and more gentle as she spoke.

I suddenly noticed that my vision had turned dark, and before another moment had passed I was unconscious.

CHAPTER 7

I heard the sound first. A beeping noise, slow, calm, and gentle. The source of the noise was to my left and above me, but I couldn't tell what it was. Another noise, softer and less sharp, was coming from ahead of me. It reminded me of a pen on paper. I smelled the very subtle scent of pure alcohol, and it immediately reminded me of a hospital.

I realized I was lying down on a bed, but that was the only familiar thing about this place. I sucked in a deep breath through my nose as my eyes flew open. I immediately closed them as the light stung my eyes, making me groan and blink rapidly.

"Oh! Look who decided to wake up," said a female voice I didn't recognize, coming from the bottom of the bed.

My eyes finally adjusted, and I could see my surroundings. It looked like a hospital, but something about it made me feel like it wasn't. The room I was in was wide, with my bed on the left side and an empty bed on the right. There was an automatic sliding glass door the middle of the room, which was closed right now. Next to the wall to my left was a couch that spanned the entire wall. There was a window over the couch, and two more on the wall my bed was against; one between my bed and the couch, and another between the two beds in the room. The windows were covered by a set of vertical blinds, which prevented me from seeing outside but showed me the yellow glow of sunlight.

The woman at the end of the bed was a brunette with her hair in a ponytail except for a short lock that hung over her forehead, almost reaching the top rim of her black glasses. She wore no makeup, and looked at me with clear, sharp brown eyes. She was skinny, and didn't have the slim muscle that Miranda had. She wore a white T-shirt that read 'shut up and let me heal you' in black letters, and a pair of deep-blue jeans. I doubted she was much older than thirty. She was pretty in a natural way. I noticed her beauty without her trying, and it made her seem approachable and likable. She held a clipboard in one hand and a pen in the other, but she stopped writing when I woke up. I sat up straighter and took another deep breath, trying to think more clearly.

I noticed a chair next to my bed, empty now, but it was clearly used.

The woman saw my gaze. "She stayed here ever since you were admitted. Of course you'd wake up within five minutes of her leaving. Men can be so cruel," she sighed.

"Miranda?" I asked, meeting her clear brown eyes.

"Who else? That girl wouldn't even leave to eat. I actually had to bring her food or she'd never have eaten anything. I had to reset her ankle here too. But the second she's forced to go give her report, you wake up. Jackass," she said jokingly.

"She had an injured ankle?" I asked, surprised.

I didn't remember anything happening to her ankle.

"You didn't know? She had to jump all the way down after you and the dark lion fell to the ground. That height probably would've killed a normal human, and even though she's an Eve, she knew she'd get injured."

"Is she alright? I remember seeing blood before I passed out," I asked, feeling a little guilty.

"Of course. It's only a broken ankle, and she had a few deep scratches from handling the lion. I just removed those bandages before she left, and her skin didn't even have a scar. She was walking on her ankle already when she left, so I'm sure it'll also be fully healed soon."

"Still …. She wouldn't have broken it at all if it wasn't for me."

"From my understanding, she would have received much more sever wounds if it wasn't for you."

I didn't respond to that, but only because I didn't know what to say. I swallowed, feeling the dryness in my throat.

The woman took notice. "I can bring you a glass of water if you want. In the meantime, try to stand up. Your injuries have all healed overnight, but your muscles might still be sore."

Her eyes snapped back down to the clipboard, the pen making the light scratching noise as it moved. A second later and she slipped the clipboard into the slot at the end of my bed, then turned around to leave.

"Thanks," I said as the glass doors opened for her.

She waved her hand in acknowledgment as she left, and the glass doors shut automatically behind her.

Scooting to the edge of the bed, I slowly lowered myself to the floor. Thankfully, I was still dressed in my own clothing, and not a hospital gown. The floor was cool on my bare feet. My legs felt stiff, but they were usable and pain-free. My arms were sore as the doctor said, but it was nothing compared to how they felt yesterday in the Outside.

I breathed deeply again, calming my mind as it raced with questions. I thought over how I got here, thinking over our journey in the Outside. It felt like a dream or nightmare—a completely different realm of existence other than the one I was in now. How could something so terrifying exist? Before I met Miranda, I thought I knew what the Outside was capable of, but I wasn't even close. The entire time we were out there, I felt an overwhelming desire to hide. An instinct was a constant pressure in the back of my mind that told me to stay alive. I felt as if the very air I was breathing was conspiring against me. It was merciless. I could remember the look on Clyde's face when the creature's tail erupted through his chest, and I could recall the sound of the dark lion's roar perfectly. I remembered what I thought as I jumped from the helicopter. I remember how much I desired to kill the creature that threatened her life.

I thought about the situation again, and I felt anger pump through my veins again. Did Miranda mean so much to me that I was willing to go that far?

"Whoa. Scary look there, fella," the woman said, standing by my bed with a glass of clear water in her hand.

Even though she sounded sincere, I didn't detect an ounce of fear in her voice. I also noticed that I hadn't heard her reenter the room, making me realize how focused I was.

I blinked and shook my head, forcing my face to relax. "Sorry. I was thinking about something."

I avoided her eyes.

"It's fine. I used to know someone who would get like that. To be fair, his expressions were less intense than yours, but it still reminded me of him."

"Who was he?" I asked, curious.

"My Adam," she replied, handing me the glass of water.

I blinked, surprised. She had used the past tense when she mentioned him.

"I'm sorry. I didn't mean to delve into your personal business."

She shook her head, making the brunette lock bounce on her forehead. "No, it's okay. It was a while ago, and I think it'd be wrong to never talk about him. Ever since his death, I've been stationed here. An Eve isn't safe without her Adam."

"Safe?" I asked.

"Yeah. I was strong, and I obviously couldn't take another limiter since they can only be implanted safely as a newborn. Without an Adam or a Limiter, there was no absolute restriction on my power. Add that to my emotional instability and I was a recipe for disaster. I understand the decision."

"What do you mean by 'absolute restriction'?"

She paused, meeting my confused eyes. "Oh, Miranda hasn't told you yet?"

"Told me what?" I asked, feeling a cautious.

She hesitated again, then spoke, "if she hasn't said anything than she must have her reasons. Ask her about it later. It's not my place to say."

I made an annoyed tsk sound with my tongue, but let it go. I drank nearly all the water before I was satisfied, and she took the glass when I was done.

"Okay, now that that's out of the way, you should go see Nathan. He'll need to scan you and take blood work for documentation. He's on floor B6, and then just follow the red line on the floor. The elevator is just down the hall," she said.

"Where am I anyway?" I asked.

"Alexandria Academy's Recovery Center."

"Recovery Center? What, like a hospital?"

"I suppose you could see it that way, but with how fast Miracle Children regenerate it's more accurate to call it a Recovery Center. They're usually fit to leave within a night." She answered.

I looked out the window, but I still couldn't make out anything through the blinds.

"Now that I think about it, how'd they find us? We never managed to send out a rescue signal," I asked.

"Your pilot managed to send out a mayday before you crashed. Even though there was some heavy interference of some sort, they managed to clean up the message and learn that something happened to your aircraft. I'm assuming they used a GPS signal to find a location."

"I see." I replied.

If we had known that, Clyde would still be alive. I closed my eyes and took a deep breath, calming my rising emotions of regret.

"By the way, Miranda asked me to tell you to meet her in the dining hall if you wake up. I don't know how long her report will take, but we might as well get a move on. I'll walk you to the elevator," she said.

"Thanks," I said, opening my eyes and heading toward the door.

She waited for me to catch up to her, then matched my stride.

"So, what makes you so special?" she asked.

Surprised by her question, I looked over to meet her eyes. They were curious and objective, studying me with a level gaze as they took in tiny bits of information. I got the feeling that she was more observant than I had thought.

"What do you mean by that?" I asked, carefully.

"You're Miranda's Adam. I heard the whole story. I know the Eve's Gaze happened between you, and something about it has me wondering …. Why you? Why did she accept you as her Adam?"

"Why are you so curious?" I asked.

"I've been Miranda's doctor for a long time now. I've watched her and listened to her subtle small talk, and I feel confident to say that I know Miranda as best as anyone can. She's had several guys approach her, interested in her, and the Gaze has even happened on a few of them, but she never accepted any of them. So why you?"

My eyes fell from her own as guilt swarmed my mind. "If you know the whole story, then you know it wasn't her choice. It was an accident that we're together."

"Hmm. Perhaps your physical connection was, but that doesn't mean she had to accept you, does it?"

I blinked in surprise and looked up. "What?"

She smiled as she hit the elevator's call button. "And even if it wasn't her choice to make you her Adam, it was her choice to stay here next to you, concerned and patient."

"Huh," I said, thoughtfully.

Her smiled flashed into a grin for a moment as the elevator doors opened, then she turned and started walking away. "I'll leave you to mull that over."

I entered the elevator as she spoke, and then turned around to see her starting to walk away. "Wait, what's your name?"

She stopped and turned around as the elevator doors had started to slide together, and I had to catch them to hear her. "Oh, I'm sorry! I'm absolutely awful at remembering to introduce myself. I'm Elizabeth. Good to meet you."

"Johnathon. Likewise," I replied.

She gave me a quick smile, and then she departed.

I leaned against the side of the elevator and crossed my sore arms over my chest as the steel doors slide together. I reached forward and hit the B6 button before relaxing against the wall again. Was Miranda okay with what happened? I took her freedom away. I stole a choice from her that should only have been hers to make. An important one, one that affected the rest of her life. The idea that she was popular with the guys wasn't surprising at all considering her looks. But she had turned each of them down. Surely there was a reason behind it. Did she want to be single? Was she waiting for someone specific approach her? Was there someone she wanted, and I'd just gotten in the way?

But she did stay here when she didn't have to. I did save her life, so she probably felt a responsibility to stay next to me all night, and if that's the case I shouldn't be reading too much into it.

I closed my eyes and shook my head. It didn't matter. None of this changed my situation. I was still here in this Academy, a place that I know nothing about.

The elevator stopped its descent, and the doors opened, revealing a darkened hallway. It was bright enough to see, but it was a noticeable difference from the previous floor. I walked off the elevator and looked down both sides of the hallway. The lighting conditions didn't improve in either direction. I heard the elevator doors close behind me, and afterward I realized how quiet this floor was. I didn't hear a single thing except the very gentle hum of the lights above me. It gave the place an almost abandoned feel. I started following the red line at my feet which lead about a hundred feet down a hallway before turning left into another hallway. The rooms I passed had the doors closed, but their silence gave me the conclusion that they were empty. I took one more left turn, listening to my own footsteps echo down the halls.

This hall had something the others didn't; a room on the left side had the door open. A light, brighter than the ones in the hallway, spilled from the room. I could see the red line I had been following lead to it, so I approached it. I didn't hear a sound as I neared, my footsteps sounding loud in this emptiness.

I expected … I didn't know what I expected, but what I found surprised me. The room was small and longer than it was wide. Mounted on the wall to the right was a panel of eight computer monitors in two rows of four over a desk. In the corner, just past the monitors was a closed door.

On the left side of the room was a single countertop that stretched the complete length of the room. It was completely covered with random electronics, most of them disassembled, and various tools that were probably used for the disassembly. The floor was clean and tiled, and the only other thing in this room was a man.

He was lounging back in a computer chair, staring at one of the monitors that was displaying line after line of numbers. As I watched, the line crawled across the screen until it reached the end, and then started over again one line down. He had his feet crossed at the ankles and propped up on the desk, leaning back in his chair. His red and white tennis shoes were completely clean, almost spotless—the only part of his apparel that was. The denim he wore had smudges of black in it, probably some type of oil or grease. He had a black, thin shirt on, which looked clean from what I could tell, but the stains could've merely blended in to the shirt. Over the shirt, he wore a used-to-be-white lab coat, also covered in various black stains and smudges.

His face was set in a serious manner as he focused intensely on the computer screen. He was pale, and had on a pair of small, crystal-clear glasses with thin silver frames. He looked like he hadn't shaved in a couple of days. His blond hair was short from what I could see, but he wore a flipped-up welder's helmet that covered most of it.

He hadn't noticed me enter, so I knocked on the steel rim of the door. He looked up, but his brown eyes hadn't focused on me, as if he was looking as something between us. A couple seconds passed before he blinked and met my eyes. He quickly removed his feet from the desk and stood up, making the chair slide back a couple of feet.

"John! Glad to see you up already! Sorry that I didn't notice you sooner, I had a troubling thought that I was trying to resolve," he said, taking a few steps toward me and holding out a hand to greet me.

His voice was slightly higher pitched than mine, but was smooth and confident, and he was just slightly shorter than me.

I nodded as I shook his hand. "As soon as I was awake, Elizabeth practically kicked me out."

He smiled. "Sounds like her. I bet you didn't even notice she was doing it until after it happened, am I right?"

I returned the smile. "That's exactly what happened."

He laughed loudly. "I'm Nathan by the way. I've been briefed about your, uh, situation, and have been tasked with finding out why."

I raised a curious eyebrow. "Why what?"

"Why you weren't found when you turned twenty-one, of course. And to determine your abilities, if I can. I tried to take some of your blood when you were unconscious, but that redhead gave me the scariest look as soon as I entered the room, so I thought it'd be best to wait," he said, laughing at the end.

"Did she really?" I asked rhetorically.

His loud laughter made me want to smile, and I got the feeling that Nathan was the type of person who got along well with everyone.

"If you don't mind me asking," I started, "who exactly are you? I mean, why were you tasked with finding out why? Are you a doctor or something?"

"Nah, that's Elizabeth's territory. I'm just someone who has a talent for technology. I invented and built the technology that allows us to take detailed brain scans and made drastic improvements on identifying genetic markers of Miracle Children traits," he explained.

"Ah. Okay. Are you a Blessed One like Elizabeth, or...?" I asked.

"No, no, I'm not. Fully normal, I am," he said as he glanced at my arms. "I see you're still dirty as hell."

"Yeah .... Haven't had a chance to clean up," I said, which was true, but I also hadn't realized how dirty I was until he mentioned it. I had a lot of dirt on my skin.

"No problem. Right this way," he said, walking toward the closed door in the corner.

He turned the handle and pushed it, letting the door swing open without him entering. He swung his arm up with his palm facing the ceiling, gesturing me inside. I obeyed, hesitantly.

The first thing I saw was another door facing me across the room. There was a wall directly to my left, so I turned to my right and surveyed the rest of the room. It was a small shower room, longer than wide. Its dimensions were identical to the previous room, but there were two shower stalls on the far side of the room connecting to the long wall. On each of the stall doors there was a stick figure, one in a blue color and another in pink with a triangle dress. There were two towels hanging on the wall between the shower stalls, and two benches on the right side of the wall, each one facing a stall.

"I'm sure it's not as glamorous as you're used to, but it's important that you get cleaned up. The dirt and grit from the Outside can interfere with the scanners in the next room. Get washed up and then step into the next room when you're done. Also, don't get redressed. You can't have any clothes on during the scan."

"Uh, sure. Okay," I replied, trying to get my head around all this.

He nodded and then shut the door, leaving me alone.

I undressed, leaving my dirty clothes on the bench as I entered the shower. I played with the different temperatures on the faucet, and I discovered that there were only two settings: cold and freezing. I decided to go with cold. There were two dispensers on the wall. I assumed one was soap and one was shampoo, but neither was labeled. I smelled each on my hand and gave it my best guess. The liquid foamed in my hair, which was very shampoo-ish, so I concluded that I made the correct choice. I didn't shower long; the temperature was too cold to make that a realistic option. I got out and dried off, then I headed over to the next door. He said I couldn't be clothed, but I kept the towel around my waist until I knew what was on the other side of the door.

I twisted the handle and opened it halfway, surveying it before I took a step inside. Just past the door was a small, four-foot hallway with a low ceiling. It was unlit, but white light from the room beyond spilt into the hallway.

I took a step forward into the hall, curious of the room beyond, but I stopped when my bare feet felt the texture of the flooring. It was rough, almost like concrete. I took a second look at that hallway walls and realized that they were made of the same, white concrete-type material as the floor. I continued into the next room, hearing only my soft footsteps on the floor.

The room was smaller than the previous two I had seen. The floor was square, but the walls were curved upward to make a dome-shaped ceiling. The curved walls and ceiling weren't made of concrete like the

115

hallway. Instead, it was made of a smooth material. I couldn't make out any more details than that because the material was also the source of the white light. There was a steel bench in the middle of the room, and on the right side of the room was three differently sized dumbbells.

"Okay John, go ahead and toss your towel on the bench and stand in front of it, holding your hands at your side." Nathan's voice was heard through speakers, though I couldn't tell where the speakers were.

I followed his instructions and stood straight with my arms at my sides. My eyes surveyed the white, smooth walls carefully, feeling self-conscious and defensive standing there in the nude.

Barely a minute had passed before Nathan's voice sounded over the speakers. "Alright, I got the basic scan done, so now I'll have to get a more detailed scan on your body structure. Go ahead and pick up the lightest weight on the right side of the room there."

Again, I obeyed. It wasn't heavy. There wasn't a weight number on it, but from how it felt it was probably twenty pounds.

"I need you two do various muscle movements with each of these weights to get an accurate scan of your muscles. The first one is simple weight lifting, so please do a few curls for me."

I stifled a sigh and took a seat on the bench, starting to wonder how long this was going to take. As soon as I got out of the shower, I had felt famished and would kill for some food. That, and I wouldn't mind seeing Miranda.

I followed his directions as he talked me through each maneuver, and it took a good five minutes to complete it. I had to do the same thing for each of the different weights, which were increasingly heavier. The last of the three was at least fifty pounds, and so the middle was probably around the thirty-five mark. Fifty pounds wasn't lite, especially when he made me try to do the awkward maneuvers like raising it over my head and lowering it behind my back. It was even more awkward doing these naked, but that feeling faded as it began to get more difficult to complete the maneuvers. I was panting at the end, and returned to my seat on the bench.

"That should be plenty of scans regarding your muscle movements, so now you can just sit there while I do the brain scans. Every now and then I'll ask you to think of something, including tastes, certain emotions, and even strong memories. This will take the longest so get comfortable," Nathan said.

I groaned softly before answering, "Okay."

Three minutes passed in silence before he finally spoke again.

"Can you think about your favorite flavor? We might as well start with an easy one," he said.

"Hmm …. Okay," I said, unsure of which was actually my favorite.

I just quickly settled on raspberries, merely because I knew it was my favorite fruit. In fact, now that I was considering it, raspberries were one of the few fruits I had ever had. Life in the Lowers wasn't exactly a luxurious one.

"That's looking good. Keep that up if you could."

Ugh. It was making me hungrier, but I tried not to let it break my concentration. Twenty to thirty seconds had passed when he said I could stop.

"I need you to remember an early childhood memory. Earlier the better, and the more emotionally powerful it is, the better."

Hmph. I knew immediately what memory I should use, but it wasn't one of happiness. I was ten years old, just a few weeks away from my eleventh birthday. I was standing in the back of a room filled with tense and silent people. They hadn't noticed me enter because they all were staring at the large TV on the other side of the room. A building was burning, a target of a terrorist attack in Los Angeles hosting a meeting to discuss founding a new power organization. I didn't know any of this at the time; only that my dad had said that he was going to L.A. last night with my mom to have a meeting. Even though I was 10, it wasn't hard for me to connect the dots. I joined the group of people in tense silence.

Nathan's voice was more somber than before when he said, "That's the earliest? Move forward. Think up something in your mid to late teens. I need a happy and sad if you can manage it."

I took a deep breath. "Okay."

Happy, huh? I had a lot of those. Most of them made from my time with Rachel. I knew which one was my favorite immediately.

Rachel was a classmate of mine. We were part of the same circle of friends, but weren't really that close at first. She was wild, adventurous, fearless, and full of confidence. She wasn't afraid to raise her hand, shout out a statement, or give her opinion. But she was also courteous toward others and kind. Watching her, I felt like I was always one step behind, following her as she dazzled with her spontaneous fun. She was mischievous too, unafraid of breaking the rules, and she accepted her current circumstances without hesitation and looked at them with unbreakable optimism.

I was the opposite. I was hesitant and careful around others, always thinking twice before doing anything. I had thought that my disposition then was due to being exiled from the Family, giving me a subconscious fear of being excluded again. However, if I was a Miracle Child, then it could explain that feeling. I was a Blessed One amongst humans; a loner amongst a group. In short, I wasn't with my own kind.

If Rachel was a wildfire, than I was a cool, still pool of water. I avoided general interaction with her at first, astounded by her brightness and never-ending warmth, but she was impossible to avoid forever—I was too drawn to her. Even after I had figured that out, I made no move to tell her how I felt. I made sure that the still pool of water that was my personally made no ripples. Any sort of disruption in my life could cause my entire social world to come crashing down—at least, that's how I felt.

One night, as the group was walking around town we passed by our school. Spontaneous as always, Rachel announced that she wanted to sneak in and head to the roof, insisting that there was a door in the back that was always kept unlocked.

No one wanted to go with her, but when she looked at me with her confident brown eyes, I found myself accepting her unspoken invitation. I usually followed along with the group, but that night, I couldn't resist her.

She was right about the unlocked door, and we made our way through the school in silence, sneaking up the stairs. I stayed just a step behind her, watching as her adventure unfolded, pleased to just be a shadow to her flame. It wasn't long before she opened the door to the roof, and I followed her out, turning the dead bolt before closing it so we wouldn't get trapped.

It was dark that night, even though the moon was full and there wasn't a cloud in the sky. "Ah! I knew we'd be able to see them up here!" she said excitedly, looking up at the twenty or thirty stars that were visible.

The school was located on the outer edge of Chicago, not far from the Wall. Any closer in and the lights from the main city would block them out.

"Pretty!" she said, taking a long look before heading over to the edge of the roof.

She waved, signaling our friends who were still at the gate of the school. I walked forward to the edge in time to see them wave back, but I didn't bother to return the gesture. This was Rachel's show after all. I was merely along for the ride. I even kept a good distance away from her, keeping her company without calling for attention. She lowered her hand and stayed still in silence for a moment, looking out over the school grounds. I looked out too, watching two of my friends goof around.

"You know ..." she started.

"Hm?" I grunted.

"You scare me," she said gently.

I looked over at her in surprise. She had her head angled toward me so that both her eyes could just barely see me, and she wore a sly smile.

"What?" I asked, a little bluntly. Even if we weren't close, I thought I'd left a better impression than that.

She laughed before turning toward me. "It's not like you think. I know you won't attack me or anything. You're a better guy than that."

"Then why?" I asked.

"How long have we known each other now?" she asked as she walked up to me.

I thought it over. She wasn't in any of my classes in school, but she was popular, so I knew of her ever since I'd started high school.

Her and her friends, however, didn't start hanging out with my group until a year ago.

"A year or so, I think," I replied.

She smiled, "a year as of today, actually."

She had a good memory.

She continued, "that's a long time, isn't it?"

"I suppose it can be, yes," I agreed, not sure where she was going with this.

"It's been long enough that I can confidently say that I know you."

"Everything about you is done confidently," I replied.

She gave me a humored smile. "I'll take that as a compliment. You, on the other hand, are the opposite."

I swallowed.

"At first, I thought it was merely indecision that was making you hesitate for just a beat before you spoke or smiled or laughed. It was as if you took just a moment longer than everyone else when deciding what to say. You seemed like you were a split second behind the rest of the world."

I stared at her in surprise. I didn't know she was this observant. I'd thought I was blending in, but someone noticed. Worst of all, she noticed.

"What changed your mind?" I asked.

"I realized it wasn't indecisiveness, but cautiousness. You heeded every action, as if you were afraid of being shunned by us."

"I'm shocked you noticed," I responded, not having the ability to lie when she stared at me so intently.

She laughed gently, which was odd—she always laughed with vigor and confidence. "I notice a lot about you."

"Like what?" I asked, not only out of curiosity, but also to stall while I gathered my wits.

I had no idea how to handle this situation. I was on the brink of panic.

"You're honest; I've never seen you tell a lie. You're kind; one of the few times you don't hesitate is when agreeing to help a friend. You're shy. I haven't heard you mention your childhood or any of your relatives. None of your friends know anything about your past either. You're very intelligent. You hang out with us every day all day long and still get perfect scores on tests while we struggle to get decent grades. You're a good person."

There was a second pause that spanned before she whispered, "and you're in love with me."

She knows. I swallowed and stared in her eyes. I recovered quickly as I asked her, "why would any of that scare you?"

I couldn't deny any of what she had just said, but I didn't admit anything either.

She broke eye contact, looking down at her hands. She reached up with her left hand and pinched her ear lope. I had only seen her do this twice before—each time was when she was nervous.

She spoke in a clear voice despite her body language. "You haven't said anything about it. You never asked me out, even though there have been plenty of opportunities."

I spent a second thinking back on my time with her, and wondered which ones she was talking about. She continued before I had thought of one.

"Any hints of affection toward me so subtle that I can't help but wonder if I'm simply imagining them. What scares me is the possibility that I'm wrong."

She still hadn't met my eyes again, and her body remained tense and nervous. I stayed still, pleasantly shocked by what I was hearing. I hadn't even considered the possibility that she might return my feelings. She was one step away from confessing her feelings for me, but still she waited, making it was clear that she wanted me to be the first to admit it. I was torn.

If Rachel and I got together, it would change the dynamic of our group of friends. What if it didn't go well and the group was ruined? With my friends was the only place where I wasn't alone. On the other hand, lying and rejecting her would still affect our group. In that case, why not choose what I wanted and hope for the best?

She pinched her ear lope again, still obviously nervous. I noticed in the few seconds that passed by in silence that her cheeks slowly became flushed.

I saw her open her mouth to speak, and I knew that my time was up. She was going to take my silence as a denial and leave it at that; probably to minimize the impact it would have on our friendship. If I didn't speak now, I would never get another chance like this.

"You're not wrong," I said hurriedly, "I've been in love with you for a while now."

My sudden confession surprised her. She met my eyes and blinked a couple times, but didn't say anything at first.

"Oh." She said, still a little surprised.

Oh? Oh? What the hell was I supposed to take from that?

She recovered finally, giving me an excited smile. "Good."

"Is it?" I asked.

"Of course." She replied, then quickly stepped forward and threw her arms around my neck.

She surprised me with this, but I recovered immediately. This type of wild reaction fit her perfectly.

"But now things will change." I stated, thinking of our group of friends.

"So what? I knew that as soon as I decided to confront you tonight. No matter what response you gave me, things were going to be different. That risk is worth it. Besides …."

She paused and swallowed as she met my eyes excitedly.

"I'm in love with you too," she confessed.

I felt relief and exhilaration flood through me; I hadn't realized how much I wanted her to say that.

She continued, "since that's the case, why not take what we both want and hope for the best?"

I blinked, and couldn't help but smile as she repeated my earlier thoughts back to me. "I suppose that makes sense."

There was a short moment of stillness between us, before Rachel cleared her throat.

"So?" She said, expectantly.

"'So' what?" I replied.

"Are you going to kiss me or what? This is going to get awkward soon."

I laughed quietly before leaning in to kiss her.

Nathan gave a yawn as I blinked several times, instantly remembering my surroundings. It wasn't hard to get sucked into that memory.

"That's plenty, thanks. Can you think of a sad one now? The closer it is to that one the better. Time-wise I mean, like within a couple of years."

I hesitated for a few seconds, then spoke in a low voice, "Sure … I can do that."

Sad, huh? There was definitely a sad memory that dominated all the others. My darkest memory. The last one I had with Rachel.

It was just another day for us, normal like any other we had together. I was walking her home like I always did, taking the route we always took. She was holding my hand as we walked in silence. This last fifteen minutes were always quiet between us, but a good quiet, since neither of us wanted the night to end. Then the rain came, and it came down hard. We were drenched in seconds, soaked completely through our clothes. There was no reason for us to run, since we were already completely wet, yet we still did anyway. We were not far from Rachel's family's apartment, and in our hurried state I lead her down an alleyway that we normally avoided. I didn't think about it; I was just trying to get us out of the rain.

As we ran, I saw a flash of steel in the near darkness, and then something hard collided with my face. I felt Rachel's hand slip out of mine as I fell backward to the ground. My nose exploded in pain, and for a few seconds it was all that dominated my mind. I immediately yelled for Rachel to run, but another assailant grabbed her before she could even hear me. The man who grabbed Rachel was the biggest one, who was broad with a large chest and bulky arms.

There were two other men there, one of them was the one who hit me with a steel pipe, who turned me over in my stunned state and bent my arm behind my back to keep me still. The other one took my wallet from my back pocket and stole the little cash I kept on me.

These two weren't weak, but they weren't very notable either. But on that night, the other two weren't important.

Dissatisfied with my cash, they complained to the broader guy, who was obviously the leader of the group.

"What are you two talking about?" he sneered, looking at Rachel, "money isn't everything. Sometimes you just gotta enjoy your work."

Rachel felt his hostility and tried to crawl away, but he grabbed her ankle and pulled her under him.

"Don't you touch her!" I screamed at him.

I felt the man that was pinning me to the ground tighten his grip on my arm as he pulled it up higher, putting a lot of pain on my shoulder. I groaned in response.

"Shut up!" the guy ordered, "I'm trying to enjoy the show."

Rachel tried to put her legs between her and the broad guy, but he had a lot more muscle then her, and easily managed to pin her underneath him.

I screamed for help, but I knew it didn't matter; the heavy rain drowned out any sound I made and we were too deep into the alleyway to be seen. I screamed away, ignoring the couple punches to the face I got from the man on top of me.

"Aw, she's a real looker. I hope you keep up the fight longer then the last one," he said as he pinned both her arms above her head with one hand.

I started shouting death threats at him for touching her, but my screams only seemed to make him laugh. The guy sitting on my back cursed at me, telling me to shut up again. He grabbed my hair with his free hand and pulled my head so I was facing the concrete, then he pushed downward, smashing my already broken nose into the ground. He didn't let ease the pressure, pinning my face where it was. I stared out the corner of my eye at Rachel, hoping—begging her to get free.

She was crying, but she hadn't given up fighting. I heard clothes rip over the broad man's delightful laughter. I felt sick to my stomach and struggled again which made the pain in my shoulder intensify.

Rachel got a hand free and swiped at his face. Her nails were long and cut deep, and he gave a loud shout in pain. He responded by giving her a sharp punch in the face.

"Bitch!" he shouted at her.

I saw the man reach into his pocket, retrieving something. Even in the dark rain I saw the flash of silver as he pulled out a knife. He pressed a button and the blade shot out of the top of the handle.

I screamed again, struggling as hard as I could to get free. My shoulder finally gave, and pain washed through my mind, telling me my shoulder had popped out of joint.

I felt my body become paralyzed from the pain and I immediately stopped struggling. I felt my voice crack as I screamed at him.

It was useless. I saw him plunge the knife into her side. Rachel screamed in pain. He didn't stop; I felt my heart break with every thrust of the knife. He stabbed her twice in the side, and three times straight downward into her chest. For the last two strikes, Rachel didn't make a sound.

The man got off her, but Rachel didn't respond. She didn't move at all. There wasn't even a slight rise and fall of her chest as she breathed. She was lifeless.

"You made a mess again," the guy that was holding me down said, as he stood up and released me.

"What do you expect after what she did to me? Shit, this might even scar. Whore," the big guy said.

"What about this one?" The guy asked, obviously referencing me.

"What a pain in the ass ... not really in the mood anymore." He said, his voice getting fainter as they walked calmly away, as if this was just the end of a normal day.

The rain absorbed them, swallowing any sound they made as they left. I was alone. I stared at Rachel's body, begging for a short moment that she'd suddenly suck in a breath of air. I crawled over to her with my good arm, and then painfully sat up. My useless left arm hung loosely next to me. I felt the hot burning sensation in my shoulder, but in my shocked state of mind I ignored it.

Her eyes were still open, staring blindly out, unfocused. I reached my right hand forward, hovering over her eyes, preparing to close them for her. My hand started shaking as I lowered it, but I gently closed her eyelids. I had no idea how much such a simple action could hurt. It felt like my soul itself was being slowly ripped apart. I wept over her, my hot tears mixing with the cold, unrelenting rain as it washed down on me.

I swallowed as the memory had caused my throat to tighten, and I shivered once as the air around me suddenly felt cold. Goosebumps had covered my arms, and I shook my head as I tried to clear the memory away.

I cleared my throat, which sounded loud in this small room, "how was that?"

"Yeah, that's all I needed …" he said, trailing off a little awkwardly.

He cleared his voice and spoke more clearly, "Moving on to the next one then, think about Miranda for me."

I blinked. "Huh?"

"Miranda. Just who she is, your experience with her, certain memories you have about her that seemed to 'pop' at you or was particularly memorable. Anything or everything." he said, his voice confident.

"Uh … right. Okay. I've only known her for a day though," I said, unsure at what he was looking for.

"True, and normally when we do scans for new pairs they have spent a lot more time together, but you're a special case. It might even be better for you, since a lot of times the new pairs don't have the same kind of life and death experience that you and Miranda went through. Just give me what you got."

"Alright, if you say so," I replied.

But I had no idea what to think about.

So, I started at the beginning. The way her crimson hair and green eyes stunned me on the street the first time I saw her. How smooth her skin was under my fingertips as I pulled out her stitches and struggled with if I should trust her or not. It seemed like a stupid thing to think about looking back, since she'd put her life on the line for me several times since then. First when the black-scaled monkey tried to grab me and she put herself in front of me.

Then when we were in the cockpit, and she stood in front of me protectively as the creatures pounded against the windows. I thought through those next moments, remembering the fear I felt when the beast sliced down the side of the cockpit like it was made of paper instead of steel. I remember holding Miranda next to me, speaking quietly to her about our next plans. I remembered her scent that mixed with the dew of the fog, and how her body would shiver next to mine from the cold every now and then. Finally, I remembered the sight of her on the ladder, climbing to safety while the black beast charged toward her, and how it felt as I watched her about to die.

Rage fumed into my mind in that moment, furious at the black lion for trying to take her, but was this reaction of mine because it was Miranda, or was it because of what had happened in the past with Rachel?

I can't let myself replace Rachel with Miranda just to satisfy my guilt. It wasn't fair to Miranda, and I knew it wouldn't solve anything anyway. However, couldn't it also be true that my desire to protect Miranda was genuine, and that it was so strong because I had felt loss before?

I shook my head at myself, pushing those thoughts away. I shouldn't keep asking myself questions I couldn't answer.

"Well that made it easy. Looks like we're done with the hard stuff. Now I just need some general scans for a while. Feel free to think about whatever you want, and I'll let you know when I have enough," Nathan said.

"Okay," I said, suppressing another sigh.

I was so hungry, and I couldn't wait to get out of this room, but I forced myself to be patient. I used the time to ponder what was ahead of me after this, but I wasn't sure how much testing was still ahead of me. I wanted to see Miranda, and she said she'd meet me in the dining hall. I was hungry anyway so that would work out perfectly. All that was left to do was to wait.

After what felt like half an hour, my patience ran out.

"How much longer is this going to take, Nathan?" I asked, failing to keep all the irritation out of my voice.

Nathan laughed a little nervously, "I can see how hungry you are, so I'll have you outta here in a few minutes. Bear with me until then."

I took a deep breath and let it out, but didn't respond.

"While the scans are finishing up, I suppose I can tell you what's next," Nathan said.

"Oh, okay. Do you need something more from me after this?" I asked.

"I just need to discuss your results while I draw some blood from you. It won't take longer than ten minutes, but after that you need to go see Paladin Samson."

I blinked. "Wait what? *Paladin* Samson?"

There was a short pause before Nathan's voice returned, "Yup. Don't worry, you're not in trouble or anything, but I'm sure he'll want to talk with you personally."

"Why?" I asked, still feeling surprised.

Paladin wasn't a title they handed out easily. There was only four of them in the entire world, and they reported directly to the Prophet, who was pretty much in charge of most of the world. Each Paladin handled a certain area of land and dealt with its problems. Even though each Paladin chooses a Miracle Child to personally assist him, there was still a massive amount of work that a Paladin must handle. Why would he make time for just another Adam?

"Dunno. Not my place to speculate really, but I assume it's because you weren't found when you were tested at the age of twenty-one. That, and your scans are rather different. Come on out and I'll explain it all to you. There's a change of clothes in the shower room for you."

"Okay then ..." I said, standing up and wrapping the towel around me.

My eyes felt relieved as I walked out of the room and back into the shower room. I hadn't noticed until now, but the white light in the previous room had started to give me a headache.

There was a small pile of clothes sitting on the closest bench, neatly folded. The shirt was a solid, light blue V-necked tee, and the jeans were lightly faded from use. Even my tennis shoes were here.

I paused for a moment, startled when I realized that these were my clothing. I recovered from my shock and started dressing myself. With as much power and resources the Church had at its disposal, it really shouldn't surprise me that they would retrieve my clothing. Still, it didn't make sense that they wouldn't just get me new ones. Did they really extend this much effort just so that I would feel a little bit more comfortable here?

It impressed me.

I exited the shower room, leaving my towel on the bench. Nathan was reclining in his computer chair, looking up at the monitors with his hands behind his head—no longer wearing the welding helmet. He leaned forward in his chair and lowered his hands when he saw me enter. He pushed a spare computer chair away from the desk, offering it to me.

I took a seat and surveyed the computer screens as I did so, curious. They were filled with different shots of what I assumed was my brain, each one had different parts highlighted with different colors. I had no idea what they meant.

"How are my scans different?" I asked, my eyes jumping from each monitor to the one next to it in turn.

I looked down to him and saw him opening some sort of reflective package.

"Straight to the point, huh? At least that saves us some time," he said with a smile.

The package he opened contained a fresh syringe, and after he got it out of the packaging he turned his chair to face me.

"Hold out your arm," he said.

I obeyed, giving him my right arm. He found a vein and didn't hesitate, poking me and filling the syringe with my blood.

"Your brain isn't exactly normal. It could be why you weren't detected when you were twenty-one, but I won't know for sure until I test your blood."

"The fact that my brain isn't normal shouldn't surprise you if you think I'm an Adam," I stated.

He shook his head. "Your scans showed that you are definitely an Adam. That much is certainly clear, since your brain activity is higher and you use different areas of your brain that normal people don't. However, your mind is not what the common Adam's mind looks like."

He pulled out the syringe and handed me a cotton ball and some medical tape to keep my wound from bleeding. I dressed the small wound while he continued to explain.

"I'm sure I don't need to tell you this, but the human mind is extraordinarily complex. Regardless, we do see a pattern in brain activity for Adams and Eves. I'll use a generalized example just for the sake of simplicity," he said, holding up both his hands so that his palms faced each other.

"Let's say that the left hand here is the logical side of your mind, and the right hand is the emotional side. A brain scan of an Eve will show that the part of their brain that controls their miracles will be more toward the emotional side. So basically, closer to my right hand. This is because Eves rely a lot on the adrenal gland to access their full potential, and adrenaline is produced when you experience emotions such as fear, anger or excitement. Adams are the opposite, and their scans will show that they're more on the left side, or the logical side. Their miracles tend to be ruled by certain laws or conditions that they must follow, but they can utilize the full potential of their miracle at any time they desire, so long as they follow those certain rules.

"The part of your brain that controls your miracle is still on the logical side of the brain, but it's closer to the emotional side then most Adams. Of course, understand that this example isn't at all how the brain really functions. I just thought this was the best way of getting you to understand," he said.

"I get what you're saying, but what does that mean for me? Is it a bad thing?" I asked.

He smiled and his eyes shined mischievously. "Not at all. It just means that your miracle is probably flexible, less solid and less defined. I expect that your miracle will be very interesting."

"Hmm?" I said carefully, meeting his eyes, "but you have no idea what my miracle is."

His smile grew bigger. "Correct."

"I haven't used any miracles yet, so how were you able to see this in the first place?"

"Are you so sure about that?"

I paused before answering, "Yeah. I haven't done anything close to a miracle."

"You think that because you don't truly know what a miracle is. When you use your miracle, it doesn't just let you do something that's beyond human understanding. It gives you something else that's impossible for a normal human being. Can you guess what it is?" Nathan said, giving me that excited look again.

I could tell from his intensity that he loved this sort of thing. He loved discovery. He loved science. He loved what he did.

"No idea," I replied honestly.

"Control," he answered, "it gives Miracle Children the ability to control their own body at a ridiculous level. They can do things a human can't, and one of the most common things for them is to remove the limitations that their mind puts on their muscles."

My eyes widened a bit when I realized what he was talking about. "But doing that would only destroy their bodies."

My mind answered my own question before he even spoke, but I didn't stop him. "Miracle Children heal a lot faster, which allows them to recover from this side effect. Sure, it hurts, but with how fast they recover, it doesn't hurt long. I'm not sure you remember, because you passed out immediately afterword, but your mind removed its limiters when you jumped out of the helicopter. There is no way you could wrestle with a dark lion without removing those."

I swallowed as I thought this through.

"Right. Well I still need to go over these in detail, but that's what I've discovered so far. I'll run tests on your blood too; it might give some insight as to what your miracle is. I'll let you know if I find anything."

"I'd appreciate it," I responded, standing up.

"Mm. There's a Crusader waiting for you on the ground floor. He'll take you to Paladin Samson, as well as answer any general questions you may have," Nathan said, standing up and shaking my hand.

"Thanks for the information, Nathan," I said.

"You're welcome. If you need anything let me know. I'm something of a genius when it comes to technology and would be happy to help you out. In return, when you find out what your miracle is I'd be very interested in seeing it," he said with a smile and excited eyes.

"I'll keep that in mind," I said, and then left

I heard my footsteps echo down the hall again as I headed back to the elevator. Even without testing my blood, Nathan had proof that I was an Adam. What was I supposed to do now?

I hit the button for the ground floor in the elevator, then looked down at my opened hand. I thought it would surprise me more than it did to have it confirmed that I was a Miracle Child. But it hadn't at all. I talked about it like it was a natural order of business, like it was supposed to have happened all along. Perhaps it was Miranda's persistent confidence and absolute assurance that I was her Adam that made this so easy to believe. I was sure that wasn't the only reason, considering that ever since I got to this Recovery Center they'd acted like I was an Adam and belonged here.

I shook my head as the elevator doors opened and I stepped out. I was in the lobby-slash-entrance hall of the Recovery Center. The room was spacious and bright; sunlight was shining in from tall glass windows on the front of the building. The marble flooring and columns only enhanced the bright light further, but it wasn't blinding; it simply gave the feeling of cleanliness. There were four columns altogether, forming a square with two on each side of the room. Between them a couple of couches and some armchairs were arranged around a small coffee table. The sets were symmetrical with themselves, and were vacant. The only real color in the room came from the green plants that were set in the middle of the small coffee tables. The room was two stories tall, and there was a glass walkway around the second story. There were two elevators on each side of the room, and a receptionist desk to my left against the wall. There were two hallways on either side of that, and signs with directional arrows and a short description on the wall.

The receptionist noticed my gaze and inclined in head to me.

"Good afternoon, sir," she said, then resumed her working.

She assumed I was an Adam. Then again, I suppose I was. After thinking that, I felt another wave of calm come over me, and I didn't know why. I started toward the exit without responding to her, caught up in my own thoughts. It felt like I was living an entirely different life than the one I had been living two days ago. I swallowed when I realized that it really was just two days since I had met Miranda. Two days ago, I was stressing about my future, now it seemed like the future was completely out of my control.

The entrance had two sets of sliding glass doors separating it from the outside. I kept my eyes on the ground as I stepped through them. But when the sunlight hit my face I looked up and felt my mind clear. My eyes grew wide and I stopped in my tracks with amazement.

CHAPTER 8

Whoa.

It was beautiful. The path leading to the Recovery Center was red brick, obviously placed by hand. It was clean and didn't look old or worn-down. The path was wide, easily fifteen feet, and stretched from this building toward another building a little way off ahead of me. Green grass spread out from the dark red brick. The grass was cut low and well-kept, and there was a variety of trees growing around the area, providing shade against the sunlight. It was warm out in the sun, but not hot, and the spring breeze felt cool on my skin. I walked off the path toward the nearest tree and knelt on the grass.

I should've expected this kind of luxury at the Church's disposal, but it still surprised me to see it. I lived my entire life in the Lower Ring, the run-down and poor part of cities. It's the area closest to the Wall, and everything there is made from concrete and steel. Pure dirt and untainted seeds are very expensive, so only the Upper Rings had that kind of money. I had heard that there were entire gardens in the Upper Ring of Chicago, but there was no way in hell I would've been allowed to go up there, let alone have enough money to enter the place.

I felt the grass slide through my fingers, feeling the gentleness and peacefulness of it. This …. This was the first time in my life that I had felt grass. It was strange feeling it. It was soft and cushioned my weight, but at the same time it was also sharp to the touch. It had a gentleness to it as it passed through my fingers, but it also poked me.

Sure, the Outside had plant life and foliage in it, but I couldn't count anything in the Outside to be like this. The Outside radiated hostility and danger. I constantly felt on edge just being around it.

But this—this was the real thing. This was peaceful, gentle, and relaxing. I took a steady breath through my nose, enjoying the subtle sweet aroma of the green growth around me. I flipped over and lay on my back, looking up at the leaves of the tree above me. Was this a dream? Surely something this good was merely a figment of my imagination. I could see a blue sky between the leaves and a few scarce clouds that made steady progress across the sky. The gentle breeze blew against the leaves on the tree, making the sunlight flash in my eyes for a mere second, and I closed my eyes in response. I felt a smile on my face, and for the first time in a long time, I felt happy.

"Great day, isn't it?" I heard a voice say.

I opened my eyes and sat up, surprised that I didn't hear him approach. There was a man standing on the edge of the path. He was tall and fit but with slim muscle. I was probably more built than him, but something about him seemed odd. Maybe it was the way he carried himself …. Yeah, that was it. I realized that he carried no threatening presence at all, and it had made me immediately underestimate his physical abilities.

He had a pair of sharp brown eyes and a young face, but despite his subtle presence his stance was one of confidence. He had short, black hair and wore a black uniform made from a flexible material, but I couldn't tell what it was. His upper shirt was close fitted, and his cargo pants were a little baggy.

"Yeah. Very nice," I responded.

He held out his hand. "I'm Zachariah Cobalt. You're Johnathon, right?"

I grabbed his hand and he helped me up, then he shook it firmly. "That's me. Johnathon Aster. How'd you know?"

He smiled and released my hand. "I've heard about you. New kid that wasn't found when he was born or when he turned twenty-one. Looks like you grew up in the Lowers, huh?" he said, looking around.

I blinked in surprise. "Yeah, that's right. You figured that out just from one look at me?"

"It was pretty obvious that you had never seen pure grass before," he explained.

"Ah. I see. Who are you, exactly?" I asked.

"I'm the Crusader that was supposed to meet you. This place is big, so I'll be escorting you around until you used to the layout. I'll also be instructing you in your hand to hand combat training over the next few days. For now, just take in your surroundings and get used to it. You're training will be hard, but you should also find time to socialize or find some sort of method to relax and recharge. If you don't, you will probably get worn out."

Hm. I had no idea if he had been briefed about Miranda or not. Since that was the case I had better keep that to myself.

"I'll keep that in mind. I've been told that Paladin Samson wanted to meet with me, but when is that exactly?" I asked, hoping I had time to see Mira—I mean, get some food.

"Oh really? I was just told to meet you here. We better get going if that's the case," he said, walking away.

I felt disappointment, but didn't express it. I started following him and realized that he was leading me to a vehicle that was parked on the side of the Recovery Center. I had missed it since I was overwhelmed with the sight of green around me. Even while walking I kept glancing around me, taking in the green grass and bright leaves as if I was afraid they would disappear.

That was when I saw it. I stopped in my tracks as my body turned rigid and went on alert. I couldn't believe I didn't notice it earlier, but now I saw it through the trees. About three hundred meters away was the Outside, with no Wall protecting me from it. It just went from clean grass to dangerous and deadly Outside. My eyes traced upward, seeing the growth of the Outside stretch up hundreds of feet, and feeling the sense of aggression it gave off. The cold, unforgiving survival-of-the-fittest attitude flowed from it and started to drown me. I swallowed and heard my heart start pounding loudly in my ears.

"Calm." I heard a voice behind me, gentle and non-threatening.

My head turned so I could see Zachariah from the corner of my eye, but also so I could keep an eye on the Outside.

"We're safe here. I know it's not something that you can easily accept after going through what you did, but trust me on this. We don't need a Wall in this place. We have something better."

Safe? Without a Wall?

"How?" I asked.

"We own generators that … aggravate the radiation in the Outside. Basically, if anything that has that radiation inside it tries to enter that shield, it'll feel like their blood was set on fire. Everything avoids it."

"That's how they kept this area from being corrupted?" I asked.

"Oh no. This area was completely corrupted in Project Regrowth, but those generators burned down this area and they had to regrow it the old-fashioned way. That's why you don't see any trees here older than thirty years."

"It's a dome, or bubble effect that the generators give off?" I asked.

"Nope. From what I understand, they can only project the effect outward, that's why I called it a shield earlier. If anything managed to get past those shields, they would be fine inside. However, this is a place that constantly has Miracle Children around, and us Crusaders can hold our own, so we're not that terribly worried about it," he said, slipping into the vehicle.

"So that's why they haven't been installed into cities yet? Because there's a chance that something could get through?" I asked.

"I'm sure that's one of them. The creatures around Unstable Walls would probably get through this since they're so aggressive and determined. But those puppies also cost a hell of a lot, and this is relatively a small area to cover. They'd need a lot of them to cover an entire city. Walls are cheaper. Hop in, I'd rather not get in trouble with the Paladin," he said.

The vehicle he got into was small, with four wheels and no doors on the sides. There weren't even any seat belts, making me think this was a vehicle designed for short distance transportation. Still, it was more expensive than anything we had in the Lowers. Most people used bikes or motorcycles for transportation if they didn't use the public buses or trains.

I walked around the vehicle and got in, having to take a step up into it since it was so far off the ground.

"Best vehicle on the planet, Jeeps are. These babies are dependable and tough," he said, patting the dashboard before turning the key and starting the vehicle.

It roared to life, but it thundered down into a steady hum as the engine quickly heated up. He put it into gear and took off, turning around first and heading toward the building across from the Recovery Center, but then he turned left and started driving away from both buildings. He stayed on the path of red bricks, even if he didn't need to. He wasn't going incredibly fast, probably 30-35 miles per hour, but it still beat the hell outta walking.

"I grew up in the Lowers too, so I felt the same way as you did when I saw grass for the first time," he explained, chuckling.

"Really? Which City?" I asked, making conversation.

"L.A." he said.

I looked over at him, surprised. "They have Unstable Walls, don't they?"

"Oh yeah. We pretty much have Miracle Children camped on the outskirts of the city constantly. It's not uncommon to hear gunfire and explosions from there daily," he said.

"It's hard to imagine. Can those creatures really break through a Wall just like that?" I asked.

He hesitated. "Where are you from, Johnathon?"

"Chicago, and just John is fine."

"Okay John. Chicago is one of the few cities that hasn't had a single breach in their Wall, so I understand why you wouldn't see how it's possible. You've grown up in an area where you could put trust in that Wall to protect you. You trusted it to hold firm, and every night that Wall didn't break, your faith in it grew, but it's not like that in L.A. We don't trust the Wall at all, but if any of us stepped outside that Wall we'd be dead within an hour, so we still depend on it."

"Depending on something you can't trust .... That's a hard thing to live with," I said, empathizing.

"It was, and it still is for them. L.A. has such a huge populace that even some creatures from the deep Outside are attracted to it. If you thought a dark lion was dangerous, you should see what those things are capable. It's pretty scary."

I silently wondered exactly what "those things" were, but I decided not to ask.

"You said that Miracle Children are a constant force in that city, so then that announcement that Gates said probably didn't bother your city at all," I suggested.

He laughed for a moment before answering, "No, it almost assuredly surprised them. In fact, it probably troubled cities with Unstable Walls even more than the other ones."

"Why?" I asked, not understanding.

"You don't seem to understand how much that daily danger is a part of our lives there. We see what Miracle Children are capable of up close and personal. We see how fast they are, how inhumanly strong they are, what they can do with their Miracles. It's one thing to see a monster move so fast and completely overwhelm you with the sense of danger they put off, but then you see a human being that can keep up with them, and surpass them .... It's scarier than the monsters themselves, and the rumors about Eve's snapping and going out of control isn't a rumor. I've seen it happen. Still, we were thankful for them, just as long as that dangerous gaze of the Miracle Children stay focused on our enemies. But Gates changed that. Now, Miracle Children will have a focused attention on the politics of each city. It'll be a difficult thing for people to accept. They won't act out, of course, but I doubt they'll have a parade welcoming that change."

"Hmm .... So, Eves really snap?" I asked, taking notice of that the most.

"Yeah. It's terrifying to see something that powerful go out of control."

"What makes them do that?" I asked.

"It's classified," he replied.

I clicked my tongue in annoyance. "I don't get to know, huh?"

He laughed then, surprising me. "No, no, that's not it. I don't get to know because it's classified. You'll find out in your training."

"Oh. I see," I said, leaving it at that.

The drive there was mostly through a peaceful and green landscape of grass and small trees. Every now and then we passed by a building, which were all different for the most part, but a few of them were tall and looked similar. Zachariah explained they were the buildings that the Miracle Children lived in for this region, and that I would get my own room today.

We finally arrived after a ten-minute drive, coming to a stop in front of a four-story building made from glass and silver steel. The glass was reflective, making it almost impossible to see inside it, and there were two men standing outside with automatic rifles. They seemed relaxed, but their eyes were clear and sharp.

I assumed they were Crusaders like Zachariah, but they wore different clothing than him, which was khaki colored and made from thicker material. It was more like a uniform than Zach's, and I assumed it was a more professional wear. The men were far from middle aged, but I guessed that they were older than me.

They looked at me, glanced at Zachariah, then stood up straighter. They shouldered their weapons and held their right hands up in a salute in a single clean motion.

"Sir!" they said, firmly but not loudly.

We walked through the doors without Zachariah saying anything, but when I heard the doors close behind us I glanced over at him.

"Are you a higher ranked Crusader than them?" I asked, curious of the solute.

"Nope. Every Crusader has the same rank. The salute was to you," he replied, stopping and meeting my eyes.

I tensed my jaw for a moment, annoyed at myself for not noticing. "This is going to take some getting used to."

"I bet. Most Miracle Children are used to it by the time they enter their teens, but you grew up outside of that kind of influence. I'm sure I don't have to tell you this, but be careful in the future. Depending on your situation you'll oversee a whole group of Crusaders, and if you don't keep it formal the order can fall apart."

I paused to think that over before responding. "Thank you for the advice. I'll keep that in mind."

He didn't respond, but I saw him nod from the corner of my eye.

The lobby was large and open, making it seem inviting. The entrance area was smaller than the room beyond, but was still a good twenty feet wide. The main room that the entrance opened into was probably double that. There were a couple side rooms that had the doors shut along the side walls, two elevators in the back of the room, and a circular receptionist's desk was in the middle.

"Okay, I'll leave you here. I'll wait outside until you're finished," he said.

I looked at him. "Thanks. I appreciate it."

He smiled. "All part of the job."

Then his back got straighter and he saluted once before turning around and walking out the door.

I turned around myself and headed toward the receptionist's desk. There was a man behind the desk, typing something into the computer. I approached him, and he looked up at me when I got close.

"I was told that Paladin Samson wanted to see me," I told him.

"What's your name, sir?" he asked, stopping his typing and instead tapping on the touch screen of his monitor.

"Johnathon Aster," I replied.

"I'll notify him that you're here, but he just received a call so it may be a few minutes for he's able to see you," he told me, tapping a few more commands on his monitor.

"Thanks," I said, turning around and walking a few steps away.

I felt like all I've done since I woke up was wait around, and the only thing I could focus on was my hunger. I looked around, hoping to distract myself.

I heard Prophet Gates' voice from a nearby television that was on the wall and turned to look at it. I hadn't owned a television so this was my first time seeing Prophet Gates, or even the God's Wall on which he stood to speak. God's Wall was a sort of monument in every city and was basically a much smaller replica of the Walls that outlined the cites. It was only fifty feet high, but was made from the same material and was constructed in the same way as the Walls. The Prophets always gave their speeches from the top of a God's Wall, and part of me always wondered if this was to show that the Prophet was greater than the Walls that kept them safe from the Outside.

Scrolling across the bottom of the screen read:

Prophet Gates' speech regarding the issues and protests about Miracle Children having permanent residency in cities. Live from New York City.

The Prophet wasn't an ugly man, but I wouldn't say he was particularly handsome either. His face was strong and composed, giving him a confidant and calm appearance. He looked out at the people that had gathered below him with a serious but kind gaze. His blue eyes were sincere and honest, and it was obvious that he really cared for the people. I could tell just by looking at him why so many people trusted him. He looked … well, *good* I suppose. He looked trustworthy. He was broad shouldered and healthy, but he didn't look particularly strong. His voice never stuttered as he talked, and his words flowed together incredibly, each one connecting to the other in a way that seemed almost graceful. Seeing him talk on the television and hearing him talk over the radio was a completely different experience, but I had no idea why.

I listened as he began to talk, carefully absorbing what he was saying. I was a part of this world now, so I couldn't just brush it off like I had earlier.

"I know that many are against this new policy. I don't blame them, and I can empathize with their unease. I have been around Miracle Children constantly since I was chosen to take up the responsibilities of Prophet three years ago, and I am still surprised when I see a Miracle performed in front of me. Even with all my steadfast belief in the Supreme and unwavering conviction that he is capable of anything, it still amazes me to see a human display such power.

"But I do not fear them, for they are our protectors. They stand between us and the Corrupted Nature when our Walls fall. They keep us alive by sacrificing their own freedom, dreams, and futures. They shield us from harm so that we have a safe home to go to at night. A place where we can rest our heads and feel safe again.

"However, even after the sacrifice those Miracle Children provide for us, we go to our homes, our beds, and our families and we realize that we are not safe at all!" his voice had risen in intensity at the end, but he never shouted, and his words weren't harsh.

"We may be protected from the Corrupted Nature by the Miracle Children, but we have become powerless against another type of corruption. This corruption never originated from the Nature. It doesn't try and break down the Walls, since it is already inside them! It comes from the people who live inside the Walls; the people that the Miracle Children sweat and bleed to keep safe take advantage of their sacrifice and corrupt their fellow survivors! They are in your businesses, in your shopping districts, in your very streets! They are your colleges, your neighbors, even your family! They take advantage because they do not see any negative consequences to their actions. They see no consequences for theft, murder or corruption and think they can do as they please—even if it causes a fellow human being suffering.

"Yes, we do already have a few Miracle Children that specialize in the fields of Law, but they cannot do everything by themselves. These Miracle Children who will be joining you in your cities are the Children that I have handpicked. They are the elite—kind, patient, and trustworthy. They have no greed or lust for fame or power. They only have a single passion; a desire to uphold what is right and just, and keep those who bathe themselves in evil from hurting those who struggle to stay clean. So, I warn you evildoers: change is coming. Justice is coming. To the righteous and upright; rejoice, for you will have an ally and protector amongst you.

"All I ask of you is if you cannot trust them immediately, give them the opportunity to earn that trust."

He paused in his speech when a loud cheering and applause from the crowd flared, and he gave them a smile filled with warmth. But the seriousness of his eyes never faded, showing them how much he meant his words.

"Johnathon, you can head up now," said the man behind the desk.

"Thank you," I replied and took a few steps towards the desk, but ten abruptly stopped when I saw that the man had no intention of showing me where to go.

"I'm sorry, but where am I supposed to meet him?" I asked.

"Oh, I apologize sir. His office is on the fourth floor," he said before resuming his typing.

"Thanks," I replied, stepping around the circular counter and walking up the elevators. I called the elevator, and the elevator on my right opened immediately. I pressed the fourth-floor button and leaned against the side, returning to my earlier thoughts.

I could easily see why Prophet Gates has become the most loved Prophet. I had heard rumors that his speeches are always spontaneous and never planned, but I had trouble believing that. It seemed too unrealistic to have that kind of grace with words without preparing it out. But the sincerity in his eyes was apparent; he loved life and genuinely cared for the people. If he had prepared it before-hand, could he really have that kind of honesty and passion after going over the words a dozen times?

I saw my reflection in the elevator doors, and I smoothed out my shirt and ran my fingers through my hair, trying to make myself appear a little more respectable. It didn't fix much; I needed a haircut.

The elevator stopped and the doors opened with a ding sound, so I pushed these thoughts from my mind as I took in my new surroundings.

The elevator immediately opened into another reception area, but this one was a third of the size of the one on the first floor. On my right was a sitting area, with two couches against the wall with a window in between them. The couches were straight, and were made from black leather. On each side of the couch was a small stand made from a polished wood. On my immediate left was the second elevator, and beyond that was a short bookcase filled with leather bound books. The walls were painted black, but it wasn't a depressing look with the rich color of the wood furniture and was comfortable on the eyes.

There was a set of wooden double doors across from the elevator, directly in front of me, and to the left was the receptionist's desk, which was made of a richly polished wood that matched the others.

At the desk sat an attractive brunette with short hair and an attentive posture. She was dressed in a cobalt blue blazer with a white blouse, and the top two buttons were undone, which gave her a respectable appeal. She wore a small wireless ear piece to take calls. Her attention was on me as soon as the doors had begun to open, making it obvious that she was waiting for me.

"Johnathon, Paladin Samson will be available shortly. Please wait here for the time being," she said.

Great. More waiting.

"Thanks," I said, stepping out of the elevator.

"Is there anything I can get for you while you wait?" she asked politely.

I was tempted to ask for some food, but I thought it would be more professional not to.

"I'm fine, thanks," I replied.

I heard my own footsteps and I looked down, surprised to see that even the floor was made from the polished hard wood. Wood was expensive. Very expensive. After all, it's not like the average human could just step outside the Walls and chop a tree down. The tree would probably try to eat anyone who did. They had to be grown inside the walls if you wanted to get the good, uncorrupted wood, and that didn't come cheap.

I looked over to my left and walked up to the bookcase. I reached out and gently ran my fingers over the leather binding of the books, then pulled out a random one and opened it up in the middle. I turned a page carefully, afraid of suddenly ripping it. This was the first time in probably ten years I had seen a book, and the first time I had ever touched one. They were expensive, and only the rich could afford to use them. There had been several books in my father's study when I was a kid, but I was never allowed to touch them. These books together probably cost more than what I had made in a year at my two jobs.

I closed the book delicately and put it back on the shelf, then turned around and walked over to the window that was between the two couches. I looked out again at the beautiful greens that were growing in the surrounding area. I was starting to feel like I was tossed into the ocean without being taught how to swim. This place was utterly different from anything I knew. The Lowers was dirty, poor, and rundown. This was clean, rich, and new. How was I supposed to act here? What was appropriate and inappropriate? I had no idea how to handle this.

A couple minutes had passed before I heard the receptionist rise from her desk. I didn't look over to her until I heard her approach me; her high-heels were loud on the flooring.

She stopped walking toward me when I met her eyes. "He's ready to see you now."

"Okay," I said, turning away from the window and taking a couple steps to her.

She led me to the doors and opened the one of the left. As it swung inward she walked into the office and held the door open for me. I entered, taking in the large office.

It was about the same size as the receptionist area, and had the same black and polished wood theme. Bookcases lined the walls, each one almost filled with books. The only other furniture in the room was the Paladin's desk—which was large and built out of a darker shaded wood—and the two chairs that were placed in front of it. The desk had a computer monitor on it, which was surrounded by neat piles of random books and folders containing sheets of paper.

Paladin Samson was older, probably late forties or early fifties, but as soon as I looked at him I sensed strength rooted in him. It wasn't overbearing, and he seemed immovable, as if he only acted on his own will and not the will of others. That look was helped by his broad shoulders and straight back. He had short, light brown hair with a few streaks of gray in it, hinting at his age. His skin was white but not pale, and his strong blue eyes were unwavering in their confidence as he looked over his small glasses.

"Is there anything else I can do for you, sir?" the woman asked.

"We have everything we need for now, thank you," Samson replied, his voice smooth.

The assistance excused herself and then shut the door behind her.

"Take a seat, Johnathon," he said politely.

"Thanks," I said, choosing the seat on the right.

He pressed a button on his desk, making the glass monitor sink down into his desk so he could see me clearly.

"So, you're Miranda's Adam," he said, stating a simple fact.

"Looks that way, sir," I replied.

His gaze and stature made me immediately feel the need to be respectful.

He didn't say anything else for a minute, organizing folders and sheets of paper on his desk. I felt pressure to speak, especially since I was uncomfortable in this unfamiliar place.

"Sir, I can't think of any reason why someone in such an important role as yourself would want to speak with me," I said.

"That's because you're not understanding what it is that I do," he said, stating a fact more than belittling my knowledge.

I hesitated. "I apologize. Why do you want to speak with me, sir?"

The corner of his mouth twitched, hinting at a smile before it fell back into a neutral position. His gaze returned to mine, and I did my best to meet it without looking like I was challenging him.

"I oversee every Miracle Child stationed in the Americas. Obviously, there's a lot of them, so you're wondering why I'd want to take time out of my busy day to speak with just one, am I right?" he clarified.

"Yes sir. I was surprised when I heard I was supposed to meet with you."

"It's actually the opposite. Since I oversee all the Adams, it should make sense that I meet with different Miracle Children daily."

"The part I am confused about is why you want to speak to me, sir."

He reached up and removed his glasses, carefully setting them down on the pile of folders to her right before meeting my eyes again.

"That's fair concern to be confused about. There are two reasons that I needed to speak with you, Johnathon. The first of which is the unique circumstances by which you were discovered. The second is the fact that you are Miranda's Adam—and that fact has more weight than you know."

"Oh. I see," I replied, not really sure how to respond.

He continued without hesitation, "I'll give it to you straight, Johnathon. ninety-three percent of Miracle Children are discovered at birth. The remaining seven percent are discovered when they get re-tested on their twenty-first birthday. However, you didn't test positive when you were re-tested. So, what you are, in plain words, is a problem."

"A problem?" I asked, surprised he used that word.

"That's right. You broke the statistics, which means that there might be other Miracle Children who were negative on their re-test but are Miracle Children. I'm sure with a brain like yours you can understand the implications of that possibility."

I swallowed quickly. "I do."

If others are Miracle Children and were missed by the Church, then they could cause a lot of trouble if they discovered they can use Miracles. Especially because of the fear among the public about what Miracle Children could do. That fear was only held in check because of their faith in the Church's power and authority. If there were Miracle Children out there who didn't have to keep their power in check, all hell could break loose.

However, I didn't test positive on my re-test because I never took it. I wasn't even inside the Walls at that time. When I came back and returned to normal life I purchased a new identity and that identity had tested negative.

"We're exploring all of the options available to us before we come to a decision, but so far it's looking like we'll have to take a new look at our testing procedures," he said.

I couldn't keep it to myself. It was too irresponsible of me too. If I allowed them to believe that I had truly tested negative it would cause a lot of money and confusion—not just for the Church, but for every citizen in the Holy Land.

"Actually sir, the reason I didn't test positive was because I never took the re-test.," I told him.

Surprise never showed in his eyes. "And what reason could you have for not taking it?"

I hesitated. "It's personal and a long story, can I just leave it at that?"

He looked at me with another steady gaze. "This issue isn't so small that I can take the word of someone who is completely new to the Church."

"Miranda knows the details; can you take her word on it?" I asked, not backing down.

His eyes narrowed in annoyance for a microscopic moment, then he relaxed again. "I'll speak to her about it."

"Thank you, sir," I responded confidently, though in honesty I felt a little intimated.

It was a gamble to ask that, but one that was in my favor. I had noticed that when he described Miranda, he had called her important. The fact that he consented meant that I was right, but also made me realize how much weight Miranda must have in the Church. I pushed that out of my mind as Paladin Samson started to speak again.

"You're educated, or was that a lie on your records as well?" he asked.

"I am. Perfect scores in high school and very high marks in my semesters of college," I replied.

"Then please humor me for a moment and walk me through history. Start from World War III to the present and only mention the important events," he said.

"Uh ...." I said in my surprise at the odd request.

"There's a point to this, I promise," he explained.

"Okay, then. The event leading up to World War III started in 2083 when the countries surrounding Israel attempted to invade. It was just small-scale battles for the first year, and at that time the allies of the countries participating in the war only provided aid through finances and supplies. However, when it seemed like Israel was going to collapse, the United States of America sent military and personal along with the supplies to Israel. The opposing countries didn't hesitate to do the same, and over the course of the next seven years, the battles increased in intensity and frequency.

Any country that wasn't involved at the beginning was starting to join; either because their enemies were strained or because the battles had overflowed into their territory. From 2091 to 2094, the entire world was at conflict. This ended with several detonations of nuclear-sized explosions that leveled most of America, and completely decimated Africa. While those were by far the worst of it, there was also some detonations on the borders of China and some in Europe.

"Almost two billion died in the blasts, and another five hundred million died from the radiation that spread outward over the next five years. That was when Operation Regrowth was initiated. A team of specialists had been researching a way to soak up the radiation that was still slowly spreading across the world and to regrow the plant life there. They're solution was a plant seed they had developed that grows very aggressively. They planted the seeds, and in three weeks the areas that were densely radiated became clean. The trees and plants and vegetation soaked it up, and besides the abnormal speed of growth and the size that they grew, there wasn't any sign that things were not as they should be."

"The specialists had planted the seeds before they were fully researched and understood, having been pressured to do so by the ever-advancing radiation. As a result, they didn't hypothesize how the radiated trees and plants would affect the animals that would repopulate the newly-grown area. The animals that ate the fruit from the trees and plants mutated, which in turn spread to the larger predators that fed on them. It wasn't very long before these mutated creatures started to attack the cities."

"Humanity became separated and broken. Travel between cities and countries was impossible, and to protect themselves each city started building Walls to keep the predators out. That was when the Church stepped forward, bringing with them Miracle Children to protect the cities. After another five years, humanity seemed to finally stabilize behind their Walls, though at great cost. The world population had been reduced to a little over a billion people, barely a ninth of what we were before WWIII. Since then, the Church has become a major authority force that offers protection to cities, and more countries are uniting under it."

I finished, and suddenly the room felt much quieter.

There was a short pause before Paladin Samson finally spoke. "The important part there was when you mentioned the Church and the Miracle Children. I know how it's taught in the cities, but haven't you ever asked where the Miracle Children came from?"

"I did. I knew it would be pointless to ask a teacher though; they'd blown off my questions that weren't nearly as serious as that one before. I couldn't research it on my own either, since the internet is tightly monitored by the Church, and they don't particularly like people investigating their affairs."

"From you're tone it seems you still found some answers," he said.

"I met some people with good memories, and they told me that Miracle Children didn't come down from the heavens in a flash of holy light, but the Church lets us imagine that because it suits their needs," I replied, carefully keeping my voice neutral.

My heart beat had sped up a little bit, and my gut was warning me not to say anything more. I knew how much power the Church had, but here I was, pointing at their dirty laundry to one of the five most important people in the world.

"That's correct," he stated, matter-of-factly.

I blinked, momentarily surprised that he was agreeing with me.

"The Church hasn't seen the need to correct that, since it gives the people a sense of understanding. If they really knew how human you Miracle Children were, they wouldn't accept it nearly as well as they do now, and they only barely accept it as it is. Understand that you're a Miracle Child, but you're also just as human as I am. You are not special or above the rest of the human race in any way, shape, or form. You are merely Johnathon Aster, and no more than that. Do you understand what I'm trying to tell you?"

I nodded. "Yes sir."

He was telling me that I shouldn't have a condescending attitude toward the rest of the human race merely because I'm called a Miracle Child. Not that I would anyway, but I bet it can become a problem with the ones that were raised in a world like this one.

"Good. Now let's talk about Miranda," he said, giving me a strong stare.

I cleared my throat a little. "Sir, before we move on, I was wondering ... where *did* they come from? I know that there was no majestic event that brought them down from the heavens, but I don't actually know their origin."

"They came to us the same way they do now; conception. They were born to us, which could certainly be described as a work of the Supreme. The Church doesn't have any more information on it than that. Even if it did, it's highly unlikely that you would be allowed to learn information that valuable," he explained.

I swallowed. "I see."

He took a deep breath. "Now then; Miranda."

I sat straighter in my chair, feeling nervous. "What about her?"

"She's a strong Eve, but she's committed herself to a career in Law, so since you are already her Adam, you will be joining her in that career," he stated.

"Sir, I'm not exactly clear on what these careers mean," I confessed.

"You'll learn all of that in training. Speaking of which, you're training will be over the next three weeks. Don't expect an easy time of it. Miranda will continue her investigations in Chicago, so you won't see her until you've finished your training and join her. Besides, I've seen what's planned for you, and to be honest I don't think you'd want her to see you in the pathetic state you'll be in after each day."

Well that didn't sound like fun.

"Also, don't tell anyone that you're Miranda's Adam, or that she was the one who found you. Her work there is classified, including her location. It's easier to keep the details of how you were discovered classified than it is to keep your entire past classified. It's alright to explain where you came from, but if anyone asks how you know Miranda, just tell them that she escorted you here from Chicago. Understood?" he asked, but the authority in his voice hinted that I had only one possible response.

"Yes sir."

He didn't respond with anything other than the hard stare he had already been giving me.

"Sir ..." I began, trying to think up a way to ask my question.

"What is it?" he asked.

"Is it possible for an Adam and an Eve to be separated?" I asked, hesitantly.

He raised an eyebrow. "Why do you ask? Do you not want to be Miranda's Adam?"

"It's not that …" I started, then paused while I organized my thoughts, "it's because of how it happened. I doubt it's what Miranda wanted."

"Have you talked to her about it?" he asked me.

"No," I answered.

"Then don't try to make a decision that effects the two of you, especially on an assumption," he told me.

"But it is possible?" I gathered from his tone of voice.

He hesitated, "Yes, it is possible."

I nodded once in response.

"I'd like an account of what transpired from the moment you met Miranda to when you arrived here in your own words please. Be as thorough as possible."

I did. I ran through everything that I could think of, only stopping to answer a few of his questions, which were mostly about the conversations Miranda and I had. When I finally finished, he only had one more question for me.

"Tell me, why did you jump out of the helicopter?" His tone was neutral and serious, as if he was only asking out of mere curiosity.

"Why do you ask?" I replied, not sure of his intentions.

"Well, looking at the situation from the outside, it didn't seem like you and Miranda were all that close, even after going through a life and death situation. Why make such a sacrifice to someone who meant nothing to you?"

I kept a neutral expression even though his question bothered me. I had skipped over the parts were Miranda was intimate with me, such as when she kissed my cheek or when I held her to keep her warm. It didn't seem important. No, that wasn't right. I didn't want to share it because I wanted to keep that private.

"I wouldn't say that she means nothing to me," I replied, a little loss for words.

"Obviously she means quite a bit, since you were willing to throw yourself out of a helicopter that was fifty feet above the ground onto a beast that had the ability to tear you to pieces. Did you even expect to come out of that alive?"

"I ... I didn't think about my own survival. I just couldn't allow myself to stand still and watch it happen," I answered honestly.

"Why couldn't you?" he asked me, his gaze steady.

The bluntness of his questions surprised me. "Are you saying that I shouldn't have acted?"

"Not at all. To be honest, I would've preferred you did that action even if it meant that you died. Miranda is that important. I merely asked for my own curiosity, and a desire to understand exactly what type of man you are, Johnathon. I'd rather take the time to figure you out now than be surprised later."

I understood that much at least. I was a risk, since they hadn't had the opportunity to observe my personality as I grew, unlike the Miracle Children that are discovered at birth. They weren't sure how trustworthy I was and that could cause a great deal of worry, considering how much power Miracle Children held.

"I just couldn't stand there and watch her die, sir. It's not who I am," I answered him.

"I see. Do you have any questions for me?" He asked.

I paused thoughtfully, trying to pick which question I should ask first. There was a lot I wanted to know.

"There seems to be some secrecy around the subject of Eves snapping. I can't seem to get a solid explanation out of anyone and I want to know why."

"I can't speak for whoever you spoke with, but I doubt that they're intentionally hiding it from you. It's just an uncomfortable topic to discuss. Don't worry, you'll learn all about that in your training. It's a lot more than building your body up to Miracle Child standards. You'll also be tutored in several advanced subjects; mainly math and tactical strategy, but we won't have time to educate you on the laws and regulations of the Church. This wasn't an oversight; we'll leave that part to Miranda while you are in the field with her."

"Understood," I replied, but inside I was annoyed.

More waiting for answers.

"Is there anything else?" he asked, his tone serious and steady, like he already knew the answer.

I could see where this conversation was heading. I was sure all my questions would be answered in training, or at least most of them.

"No sir," I responded.

"Good. Go enjoy your day, and I recommend getting a good night's rest tonight. You start you're training as soon as the sun rises," he said, pressing the button on his desk to make the monitor rise back up. "You're dismissed."

"Thank you, sir," I said respectfully, then got up and left the room.

I shut the wooden doors behind me, then walked over to the elevators. I glanced at the receptionist as the elevator doors opened.

"Have a great night, sir," she said, her attention on me as I stepped inside.

"Thank you. You too," I responded as the doors closed, then leaned against the back of the elevator as I felt it start to drop.

I sighed as I stared at myself in the reflective steel doors, and immediately thought about the last thing the Paladin and I discussed. Surely Miranda knew that it was reversible …. Is that why she tried to get us to this place so quickly? I wouldn't blame her if that was the case.

But I couldn't help but think about the way her eyes met mine, and that moment before we left the cockpit, where she grabbed my hand and kissed my cheek. Was it all an act? Just a way to keep me calm in that difficult situation? I could see it as a possibility, but I didn't want to believe it. I quickly ran through a few different arguments in my head about her intentions, but in the end the most logical conclusion was that she was just trying to keep me calm. She had known me for less than 24 hours, so there was no way she could have any emotional attachment to me.

The doors opened, and I pushed this topic out of my mind as I stepped out of the elevator. For now, I had a much more pressing concern; I was starving.

CHAPTER 9

The vehicle ran smoothly over the red brick, and I looked at the fresh green trees and the sun-soaked grass as we passed. My eyes traced over each detail as I saw it, but I didn't take any of it in. My mind was already filled to the brim with what Paladin Samson had told me. It looked like the next thing for me was my training, even though I didn't have a clear explanation of what that entailed. From what Paladin Samson had said, it seemed like I was going to be put through intense physical training and advanced education at the same time. They said it would take three weeks, but why so short? Surely it took longer for a Miracle Child to master their abilities.

I felt my jaw tense when that thought flashed through my mind, and I started to stress about it. Not knowing my Miracle bothered me severely, since I already had trouble trusting myself in certain situations, and now I had an unknown ability that I needed to keep an eye out for. Who knew what could happen ....

"John?" Zachariah asked.

"Hm?" I said, turning my attention to him.

"I asked if you were okay with that," he said.

Crap. I hadn't been paying attention to a thing he had been saying. I apologized and asked him to repeat himself.

"I should have known that was the case since you were so quiet. While you were upstairs with the Paladin, I was informed that I would oversee your muscle training. While it's an order for me, they do give you the right to choose someone else to do it."

"Oh. That's okay, you're the only one I know here," I replied.

"True, you did just arrive. Still thought asking would be better than to just assume you were fine with it. Regardless, I doubt that we'll be training together for longer than a couple days," he said.

I raised my eyebrow, "You think I won't last that long?"

He laughed. "No, no. It's not that. I'm just a normal human, so you'll outgrow what I can keep up with in just a few days. After that, another Adam will be taking over you're training, since they have a better understanding of what your muscles limitations are."

I half-smiled. "Oh, I see."

It was only a minute later when we pulled up to a large building. It wasn't especially tall, probably two stories, but it was long and wide. The building was made from stone, but not the run-down, cracked and rough stone that I saw in the Lowers. This was smooth and set together in near perfection, making the entire building look impressive even though it was created out of relatively inexpensive materials. Hell, no matter what it was made from, it had to be better than the cheap steel that coats everything in Chicago.

"This is food, right?" I said.

He chuckled. "Yeah, Miracle Children eat here if they don't feel like making something at their apartments."

"Hmm," I said, looking over the building.

"Come on, I'll show you inside," he said, stepping forward.

I followed, stepping through the double set of glass doors that led inside.

As soon as I entered I saw exactly what I expected to see by now; it looked opulence. The ceiling was high, clearly spanning the entire building's height, and hanging from the ceiling were chandlers made of glass and gilded with gold. The light from them clearly illuminated the room, but was also gentle, making the room welcoming. The area was filled with round tables set with tablecloths and silverware wrapped in white napkins made from a thick cloth. There were six padded chairs around each table so that each chair had a comfortable space between the others.

Classical music, mostly piano, was playing softly through speakers. There was less than fifteen people at the tables, giving the place an empty feeling; this building could easily feed two hundred people. The people sitting didn't look up when we entered, but I noticed that they were around my age.

"Damn," I muttered, taking it all in.

"You said it," Zachariah agreed.

"Do we need to do anything particular or do we just take a seat …?" I asked.

"I'm not really sure," he confessed, and I noticed from his body language that he had no intention of joining me.

"You're not hungry?" I asked.

"It's not exactly that …" he said, and it was obvious he wasn't relaxed anymore.

I heard a voice from behind us. "You're new, aren't'cha?"

I turned to see a man around my age and about my height, maybe a little taller. He had dirty-blond hair that was long for a man, but he kept it tidy in a short ponytail. He had clear brown eyes and a dark tan. When he turned his head to the right you could see a scar on the left side of his face that stretched from his mid-jawbone and down his neck, then disappeared under the collar of his shirt. He wore a black shirt with the sleeves rolled up and the front unbuttoned, which showed the dark gray shirt he had on underneath. The gray undershirt was tucked into his dark blue jeans and he wore a black belt. He had a good amount of muscle on him, but it wasn't bulky.

He was relaxed and at ease, as if nothing in the world could bother him. He had both his hands in the pockets of his jeans.

Zachariah stood at attention and saluted, but the newcomer took out his hand from his pocket and waved at Zachariah, telling him to be at ease. His brown eyes steadily met mine, and I knew he was sizing me up, but not in a challenging way.

"Was I that obvious?" I asked.

"Pretty much," he said with a smile, then looked at Zachariah, "I'll show him around from here. You're dismissed."

"Sir!" he said, saluting again, then turned and walked out.

I watched him go, a little surprised, then the man got my attention when he stuck his hand out in greeting.

"Benjamin Powers," he said, giving me a smile.

"Johnathon Aster. Nice to meet you," I said, shaking his hand. "Are Crusaders not allowed to eat in here?"

"It's not that …. In fact, I'm pretty sure we've never had to have a rule like that," he replied.

"Then what was with his reaction?" I asked.

"You grew up having no idea that you were and Adam, didn't you?" he surmised.

I nodded.

"That's why you don't really understand it. You have a foot in both worlds, so to speak. That Crusader felt at ease around you because you had the feel of a normal human being, but it's not the same around the other Miracle Children. Crusaders and normal humans alike are uncomfortable around us. They've seen what we can do, and, even if it's subconsciously, they fear us. So they tend to avoid this place because this is where the Miracle Children eat. I've never seen anyone who wasn't a Miracle Child eat here."

"Hm," I acknowledged, but not knowing how to respond beyond that.

I couldn't blame them, especially with thinking back on how I first met Miranda and immediately felt that she was a threat.

"Well, it is what it is, and we can't change what it is. So, we might as well eat," he said, walking toward the tables.

I followed him, realizing this was my best chance at finally getting some food. He led me through the tables until we reached his destination, a table that already had two others sitting at it.

The first was a woman, again around my age. She was very pretty, with a serious face and strong amber eyes. Her blond hair stretched down past her shoulders, and she had pale-white skin. The man next to her had the same brown hair, brown eyes, and dark tan as Benjamin, but those were the only features they shared. His face and posture were less welcoming, but he also looked at ease with his surroundings. His muscles were bulkier than Benjamin's, but wasn't over the top and didn't look like it would affect his agility. He was reading a book, but from the cover it looked like some sort of comic book in a language I wasn't familiar with.

The woman's eyes looked over Benjamin's face, and for a small moment her serious face was broken by a gentle hint of a smile on her lips, but then it vanished as soon as her gaze switched over to me.

She rose from her seat when we reached the table, and stretched her arm out in greeting. She was tall for a woman, but still a couple inches shorter than me.

"Anastasia Martin," she said, her voice clear and sharp.

"Johnathon Aster," I introduced myself, realizing that my own voice must sound mundane next to the beauty of hers.

The man sitting next to Anastasia stood up then and reached out a hand in greeting as well. He didn't stand up completely, but still reached eye level with me. He was probably three to four inches taller than I was.

"Dylan Powers," he stated, his voice deeper than mine, and a little rougher.

"Good to meet you," I said, realizing that he was Benjamin's brother.

Right before our hands clasped in a handshake, he pulled his hand back, as if he suddenly realized what he was doing. I was stuck holding my hand in midair, a little awkwardly.

"Uh ..." I said, not sure how to respond.

"Sorry," he said, "don't take it personally. I just ... have trouble with physical contact sometimes."

"Oh. Sorry about that," I said without really having a reason to apologize.

I felt Anastasia's eyes on me so I looked over at her. Her amber eyes bore into mine cautiously, as if she was searching for something. I got the distinct feeling that Dylan not shaking hands with me meant something more than just him having a phobia of some sort. Her eyes were strong and fierce, and I got a sudden sense of unease, as if my body was getting ready to defend itself.

Then I saw Benjamin kiss her on the check.

She blinked, momentarily surprised, then I saw her interest in me disappear and she turned toward Benjamin.

"What was that for?" she asked, but I saw that small hint of a smile on her lips again.

"Just showing you off to John, while also making it clear that you're off limits," he said, giving me a wink.

Her eyebrows twitched in slight annoyance as she promptly took her seat. "I'm not an object."

Ben took a seat next to her. "Really? That's definitely not the attitude you had last nigh—"

He was cut off sharply by something that sounded like a foot stomping underneath the table. Benjamin groaned in pain and reached down under the table.

"Are you alright?" I asked, suspecting what happened as I took a seat next to Benjamin.

"Just fine," he said in a strained voice that made it sound like he wasn't fine at all. He looked over at Anastasia, who wore a very neutral face. "Baby take it easy on me. You're in heels today."

"I haven't the faintest idea of what you're talking about," she said, that small smile returning to her face and mischievousness clear in her eyes.

"You're so sexy when you're cold to me," he said. His voice was starting to regain some of its strength, but he was still obviously caressing his foot under the table.

"A smarter man wouldn't put up with it," she said, still not looking at him.

He sat straighter in the chair, finally having recovered. "Then it's a good thing for both of us that I'll always be an idiot."

She met his eyes again this time, the romance back again.

"Shall we order?" Anastasia asked, reaching forward and grabbing a small electronic touch pad that was part of a group in the middle of the table.

"Give me just a minute," Benjamin said. She must've gotten him good.

"Are you sick or something? We can skip dinner if you aren't feeling up to it," she said, her voice now definitely dripping mischievousness.

"Nah. We already skipped dinner last night in favor of something a little more fun—" Benjamin said, but cut off when Anastasia cleared her throat and tapped on the table with her index finger loudly.

"Uh, I mean, I'm rather hungry, and I'm sure that my sudden discomfort of unknown origins will pass shortly," he said, correcting himself.

"I'm glad to hear that. Don't worry, I think I know you well enough to order on your behalf," she said, taping a few options on the tablet.

"Thanks, baby. Where would I be without ya?" he said, finally straightening.

"Starving probably, but with healthy feet," she replied. "Steak and fries again?"

"Hmm, sounds perfect," he replied, leaning over and looking down at the tablet.

"We, uh, order with these things?" I asked, grabbing my own tablet.

"Yeah. Anything on there is made fresh for ya, and it's free, so don't be shy about trying new things," Benjamin explained as I scrolled through the huge list of possibilities.

"Everything on here is new to me," I muttered to no one.

People in the Lowers pretty much lived on rations, which mostly consisted of noodles or rice, potatoes and sometimes a few meat choices that was always freeze-dried. Only the wealthy people in the Lowers ever got fresh food, but it was rare even for them.

"What'd you order again, Benjamin?" I asked, starting to feel overwhelmed at all the options.

"Call me Ben. We don't gotta be so formal with each other. And I got steak and fries," he stated.

I scrolled until I found the steak, and when I tapped on the option it gave me another whole list of how I wanted it prepared and seasoned. I placed my order as best as I could, ordering the fries as well. I even got ketchup as a side for my fries, since I've always heard that was how they were usually eaten.

What kind of world had I stepped into? The amount of resources they'd have to have on hand to manage all of these options was ridiculous. Did the Church really have this kind of wealth that they could afford this amount of money just for food?

I heard Anastasia and Benjamin talking next to me, but I let it fade into the background and didn't pay attention as my eyes slowly looked around the room, taking in my surroundings again. Was this the new normal for me? I didn't particularly have any complaints but ... I couldn't help but think about how unfair it was to the rest of people who struggle to get by in the Lowers. The food I had just ordered was as expensive as an entire month's salary for my neighbors. No, more realistically, two months.

I didn't have this overwhelming responsibility to care for that city or anything, but evidently, I wasn't as neutral about it as I had thought. I suppose it wasn't unnatural to think that though, since I still had Vivian there.

I blinked, and felt my shoulders tense up for a moment as I suddenly realized that I hadn't contacted Vivian about this at all. She was a friend from high school, and I should find a chance to talk to her when I could, or else she'd have every cop in Chicago out looking for me.

I snapped out of my daze when a plate of food was placed in front of me, and I realized that there was a man dressed in a black and white suit setting our dishes around. I thanked him along with the others as he left, then looked down at the food in front of me. The smell alone was better than anything I had experienced before.

It was delicious, and I suddenly realized that I would have trouble going back to rations. That's when I had to stop again, and remind myself that these were my new rations. I wasn't going back to Chicago anymore. This was my path was now.

"So, John," Anastasia started as I was half way through my steak, "you're a newly discovered Miracle Child?"

"Yeah, that's what they tell me, but to be honest I think part of me is having trouble believing it," I confessed.

"Wait, so you haven't used your Miracle?" Benjamin asked, surprise traced in his voice.

I looked up, suddenly realizing that all three of them were staring at me, their plates momentarily forgotten.

"No, I haven't. Is that a problem?" I asked, concerned about their reactions.

"Not at all. You'll discover your Miracle eventually," said a voice behind me, and I turned in time to see Miranda take a seat next to me.

She tucked her crimson hair behind her ear as he emerald eyes met mine. Damn, I knew that she was gorgeous, but apparently my eyes had forgotten in the short time that I hadn't seen her.

"Hey," she said, as if I was the only person in the entire world.

Her eyes made me smile, and I hoped it came across merely friendly, "Hi."

"How are you feeling?" she asked.

My eyes jumped between her eyes as I realized that I had missed her scent. I needed to get a hold of myself. She just caught me by surprise is all.

"I'm fine. What about you? I heard your ankle ..." I started, but died off when she raised her hands and smiled.

"All better," she said, as if a broken ankle was nothing more than a scratch.

Then again, maybe it was to a Miracle Child.

"Mm, those look good," she said, taking a fry.

"They are," I said, not knowing what else to say. Her eyes seemed to force my mind into a constant state of disarray.

"I think I'll order some," she said, reaching for a tablet.

Anastasia cleared her throat, and I suddenly remembered that we were sharing this table with three other people, "Um, Miranda?"

"Yes?" she asked, eyes looking down at the tablet.

"What are you doing?" Ana asked, her face showing confusion.

Miranda looked up at her, "What, can't I join you?"

"Well yes, I suppose, but—" she started, but Miranda interrupted her.

"Then what's the problem, Annie?" she asked, her eyes returning to the tablet.

Anastasia's eyes grew wide in surprise at the nickname, and when she recovered she responded, "Nothing, I guess."

"Err, so how have you been, Miranda?" Ben asked.

Dylan was giving me a steady stare over the top of his book, and only after I stared back did he return to his reading. It made me uneasy, as if he had guessed a secret that I didn't know I had.

Miranda sighed gently. "Busy. Very, very busy."

A moment of silence passed as Miranda finished placing her order and put the touch screen back in the middle of the table.

"And you? I haven't seen you with the scar before," she said.

"Oh this?" he said, turning his head so we could see it better. "Pretty sweet, right? Turned out quite well I think. This pride of Dark Lions we went against had some excellent reflexes. I only had time to choose what side of my face I wanted it—" he started, but was interrupted when Anastasia cleared her throat.

She looked annoyed. "You will not be so careless again."

It was clearly an order.

He scratched his chin with his right hand and laughed a little nervously. "Well it's not like it was intentional baby. You shoulda seen her freak out when it happened though. I feel a little bad for those lions, actually. Very few things deserve that kind of wrath."

"Keep talking and you might get a piece of it yourself," Anastasia said, her face a little red.

He grinned as he shot her a look from the corner of his eye, "Well save it for tonight, oka—"

He grunted in pain again, "Baby ... your heels ...."

"Still having foot problems? I thought you'd learn by now," Miranda said.

"Ana is so mean," he muttered in a teasing tone.

"Looks perfectly justified from my prospective," Miranda replied.

I shifted my feet a good six inches away from Miranda under the table.

She shot me a sly smile as she noticed me do so.

"How do you two know each other?" Anastasia asked, looking between Miranda and me.

"Johnathon and I shared the flight from Chicago," Miranda said before I got the chance, "I was tasked with escorting him here."

I was glad she was taking the lead on this, because I wasn't sure what could be disclosed and what wasn't.

"So, you're originally from Chicago, John?" she asked.

"Yup. The Lowers," I replied as a waiter placed a small plate of fries in front of Miranda.

"Whoa. Big change," Ben said, having apparently recovered again.

"No kidding," I added.

Miranda changed the subject. "How fares the front lines?"

"Very front line like," Ben said, "but we're making progress. A few cities have successfully expanded their Walls, and a few of the wealthy cities even have room for agriculture."

Anastasia spoke, "Still, I'm sure the Church will instigate a limit on human reproduction soon. It doesn't look like we can build the walls fast enough to keep up with the room we'd need for the expanding population in each city, and when you have too many people inside a space with nowhere to go, things can get nasty."

"You think that's one of the reasons Prophet Gates plans to have Miracle Children live in the cities?" I asked.

"Probably one of them, but if he's smart—and he is—then another reason is so he can have a reliable source of information on the current status of each city's political matters. There's been a couple times where we've had requests for aid from the cities and when we arrived they told us that the reason they requested our services was because they'd heard sounds from outside the wall. An entire task force of Miracle Children wasted their time because the city Mayor was afraid of a few growls," Anastasia mused.

"Hm. When you put it like that, I'm actually surprised that the Church hasn't had representatives in the cities before now," I said.

"Yeah, well, some Miracle Children will be lucky enough to get that deal," Ben said.

"How are they chosen?" I asked.

"Probably by years of service. Ana and I have only put four years in, so we won't be on the list. Though, they might only choose from

Law careers, since they have more experience in political areas, and with dealing with normal humans in general," Ana explained.

"You both are in the War career?"

"Yup. We get to go kill monsters," he said, shooting me a grin, but his eyes didn't seem that into it.

"Sounds like so much fun," I said dryly, thinking of my own experience with the Outside.

"It definitely has its ups and downs, but at least it's good adrenaline rush," Ben replied.

Miranda pushed her half-eaten plate a few inches away from her as soon as he commented, and for a moment I felt like it was a reaction his comment, "Well, I'm going to go get some rest, even though it is a little early yet. John, I can show you where you'll be staying."

"I'd appreciate that," I said.

That steak was incredible. I had eaten almost all of it but hardly touched my fries before I got full.

"Mind if we walk with you?" Ana asked, standing.

"No, not at all," Miranda replied, standing as well.

Ben and I stood up in unison, and Dylan followed suit. They left their plates on the table, so I did the same, assuming someone would come to clear it off for us.

Miranda lead the group outside, with Anastasia following right behind her. Ben and I walked at a similar pace behind them, and Dylan walked behind all of us, somehow managing to read as he walked.

It was dusk already, with just a little bit of light left slipping over the horizon. Lamp posts that I hadn't noticed before were now lit up along the red stone paths, lighting the way, and the moon was bright up in the sky.

Miranda held her right arm straight up and grabbed her elbow with her other arm. She stretched, arcing her back as she did so and showing off her curves. I managed to resist tracing her curves with my eyes for about half a second, and to my misfortune I didn't manage to look away before she turned her head to get a glimpse of me. I saw a sly smile on her lips before she faced forward again, and I had the very distinct feeling that I was set up.

"How far is it to where I'll be staying?" I asked, curious.

"Just a few minutes' walk," Miranda answered, "you'll be staying in Law apartment complex."

"He's already decided on his career? At 21?" Anastasia asked, surprise clear in her voice.

"I'm 24 actually," I clarified, and for a moment I wondered how old the others were.

Anastasia and Ben stopped in their tracks, "What? I thought you were just discovered."

Whoops. I was sure that was some of the information that Paladin Samson didn't want me to give out.

"I was. It's ... complicated. Same with my career choice," I answered, trying to recover from my mistake.

They didn't get a chance to press further, since our attention was suddenly on the vehicle that drove up to us. The headlights prevented us from seeing who was driving until the vehicle was turned off.

Zachariah got out and saluted, then turned his attention to Miranda, "Ma'am, Paladin Samson wishes to speak with you again concerning your next orders."

Miranda sighed, "It can never wait until tomorrow with him. What a workaholic."

"I have no comment on that, Ma'am," he said.

"That's probably smart of you," Miranda said with a humorous tone. "Can you give me a ride there?"

"Of course Ma'am," he replied, then turned around and entered his vehicle.

Miranda turned to us again. "Annie, can you please show John where he's staying?"

"I don't mind," she replied.

"Thanks. His key has already been loaded, and its apartment 414," she explained, then her eyes flashed to me. "Sorry I couldn't take you the whole way."

"Don't worry about it," I replied.

"I'll see you later, John," she said, then got in the passenger side. The vehicle started up and left, leaving the four of us behind.

"Well, we'd better get going. I don't really like being outdoors this late," Anastasia said, leading the way.

"You need to go to the Recovery Center, right Dylan? Lemme tag along," Ben said as he started to follow after Dylan, who had apparently started walking away from the group without a word.

"Huh? Are you sure? You and Ana usually go straight home after dinner," Dylan said as they walked away.

"True, but I don't think Ana is in the mood tonight, if you know what I mean," Ben said, disappointment in his voice.

Anastasia stopped in her tracks as their words floated over to us.

"Really? It didn't seem that way to me at dinner," Dylan said.

I saw Ana's hand clench into a fist as she turned toward them and yelled, "*We* can still hear you!"

"Shit. Run for it," Ben said, then placed his hand on Dylan's shoulder and they disappeared into thin air.

"Honestly ..." Ana said, her tone not angry, but obviously still annoyed.

I stared where I saw Ben and Dylan vanish for a moment, "can he turn invisible?"

I kept blinking as I spent a few moments doubting what my eyes had just seen.

"I'll tell you because Ben wouldn't care, but around here it's considered rude to ask. His Miracle is teleportation," she said as she resumed her walking.

"Oh sorry. Why is it rude to ask that?"

"It's personal for one thing, but it's mostly because of how Miracle Children view one another. If you have a useful and respectable ability then it's no big deal, but if you're ability is useless then how would they view you? It'd be like feeling you were born with a birth defect."

"Huh, I see. Thanks for letting me know," I replied.

She didn't respond and I followed behind her in silence, listening to her heels hit the stone pathway. Then she stopped and turned around to face me, meeting me with that strong gaze.

"So, who the hell are you?" she asked, rather bluntly.

"Uh, excuse me?" I asked.

"Well I already know that you're Miranda's Adam, but what I want to know is why *you*?" her eyes narrowed a bit, focusing on me as if the answer was etched in my irises.

"There are some things that I've been ordered to keep classified, and one of those things involves my Eve," I replied, trying to get some momentum in this conversation. I felt like I was being interrogated.

"Oh please. If you two wanted to keep it a secret, then you both should not have been so incredibly obvious at dinner."

"We weren't obvious," I retorted.

A mischievous smile appeared on her face, and I realized that I practically told her she was right.

"Because there's nothing to be obvious about," I spit out hurriedly, but it sounded pathetic even to me.

"Oh of course," her tone was one of complete sarcasm. "It wasn't obvious at all that as soon as you two met each other's eyes the entire world disappeared around you. Honestly, if I hadn't said anything you two would have stayed that way for hours."

I felt annoyed at how on the mark she was. "Regardless of how accurate your wild guesses might be; I can't tell you anything about it."

"You don't need to. It doesn't matter much, since I know that recently, probably just a couple of days ago, something happened and you became her Adam. What I don't know is who you are and why she's ..." her voice trailed off as she turned around away from me.

I felt my back straighten slightly as my interest was suddenly captured. "Why she's what?"

A short moment passed as Ana stood there, thinking.

Then she turned halfway around so that she could face me. "It looks like you didn't know her before becoming her Adam."

"Obviously not," I said, but I kept my tone gentle.

"Miranda ... Miranda wasn't like how you saw her tonight. She rarely stays long at this Academy, only stopping in when her reports are too classified to transmit digitally and then she leaves that same day. Even if she spends the night, she never goes into the dining hall. She has no friends or lovers or even people she's on good terms with. She was alone, isolated and distant, but completely by choice." She tried to keep her voice neutral, but I could hear a soft hint of sadness to it.

"And then what do I see today, out of nowhere? She comes in the dining hall and sits with us, with no warning or any kind of explanation, as if nothing had happened. She even called me 'Annie,' which she hasn't done in five years. And she smiled. She actually smiled. It was as if the last six years never happened."

"Something bad happened that isolated her, didn't it? Even though you said she chose it, something happened to her," I probed.

Her amber eyes bore into mine again as she spoke. "I'm not at all surprised that you don't know, and it's probably something that you should discuss with her alone. But at this point you have to know: Miranda killed her best friend."

CHAPTER 10

I placed my hand on the touch pad. The pad scanned my hand and then flashed green as the door to apartment 414 unlocked. I twisted the handled and entered, then let the door swing shut behind me. I heard the door lock again as soon as it shut.

I didn't turn on the lights, since the moonlight that came in from the tall windows on the far side of the room was enough. I couldn't see any details, but the gentle blue-white light felt better on my eyes. I didn't pay much attention to anything in the apartment as I walked through it, seeking only one thing in particular. I left the first room and entered one on the left wall. Separating the two rooms was a double set of glass-paned doors that I opened as I entered. I didn't close them behind me, since I found what I was looking for.

I fell onto the bed and pushed off my shoes with my feet. Then I flipped over onto my back and stared at the darkened ceiling. Finding out about Miranda killing her best friend was definitely a shock. I was a little irritated that Anastasia wouldn't tell me more. She had brushed off my questions by saying that Miranda should be the one to talk to me about this. I had begun to wonder if being cryptic with information was a common hobby among the Church members.

I pushed those thoughts from my mind, knowing I wouldn't get anywhere by over thinking it. I would just have to ask Miranda later about it, but I wasn't sure how I could approach that subject.

I took a deep breath slowly, listening to the sound of my breath as

I accepted that I was alone here. No one was watching or waiting on me, and I didn't have any more responsibilities tonight.

So I let in the thoughts that I had been avoiding all day.

I could see it if I closed my eyes. Clyde's face as the tail of that monster burst out of his chest, and the realization that he was going to die fill his eyes. Then he was yanked away from me into the darkness, and I knew he was eaten. Why wasn't I more careful? I'd let my guard down just because we were next to the plane, as if that actually made us safe.

I hit the bed with a clenched fist. "Damn it!"

My voice was merely a whisper, but it still sounded loud in the peaceful darkness that surrounded me. I felt responsible. His death felt heavy on my mind, even though I hardly knew him.

"What were you thinking, John?"

I closed my eyes tightly as I pictured that scene in front of my eyes again and again. I went over all the things I could've done differently in multiple ways, each one having a better outcome than his death. I cursed myself a few more times and I felt my heart beat fiercely as my body remembered the experience. Somewhere in my self-inflicted torture, I feel asleep.

I woke up some time later when I felt something fall on the bed to my left. That something then let out a small sigh, and I heard her shoes hit the floor as she pushed them off with her feet.

Barely half-awake, I opened my eyes that had become accustomed to the darkness. The moonlight was plenty enough to see by now, and that same light made her hair appear dark, almost blood red.

"Miranda?" I muttered.

"Oh, sorry. I didn't mean to wake you up. That damn Paladin wouldn't shut up about tomorrow. I probably told him five times that I was tired," her voice wasn't as sharp as it normally was, and I could tell that she really was sleepy.

"What are you doing in my bed?" I asked her, my voice also sleepy.

"Yours? If I remember correctly this is mine," she replied.

"What?" I responded cleverly as my mind was still waking up.

"Apartment 414 is my apartment. Has been for six years now. You're my Adam, so you're automatically transferred into my apartment," she replied, and I saw her flip over onto her side and look at me.

"Oh. Sorry, I didn't know this was your bed," I said as I sat up.

"Are you leaving?" she asked, her voice had a trace of disappointment in it.

"I'll go sleep on the couch," I said, starting to get out of the bed.

"Wait," she said quickly.

Still sitting on the edge of the bed, I turned to look at her from over my shoulder. She had pushed herself up so that she was leaning on her right arm in a half-sitting, half-laying position.

She tucked a lock of hair behind her ear. "Can you stay?"

I was about to ask her why, but I had a sudden feeling that I shouldn't, so the question died in my throat. I hesitated a moment before I decided to lay back down. She wrapped her arms around my left arm as she pulled herself closer to me. I felt her forehead hit the side of my shoulder as she took a deep, comfortable breath.

"This is okay, right?" she asked, her voice soft and coated with that almost-shy tone that she rarely used.

Very much so. At least, that was my initial response, but I held my tongue. I was conflicted as usual with her. I didn't know her—at least, nowhere as well as she knew me, thanks to the Eve's Gaze. Even so, I couldn't deny that her touch was electric. For a long moment, my entire focus was on her simple contact with me and on how good she smelled. After a few minutes, she spoke.

"I should apologize."

"For what?" I asked in a soft tone, matching hers.

"I was the one who insisted your training be done in three weeks, so you're in for some hell. I, err, also made up the training regime. So, I'm sorry," she confessed.

"Paladin Samson said that my training schedule looked awful too."

"*He* said that?!" she asked, surprise in her voice. "Damn, it must be really bad …."

"Great," I replied.

"Sorry," she said again. Her grip on my arm tightened for half a second.

"Why three weeks?"

"I think I'll be at the point in my investigation where I'll need your help in three weeks. They won't let you out into the field until you've completed your training though. They also have me on a tight leash now, since my limiter was disintegrated, so they won't let me do anything that would be combat related until you're with me. But I have three weeks of recon and general investigation before I'll be ready to make a move anyway," she explained.

"And why aren't you allowed to fight anyone without me being there? Even after three weeks, I doubt much will change. I'll probably be a hindrance to you still."

"Don't underestimate the training. You'll be shocked at what a Miracle Child's body can do. If we were on the front lines fighting the Outside, then you would definitely need more than three weeks training, but since you'll just be facing humans, three weeks should be okay. We'll be facing an Adam, but one that hasn't been trained. It shouldn't be much of a concern."

"Still, why couldn't you handle that yourself?" I asked.

"It's not that I *couldn't* handle it. It's that I might be *too strong* to handle it."

"What?" I asked.

She sighed. "You'll find out in training. I'm too tired to explain."

I suppressed an annoyed sigh. "Okay."

Ana's words replayed in my mind. *She killed her best friend.*

A moment of silence passed before I said, "Hey Miranda …"

"Hm?"

Her response was comfortable and sleepy, and it made the question die in my throat. I couldn't ask her about her past right now. She was totally at ease, resting peacefully. I didn't have the courage to break that by digging up a painful memory.

"Nothing. Never mind."

She pushed herself up, leaning on her arm so she could see me. I stared at the ceiling, not wanting to meet her eyes right now. She pulled herself forward so that she was half on top of me and looked down, forcing me to meet her eyes. Her hair hung down on the left side of her face, letting the moonlight illuminate her.

"What is it? You can ask me anything," she said.

I swallowed. She was close. Really, really close, and I didn't have a single complaint about that. In fact, my thoughts were pretty much non-existent. I couldn't even remember what it was that I didn't want to talk about. I met her eyes, and even in the bright moonlight, I couldn't see anything more than the gentlest shade of green.

Her eyes glanced down at my lips once, and after only a moment's hesitation, she moved. She leaned closer slowly, while I stayed very still, my mind battling over what I should do. She noticed my stillness, and she pulled back in the instant before our lips met. She didn't retreat very far, but just enough so that her eyes could focus on mine again.

"Do you not want to kiss me?" she asked in a soft voice.

"It's not about wanting to or not wanting to," I replied honestly.

Because if it was, I would not have hesitated to find out what she tasted like.

"Then what is it about?" she asked, her voice still soft.

It was hard to tell in the moonlight, but looked as if her eyes were worried.

"Whether I should or shouldn't," I answered.

"That's so like you," she said humorously.

"Sorry, but this is happening rather fast, and to be honest if I kissed you now it would be more because you're damn gorgeous than because you're important to me emotionally."

"I see," she answered. It was very apparent that she was relieved.

"What if I kissed you anyway?" she asked playfully.

I narrowed my eyes as if I was suddenly serious, "Then I'd blow my rape whistle."

Her eyes widened in surprise then her forehead sank into my chest as she started laughing. I felt her hand tighten into a fist as she laughed, which clumped up my shirt, and I felt myself smiling at the sound of her quiet laughter.

She stopped laughing and met my eyes again. "So I'm not important emotionally to you?"

A flash of memories ran through my mind as I thought about the time that we'd spent together, then I answered her honestly. "If I had to choose one way or the other, I would say that you are important to me, but I haven't done anything to deserve a kiss from you."

She raised an eyebrow slightly. "Oh? A kiss from my lips must be earned?"

"Well …" I started, not sure how to respond to that.

Her eyes sparkled mischievously. "Then if some other man saved my life, I should kiss him? It would be earned, wouldn't it?"

"No," I answered instantly.

"Oh really? Then I guess it's up to me to decide who deserves my kiss, isn't it?" she asked.

I frowned in defeat. "I suppose."

Her eyes danced playfully between mine, then she retreated and rested into my side, so her head rested on my shoulder. My arm was around her and I automatically placed it on her waist. She smoothed out the wrinkles she made on my shirt.

"I've decided that I won't kiss you," she said.

"I knew the rape whistle threat would work," I answered her.

She laughed again, and I felt her body shake gently against me. I was already severely regretting my decision not to let her kiss me.

She stopped laughing a moment later. "Hardly."

"Then what made you decide that?" I asked her.

"I realized that I didn't want to kiss you. I wanted you to kiss me. I'm not going to make another attempt to kiss you, or even hint that I want one. Instead, I'll simply wait until you can't resist any longer."

The way she coated her words with a flirtatious tone was appealing. The way that it wasn't quite seductive made it seem all the more alluring.

"Just don't keep me waiting too long," she added.

"Okay," I answered her. I was starting to think that keeping her waiting wasn't going to be an issue.

I felt her body relax into me, and I suddenly realized that she had been tense.

"Were you nervous?" I asked her, surprised.

"Err, maybe. A little bit," she admitted.

"You hid it well," I told her.

"I'm just not used to this ..." she replied.

"You're not used to trying to kiss guys in your bed? Or are you not used to them resisting?" I teased.

She laughed a little. "Very funny. I meant physical contact in general. My Miracle ... because of its nature it's dangerous to touch other people since I could hurt them if I'm not consciously suppressing it. But it doesn't matter with you, since you're immune to me."

Now that she mentioned it, I could feel it. It was that electric feeling from before, but softer and less powerful. Like a calm stream, this was more relaxing and less exciting and energizing. It was nothing more than a very subtle tingling under my skin.

I also realized that she was actually pretty shy when we first met. I wonder what changed that made her more open and forward around me.

"Is your Miracle electricity?" I asked her, pushing her shyness to the back of my mind.

"Yup. I suppose I never did properly show you," she held up a hand above us, and a small arc of blue light flowed between her thumb and forefinger.

"I saw something like that happen to you a couple times when we were Outside," I admitted, holding my hand up next to hers.

I hesitantly placed my hand between her thumb and forefinger, letting the electricity pass harmlessly through my hand. I felt just a gentle pressure.

She moved her hand so that it was facing mine, and the electricity jumped between the small space that separated us, but half a dozen more arcs appeared as well.

"I can use it to enhance the speed that my muscles contract—basically, it makes me move faster," she explained.

"Faster than other Eves?" I asked, surprised.

"Usually, yes. It takes a lot of concentration though."

I raised an eyebrow, "how's that work?"

"Good question, but it's not one that anyone has been able to answer yet. Not only with my Miracle, but also with others'. What they can do with them shouldn't be possible from a scientific standpoint, yet we make it possible. Anyway, it's a pretty handy ability. It has a lot of uses," she said, her voice soft.

"I can imagine," I replied as she lowered her hand back down to my chest.

I could tell from her voice that she was on the edge of sleep, so I didn't press for more information. Time passed as we lay there, and I felt her breathing slowly get gentler as she fell asleep.

I took a slow, deep breath and let it out, noticing my body relaxing. I suddenly noticed that she wasn't the only one that had been nervous.

She'd been alone for years, isolated for a killing her friend, though I didn't find out why she killed her friend. Possible outcomes had already raced through my mind, such as it being an accident and she blamed herself. Additionally, I wondered about what Ana had mentioned. Her Miracle didn't even allow for simple contact. What if one of her friends touched her by surprise, when she wasn't being careful? Maybe she isolated herself in an attempt to keep people safe? I couldn't really see that though; the reason was too simple.

I didn't know the details, but I did know she must have been alone for the past few years.

"I'm sorry I didn't kiss you," I whispered.

Miranda's only response was her gentle breathing. The sound of it was so subtle that it was barely audible, yet it was a sound that completely captured my focus. It was only a few moments longer before I joined her in slumber.

CHAPTER 11

When I awoke, I realized that the bedding didn't feel familiar. I sat up and opened my eyes, not remembering where I was. It came back to me after a short moment; the Church, the training ahead of me, and Miranda all swirled around in my mind. I closed my eyes and rested my head in my hands, blocking the morning sunlight from my eyes. I heard water running on my right, and once my eyes adjusted I took a better look around me.

The bed was in the center of the room with the head of the bed against a wall. On the left were four long windows, stretching from the floor to the ceiling. The middle two were actually a set of glass doors that lead out to a balcony. There was a nightstand next to the bed on my right, on which was a small lamp and a digital clock but nothing else. The sound of the running water was coming from a closed door on the right side of the room, and now that I was more awake I recognized the noise as a shower running. I assumed Miranda was in there. The only other thing in the room was a dresser, which stood in the left corner next to the bed.

I yawned, and then stayed still for a moment as I fought off the temptation to lay back down. Eventually, I managed to stand up and stretch, trying to squeeze the tiredness out of my muscles. I was still in the clothes I wore yesterday, but I suppose that couldn't be helped for now.

A noise I hadn't noticed before suddenly took full focus of my mind. A chirping noise was drifting in from the balcony, and I knew what that noise should represent, but it was difficult for me to believe. The sunlight felt bright on my eyes, and I had to blink several times before I could stand it. I didn't know what time it was exactly, but it was at that time in the morning when the warmth of the sun first chases away the cold night air.

The balcony was made out of stone and stretched the length of the bedroom. The railing on the balcony was made out of the same stone, and was decorated eloquently. I saw that there were other balconies similar to this one on the building, but no one else was out on them. The stone was cold beneath my feet where the shadows still protected it from the heat of the sun.

My eyes searched the surrounding trees for the birds that were making the chirping noise. I had never seen one with my own eyes. I knew it shouldn't by now, but it still surprised me that the Church would have pure animals here of all places. I stayed out there for several minutes, enjoying the green and peaceful scenery before me. I saw a small creature with a brown, fluffy tail run down one tree, across the lawn and up another. I took a moment to recall the name of the creature.

Distracted by my thoughts, I didn't even notice her until I heard a coffee mug being placed next me on the stone. Her hair was still wet, giving it a much darker red color than normal. It had a strange sort of intimate feel to it.

"Morning," she said, giving me a lovely smile before taking a drink from her own coffee mug.

"Morning," I replied, returning the smile and picking up the cup she had made for me.

"It's beautiful today," she said, taking a deep breath and looking out over the scenery.

Her eyes held no traces of wariness and her face seemed full of energy. If I didn't know better, I would've guessed that she'd been awake for hours already.

"You're a morning person, aren't you?" I asked, curious.

"Hmm … I hadn't really thought about it before. If all my mornings were like this one, then I'm sure I would be," she replied.

Her gaze left my eyes and looked at the green scenery. Freed from the beauty of her eyes, I glanced over her, noticing that she was already dressed for the day ahead of her. She wore dark denim jeans, but they were a lighter color than the ones she wore yesterday, and her top was a silky shirt that was green—just a couple shades lighter than the deep, rich color of her eyes.

We watched the sun as it climbed slowly away from the horizon. It was early still. The sunlight hadn't reached the grass yet, but it reached us since we four stories up. I saw another one of those brown creatures run across the lawn.

"That's a squirrel, right?" I asked.

She smiled, "Yes."

"Where are the birds?"

"They like to hide in the trees when it's this early. When they leave their nests, you can see them," she explained.

"Thank you for the coffee," I told her as I raised it to my lips.

"No problem," she replied.

I blinked in surprise as the hot liquid ran down my throat. This was exactly how I liked it. Black with a little bit of sugar to give it that subtle sweetness.

I looked down at the black liquid that swirled a little in the mug. "How did you know I liked it like this?"

She looked over to me with a clever smile. "It was in one of the memories I saw."

"Which one?" I asked, curious.

"Nope. Not telling," she said, looking away from me, her tone playful.

"What—they're my memories!" I argued back.

She turned and closed the space that separated us, looking up into my eyes. The scent from her was stronger than normal, making me realize that the scent I had been smelling wasn't perfume but her shampoo. It was some sort of flower scent, but I didn't know the name of it.

"Well then, don't let them be viewed so easily," she said with a smile, then turned, going back inside with her coffee mug.

I watched her leave, enjoying the way she looked in her denim jeans.

Her comment annoyed me and I muttered under my breath, "As if I actually had any control over that."

I looked down at the coffee. It was rare for me to have coffee, and I've only ever had it maybe a dozen times. It was a luxury in the lowers. Most of those times I was with Rachel, so I wondered if it was one of those that she saw. I was uncomfortable with that thought; my memories with Rachel was all I had left of her. It wasn't fair that Miranda got to view them without my permission. I didn't like it. I wanted them to be mine and mine alone.

I couldn't blame Miranda for it, of course. It wasn't something under her control, and it wasn't like she enjoyed the experience. She had felt the same heartbreak that I had.

I took another drink from my coffee and followed her inside. The apartment was larger than I had originally thought, but that was last night with nothing to go by but the moonlight. Now, in the sunlight, it was very clear how open her apartment was. I was standing in the double doors that separated the bedroom from the rest of the apartment. To my left was more glass windows, similar to the ones in the bedroom but without the balcony. Straight across from me was a sitting area with a large TV in the corner. Along the far wall was a door to an unknown room. Directly to my left was the kitchen, and beyond that was the door out of the apartment.

Miranda had the fridge open, her eyes looking over what there was to eat. I leaned against the side of the counter and yawned again.

"In the mood for anything particular? Sorry, but we're out of rations," she said, sticking her tongue out at me for a second before looking back into the fridge.

I chuckled. "That's okay, I'll manage. I'm not a picky eater."

"Hmm ... eggs it is then," she said as she started to pull items out and set them on the counter.

"Is there anything I can help with?" I asked, unsure what to do.

"Seeing as you haven't cooked a day in your life and I prefer to eat unburnt food, I'll manage on my own. The offer is appreciated though," she said, giving me a smirk.

I sighed and walked around the counter to sit on one of the stools. "It's a little freaky how much you know about me."

"I still don't know a lot about you," she admitted.

"Like what exactly?" I asked her.

"Hmm ..." she said thoughtfully, looking up at the ceiling.

There were a couple seconds of silence before she met my eyes again with a sly smile. "Then again, maybe I do know everything about you."

I sighed again, and took another sip of my coffee. I watched her smile widen at my reaction before she turned back to her cooking.

I watched her as she started to cook the eggs and toast the bread. I had never seen actual cooking done in front of me before. The most rations required was to boil water for noodles or rice, and a microwave covered everything else. While I watched, my mind drifted onto other topics. Vivian was at the top of my list, but I had no way of contacting her. I wasn't sure I wanted to get an earful of how I should've contacted her sooner anyway.

I remembered Anastasia's words from last night, and I knew that I should ask Miranda about it, but how on earth was I supposed to bring that topic up? There was also the matter of my training, and judging from the reactions I saw, I was sure it was going to be a living hell.

What was my future like now? Where was I headed? The life of an Adam was one where I would often be fighting against the Outside—a battle that often claims the lives of Miracle Children. Even if I didn't have my own survival to worry about, I no longer had any sort of control over my life. In every way that mattered, I was the property of the Church.

I forced those thoughts out of my mind as Miranda finished cooking. She set the plate full of food in front of me before taking a seat next to me.

I looked over at her. "Thank you."

"You're welcome. I know this is a lot to take in, and it's definitely a drastic change, but hang in there. I feel like this is where you're supposed to be."

I looked at my plate of food as she talked, not really knowing how to respond. Where I was supposed to be? I haven't felt anything like that since Rachel died. I'd only been coasting through everything so far, since all of this seemed over my head. Miranda was strong and confident, so I chose to follow her lead thus far. I was still unsure if that was the right choice, but there was no use fretting over it now.

I saw her use the toast she had made to break the yoke on her fried egg, and I followed suit since I hadn't ever eaten anything like this before. It was delicious.

We mostly ate in silence, but toward the end of it Miranda spoke. "I'm sure the Paladin told you, but I won't be here during you're training."

I swallowed. "He did."

"I want to stay. I do. But this case is giving me a bad feeling, like I'm missing a small detail that could cost people their lives. I have to return and investigate more. I'm sorry for leaving you on your own," she said and pushed her plate a few inches away to signify that she was done with it.

I swallowed the last bite of food that I had taken while she was talking. "It's okay Miranda. I'll survive three weeks."

"I hope so," she said, meeting my eyes.

Seriously, what the hell was this training?

"You should change your clothes, but I don't think you have time for a shower before your training today," she said, her eyes glancing at my apparel.

"They only gave me this yesterday. I don't have anything else other than what I'm wearing," I told her.

"There's a suitcase full of your clothes in the bedroom. I tucked it under the bed so it was out of the way. I forgot to tell you," she said, giving me an apologetic look.

"Oh. Cool," I said, entering the bedroom.

I found the suitcase she was talking about, and it indeed did have a lot of my clothes in it.

"So when will you return?" I asked her, shouting through the cracked door to the bedroom.

"The day after you finish training. I'll come pick you up and we'll go back to Chicago," she replied.

Today was Monday, and the first day of my training. I don't know my exact schedule, but if it lasted three weeks, then she'd probably be back on a Sunday or a Monday.

"You won't be returning any sooner?" I asked, curious. There were a lot more questions I had for her.

"Trust me—I would if it were possible. I might be here for a day if I have to give a report in person, but it's unlikely. What, miss me already?" she teased.

"What if I said I did?" I said as I stepped out of the bedroom, teasing her back.

She surprised me by immediately hugging me as soon as I got through the doorway. I stood still for a moment as I processed what was happening. Hesitantly, I hugged her back.

"Joking aside, I will miss you," she said gently.

"That's not fair," I accused. She knew that I didn't know how I felt about her. She knew that I wasn't sure I could say those words back to her honestly.

"I'm not going to apologize. You're my Adam, so I have every right to say those things," she replied, calmly, and showed no intentions of letting go.

I paused before responding. "I can't argue against that."

She pulled away from me and looked up at my eyes. "Damn right you can't."

I noticed she was taller than before. She had her shoes on.

"You're leaving?" I asked.

She nodded. "You need to be downstairs for your training in five minutes anyway, so now is a good time to leave. If we left at the same time, someone could see us."

"I suppose that's true," I agreed.

She winked at me, then stepped away, heading toward the door. Her hair was dry now, and she started to put it up into a ponytail.

I followed behind her as we headed to the door. She managed to finish with her hair right when we reached it.

"Okay. I'm off. See you in a few weeks," she told me, giving me a breathtaking smile.

"Be safe, okay?" I told her.

I couldn't believe I was telling a Daughter of Destruction to be safe.

"Don't worry about me. Worry about yourself," she said, then her face turned into an expression of guilt, "again … sorry."

"I'll get through it. See you soon," I said.

She gave me one last smile, then the door shut behind her, and I was alone.

I took a deep breath as I waited a few minutes before exiting. I noticed that the dishes from breakfast had already been washed and set out to dry. She must've done them when I was changing. I hadn't even heard her.

After five minutes had passed, I put on my shoes and left the apartment.

The next three weeks were a hellish, exhausting, muscle-tearing, bone-breaking training, and the harshest studying I had ever experienced.

Honestly, it was horrendous. The days went by quick, but that was because every single second was spent focused on something, whether it was weight exercises or studying laws and rules of the Church and investigative tactics and undercover methods.

I also studied the political situation of the Church. It governs eighty percent of the world, which is referred as the Holy Land. The nations that join the Church retain their individualism, however they are required to adopt the Church's laws and regulations. The Church then protects the nations that joined with them, sending their Miracle Children to help ward off the Outside. Only a few nations had successfully survived without joining the Church, but if their Walls are breached, they usually come to the Church asking for protection.

The Church only has one enemy, which is more of a terrorist group than anything else. They called themselves Deliverance, and they gained some popularity among the people fifteen years ago. However, that rapidly faded after they bombed a building that was housing a negotiation between several cities and the Church.

My parents were among the casualties, so I knew the event well, but I got a better understanding of Deliverance's motivation during my studies. If the Church and the cities in the Americas reached an agreement, they would lose the support of the people. Deliverance wanted the Church eradicated, but the people wouldn't support that if the cities received more rights and freedoms. In an attempt to stop the negotiations, they rigged the building to explode. A dozen priests of the Church and over two hundred representatives from the cities in the Americas were killed. They carefully planted evidence so that it looked like the Church was the ones behind the explosion. It was so well put together that Deliverance would've succeeded if a Blessed Pair had not captured a Deliverance agent fleeing the building moments before it exploded. The bombing put a hold on the negotiations, which still had not been resumed, but the public outcry against Deliverance was understandably enormous. They lost all support.

Even though my study work load was triple that of anything I have had to handle in college, the real majority of my time was focused on physical training. I had to force my muscles to go well beyond what was safe for them. They would tear themselves, and it hurt like hell.

It was the same thing every day. I'd wake up and immediately start training. I had to eat four times daily to keep my energy up, and five times if I managed to get up in time for breakfast. I had to combine my studies with meal times, so I technically didn't get a break until I arrived back at the apartment late each night. I found out that the other door in the apartment lead to a small laundry room, and if I had the energy, I would wash my clothes. My muscles pained me to the point where it was difficult to fall asleep, but it wasn't long before I got used to the pain and would fall asleep as soon as I hit the bed.

Zachariah was in charge of my muscle training for the first few days, but I quickly reached the point where I wasn't struggling with the tasks he set before me. That was when Benjamin took over.

"Yo," he said, leaning against the side of my apartment building as I came out.

The morning air was chilly enough that I saw his breath.

"Mornin' Ben," I replied after I recovered from my surprise.

"I'm your new instructor for muscle training. I'll also be running through a few topics you'll need to memorize while we train, and you'll be tested on these afterward," he said, taking a few steps toward me.

"They told me that they were putting another Adam in charge of it, but I didn't guess it was you," I said, feeling a little more comfortable that I wouldn't have to worry about getting along with someone new. "Is this your way of apologizing for abandoning me with Anastasia the other day?"

He laughed. "Sorry mate. I knew she'd want the opportunity to talk about Miranda with ya. No matter what she says, Ana does care about her. Now and then I catch her worrying about what Miranda was doing and wondering if she was okay, so I had to give Ana that chance to find out what was going on. As to why it's me that's in charge of your training, well, the Church gave me a very nice offer. Extending my vacation time here in exchange for me training you. Definitely worth it."

"So, you can't normally crash at Alexandria Academy for a couple days?" I asked.

"Eh, sorta. We have to appear here and give detailed reports in person if something went wrong with one of our assignments, which can take a couple days depending on what's needed from us. Also, The Church gives us some time to ourselves every now and then. We call it vacation, but it's pretty much just givin' us a break from the fighting. There's a certain amount of time per six months allowed, and a minimum amount of time required. Basically, the Church does force vacation on us, but we get to manage how much of it we want. They gave me and Ana more time since I'm training you, and we jumped at the chance to have it, but I'm worried Ana might get a little restless."

"In what way?" I asked.

"Ya won't really understand unless you take the front lines yourself, but in cities with unstable Walls, the fighting is pretty damn intense.

It pushes us to our limits and we don't have to hold anything back. I don't want to say that it's particularly fun, but it does get your heart pumping. Ya don't love it, but you're out there, with the lives of everyone in the city resting on your back, fighting your damnedest every day. Then ya come here, where it's peaceful and beautiful and after some time passes ya start to think, 'why am I wasting my time here, when there's people out there who need me?' I don't want Ana to go through that, but at the same time we don't get many chances to spend together intimately when we're on the front lines. We think this is the right call," he explained this while stretching out his legs, so I followed his lead and did the same.

"Hmm, I see. Miracle Children of Law don't get vacations?" I asked, thinking about how Ana said Miranda never stayed here for longer than a day.

"Nah, they do. It's just not required like it is with us. Though to be honest, I think it probably should be."

"Why?"

"'Cause although the Law career does sound like it's safer than the front lines, it takes a stronger mind to handle that task. You have to see the darkness in humanity, and we are the most powerful species on this planet. They see an evil that the War career doesn't have to see, so it can mess with you up here," he said, tapping his temple.

"Hm," I said, thoughtfully as I stretched out my leg.

"Anyway, let's get going. We're gonna start with a run, but we don't have much time since we talked for so long, so we'll have to sprint in some places."

"What?! Dammit! We could have talked and jogged, Ben!" I said, annoyed.

"Yeah, but where's the fun in that?" he said, starting to run.

I cursed and followed after him, beginning another day of hell.

I had to do this for three more days, and on Sunday I had a day to recover. I spent my entire first Sunday sleeping. Most of my muscles stopped hurting toward the end of the day. When I finally got out of bed to eat and shower, the sun was already setting.

On the kitchen counter was a handwritten note, with my cell phone next to it. Surprised, I read the note.

Hey John,

Sorry to only leave a note, but after the week you had, I didn't want to wake you. I came out here to give a report, so I thought it would be a good opportunity to drop off your cellphone. I met Vivian at your apartment. She had no idea who I was and why I was in your apartment, and it took a bit to calm her down and explain everything. She was really worried about you. Though, after I explained everything, she seemed more angry than worried. We talked a great deal about you, and she asks that you call her as soon as you get the chance. Don't leave a girl waiting.

--Miranda

I swallowed as I read the letter, very much relieved that I had missed introducing those two. Part of me was genuinely curious what they talked about, the other part was genuinely terrified to find out.

I turned on my phone. "Oh, shit."

There were twenty-four unread text messages and 103 missed calls. All from Vivian. They abruptly stopped after last Tuesday, so I guessed that was when she met Miranda.

I started to feel guilty as I quickly read the lines of text messages she sent me, which alternated from worried responses and threats of violence if I didn't answer her. I opened my contacts to call her back, but was surprised to see that there was something different.

I had six contacts in my phone. Popular guy, I know, but my only friend was Vivian. The other five were my two places of work, my college, and a couple professors who were useful to contact about assignments. Now, however, there was a seventh labeled Miranda Pierce.

I shook my head, humored. I guess this was a hint that I should call her too. First, though, Vivian.

She answered on the second ring, but the line was silent.

"Um, hello?" I asked, unsure.

"I'm pissed, and you only give me a 'hello'?" said a clearly annoyed female voice.

"Err, sorry. I forgot my phone—" I started, but was cut off.

"Don't. Even. Seriously what the hell did you think I was going to assume? A member of the Guards shot dead in your apartment and you missing? And then the investigation shut down a few days later by order of the Church. I was worried sick, but then I find out you were fine all along, and were getting rather friendly with that pretty redhead."

"I was not—"

"Oh, save it. She never said anything directly but it was incredibly obvious that there's something going on between you two. I know better than to expect you to admit anything, but don't try to pretend that she's not your type. What I do expect is an explanation. Where have you been?"

I paused, not sure what I was allowed to tell her. "What'd Miranda say?"

"She didn't give me any details, but she did say that you're working with the Church ever since the break-in at your apartment," she explained.

"Sorry, I probably shouldn't say any more than that to someone who isn't a part of the Church. I'm fine though, and you don't need to worry about me."

She sighed, then stayed silent for a few seconds. "So, in our current situations it looks like we won't be able to be such good friends anymore."

I found myself frowning, not liking where this was going. "I don't know what the future will be, but I don't want us to stop being close friends just because I got caught up in this."

"Oh, you misunderstood me," she said, "we won't stop being close friends. I'll just have to join the Church as well."

"What?" I asked, surprised.

"Well I told you before that I've been invited to join the Crusaders because my good record as an officer. I was aiming for a higher position inside Chicago since you were here, but if you moved on then there really isn't any reason to hang around. Besides, you found a hot girlfriend in the Church, maybe I'll get lucky too," she said in a teasing tone.

"She's not my girlfriend," I replied, annoyed, "and you can't just make a decision like that based on my current situation."

"Sure, I can. It's my life after all, and I don't want to lose my best friend. Bye now, John."

"Wait—" I started, but was interrupted by a click, signifying that she had hung up.

I sighed and gave my phone a look of annoyance, as if it was to blame.

"Why don't you ever listen for once, instead of just charging full-throttle into everything?" I muttered, pointlessly.

Part of me wondered if she had wanted to join the Crusaders all along but hadn't because of me. If that was true, how else had I been holding her back?

I went back into the bedroom and flopped down onto the bed, starting to feel tired again. I needed to rest as much as I could if the week ahead of me was anything like the one I had just survived.

I rolled over onto my back and held up the phone, looking at the name *Miranda Pierce*. Even if I called her, what would I say? Did I have anything to talk about? What if I called her at a bad time? I sighed and gave up, deciding to call her another day, and went back to sleep.

I started martial arts training the second week, and to make time for it, they cut back my muscle exercises. At first, I was relieved, but the toll that the martial arts put on my body was more severe than the weight training had been.

The second week was also the week I learned more about how Miracles work, though it was extremely vague and I heard a lot of *this is a new science* and *we have barely scratched the surface of this field* when I asked my instructors questions they couldn't answer.

The differences between Adams and Eves were significant when it came to their Miracles. It was difficult to even compare the two, since there's such a variety of Miracles, but Adams seemed to have more powerful Miracles. Theoretically, a really powerful Eve can outperform an Adam in combat, but the instructors told me that it was dangerous and difficult for an Eve to reach that level of power. They wouldn't explain any more, telling me that I would learn more about it later.

An Adam has a single Miracle that is unique to him alone. The Miracles are never effortless to use, so there are always limitations to what an Adam can do with his Miracle. I asked Ben about this later, and he explained it more thoroughly than the instructors.

"Hmm," he started, not even out of breath even though we were practically sprinting, "you know my Miracle is teleportation, right?"

"Yeah." I heaved, sucking in air.

"Well, it's not like I can teleport anywhere in the world as many times as I want. I can only teleport x amount of mass y amount of times before I get too exhausted to use it anymore. And of course, there's a distance limit to all of this," he explained as he started to speed up.

I gritted my teeth and did the same, "sounds complicated."

"Oh, it is. I must do several calculations to estimate how much effort it would take to teleport something before I do it. Otherwise I might be too exhausted to use my Miracle when Ana really needs me. It would be irresponsible."

"How far can you teleport yourself?" I asked.

"Two and a half miles in one step. If it was only myself, I could probably go fifty or sixty miles before I reach my limit. I haven't tested it though."

"So, my Miracle, whatever it is, will have restrictions like that too?"

"Yeah, undoubtedly," he said, and then gave me a mischievous grin, "maybe I'll get you to use it today."

I groaned. Whenever they tried to push me far enough to use my Miracle, I would always end up in some kind of pain and still be unable to use it.

After surviving the torturous workout that they put me through, I retreated to Miranda's apartment and immediately went to bed.

The following day was one I had been looking forward to, since I was going to be learning more about Eves and how their Miracles function. I don't know what I expected, but once again, the majority of my questions were deflected into some excuse of why they didn't know.

Even so, I learned a lot. Eves had at least two, sometimes three, different Miracles they could do. The first of which was the fundamental aspect of their Miracles and is known as Blood Forging. Every Eve could do this, although some Eves were better at it than others. It's the Miracle I had seen Miranda do several times already; the ability to teleport—or summon—an object to them. Whatever their blood touched, they could teleport it back to them. Not only that, but they could also manipulate the object to whatever they want. They showed me videos of an Eve dripping her blood over an ingot of iron and crafting all sorts of weapons and tools out of it with nothing but her mind. However, since this takes immense concentration, it was deemed impractical to use it in combat. To get around this, Eves would store weapons that are already crafted and then summon whatever ones they want whenever they needed them. The process of storing weapons is called the Ceremony of the Red Steel, and I was shut down quickly when I asked about the ceremony. Basically, *Eves only; Adams keep out.*

Eves also had something called a Minor Miracle, or just a Minor for short. It wasn't something that was present in all Eves, but it was common. A Minor was similar to an Adam's Miracle in that it can be any sort of ability, but it's usually not very powerful—at least, not on the level of an Adam. The Minor Miracle was used more as a helpful talent or skill and not for combat, with one exception, which led to the explanation of their third Miracle.

Eves could create something known as a Core. I had thought that the lecture on an Adam's Miracles was a complicated mess, but this was on another level entirely. These scientists hadn't a clue as to what a Core was or why Eves could summon one. From the tests they performed— and most of them were actually designed by Nathan—they discovered that Cores are the true power of an Eve, and hypothesize that Blood Forging is simply a side effect, or lesser version, of this Miracle. A Core, at the most basic description, was a weapon. An Eve doesn't really summon a Core, but creates it—similar to how they shape things by

Blood Forging, just without the blood part. The weapon crafted from something in their environment, such as stone or wood that they compress and harden to the strength of steel. It's form and abilities are unique to each Eve, and it's usually a weapon of incredible power. I was shown another video, but unlike the others, I recognized the Eve that was in this one.

She looked younger in the video, with her blond hair shorter and her expression somehow less composed and more innocent. Her amber eyes bore into the camera at the start of the video, but they switched to a man in a lab coat that was sitting in a chair, with his back to the camera. She was standing a short distance away and was obviously the focus of the video. At her feet were two ingots of iron.

The room they were in was the same room that Nathan used to take scans of my body. There were a few changes, such as a lack of a steel bench in the middle, but I recognized the white walls and the strange dome shape of the room.

"Okay, let's get started. First, state your name for the record, and the purpose of this video." I recognized the voice as Nathan's, apparently the he was the man in the chair.

She looked at the camera again. "Anastasia Martin. I will summon my Core and attempt to explain its effects in detail."

"Excellent," Nathan said, then he turned around in his seat, and looked at something that was behind the camera.

"Is everything running optimally?" he asked.

I heard a man's voice I didn't recognize respond with, "Yes, but are you sure this is going to get any accurate or helpful readings from her?"

"The moment a scientist starts being sure of anything is the moment that he stops being a good scientist," Nathan replied.

"So ... no then," responded the voice.

Nathan gave him a smile and turned back around to face Ana. "Whenever you would like to start, Anastasia, you may."

"Okay," she replied, then readied herself.

Her posture changed, going from a neutral pose to a tense one as her back straightened. Her expression tightened into one of focus and determination. She raised her right hand out in front of her, as if she was about to grasp something. Her mouth moved subtly, muttering some unheard word.

The iron morphed, slithering up into the air toward her outstretched hand like a silent snake obeying its master. The iron bent into a gentle curve before recurving out at the tips, forming a bow. A strip of iron split into very fine strands, and then twisted around each other, creating the string of the bow. It strung itself, bending the bow back slightly.

"Heartrate just shot up to 130, and it's steadily climbing," said the voice behind the camera.

"Well naturally. I'm sure summoning a Core isn't an easy thing to do," Nathan replied without turning around. "Anastasia, how do you possess the strength to pull back a bow of iron? And even then, iron isn't flexible enough to make the bow very useful."

"I reconstructed the molecular structure slightly to accommodate my strength," she said calmly, turning to her right and holding up the bow.

She slowly pulled back on the iron string in a smooth motion, making it seem almost effortless. "When I release the string, I modify it again to give it increased flexibility and pull strength. This allows for a devastating amount of force to be released."

"You can modify the iron all the way down to its molecular structure? So, your Core is similar to Skyfall?" Nathan asked.

The mention of Miranda's Core momentarily surprised me.

"Hardly. I can only make minor changes to my Core. It's impossible for me to do anything drastic to it. You should know this; after-all, the reason you asked me for this favor and not Miranda is because you haven't the slightest idea where to even begin studying Skyfall," she replied as she turned back to face him again.

I heard a hint of humor in Nathan's voice. "True. Skyfall's existence makes us question everything we know about nature's laws."

"Heartrate has reached 160," said the voice behind the camera.

"Already? I've barely started the study," Nathan complained.

"Don't worry, with no threats to my life the Break Phenomenon won't happen until I reach somewhere past 240 beats per minute. The strain of wielding my Core will push my heart to 180 quickly, but then it will hold steady. However, because of the strain it puts on me, I'd like to rest after a few minutes."

"How could you possibly know this?" Nathan asked.

"I've experienced it once before. I remember," she explained simply.

"Interesting. What do you use for ammunition? Do you make it when you need it—like the bow?" he asked.

She shook her head. "I don't have any physical arrows or ammunition. When I'm using the Core, my Minor is much stronger and easier for me to use. I use that in place of ammunition."

"Your Minor is the slight influence over air, correct?" Nathan asked her, looking down at something in his lap. From his body language, it looked like he was taking notes.

"Yes. I can move the air around and change the temperature and pressure of it. Without my Core, I can only use it on a limited scale."

"But with your Core, how much is this amplified?"

She took a deep breath before replying, "I condense the air until it's tough enough to pierce flesh and bone. Before I entered the Break Phenomenon, I remember that my air was dense enough to pierce through Blackscale."

"Damn," Nathan responded.

She gave a delicate shrug. "It's not as impressive as others, but I am confident in the strength it gives me."

He nodded while he jotted down some more notes.

The video ended there, rather abruptly. I had questions, but most were deflected and left unanswered. I asked about the 'Break Phenomenon' they mentioned in the video, but I was again told I would learn about it later.

Sunday came again before I knew it, and like the week before I slept all day. I woke up when I heard the door to the bedroom close, and felt the mattress dip, as if someone had sat on it.

I sat up and ignored my muscles as they complained. I blinked a couple times, trying to get my sleepy eyes to focus in the dark. The moon was only half full tonight, but it was bright enough to make out shapes. To my left I saw an outline of someone sitting on the edge of the bed. I heard the soft but recognizable sound of shoelaces being untied.

"Miranda?" I muttered as my brain tried to piece together what was happening around me.

She looked over her shoulder at me, a humored smile barely visible in the dark. "Of course."

My brain started to work again, and the room got clearer with every second that passed. Miranda was here. I thought she wasn't going to be here until next week, but here she was.

She straightened up as she finished taking off her shoes, then turned so she could look at me more comfortably.

"Don't tell me that you've had other girls spending the night while I was away ..." she accused, teasingly.

"Of course not," I replied instantly. "Not the whole night, anyway," I added, and was rewarded with her surprised look.

She recovered and smiled. "You're more alert than I expected. I was hoping I could tease you for at least a few minutes."

I smiled back and lay back down. "Sorry to disappoint."

I felt her crawl toward me, and I automatically raised my arm so she could rest against my side. She didn't hesitate, and lay against me like she had the last night we spent together. She smelled nice, as always. Her mere presence against me was comforting and relaxing— even with my sore muscles.

"Think of it as raising my expectations," she replied.

I chuckled.

"I like the haircut, by the way," she commented.

"It was pretty much the first thing they did to me."

"I thought they would. You don't look like you live on the streets anymore."

"It wasn't *that* bad," I remarked.

She laughed for a moment. "If thinking that makes you feel better ...."

I let her comment go unchallenged and changed the subject instead. "So why are you here? Did you have to give a report in person?"

"No," she said, pushing herself up with her right arm and leaning on it, so she could see my face easier. "That was my official excuse, but really it was because I wanted to see you. Paladin Samson saw through it immediately though … I got scolded."

I stared into her eyes for a long moment before I muttered, "Well you've seen me."

She raised her eyebrows and spoke in a teasing tone. "Fine. If you're going to be like that, I guess I'm done here. I might as well leave."

She was trying to make me feel guilty for my comment, and was succeeding, but I wasn't going to give up that easily. "Good. I needed to get some sleep anyway, since this training schedule *someone* made for me is extremely vicious. I swear, they must really hate me or something."

Her eyes sparkled, enjoying that I was playing along. "I certainly noticed that you were busy. Too busy, it seems, to even give a girl a phone call."

"What are you talking about? I called Vivian," I replied, trying to keep the grin off my face.

Her eyes narrowed in honest annoyance at me, "I meant *me*, John."

I smiled gently at her. "I know, I know."

I felt her body next to mine and could smell her shampoo. I could hear her gentle breathing and see her lips curve into a stunning smile. I must have been too busy during the week to notice, but now that she was here next to me it was obvious. I had missed it. I missed her, and much more than I should have.

I reached up with my right hand and tucked her crimson hair behind her ear so that the light from the half-moon illuminated her features better. "Sorry. I should have called."

Her face relaxed out of her annoyed expression into a more natural look. "It's 'kay."

Her eyes switched between mine as the sides of my fingers followed her jawline.

This wasn't good. I knew it wasn't. I knew I shouldn't be doing

200

what I was doing. It couldn't be right. I didn't know her and I didn't have the right feel this way, or to want to do what was going through my mind.

My fingers reached her chin, and I traced her lips gently with my thumb. I wanted to kiss her, and if I didn't distract myself immediately, I was going to.

I hesitated a moment longer, then I swallowed and lowered my hand. "Can I ask you something personal?"

She blinked, surprised, then lowered her head down and placed her forehead against my chest. She sighed disappointedly, and I felt her warm breath go through the thin black shirt I had on. Then she looked up again, and rested her chin on the back of her hands as she lay on top of me. She gave me a look that was almost pouting.

Her expression was undoubtedly the most adorable thing I had ever seen, and it made me immediately regret not kissing her. I wanted to, there was no getting around that, but I couldn't let myself take that step when I had no emotional attachment to her. It wasn't fair. I couldn't just listen to my hormones.

"So, what was it that you wanted to ask me? Or was that just an excuse?" she accused.

I couldn't admit that it was both. "I heard something about you. Something bad about your past … it involved your best friend."

The sparkle in her eyes died immediately. "Oh."

"I don't know the story, but I was told the ending," I explained.

"I suppose I shouldn't be surprised that you heard this," she in a sad tone.

"Was I not supposed to?" I asked her.

"It's only fair. I've seen all the secrets you didn't want people to know, so you should have my secrets as well."

She moved, sliding to my left. I assumed she was going to settle into my side, so I raised my arm. Instead, she pulled my arm in front of her so it separated us. She embraced it and rested her forehead against my shoulder.

I started to sit up so I could see her face, but I didn't even get halfway up before she stopped me.

"Wait," she ordered. Her voice was tense and serious.

"What is it?" I asked, confused.

"I'll tell everything, but don't look at me as I do so," she said, her voice soft.

"Why not?" I asked.

"Please."

I stayed still for a moment before I conceded and lay back down.

"I have to start at the beginning for it to all make sense, so bear with me," she started.

"That's fine," I told her in what I hoped was a supporting tone.

Her voice was quiet and gentle when she spoke again, "As I told you before, I was born into the Church. I was discovered to be a Miracle Child at birth, so I grew up under the complete supervision of the Church and started my education at a young age with other Miracle Children. Our parents were allowed to live with us until we turned eleven, and then we lived in dorms with until we graduated at eighteen. My roommate was Titania West, a very talented Eve. We got along well, and it wasn't long before we became best friends. She was kind, open-minded and popular. I don't know anyone who disliked her."

When she spoke again I heard her tone soften. "Titania loved the stars. She'd convince me to sneak out of our dorms at night. We'd dodge the security patrols and cameras till we got to the very edge of the Outside. Far enough out that we could reach one of the huge trees but still close enough to the barrier that the Outside creatures avoided us. We'd climb to the very top of the tree and spend hours staring up at the thousands of stars and talking."

She paused and smiled as more memories came to her. "One time we got caught sneaking back in, but Titania convinced the two Crusaders that we were just using the security patrols as extra training. Somehow they let us off with only a warning."

She paused again, spending a moment lingering in the past before continuing, "Anyway, we were a part of the same group—or class you could call it—of twenty-two others. Ana and Ben were in this group too, and the four of us were friends. Titania and I competed in everything. We would lord it over the other when one of us succeeded at something. But we always encouraged the other when they needed it. I always had a lot of fun with her. She would typically beat me in combat scores, but in academics I usually had the upper hand. She was the first one in our class to be able to summon her Core, and she didn't let me forget it for weeks. They taught you what a core was, right?"

"Sort of," I answered, my voice sounding odd after only hearing her voice in the silence.

She gave a humored chuckle, "I know what you mean. Miracle Children have been a part of this world for fifty years and scientists still have no clue what makes up a Core."

"Well the important part to know is it's difficult to summon one as early as Titania could summon hers. They called her a prodigy. They expected great things from her, and I was ... very jealous. No matter how hard I pushed myself, how hard I tried, I could never summon my Core. It wasn't uncommon for an Eve to graduate without having summoned her Core, but the strongest Eves always had."

"Why is it called that?"

"A Core?" she clarified.

"Yeah."

"It has to do with how one of the first Eves described it to the researchers. She called it the source of her power and the Core of who she was. To an extent, all Eves have that feeling when they grasp it in their hands, so I don't disagree with the name."

"So Titania and I were the top of our class, which was probably to our competitive nature with each other. Graduation arrived, but it's not the type of graduation that you're probably thinking. Graduation is a final test—everyone is flown to the Outside and told to survive for a week. Staying alive earns you a Seal and allows you to advance into doing field work, but each individual was given a ribbon that they must protect. Other Eves can take these ribbons, and we're ranked based on how many ribbons we have at the end of the week. The more we collect, the better rank we achieved.

"Naturally, as soon as we heard this, Titania and I grew competitive, and when we ran into each other half way through the week, we fought each other. It was fun at first, but fighting in the Outside was completely different then fighting in training. It felt so … real, I guess. We had total freedom in our choices—no longer restricted by weapon choice or tactics by our instructors. It was exhilarating and heart-pounding, and every time she pushed herself farther, I did the same.

"Neither of us hesitated for even a moment as the fight escalated. We had this trust and respect in each other's abilities; I never once thought that she wouldn't be able to counter me, and I don't think she thought that either. She gained speed, and then so did I. Her hits became stronger, so I retaliated even harder. I don't know how much time had actually passed, but the fight changed when Titania summoned her Core. I wasn't a match for her anymore, and I quickly began to lose. I remember knowing what I needed to do …. Maybe it was the adrenaline or the atmosphere of the Outside, but for the first time, I knew I could pull it off."

Her voice was steadily getting quieter, and I let silence stay between us for a moment before I spoke.

"Your Core?" I asked gently.

Her grip on my arm tightened, and I felt increased pressure from her forehead on my shoulder as her body tensed. She never affirmed it, but her reaction made it clear that I was right.

"Neither of us noticed what was happening," she continued, but her voice was tense and it was obvious that she was holding back tears. "I … I was trying to kill her, John. How did I—"

She cut off abruptly when her voice broke, and she took a moment to recover. Her breathing was unsteady, and it sounded loud in the momentary silence. It wasn't long before she was able to continue, but her voice was still full of pain.

"I don't know why we didn't notice. I don't know … why it wasn't obvious to me that I was only seeing her as an enemy, and not a friend—not Titania. I was putting everything—every ounce of muscle into my attacks. I couldn't stop myself; I know that. I know that and I could forgive myself if that's all it was, but … I didn't want to stop. I was loving every single second of it."

I heard her give a gentle sniffle. "My sense of time was gone—it was as if I had no need of time, like it didn't matter to me anymore. There was the moment and nothing else, and in one of those moments she made a mistake. I don't even remember what it was exactly, but it was something small and simple—her defense was imperfect for just a breath … and I didn't think twice before stabbing her in her chest." Her body started shaking gently, and my shoulder started to feel wet from her tears. "Right in her heart."

She couldn't stop herself now; she cried. It was soft and quiet, but there was nothing gentle about it. She was weeping with anguish.

Her next words were filled with self-disgust. "What kind of human does that? What kind of person feels triumphant after killing her best friend? I hate what I am! Holy Demon is a perfect label for a creature like me."

She stopped speaking, and she spent several moments calming down. Her sobs lessened and her breathing became more even, but her tears hadn't ceased. I didn't answer her. I had no idea what to say, and it seemed best to say nothing than to say something half-assed.

She spoke again, the sadness in her voice was practically painful for me to her. "I realized what had happened instantly. The shock of that realization brought me to my senses—I couldn't believe what I had done …. I held her and wept."

The silence that followed was suddenly deafening, and it was only broken by Miranda's occasional sniffle. I let another long moment span between us, trying to decide what I should do. Eventually, I pulled my arm from her grasp. At first, she tightened her hold on it, but after a few seconds she relaxed her grip and let go, curling her hands into her chest. I turned onto my side so I could face her, and saw in the dim moonlight that she had her eyes shut tight.

Here was a Daughter of Destruction lying next to me, with tears sliding down her face. Her hair was spread out on the bed behind her; it looked dark in the feeble moonlight. She was wearing a white T-shirt which had slid up from her hip bone, revealing a small section of her pale skin. Her denim jeans were a dark blue and complimented her skin in the moonlight. She had her legs half curled up, as if the only thing preventing her from being in a tight ball was my presence.

She looked so incredibly fragile, as if I would hurt her if I exhaled too sharply.

I carefully cupped her face with the palm of my right hand, and gently brushed away her tears with my thumb. Even in the bad lighting, I could see her open her eyes in surprise, and I gently took her hand with my left. Had she honestly thought I was going to leave her in this state? Hadn't she seen my memories? Didn't she know me better than everyone else? How could she think that?

Her expression gracefully changed from surprise to one of relief, and I suddenly understood why she was surprised. Miranda had been alone for the past five years; not only physically from her Minor Miracle, but emotionally as well. Now, through an accident, I was suddenly a part of her life without having the time to develop trust. She was afraid of getting hurt, and I held the power to hurt her most. The thought bordered on ridiculousness to me after witnessing her strength and ability. Someone so strong was curled against me, crying and worried what I might think about her.

I didn't have any wise or graceful words to say to her. So, I only did what I could, and told her my honest opinion.

"Miranda, don't hate yourself. I am here for you and you alone. I like you for who you are."

She stared back at me, her eyes no longer in pain. Her tears hadn't ceased, but they were slowing. Empathy stirred in me, and I struggled to find a way to comfort her.

Even though I knew that Eves snap and lost control like that … it was one thing to hear it in casual conversation, but completely different seeing someone hurt and affected by it.

Was it possible that it only bothered me this much because the girl that was hurt by it was crying in my arms?

I swallowed. No, that wasn't right. It was more likely that it bothered me because the person who was hurt by it was Miranda.

I didn't have the time or focus to think about it, so I pushed that thought out of my mind.

"I don't understand," I stated, stroking her cheek with my thumb.

"What part?" she asked, wiping the tears off her other cheek with her free hand.

"Anastasia said you were alone because you choose to be. After hearing the story, I agree with her, so why have you been hiding?" I asked her.

She sniffed gently, her tears had finally stopped and she was recovering. "Ugh. I knew it was Annie who told you."

I smiled gently, glad to see that she wasn't crying anymore. She reached up and took my hand from her cheek and pulled it down so she could speak more comfortably.

"It's not fair to say that it's all my fault that I was isolated .... Annie was referring to the friendship we shared. Annie trusted my testimony—trusted that I didn't purposely kill Titania."

"What? Why would anyone think that?" I asked, offended by the injustice of that accusation against Miranda.

"John, I know you haven't been taught about Eve's snapping, but—" she cut herself off and took a deep breath before continuing. "It's called the Break Phenomenon, and without going into details, know that an Eve doesn't return from that state on her own. It just doesn't happen, but there I was, claiming to have come back from that after I—at the end."

"Still..." I said, not understanding.

She cleared her throat, "John, Ben and Annie were the only ones that really knew how close Titania and I were. Everyone else only saw our competitive nature, so it was easier for them to think that I ... out of jealousy. I will admit that I didn't fight those rumors. I deserved their suspicion and even hate. I welcomed their isolation because then I wouldn't have to worry about hurting anyone else."

"Don't talk like that," I said, bothered by her words.

She shrugged gently and wouldn't meet my eyes, "it's not untrue, but it doesn't matter anymore."

"Because?" I asked.

She shook her head, telling me she didn't have anything else to say.

I spent a moment thinking over everything she told me, and I was left with a very evident question.

"Miranda, why tell me all this?" I asked, keeping my tone gentle.

"What do you mean?" She responded.

"I mean, you've only known me for a few days, but you're willing to tell me something that you're so deeply ashamed about. Why? What could I have possibly done to make you trust me with something like that?" I said.

She didn't respond right away, and instead just stared into my eyes. She pulled herself up into a sitting position, and I rolled onto my back. She leaned over me and looked down, supporting herself with an arm on the other side of me. She placed her other hand on my chest as she stared into my eyes.

"To me, you're absolutely invincible. No matter how much electricity I could ever channel into you, and no matter how many times I attempt to stab you, it's futile. Even in the Break Phenomenon, there isn't a single thing I can do to you."

She lowered herself down and placed her ear to my chest. "No matter what, there isn't a single thing I can do to make this heart stop beating. Nothing at all. I can trust you to safely stop me if I lose control, and keep me from hurting anyone. I trust that, John, more than anything."

She looked up and pulled herself close to me, now fully resting on top of me. Her face was close. I could feel her warm breath and a soft smell of peppermint.

She placed her hand next to my face, and ran her fingers through my short hair on the side of my head.

"Aren't you afraid of me? Afraid that I might misuse that outrageous advantage?" I asked.

"How could you? In the same way, I am invincible to your power as well, whatever it may be," she replied.

"I don't mean it like that. Aren't you afraid that I might not stop you? Or afraid of me rejecting you, not feeling the same things you're feeling?" I asked.

I was sure of it by now. She wasn't just fooling around with me. Yet what of me? What did I feel in return?

She was suddenly hesitant and cautious. "Are you going to? Do you not like me?"

"That's not really it …" I started, not knowing how to say what was on my mind.

"Am I attractive to you?"

"Of course you are." Was it possible for a guy *not* to be attracted to her?

She paused, and her tone lowered, "is it because of what I just told you?"

She thought it was because of her past? "No, definitely not."

"Than my personality? How forward I am? I know I invade your personal space but—"

"No, no, no. It's none of that. I like those about you," I interrupted her before she could mention something even more ridiculous.

She had courage, but at the same time she had her shy moments. It was a mixture I found alluring.

"Then what's the problem? Why do you always hesitate around me?" she asked, impatiently.

"Because I don't understand how you can so easily trust me. You've only known me for a few weeks, how can you trust me so completely with something as important as keeping you from losing control? What have I done that's earned that?"

Her eyes widened slightly. "Oh. I see," she smiled gently. "I know it's completely one sided and unfair, but I've seen your life. I saw important memories that make up your character, and so I know you enough that I know you won't leave me when I need you. You're reliable."

"Don't you have any doubt? You only saw a few memories, so what? Why can you be this comfortable around me based on that?"

Her expression turned serious, but still soft. "You're my Adam. You are linked to me with something more powerful than just words; blood. You're so important to me that it's changed my body on a fundamental level. How can I not trust that?"

I didn't respond and instead looked away. I didn't want to argue with her.

She pulled my face back to her with her hand so she could meet my eyes, "I'm yours, John. I'm your Eve. Isn't it a better question to ask why you're hesitating to trust me back?"

"Miranda, how can you expect me to have this trust in you when I don't know you?" I asked.

"Is knowing who I am important?" she asked in a tone that made it clear she thought it wasn't.

"Yes!" I exclaimed back, surprised by her question.

"Why? John, even if everyone you know and love betrays you, I would never do so," she stated.

"Again, how can I trust you on this when I don't know you?"

"Because I don't have a choice but to stay by your side," she answered.

I gave her a questioning look.

She took a deep breath. "John, now that you are linked to me, my one weakness is you. Nothing I can do would work against you if it came to a fight. Likewise, I am your weakness. You can't stop me, John. Your Miracle, whatever it may be, will be powerless against me. The safest place we can be is with each other. If we're together, we are without weakness—quite literally. I won't betray you because I can't afford to betray you, John."

"How romantic," I said sarcastically.

"Logic rarely is," she responded.

I stayed quiet, thinking over what she had said. Although her reason made sense to me, part of me wondered if that was the sole reason for her trust in me. Perhaps that reasoning was enough to someone who's been with the Church all their life and been around Blessed Ones constantly, but as for me ... I needed more.

"I'm sorry, Miranda. I don't think that's good enough for me," I confessed.

She sighed and retreated to my side, seemingly admitting defeat.

"Just give me some time, okay?" I asked.

"Mm," she replied, and I could tell she had her eyes closed. "If there's anything we have, it's time."

I took another deep breath and used the silence to think.

Maybe I was being ridiculous. Miranda was clearly a woman I could come to care about, so what *was* I afraid of? What was holding me back? Was it my past? Was losing Rachel even more traumatizing than I thought? I wanted to trust Miranda. I did. I wanted it more than I cared to admit. She was beautiful, graceful, and strong. I was aware of the pull she had on me from the moment I first saw her.

I closed my eyes, thinking, and eventually I drifted off to sleep without an answer for my question.

CHAPTER 12

I woke early after hearing movement in the room. I realized Miranda wasn't next to me, and my mind settled on the satisfying conclusion that she was the one in the room making the noise. I liked that conclusion, since it meant that I could go back to sleep.

Before I made any progress, some part of my mind noticed that the sound of footsteps was getting closer to me. My alarm went off, signaling that it was time to start another day of hell. Over the previous two weeks, I had realized that I despised that alarm more than I did my actual training. That morning, though, was different. My alarm was shut off almost immediately by Miranda.

I heard her whisper in my ear, "Time to get up."

Her voice had a stronger effect on me than my morning coffee.

"I gotta go, or I'll be late to my plane." I felt her soft lips against my cheek for a moment. "I'll see you next week."

I heard her start to walk away. Her footsteps were audible on the hardwood floor, which made me realize she had her shoes on. I managed to sit up and look at her as she reached the door leading out of the bedroom.

"Be safe," I muttered sleepily.

She looked back as she stepped through the door. I blinked the fog out of my eyes, trying to get a clear look at her. She had showered, so her hair was that darker shade, and she had it up in a ponytail, reveling her neck in an attractive way. She wore a white t-shirt that had a black outline of different flowers in an abstract, stylish design, and a pair of denim jeans that fit her curves so perfectly that it seemed to be made for her. Then again, with the resources of the Church, they probably were. Her eyes met mine for a long second, before she winked and waved goodbye with her fingers, somehow making that gesture flirtatious. She left the room, and a few seconds later I heard the front door shut behind her.

I flopped back down on my back and worked on sorting out my thoughts, which were still a jumble after sleeping. I took several deep breaths to help wake me up.

I could just faintly smell Miranda's scent, but it faded quickly. I rested there for a few more moments before I forced myself out of bed, and began the last week of my training.

I didn't have any more muscle training. By now, I was automatically removing my muscle restrictions when I knew I should. My strength was unbelievable. When they told me how much weight I was lifting it felt like there was a secret trick being played on me. It felt surreal.

The martial arts got more intense, and at the end of each day Ben sparred against me. He broke a few of my bones, including my wrist and ankle, and dislocated my shoulder. Each time I recovered easily after a night's rest, which only added to my uneasy feeling I was having.

The first few days I was actually quite distracted. I couldn't seem to get Miranda out of my mind. Whenever the training didn't require my full attention and concentration, I somehow found myself thinking about her. I had just managed to go a full day without her intruding on my mind when Saturday came, on which my mind was again filled with thoughts about her—just not in a good way.

Right from the beginning of the day, I was instructed to wait in the room that I was using for my study sessions, even though my mornings usually had been dedicated to martial arts. The room was very much like a classroom, and had a dozen desks that each sat two people, and a wide area for the various instructors that taught me. I felt a little uneasy in this room at first, since it felt much too big for being the only student, but after three weeks I was completely used to it. I sat in the first row, center desk, which was the same one I had used all week. I waited for my instructor to enter. Finally, ten minutes after he was supposed to arrive, Benjamin walked through the door.

I blinked and raised my eyebrows. "Ben?"

"John," he said, nodding to me.

His smile and relaxed demeanor were absent, which was an immediate red flag to me. Something was wrong.

"I was told that I had studies this morning. I didn't think I'd see you until this afternoon," I told him as he approached me.

"I'm your instructor today, and after this you will have the rest of the day off." He grabbed a chair from one of the other desks and brought it around my desk so that he was sitting across from me.

"Why do I have the rest of the day off?" I asked, feeling like there was a major catch to getting such a reward.

"You'll need time to process what I have to say," he said, still serious.

I realized that Ben was controlling his words carefully, and his usual, lazy jargon was gone.

"Why are you my instructor instead of the usual professors?" I asked.

"The subject you'll learn today shouldn't be taught by someone who can look at it objectively. It should be taught by someone who has experience with what we're about to discuss," he answered.

"From the way you're acting, I get the feeling that I won't like this topic," I surmised.

He shook his head. "Even though I've only known you for a few weeks, I already know that you'll have trouble accepting this."

I swallowed, getting uneasy. "Okay, let me hear it."

He nodded, and then hesitated. Several seconds passed, and I knew he was gathering his thoughts, but that was rare for a Miracle Child. We think faster than normal humans—Ben shouldn't need this much time to know what he was going to say. It only added to my unease.

His eyes were glued to his hands on the table. "Has Miranda ever talked to you about Eves snapping?"

Oh, so this is what it was all about.

"A little. She told me it's called the Break Phenomenon, but that's about it," I said.

He nodded again, almost absentmindedly. "Okay, then I'll have to explain everything. Adams have … a very difficult responsibility. One that the public doesn't know about. It's not an easy thing to live with."

"And what is that?" I asked, wary of this conversation.

"Even for a Miracle Child, an Eve's brain is unique. When under extreme physical and emotional stress, their brain starts producing a unique compound called the incognita chemical. I'm not sure if you heard it mentioned from any of your professors."

As he talked, he inserted a small memory drive into the side of the desk, and a small monitor slowly slide up from the desk. It powered on immediately.

I shook my head at his not-quite-asked question.

"Well, for lack of a better word, the incognita chemical is incredible. The effects it has on an Eve is unbelievable."

A video opened up on the monitor, automatically playing what was on the memory drive Ben inserted. The video was obviously taken in a helicopter or a hovercraft, for it was shot from above. It was a view of the Outside, that much was clear, and I could see a single Eve moving on the ground, a couple hundred feet below. The video enhanced, zooming in closer on the Eve and following her.

"It enhances muscle strength and control, quickens reflexes and increases cognitive responses. Basically, it makes them stronger, faster and smarter, and when this chemical hits their system, they enter the Break Phenomenon. At this point, they're combat prowess usually surpass an Adam. Whatever they would normally lack in raw strength or power is made up in agility and tactical superiority."

His words were emphasized by the pure ferocity of the Eve on the video. The creatures she was fighting looked like gigantic centipedes, except these ones had legs coming out of every direction of their body, leaving some kicking aimlessly in the air as the creatures would charge toward her. There were dozens upon dozens rushing her, lunging over their slain brethren from the shadows of the trees. She moved with a speed I had trouble comprehending. My mind kept wondering if the video was purposely being sped up. She was moving so fast that I couldn't make out any details about her, except for her long blonde hair. The strange behavior of the centipedes contributed to my confusion, as I would watch them charge at her with superhuman speed, then suddenly slow down when they were almost upon her. She wielded a long weapon similar to a halberd, except that the axe at the top of the pole was elongated and thin. The entire weapon, shaft and all, seemed to be over eight feet long and made entirely out of stone. She kept spinning and twirling the weapon around her—a style that allowed her to use the heavy weapon's momentum to cleave through the mutated centipedes.

"I'm guessing there's a large price to such power ...." I commented, still watching this unnamed Eve slaughter these centipedes.

He continued, "Yeah, a big one. It prevents emotional responses and a large amount of rational thought. The fight instinct has pushed their body into this destructive force to defend itself, but in this state, they don't recognize anything. It's a body devoid of any kind of personality or complicated thought process. It's driven by merely instinct, and that instinct is to fight and to survive. Now, understand that once an Eve enters the Break Phenomenon, they cannot snap out of it—the chemical is just too strong. They keep pushing themselves, forcing their body so far past their limits that they end up killing themselves."

"They die? How?" I asked, surprised. My surprise made me look up from the video to meet Ben's eyes.

"What happened when you pushed your muscles too far in training, John?" He asked.

"They tore," I replied simply.

"Exactly. That happens, except with muscles all over the body, and eventually happens to the heart," he said softly.

"How do we stop it?" I asked, my voice tense.

"Well, at first there was no cure. Once an Eve entered the Break Phenomenon, all an Adam could do was restrain her so that she wouldn't kill other humans. Naturally, the biggest thing to do then was to make sure that you never got put into a situation that would push her to that point, which was an incredibly hard thing to do, since our job is fighting monsters like that." He nodded to the screen between us, referencing the black centipedes. "It took them a while to come up with a ... cure, if you could call it that."

I briefly imagined what that would be like—forcibly restraining Miranda as she struggled against me until her heart finally destroyed itself—and immediately recoiled at the thought.

"Which is?" I asked, eager to hear some sort of salvation from the thought.

He reached behind him and pulled out a medical device I recognized; it was an autoinjector. It was a small, steel tube-like device roughly six inches long and an inch in diameter. There was a small section made of glass, revealing its contents of a bright green liquid that very faintly glowed.

"This one is mine, and it's specially created for Ana. One injection, and it snaps them out of it—cures the Break Phenomenon," he said, but his tone was still somber and serious.

I felt my shoulders relax, but part of me wondered if it was that easy.

"That's not so bad," I replied.

He frowned a little. "Well, actually using the injector isn't a walk in the park, John."

"Yeah, but it could be worse ... couldn't it?"

He gave a snort, "I guess."

I could tell that something wasn't right by his behavior. It was as if he hadn't gotten to the bad part yet.

"Do I have to inject her somewhere specific?" I asked.

"No, thank the Supreme. Anywhere will suffice."

I gave him a questioning look, a little put off by his response.

He took a deep breath, "Yeah, I figured you didn't quite comprehend what I just explained."

"Then reexplain it," I responded, feeling a little impatient.

He nodded to the monitor between us. "Keep watching."

I did.

"The Church has a very, very scarce amount of video of the Break

Phenomenon. This is the only real video that gives a clear showing of what the Phenomenon does. That's Jennifer Gram. She didn't get the cure in time."

I looked up at him. "What? Why not?"

He gestured at the video, "don't look away, or you'll miss it."

I returned my gaze to the screen, watching her finish off the last of the centipedes. After dicing it into several, bloody pieces, she moved back two paces before bending back and shifting her weight forward into a heavy, powerful throw. Her weapon hurled skyward with incredible speed, heading straight towards the camera. The screen immediately went black, signally the end of the video.

"Woah!" I replied, reflexively leaning away from the screen, "Did she just—?"

"Destroy the helicopter and the three Crusaders in it? Yes, and she did it without hesitation," Ben responded.

I looked up at him, confused.

"That's the fight instinct for you. I told you earlier; Eves lose all emotional responses and most their rational thought. She was driven with a need to fight against anything that could be potentially dangerous to her in anyway."

"Where was her Adam? Why didn't he stop her?"

He reached forward and touched the screen, replaying the video. We watched it in silence for a short minute before he paused the video.

He pointed to the bottom left corner of the screen, "He's right there."

I searched the area he pointed in. "I don't see him."

He pointed again, this time indicating more specifically to a downed tree. "He's under that."

"So, he died? You couldn't just say that?" I asked, annoyed.

"You don't understand, John. He wasn't killed fighting against the centipedes."

"Then how—" I started, but cut myself off when it finally clicked. I leaned back in my seat, stunned, then muttered, "no way."

Ben removed the memory drive from the side of the desk, and the monitor slowly lowered back down.

"She killed him?" I asked softly, shocked. "How? He's immune to her."

"Yeah, but he's not immune to a tree falling on him," Ben replied coldly. "I wasn't exaggerating when I said that Eves have tactical superiority in the Break Phenomenon. She maneuvered the battle to her favor. He was struggling to deal with the mass chaos of all the centipedes and with trying to reach his Eve, and didn't notice the tree crashing down on him before it was too late. Do you understand now, John?"

I stared at him, not responding.

He leaned forward with an intense expression, "John, if Miranda Breaks, she will do everything she can to try and kill you."

"Why?" I whispered.

"On some level of their fractured mind, they know that we are immune to them. That makes us their biggest weakness, and the highest threat to them."

"God in Heaven," was all I could respond with.

A long silence passed between us while Ben let me absorb everything he told me.

"But the autoinjectors ... just use that on Miranda and she's back to normal, right?" I said, breaking the silence.

He hesitated for barely a moment before responding, "Yes."

I tensed, "you're hiding something else from me."

He sighed, "No, it's not that .... Look, John, since you didn't grow up in the Church, you aren't influenced by some of the rumors that have floated around here, and those rumors have caused me a great deal of turmoil. I haven't decided if it's better to tell you or not."

"Turmoil?" I questioned.

He nodded, "I'm terrified of the possibility of a certain rumor in particular. John, sometimes I can't sleep because of it. Part of me honestly believes that, in this case, ignorance is bliss."

What the hell could be worse than what he's already told me? Worse than not only having to use the autoinjector on Miranda before she destroys her own body, but also try and not be killed by her in the process?

I stayed quiet for a moment before saying, "tell me."

He sighed through his nose, "okay, but … okay."

He spent another moment gathering his thoughts. "It's happened to Ana only once. We were sent to Phoenix and assigned to protect the workers that were repairing a breach that happened the day before. We were attacked by some sort of bizarre black scorpions with multiple stingers. You remember the blackscaled monkey you told me about?"

"Yeah," I replied.

"Imagine fighting fifty of those, except that the monkey has stingers and is twice as vicious. It was one of the most difficult conflicts I've ever been a part of. Ana and I became separated from the rest of the Pairs, and it wasn't long before I got pushed away and separated from her as well."

He paused long enough to take a deep, steady breath before continuing. "When I made it back to her, I knew immediately that something was wrong. Her movements were … too controlled—too precise. She was fighting one last scorpion, but she stood in a pile of gore. Both her and the area were covered in the greenish blood of the mutated scorpions, yet she seemed calm. I … can't really describe it, but her movements were so calm and controlled … it had this inhuman feel to it. I knew it in my gut that she Broke."

He paused, and I shifted in my seat. If the autoinjector was as fool proof as Ben made it sound, then why was it so difficult for him to recall this memory?

He swallowed. "She finished off the last scorpion in seconds, then turned to me. It was apparent that she was gone. She didn't recognize me—not in the ways that it mattered anyway. She knew of my abilities and knew of how I would respond to her fighting technics—that much I figured out as we fought. But not as her lover, or even as her friend. She was empty, void of emotion. She attacked first. She was *fast*, John."

That meant a lot coming from someone who could teleport.

"Anywhere I moved, she was already there. She predicted my moves as I made them. Her combative superiority was obvious. If I wasn't immune to her Miracles, I would have been soundly outmatched. It wasn't long before I managed to get ahold of her and overpower her," he said, his tone becoming more somber as he spoke. "I had heard the rumors, but I was panicking. I knew she was going to die if I didn't get her out of the Break Phenomenon. I used the autoinjector."

He stopped there, and after a long moment of silence I asked, "What happened?"

"I don't know. The next memory I have is waking up in the Recovery Center, a day of my memories missing."

He noticed my confusion. "John, after an Eve Breaks and is saved by use of the autoinjector, all memory of what happens afterword is erased."

"What? Why?" I asked, surprised.

"That's an extremely important question, and gives some credibility to the rumors," he replied.

I exhaled annoyedly, "What rumors, Ben? You still haven't told me."

"I know. John, before the autoinjectors, there was a generation of Adams that was instructed to cure their Eves a different way—through torture."

The mental thought of it sent an electric shock of disgust through my body, and I immediately stood up. His last word seemed to hang in the air for a long time as my mind tried to process what he was telling me.

"I know," Ben said, agreeing with my response.

"How could Adams go through with that? How would that even cure the Eves?" I asked, the disgust in my voice plain. I barely noticed that my voice was raised.

"I'm guessing it was some sort of indoctrination from the Church that gave them the mental fortitude to go through with it—and most of them, understandably, couldn't bring themselves to torture their Eves to save their lives. The few that did resulted in a broken relationship between the Pair. They couldn't trust each other, and their combat effectiveness was damaged. The casualty rate of a pair who survived a Break Phenomenon was extremely high. As for the way it could cure an Eve, it has something to do with changing their mental state. Instead of their need to survive by fighting and defeating their opponent, you make them give up and desire to flee. You make them feel an emotion of terror, and that gets them to stop producing the incognita chemical. The important part is that it wasn't long before they introduced the autoinjectors. You know where I'm going with this, don't you?"

I gave him an appalled look, "the autoinjectors cause pain to the Eves?"

"I have no idea, but that's the rumor. I don't see a reason that the Church would make us forget about curing our Eves ... and sometimes I get this feeling when I look at Ana. A crushing, overwhelmingly dreadful feeling of guilt and shame. I wouldn't say I'm a believer in the Supreme, but I do pray that it's just a rumor."

Silence came between us again, and lasted for several minutes this time. Neither of us moved. I was reprocessing everything that I had just learned, but it felt hard to think. I had trouble accepting this as a reality—as if I was going to wake up from this twisted dream any minute. I didn't have a positive opinion of the Church to begin with, but now I felt this sense of nausea and disgust when I thought of it. I couldn't believe they were hiding such a dark secret. Finally, after what felt like an hour, I had something to say.

"You shouldn't have used it on Ana," I told him in an accusatory tone.

He met my eyes, surprise on his face, but that quickly tightened into anger, "What?"

"You heard the rumors, Ben. You knew better than to use it."

"The hell do you think you are? Do you have any idea what it's like to watch the woman you love dying right in front of you?" His voice was rising in anger.

"Yeah, I know exactly what that's like," I hissed at him.

He paused, surprised again, but he recovered quickly, "Then what the shit, John? You should know that I would do absolutely anything to save her! I would take any risk, and I wouldn't stake her life on a rumor!"

"Oh, COME ON!" I shouted at him, "you knew the credibility of that rumor."

He stood up now and stared me down across the desk. "Well since ya know fucking everything," he started, sarcastically, "What would you have done?"

He had reverted to his lazy slang in his anger.

"I would have found another way!" I replied.

"DAMMIT JOHN!" He roared, losing control over his anger.

He kicked the chair next to him and it flew twenty feet in a straight line before colliding with the steel wall. It left a good-sized dent before ricocheting off and bouncing on the floor a couple times.

"THERE IS NO OTHER WAY!" He continued. "They told me it was safe! They told me 'use this, and she'll live!' What the hell else was I supposed to do? She was dying right in front of me!"

He started pacing a short distance, breathing heavily. I stayed stubbornly still, not granting him amnesty.

He suddenly stopped and looked at me, "John, you need to realize that Miranda is going to expect you to save her. She is going to trust you with her life if she ever Breaks, and in her mind, that means using the autoinjector."

I shook my head at him.

"I don't know what the Church is hiding from us by erasing our memories every time, but what I do know is that this is the only way to keep her alive."

"I'm not hurting Miranda like you hurt Ana," I shot at him.

His eyes narrowed at me, and I saw his jaw tighten out of anger. He spoke through clenched teeth, "either you use the autoinjector—risk and all—or she dies."

"Yeah, I'm sure telling yourself that lets you sleep at night." I told him angrily.

He scoffed almost painfully, and looked away from me. Barely a moment passed before he looked back at me aggressively. He put his hands on his hips, his body tense from anger.

"Get out," he commanded.

I knew I had gone too far. My words were hurtful and served no purpose except to lash out at him. But my pride refused to back down, and I was still angry, so there was no way in hell I was going to apologize. I left in silence instead.

I noticed that the door was ajar, but I didn't think anything of it until I closed the door close behind me, and I saw Anastasia's silhouette from the corner of my eye. I turned to look at her out of surprise, but then I saw a blur of motion and pain flared up on my cheek. The force jerked my face to the right and made me off balance, forcing me to place a hand on the cold steel wall to keep myself on my feet. The sound of the slap echoed down the empty hallway. I didn't even have the chance to recover before she grabbed my shirt with both hands and pushed me up against the wall.

Anastasia was furious—an emotion I hadn't seen her display before. She was like a different person. Gone was the calm and collected amber eyes and gentle expression. In its place were the intense emotions of anger, and I saw the faintest hint of guilt in her eyes. In her anger, she looked like she was on the brink of tears.

I was suddenly surprised at how *strong* she was. The pressure she was putting on my chest was painful, and I instinctively grabbed her left forearm. I couldn't look away from the intensity of her amber eyes as they bore into mine.

Her smooth voice had layers of sincere fury as she spoke, "I'm not some weak damsel that you need to protect, nor is it your place to lecture a man who would walk through Hell itself if it meant keeping me alive. You don't have the faintest idea what it's like for us in the Church—I would bear any amount of pain if it meant a lifetime Ben. So just shut the hell up about things that you can't comprehend."

She released me and took a step back, but powerful anger was still very apparent. "If you ever hurt him with your arrogant words again, I will never forgive you."

She made it sound like a death threat, and with the look that was in her eyes, part of me believed it was. She gave me one more hard, angry look before opening the door and entering the classroom. The metal door slammed shut behind her, echoing down the hallway.

It took me a moment to get my thoughts back in order and when I did I felt regret at how I handled this situation, but instead of facing them and apologizing for my careless words, I left and hid in my apartment.

I sat on the couch and immersed myself into deep thought. Over and over, I ran through what he said, word for word, trying to understand the world I was a part of now, but each time I did, I resisted accepting it. I wasn't stupid. I knew he didn't want to do what he did, but even so I hated that he had admitted doing what he did, and claiming that it was the right way to handle things. There was no way in hell I would do that to Miranda. There was no way I would ever risk having her go through such pain.

Either you use the autoinjector—risk and all—or she dies. I heard Ben's voice.

I shut my eyes and shook my head. "Shut up."

He didn't know me. He didn't know what I went through, what I've experienced. Asking me to do the kinds of things the animal that killed Rachel did? Ludicrous. I'd never be able to live with myself. Rachel's screams of pain haunted me. I wouldn't add Miranda's screams to my nightmares as well.

Selfish much? I asked myself.

I'm the selfish one for not agreeing to hurt her? Bullshit.

Is it?

I breathed sharply out of my nose in aggravation and stood up. I went to the window and looked out it, but I wasn't really looking at anything.

Miranda's would be worse. Her screams would be caused by my hand. It didn't matter if it was indirectly or not—it was unacceptable.

I hit the bottom of my fist against the window. "What bullshit."

I closed my eyes and rested my forehead against the window, listening to my own angry breathing. I slowly calmed myself. Getting angry wouldn't give me a solution out of this.

I looked out the window in surprise, suddenly realizing that the sky was orange and the shadow of the apartment building was long. The sun was setting already.

I gave a long sigh. I knew I needed to eat something, but it just seemed unimportant. I returned to my seat on the couch and became absorbed with my thoughts again.

What was I going to do? Was this my only choice?

I shook my head. No. I was thinking about this the wrong way.

Miranda shouldn't pair with me. Paladin Samson said it was reversible, so I should look at this as a serious option. I wasn't sure I could bring myself to use the autoinjector if she ever Broke. In fact, I doubted I could. The best choice was for her to reverse our pair, that way I don't fail when the time comes.

I closed my eyes and leaned my head back against the couch. Was that the best choice? I hated this. It seemed like my only choices were inject Miranda or to separate with her. Isn't there some middle ground between what was best and what was easy?

I drifted off into sleep, still battling what I was to do.

Sunday came immediately. I opened my eyes as the sunrise light up the living room. I didn't dream that night, so my mind had instantly remembered what was last on my mind.

Miranda. Break Phenomenon.

I took a deep breath and rubbed my eyes awake. She was going to be here today, though I didn't know what time. My stomach growled, and I felt hunger, but I promptly ignored it. I didn't have time to bother with that. I needed to think. I felt that it was important to have my mind set on a decision before Miranda came back, or I'd lose my chance to make the right decision. If I was still battling with myself when she arrived, I would be influenced by the mere sight of her.

I went to the kitchen and made coffee. I was starting to feel like my mind was on repeat, asking the same questions over and over without finding any answers. I returned to my seat and sipped my hot coffee slowly.

I shook my head, agitated. Thinking in these loops wouldn't help me. I needed to reorganize my thoughts.

First, I knew that Miranda had an honest romantic interest in me. I saw no reason for her to be lying to me about that. How I felt about her in return was a little complicated. I knew my feelings for her wasn't as strong as her own for me. At this point I could see myself falling in love with her given enough time, but right now I knew her effect on me was merely hormonal and not emotional.

Second, I knew what my responsibilities were as an Adam, and what it would require me to do to Miranda if she ever lost control. My thoughts were too focused on Miranda, but now that I had laid it out I realized that the same would be expected of me if I had any other Eve.

I drank the last little sip of coffee that was in my mug, though it had grown cold by that time, and refilled my mug before returning to my seat on the couch.

Third, I knew that my link with Miranda was reversible, and that I could probably convince her to go through with it. I didn't know what methods were used to make it reversible, but for now that didn't matter.

Lastly, I doubted that there were any other positions in the Church that I could take up other than the one of Adam. I also knew that it would be impossible for the Church to let me go back to my previous life now that they've tested me and proved me to be an Adam. Not that I really wanted to go back to that life anyway, but part of me felt cornered since I didn't have that option. There might be opportunities—such as Elizabeth. Her partner died, so she was too dangerous to use in combat, since there was no way someone could inject her if she Broke. That option was very slim, since our situations are different.

I concluded that I had three options before me. The first of which was stay as an Adam and stay paired with Miranda, and hope that I had the strength to do what was needed when the time came. The second was reverse my link with Miranda, which would give me enough time to prepare myself mentally for what was required of me before linking with another. That option I valued the least and quickly dismissed. If there was no way to get out of my responsibility, I felt like I should stay with Miranda, for I knew how I could feel about her in the future.

The other option was to reverse my link with Miranda, and fight against my role as an Adam. I wasn't sure how I could, or even if it was possible. Nor did I know where that path would take me, but this option appealed to me the most. I didn't want the responsibility that an Adam bore. Even knowing that, part of my mind kept reviewing the option of staying with Miranda.

I suppressed that option. Thinking about what I'd have to do to Miranda if I went down that road was impossible for me. I recoiled at the thought. Still, part of my mind couldn't help thinking, *what if she never Breaks?*

I sighed. I was pathetic, grasping at every straw to get what I wanted. Choosing to stay with Miranda without knowing if I was capable of protecting her from herself was unbelievably selfish of me. I couldn't let myself do that.

I heard the door to the apartment give a click, signaling that it unlocked.

She was here.

I quickly set my empty coffee mug on the glass table in front of me and stood up, facing the door. The handle twisted.

Was I really ready for this conversation?

She entered, and immediately her green eyes locked on mine and she gave me a warm smile. I felt my face automatically relax into a small smile in response.

She slipped off her shoes quickly and started walking towards me. "Hey."

"Hey," I replied.

My response wasn't anywhere near cold, but it sounded like it had less warmth than hers had.

Walking towards me, she reached the point where it would've been a polite distance to stop, but instead she took another two steps into my personal space. She placed her hands on my shoulders and pressed her body against mine with her head against my chest, giving me a gentle yet graceful hug.

"I missed you," she said softly.

Again, she lacked any hesitation. Again, she did all of this without asking for permission, as if she didn't need it. I took a small breath, inhaling her scent. I felt her warm skin through my shirt, and I felt her body against me. Not fair.

"I missed you too," I replied without thinking.

She looked up at me with raised eyebrows. "Really?"

Her voice held surprise mixed with suspicion.

"You're surprised?" I asked.

She gave me a witty smile. "I'm happy you are, but surprised you admitted it. It's been quite a struggle getting anything at all out of you."

I was a little surprised myself, but thinking over how I felt over this last week and how I couldn't get her out of my head ... I had no choice but to admit it.

"Well it's true," I told her.

Dammit. This definitely wasn't the right mood to lead into the discussion that we needed to have.

"Good," she replied.

Her emerald eyes flipped between mine, and she wore a gentle but happy smile. I realized I had my hand on her lower back when her long crimson hair brushed against it. I saw that she had a strand of hair that refused to be kept behind her left ear. My hand tucked it back before tracing her graceful jawline, all without asking my brain if it was okay. My body was moving on its own again. Time to end this mood before I get myself into trouble.

"We need to talk," I told her, my tone serious.

"Hmm, I know," she replied.

"Do you?" I asked, surprised.

"I planned your training schedule, remember? That, and I spoke to Ana before I got here," she explained, her tone had turned a little hard at the end.

"Oh. Great," I replied sarcastically.

She watched me with strong eyes and a patient smile for a moment before saying, "You didn't apologize."

"Nope," my tone had turned stubborn.

"Why not? Ben was doing you a favor. You probably would've flipped your desk if an instructor explained it all to you, and it wasn't free. It's not easy for him to talk about it, especially to another man," she said.

I knew she was right. I wouldn't have known about the risk of using the autoinjector. Of course, she was right in everything she said, but that just made it worse somehow. She wasn't there. She didn't hear what he said. It wasn't fair.

"Miranda, I can't accept this. This autoinjector could cause you immense pain. Why would I ever be fine with doing that to you?"

"I would hope that you wouldn't fine with it, John," she replied, "but I do hope you would do it anyway."

I sighed and looked away.

A short moment passed before I felt her soft hand on my cheek as she gently forced my eyes back on her.

"It's a rumor." Her words were soft, and her tone was almost pleading.

"One that makes sense," I countered, mimicking her voice.

"I don't care. A rumor is only a rumor. Don't let it get to you," she replied.

I scoffed, "how am I supposed to do that, Miranda? If it turns out to be true, I would hate myself. It would destroy me. I can't take that risk."

"And watching me die as you restrained me wouldn't?" she asked.

I frowned at her.

"Ben and Ana are very much in love, even after a Break Phenomenon. It can't be that horrible."

"Yeah, I'm sure that the Church just erase memories of it for shits and giggles."

She sighed and looked away. We stood there, half-embracing each other while arguing.

Her hands rubbed my shoulders gently. "Your tense, and you need to shave. Take a hot shower and relax, then come back to me and we'll discuss it at length, okay? If it stays like this we might end up fighting, and I doubt either of us wants that."

I swallowed and nodded, but my thoughts were more one sided then that. It was true that I didn't want to fight with her, but I didn't see this coming to a peaceful agreement. I was a million miles away from agreeing to torture her.

CHAPTER 13

I shaved and then showered, putting the water temperature as hot as I could stand it. I felt my shoulders relax after a couple minutes, but I didn't get out for a while. I was dreading the conversation that was going to happen when I did, but I knew that staying any longer than I already had would just be pathetic.

I dried off and put my jeans back on. Although I wore them for a day already, I didn't do anything to make them dirty. However, my shirt was a thinner material so I decided to switch it out with another black one. I exited the shower, but I froze when I heard voices coming from the main apartment through the door that was slightly ajar.

I heard Paladin Samson's voice, "—did impress me. His muscle training was finished two days ahead of schedule, which allowed us to begin martial arts training earlier. On top of that, he seemed to have learned the basics to a variety of different martial arts before you met him, which also gave him an advantage and allowed us to teach him more advanced techniques than what was assigned. He demonstrated a strong willpower and concentration. When it comes to physical abilities, I'd say he's still below a normal Adam, but not by much. It's very impressive for only three weeks of training. His studies weren't perfect but above the passing threshold. He can think on his toes and has a knack for strategy. When only looking at these things, he'd make a capable Adam."

"But?" Miranda asked, her tone slightly defensive.

Paladin Samson sighed. "He showed not a trace of his Miracle. Even when we pushed him to his absolute limits he'd either surpass them or fail trying. We never got his miracle to surface. It happens rarely, but his might not show up unless he's mentally pressured to the point of breaking. At his age and his mind's maturity level, along with his stubbornness and willpower, I'd say it's impossible to put him in that situation safely. He probably won't show it until he's out in the field."

"Hm. Although problematic, it's not a huge concern," she said with confidence.

"No. Normally it wouldn't be," he replied.

"Normally?" Miranda asked.

Paladin Samson hesitated, obviously choosing his words carefully. "Miranda, you're powerful and he's not a very strong Adam—not yet at least. If we don't know what his Miracle is, how can I be confident that he is capable of stopping you? The risk is too high."

Hearing all this, I was tempted at first to make a loud noise so that they'd know I could hear them, but the Paladin's words interested me. Additionally, Miranda's tone was not like she was speaking to someone of a superior rank. It was casual and defensive, as if they were equals. The Paladin also didn't rebuke her for this, and in turn his voice had concern in it. While all of this was going on, I made smooth, quiet movements to put my shirt on, and then I took a seat at the end of the bed.

"I'm a Law Eve. Intense combat isn't common for me. The risk of Breaking isn't high at all," Miranda argued.

"Don't give me that when you know what your next assignment is."

Miranda's voice was a little hard. "Miracle Children have the freedom to choose whatever partner they desire, as long as it's mutual. Not even a Paladin has the authority to take that decision away from them."

"I'm not here as a Paladin, Miranda," he answered strongly, but his concern never left his voice.

"It's pretty convenient that you can just turn off that title whenever you feel like it." Miranda shot. "Let me guess; you don't like him."

"No," he growled back a little irritably. "I'm actually a little grateful towards him. You haven't looked this alive in years."

"Yet you wish to take that from me?" she said softly, letting a little emotion leak into her voice.

"I don't. If this was a different world, or a different time, it would be a different story. While your happiness is a priority for me, your safety is a higher one. Please, while there's still time, reverse this. Today is your last day, and each minute makes it more unlikely to succeed."

I felt jealousy linger on the edges of my mind. What the hell was their connection? It was most certainly more intimate than a superior-subordinate relation, but I couldn't put my finger on it. He sounded almost fatherly, but they had different last names. It didn't seem like a romantic relationship either, considering that he wasn't expressing jealously. Another thing that he had mentioned was very important. I had no more time. If I was going to reverse this with Miranda, I would have no other chance. I would have to do it before the day was over. My attention returned to their conversation when heard Miranda's voice.

"If that's all you wanted to say, leave," she said in a low, angry voice.

"Miranda, take this seriously—" Samson started, but he cut off mid-sentence, making me think Miranda's body language instructed him to.

She spoke two words in response, emphasizing them in her anger, "get. Out."

He sighed, and after a moment of pause, I heard his footsteps walk over to the door, which opened and then closed.

Miranda gave a long sigh. I was tempted to return to the bathroom and pretend like I didn't hear anything, but I pushed that immature thought out of my head and remained seated at the edge of the bed.

After a short moment, I heard her approach. She opened the door, but froze when she saw me. Her eyes widened in surprise for a moment, then she gave another sigh and relaxed.

"And of course you heard all of that," she stated.

"Sorry," I told her. I meant it, but at the same time I knew I didn't regret eavesdropping.

She walked forward and took a seat next to me. Her hands were at her sides, grabbing the edge of the bed, and she was on the balls of her feet with her heels against the side of the bed. It was obvious that she was nervous. We sat there, not looking at each other.

"I bet you're even further from changing your mind now, aren't you?" she whispered.

I stayed silent, having no answer for her. While I wasn't close to changing my stance before, hearing that Paladin Samson agreed with my view point made me feel like I was in the right.

"John, I don't want to reverse this," she whispered again.

"Why not? It'd just go back to before, as if we never met," I told her.

"All the more reason not to," she said.

I couldn't disagree with that comment, so I took it a different way. "It's the right thing to do. The Paladin was right. I can't keep you safe."

"Why do you say that?" her whisper had more bite to it, but it was still soft.

"Why don't you agree?" I countered.

We still didn't look at each other, but her left hand slid over my right one, which was on the bed next to me. "Because you're strong. You'll do it. I know it."

"You're wrong," I told her, but I managed to keep my tone gentle.

I pulled my hand out from under hers as I leaned forward and rested my elbows on my knees.

"No, I'm not," she whispered.

"What makes you think that? What have I done that makes you think that I'd torture you?" I asked, my voice rising.

I stood up and took two steps away from her. I kept my back to her. I didn't want to look at her. I was sure the sight of her would influence my thoughts.

"Stop saying that. It's just a rumor. But I know you," she said softly again.

"Know me? From a handful of memories?" I shot.

"There was more than a handful," she replied.

"The actual number hardly makes a difference." I replied.

"Even if that number was in the thousands?" she replied, her voice a little louder now.

I froze, then I turned to look at her from over my shoulder. She was looking at me from the corner of her eyes, which were guarded and unsure.

"What?" I asked.

"I saw a lot, John. More than what I originally told you. More than I have ever seen in a Gaze. I saw your life, and I can say with confidence that I know who you are."

I swallowed and looked away from her again. "Why didn't you tell me?"

"Are you kidding? It's bad enough that I invaded your mind and saw a few, how would you react if I told you I saw everything? It'd take even longer for you to trust me."

She wasn't wrong on that part. When she first spoke to me, it was hard for me to accept it, but if she said she saw everything, I most certainly would've reacted differently.

"Regardless Miranda, if you know me that well, then you should know that I'd never be able to ... to take that risk," I replied.

"No," she started, standing up and taking a few steps forward. "I know that you would."

I shook my head in silence, disagreeing with her.

I felt her hands on my shoulders, which clenched my shirt as she tightened her hands into fists. I felt her forehead rest against my upper back.

"I know you. I do. If you came to love me, you would do absolutely anything to protect me. No risk would be too great."

I swallowed. She wasn't wrong, yet again.

But, "I don't love you."

I felt her move. She let go of my shirt and somehow slipped around me, so we were suddenly facing each other. Her raw beauty hit me as hard as it always did as I gazed upon her face. Her green eyes against her red hair was an alluring contrast—she was beautiful even with her features strained in worry.

Her voice was silk, but still held strong emotions that I couldn't identify. "But isn't it a possibility that you will come to?"

Ugh. She keeps saying things that were hard to argue against. I suddenly had the feeling that if I told her the truth, I would lose this argument. I would lose if I told her that the possibility was there.

I placed my hands on her sides and slid past her, walking towards the balcony. "This isn't something that can be risked with a possibility."

"That's not true!" she said, and I heard her following me.

She chased me out to the balcony, and I leaned forward on the stone railings and didn't face her.

She stood on the right side of me, facing me, but I still didn't turn to look at her.

"Love is always a risk, and if that risk succeeds then you would protect me. You would have the strength, John."

I felt irritated. "This isn't about love, Miranda!"

"Then what is it about?" she asked, matching my raised tone of voice.

I turned to face her, meeting her eyes. "I don't want to hear you scream, okay?"

She stared back at me, but her eyes held no surprise. She stayed silent, and her face relaxed into a gentle sadness.

I felt like the silence between us was going to suffocate me, so I continued, "I still hear Rachel. I know how she sounded when she was stabbed, over and over. I don't want to hear you make those same sounds, and yet you ask me to be the one to cause them?"

Her eyes dropped from mine, and she turned around and took a step away from me. Her body was tense, and I saw her hands tighten into fists at her side. Even then, I found her beautiful. Her body looked strong, but because her body was smaller than mine, it made her seem vulnerable at the same time. Her crimson red hair was gently tugged by the light midday breeze.

She stayed motionless for several seconds, then spoke in a tight voice, as if she was on the brink of tears. "Fine. But I'm not going to reverse this willingly. You have to tell me to do it."

I opened my mouth to tell her just that, but then no sound came out. My body had frozen in this moment, stuck on replaying what she had just said.

It was this moment that truly mattered. If I told her what I knew was right, she'd be gone. She'd vanish like smoke, and she'd eventually find another man to take my place. Another one she Gazed upon. Another one she'd come to love.

I felt my mouth close and I swallowed in my stunned state. Tell her to vanish? Tell her that the last three weeks was a waste?

I didn't want to.

I clenched my teeth in frustration at my own indecisiveness. I knew what was the right choice. I did, but it was much harder now that I had to be the one to say it. It angered me at how selfish I was. It was one thing to convince her to make the choice herself, but if I was the one to do it, it made it much more difficult. She had me in checkmate. She had said the one thing that I knew I couldn't fight against.

I took a deep breath and slowly relaxed as I exhaled. I will hate myself for my decision, but there's no reason to torture myself over it. I knew what I wanted, and what decision I would make.

I took a step forward and grabbed her arm, gently tuning her to face me. Her green eyes matched her tone of voice. They weren't guarded, but they were worried and afraid. She feared my next words. I decided to say nothing.

I placed my left hand on her hip and pulled her against me. She automatically put her hands on my chest, but she didn't push me away. I saw her eyes show confusion amiss her other emotions, but I didn't hesitate. I was done with hesitation. It didn't make it any easier to be around her, nor did it make it any easier being away from her.

My right hand traced behind her ear and went down to the back of her neck. I gently pulled her up towards me, and I bent down the couple of inches it took to meet her lips with my own.

A second had passed before she recovered from her surprise, and then her lips melted against mine as she began to kiss back. I felt her hands slide up my chest and ran through the short hair on the back of my head, and as she did I pulled my right arm out from in front of her and placed it on her lower back. I traced up her back with my left hand, following along the natural curve of her body that formed since she was against me. I felt her tight skin under her thin shirt and her silky hair flowing against the back of my hand. The distance that separated us, which was very little to begin with, disappeared entirely as she wrapped her arm around my neck. She went up on her toes, making our kiss more comfortable for us.

Our kiss intensified as we began to move in sync with each other. I tasted her, and I felt her hand run against the back of my head again. Our lips would part in unison, though it would only last for the half-second that it took to take a small breath of air.

I don't know how long it lasted. It was a long kiss, but at the same time it felt like it went by much too quickly. When we finally parted, she hugged me, putting her forehead against my chest. I felt my blood pump through me excitedly, and I realized that I wanted *more* of her. I wanted to bring her chin up and meet her lips again. I wanted to feel her warm breath against my skin in those short moments when we parted. I was overwhelmed with her in that moment, but at the same time, I knew that my desire for her didn't end there. I wanted to feel her smooth skin, not just the hints of it through her thin clothing, and I wanted to feel her warmth of her body against mine. I swallowed as my mind started to think clearly again, and I realized I needed to be more careful. It had been awhile since I had these thoughts, so I wasn't used to moderating them. I didn't want to rush this, but to savor it. She was more to me than what my hormones desired.

"You can be cruel sometimes," she said in a quiet voice.

I blinked in my surprise. I personally didn't think it was that bad.

She continued before I had the chance to respond, "finally kissing me and it's a kiss goodbye. On top of it it's a kiss like *that*."

She empathized the word in a way that made it clear she enjoyed it.

"Goodbye?" I asked. "You decided to get the reversal after-all?"

"Of course not. I don't have the strength to do that, even though I know it'll hurt you," she replied, still speaking to my chest.

"Well ... I don't have that strength either," I replied.

She looked up now, surprised. Honestly, why would she think that I'd kiss her like that only to leave? Her surprise was a little humorous, but I kept it off my face.

"Oh," she said, as if she just now understood something. I saw relief in her eyes, which intensified into what I could describe as happiness.

"Well if I had known that I wouldn't have ended that kiss so early," she said, her voice now full of confidence.

"Ended? We weren't just taking a break?" I replied.

She raised her eyebrows in surprise and she laughed gently. "It's not like you to make a comment like that."

I pulled her against me, closing the small gap that formed while we were talking and stared into her green eyes. While it was true I was done hesitating, she was right. I was feeling intoxicated, which I was sure was a mix of the taste of her lips and the feeling of freedom that I felt from not having to restrain myself around her anymore.

"I suppose it's not," I mumbled, agreeing with her.

She went up on her toes again and muttered back, "Looks like our break's over."

Nope. Pretty sure my intoxication had nothing to do with my newfound freedom and everything to do with the lips I was about to meet.

"Ahem," a female voice sounded from behind me.

My heart nearly jumped into my throat in my surprise, but the first thing I noticed after that was Miranda's body tense against me. I automatically spun around. Miranda was faster than me, and managed take a step to the side so she was almost beside me while facing the woman defensively. Out of reflex, I held out a hand protectively in front of Miranda, even though I knew she was more powerful than me.

"I heard you had an Adam, Miranda, but seeing you kiss him like that, well ... I think you've made me envious. Though you two were overly lovey-dovey for my taste," her voice was smooth and attractive, but it lacked the grace of Miranda's.

The woman was standing on the stone railing, but was perfectly balanced and at ease. She had dark skin and long black hair that was up in a ponytail. She was older than me, but I doubted she was past her early thirties. She was attractive, with smooth skin and delicate facial features, and her body was built like Miranda's; fit but with curves in all the right places. Her eyes were a warm brown. Perhaps it was the contrast with her skin, but they stood out in a way that was alluring and easy to look at. She had on a black, close-fitted T-shirt and black pants that were a little baggy. The material of her clothes looked flexible and strong. I got the impression that she was a Crusader because her outfit was so similar to Zachariah's, but that quickly faded as I observed her more closely.

I realized that the reason I thought she was older than me was not because of her physical appearance, but because of the experienced and confident air that surround her. It was immediately apparent that she didn't have a single shred of doubt in her abilities. She knew exactly what she was capable of and exactly what her limits were. However, since I lacked the information on her abilities, the most I could discern from her in that few seconds was how dangerous she seemed.

She spoke again, continuing, "But I guess that's understandable for your first kiss."

"Be careful, John. She's no friend of ours and extremely dangerous," Miranda said to me in serious, low tone of voice, and I saw her summon a sword to one hand from the corner of my eye.

"Don't worry, little Miranda. He knows. I can see it in his eyes. Though he did under-estimate me at first, he wised up very quickly," she said, meeting my eyes.

I hoped I managed to contain my surprise as I heard her words. She was a natural at reading body-language. She had known exactly what I was thinking during those few seconds, and if she could do that, I bet she could do the same thing in a fight. She was definitely dangerous.

It was her eyes that put me off the most. While warm and excited, I could tell that there was something else about her … I just couldn't put my finger on it.

"Who are you?" I asked.

I was curious, but I was mainly buying more time to assess her as an opponent. Miranda hadn't immediately attacked her; instead she had told me that this stranger wasn't an ally, but that didn't mean she was an enemy. I didn't know this person. My only choice was to let Miranda take the lead completely on this. I would have to support her however I could.

I slowly lowered the arm that I had out in front of Miranda. Although the woman's eyes never left mine, I knew she was tracking my movements and reading them perfectly.

"I like him, Miranda. He will suit you very nicely. To answer your question, I will introduce myself. I am Aryanna Carter, but please call me Ari. It's cuter. Oh, you should also know that I'm an Eve, though unregistered and utterly opposed to the Church and all it stands for," she winked at me. "Pleased to make you acquaintance, Johnathon Aster."

I swallowed. I suddenly had an idea what it was that I saw in her eye.

"I don't need your approval, nor are you in a position to give it," Miranda replied in a steely tone.

"This is the attitude I get after I rushed over here as soon as I heard about John?" she made a tsk sound with her tongue. "You sure love to play the part of the cold beauty, don't you?"

She stepped down from the railing gracefully, making her body appear weightless, and took slow steps toward Miranda.

I was positive I knew what was bothering me about her now. She was utterly relaxed, but not in a good way. She wasn't relaxed because she didn't think we'd attack her. She was relaxed because she had absolute confidence that she could kill both of us.

As soon as I realized that I started to feel a pressure with every step she took toward us. Her movements seemed predatory in their control and precision, and her eyes suddenly had the excitement of the chase in them, as if they were begging me to run from her. I knew I should fear it, but all it did was make me more cautious and nervous. It was probably due to the fact that I knew exactly how it felt to be in her shoes. To want your prey to run from you as they struggled to save their own life, and the dark humor you felt knowing that their struggle was absolutely futile. I was the same way when I put down the animals that killed Rachel.

I didn't retreat from her for two reasons. The first was because although I could feel that predatory nature in her, it lacked blood lust. I didn't think she was here to fight. The second and stronger reason was that I couldn't leave Miranda here.

Ari's eyes, which had been locked on Miranda as she walked calmly toward us, moved to look at me.

"He's got better instincts than you, little Miranda. He's definitely a good pair for you," she said.

"What do you want?" Miranda asked, her voice still stern.

"I already told you. I simply wanted to see the man that earned a second glance from the cold, emotionless Miranda Pierce. Unlike my previous visits, I am not here for a duel," she said calmly. She had come to a halt right in front of Miranda, who had her sword raised and ready.

"As if I could take your word on that. Why would you care about my Adam? What is your interest in me?" Miranda's tone held genuine curiosity, and it sounded like that last question had been bothering her for a while.

Ari took a step forward, getting well inside Miranda's space and looking at her with a strong gaze. Miranda's sword was pressed against Ari's neck, but Ari was still collected and confident.

"Because you are special, Miranda. You're strong, so I have been challenging you to get an idea of how strong you'll become. Because when lies start getting dragged into the light, I'm worried that you won't have the courage to choose the right side. If you don't, you will certainly become my enemy. And now, your Adam looks like he could be quite strong as well. But that's all just speculation."

Miranda's eyes hardened. "I should just kill you here."

Ari smiled at her. "You certainly could, but you won't. You don't know who I really am, or what organization I am really with. You only know that I am an unregistered Eve, and you need me in order to find out how dangerous that organization is. I am you're only source of information."

Miranda's eyes narrowed in response.

"Oh, and I'm sorry. I lied just now," Ari said, and she moved forward ever so slightly so that Miranda's sword pierced her dark skin. A thin, gentle stream of blood slid down the perfect silver edge of the blade. But Ari gave a kind smile that was sincere but with strange hint of wickedness.

Her voice was a whisper, "Even from here, you would not be able to move quickly enough to end my life. That's how much you still have to grow. But don't let this get you down, okay? You're improving rapidly."

She took a step back then, and gave her another kind smile before turning her eyes toward me. "It was great to put a face to the name, John. I do wish I had the time to get to know you better. Someday, I'm sure we'll be able to have some small talk, but I don't want to overstay my welcome."

She walked toward the stone railing and gracefully jumped up on it. She turned to look at us from the corner of her eyes. "Until we meet again. I'm already looking forward to it."

She jumped upward, easily clearing the thirty feet that spanned this balcony and the one a few stories above us. She disappeared from sight after that. I looked at Miranda, who was clearly pissed.

"Damn it!" She hissed, and after her sword disappeared with a quick flash of light, she went inside the apartment.

Interestingly, only the sword was teleported away, so Ari's blood immediately dropped to the ground.

I followed her inside, unsure of where to start with the questions that were buzzing around in my head. "Who was she exactly?"

"I don't know, and that's the problem," she replied, still angry.

I followed her all the way to the kitchen, where she started pacing back and forth, obviously restless.

"Is Aryanna Carter her real name?" I asked.

"I don't know. The only thing I know for certain is that she isn't registered as an Eve. I searched for her physical description and came up empty. She's strong, John. And she was absolutely correct when she said I can't afford to kill her; it could have disastrous consequences."

"So could leaving her alive, especially if she can sneak in and out of this Academy so easily," I stated.

She shook her head and stopped pacing, leaning against the kitchen counter. "That's not the scary part. This was the first time she's met me here, but I wasn't surprised she was able to. She's come to me several times on my investigations, and those are always confidential, which means she has a source inside the Church."

"Really? Hm …. Shouldn't that make it easy to find who it is? Just make a list of who has the information available for each mission and compare the lists to narrow down a suspect pool."

She shook her head. "By confidential, I mean no one outside of the Church can access that information, but the list of people who could access that information is still very large. Any other Miracle Child could have that information—as could several Crusaders. I wish I could rule out other Miracle Children on faith alone, but that would be foolish, especially now that it's clear other Blessed Ones are working against the Church."

I nodded, understanding. After thinking over my suggestion again, I realized that it assumed that there was only one leak within our network, but it was possible that there were multiple. The fact that Ari could find Miranda so easily actually made that possibility very likely.

"Have you told Paladin Samson about this?" I asked.

"No. You're the only one other than me who knows of her existence," she explained, staring at the floor thoughtfully.

"Do you suspect Samson of being the leak?"

She laughed a little. "No, not at all. I do trust him, but I don't tell him because who he trusts and who I trust are different people. I'm unsure who he would assign to the case to. The less people involved the easier our job becomes. If she learns that the Church is investigating them, then she might take more drastic moves in the future, instead of just playing around with me."

"Hm," I replied, thinking.

Silence stayed between us for a short minute as we both were in deep thought. I was the one to break it.

"How strong is she, really?" I asked.

"That's a difficult question to answer since I haven't been able to push her to her limits yet," she replied.

I raised my eyebrows and looked over at her. "Really? She's that powerful?"

"Powerful isn't the right word to describe her. I'm more powerful, but she's a stronger combatant. What did you think of me when you saw me fighting against the Outside creatures?" she asked.

I thought about that for a moment, remembering how I felt watching her movements. She displayed grace, control, and precision.

"I thought you were beautiful, to be honest. Even though all of those times were life threatening, I couldn't help but think that when I watched you move."

She stepped sideways, closing the short gap between us by sliding down the counter. Her wide eyes were shining as they met mine and she gave me a small smile.

Her mouth opened, and then closed, like she wasn't sure how to respond. Then she said, "Thank you. I like that you felt that way. I know I am not unskilled when it comes to sword play. In fact, I'd say I'm one of the strongest ones in the Church. But compared to her, I look like a monkey swinging a wooden stick around."

I had trouble imagining that sort of difference. Miranda seemed amazing with her ability to wield a sword.

"Is she really that good?" I asked.

"Yes. The amount of experience she must have … she can read my moves so easily. I can't ever hit her; it's as if she's made of air," she explained.

For Miranda to praise an enemy so highly made me nervous. Aryanna made it clear that she intended stay involved with Miranda— no, she intended to stay involved with us. If worst came to worst, we'd end up fighting to the death.

"Is there no way to beat her?" I asked aloud, thinking of possible futures.

"I don't know. If I summoned my Core and threw all of my power at her, then I could probably win," she said thoughtfully.

Hearing that lead me into my next question, "But you haven't done so yet because …?"

"There's a few reasons. The first of which is because it is dangerous for me to use that much of my Miracle while I had the Limiter still. I also need her alive, and the amount of power I would need to beat her would be lethal. Those are both facts that stopped me from going that far, but in all honesty the main reason was that I didn't want to."

"Why not?"

"Well … I didn't want to beat her skill with my power. If the only way to beat her was to drown her in raw power, it wouldn't feel like a victory. I would still know that she was stronger than me, more skilled and more agile. I've always wanted to beat her with my own skill. Otherwise I'd just feel like I cheated, or played dirty just to win," she explained.

"I see," I responded.

I could understand the feeling she had, but at the same time, a victory was a victory. If you needed to get your hands dirty in order to achieve that victory, then so be it. At the end of the day, it was more important that you stayed alive, not what you did to stay that way. In this case, Miranda's pride wasn't worth her life. I figured she already knew that. Still, thinking about what Ari told us ….

"Miranda, are you the strongest in the Church?" I asked.

"No. I'm sure I'm high up there, but not the strongest. Of course, it all depends on the situation. Concerning skill with a sword, I'm in the top one hundred probably. When it comes to the power of Cores, I'd say the top ten. With our Miracle ability … top twenty-five maybe," she explained.

I knew it was all guess work, but those numbers were impressive, considering that there was hundreds of Miracle Children in the Americas alone.

"By Miracle ability, do you mean your Minor—your electricity?" I asked.

"No, there really isn't an accurate way to gauge those, since each is useful in multiple ways. I meant how well I can use our main Miracle. How quickly I can summon a weapon, and how complex of a machine I can summon. The majority of Eves cannot summon anything more complex than a bow or sword. Firearms are usually out of the question. Some Eves can summon revolvers, but most of them don't bother, since their combat effectiveness is very limited. I can summon semi-automatic pistols, but it's never an easy thing to do and takes a lot of concentration," she explained.

"That sounds like you're more skilled than what you claimed," I responded.

If it was hard for Eves to summon a revolver, but Miranda could bring up semi-automatics on the fly, why didn't she rank herself higher?

"No, I think my ranking was fair. By comparison, Anastasia is probably the most skilled at summoning. She can even replace her magazines by exchanging them directly though summoning. She undoubtedly has the skill to summon more advanced or complex weaponry than pistols, but I haven't ever seen her pushed the that limit."

"I see," I replied, understanding the difference now. I stayed quiet for a long minute, pondering what she told me.

"Considering all of those attributes though, if it came into a real, all-out battle between the other Eves, what rank would you give yourself?" this was the question I needed to know.

"I'm not sure why you're asking, but … hm, probably the top fifteen. After that, we get more evenly matched and more luck is involved to determine the winner. I probably would lose to the top five. Of course, this is only considering the Eves. If I count Adams it'd be a different ranking altogether. Why?"

I had thought so. That was the part that didn't make sense.

"Ari said—"

"Nickname already?" Miranda complained.

"Sorry. Aryanna is just a bit of a mouthful," I replied.

Though that wasn't the whole truth. Ari's personality made it easy to like her, in spite of our circumstances.

Miranda sighed. "It's okay, I get it. I was calling her that by our third meeting."

I smiled a little and continued, "She said that she was interested in you because you're special and strong and she's wary of you as a future opponent. However, you're not the strongest out there, so that doesn't really hold up. In fact, she should be more interested in the top five than she is in you."

"Hm. That's true. However, we don't know for sure if she's not fighting them as well. They could be keeping quiet just like us, so we should keep that in mind. There's one last thing that worries me," she started.

"What's that?"

She looked up and met my eyes. "She knew that you were my Adam. Where did she learn that information? If we counted it out, there should be less than ten people who know that. Unless you've been bragging about it to everyone you meet."

I smiled. "As much as I would like to, I haven't. It's not like I've had time to socialize this past three weeks, if you remember."

A flash of guilt showed in her eyes, but quickly faded. "Ah. Right. Sorry. We'll keep on our toes about it, and after this investigation we can take a deeper look into it."

"What investigation?" I asked.

"The one I've been busy with in Chicago. We're going back there early tomorrow to pay the Guards a personal visit," she explained.

I froze in surprise for a moment, then intelligently responded with, "What?"

She gave me a smile. "It seems the Guards have been misusing the freedom we've given them. I have no proof of this, but something dark is lurking around them. I can't really explain it, but I've never been wrong about these feelings."

"Hm," I replied, thinking.

The Guards? I had history with them. Important history. I wasn't sure how well I'd be treated if I came back. Miranda must know this, for she has seen all of my memories. I knew that the Guards weren't saints, but still ....

"What have you discovered so far?" I asked.

She gave a gentle sigh, "let's discuss this on the plane tomorrow."

I half-frowned before I could keep it from showing. I was curious, and I knew it would bother me all night if I didn't know.

She turned to face me and stepped closer, wrapping her arms around my neck and leaning her body against mine.

"In the meantime, let's get some food. I'm starving," she told me.

The combination of Miranda's presence and the suggestion of food immediately killed my curiosity. I eagerly agreed.

The next day, I opened my eyes as I awoke. The morning light was just barely brightening the dark sky, but it was enough light to make out my surroundings. Though it wasn't necessary; I knew where I was immediately from the sight of the bedroom ceiling. I looked to my right at the digital clock on the nightstand out of habit, but I pretty much already knew what time it was.

Yup. If I had set my alarm the night before, it would've gone off two minutes ago. My body was used to waking up at this time for my training.

I looked back up at the ceiling and listened to my surroundings. The loudest sounds were the birds outside, which I could hear even through the closed windows. My mind faded that out immediately as it focused on another, much more interesting sound. It was a slow, steady breath coming from my left. When she fell asleep last night, she was resting against my side with her head on my chest, but now my arm was between us, and she had her arms wrapped around it. I felt her gentle breath against the skin of my arm, and her long silky hair was somehow against the back of my hand. Her breaths were shorter than mine, but both were quiet in the still of the morning. I held still, not wanting to disturb her sleep.

I realized what a contradiction she was. When she was awake, she was confident, strong, assertive, powerful ... yet when she slept next to me she was so gentle, small, and fragile. I felt as if I knew a secret about her that no one else did, and I liked that feeling.

I knew I should get up and stay awake, since it doesn't do me any good to oversleep, but I had no desire whatsoever to move. I closed my eyes and focused on my breathing, trying to fall back asleep.

I sighed and looked at the clock, which showed me that twenty minutes had passed. It was no good. I wasn't going to be able to go back to sleep. I looked back at the ceiling and let my mind wonder. The previous day had been my last chance to try and get out of being an Adam, and I didn't take it. I didn't regret it. In fact, feeling Miranda's gentle breathing next to me, I was glad about the choice I made. I got out of bed, slowly removing my arm from Miranda so that I didn't wake her. She shifted a little bit, but it didn't look like I woke her.

I changed from my shorts that I wore to bed into normal clothing before I walked around the bed and went out onto the balcony. The morning air easily seeped through the T-shirt and jeans that I was wearing, but it didn't make me cold. I watched the sky get lighter as the sun slowly climbed its way up toward the horizon.

My thoughts drifted over last night's dinner. We saw Ana and Ben stop in, and I used that opportunity to talk with Ben. I apologized for acting as if I knew better and judging him for something that was between him and Ana. He forgave me quickly, and afterward they joined us for dinner. As my thoughts continued on this subject, I eventually remembered first meeting them, and their reactions when they had learned I didn't know what my miracle was.

I opened my right hand and looked at it thoughtfully. What *was* my Miracle? Was it really so bad that I don't know what my Miracle was?

I recalled Miranda's words to Paladin Samson yesterday, *although problematic, it's not a huge concern.*

He agreed with her, but then what was with their reactions earlier? Was there something I was missing?

I hadn't noticed even noticed her until she placed a gentle hand on my arm. "John?"

I returned my focus to my surroundings and met Miranda's eyes. Her hair was messy this morning, but it didn't deter from her beauty.

"Hm?" I replied in my surprise.

"What's got you in such deep thought first thing in the morning?" she asked, a small smile on her lips.

"Just thinking …" I replied, unable to keep myself from smiling in return.

"About?" she asked.

I looked out over the grounds below as I thought about the best way to describe my uneasiness. She didn't pester for an immediate answer. Instead, she leaned on the stone railing next to me, purposefully getting close enough that our arms were against each other.

"You've said before that me not knowing what my Miracle was or how to use it isn't a problem, right?" I asked.

"It isn't really, but I was hoping that you would discover what it is," she answered.

"Why?"

"Well, having that extra tool is helpful, regardless of what that tool is. Additionally, because we don't know what this Miracle is, there's a higher risk that bystanders could get hurt when you first use it," she explained.

Oh great. She made it sound like my Miracle could be a ticking time bomb.

She must've noticed my reaction because she quickly added, "But don't get stressed about it. The risk of that happening is small. You will have to be under a lot of mental pressure and in a life or death situation before you would be able to draw it out. It's unlikely that you'll be in a situation like that with innocent bystanders nearby. Most likely, you won't use it until we fight against the Outside when a Wall is breached."

"I see," I replied, taking it all in.

"Why do you ask?" her voice was curious, but I noticed concern in it too.

I met her eyes in an attempt to relieve her of her worry. "It's just that when I met Ana and Ben, they were surprised when they learned I hadn't used my Miracle. I think it made them uneasy."

Her eyes narrowed slightly and she looked down, thinking. "Did anything else happen before that?"

I hesitated, trying to remember. "No. Not really. I met Benjamin first, and he introduced me to Anastasia and his brother, Dylan."

"Oh, right. Dylan was there." she asked in surprise, as if this was important.

"Yeah." I replied, my mind suddenly focused on my memories with Dylan. "He refused to shake my hand."

"Well I don't know what not shaking your hand would mean, but I do know that Dylan's a special case," she said.

"How so?"

"Dylan is the only Adam that's not allowed to take on an Eve. The only explanation they gave us was that his Miracle is unstable. He's not sent on any assignments nor is he in any career. As far as I know, he doesn't even leave this Academy. Dylan is Benjamin's older brother, so Ben knows what Dylan's Miracle is. However, out of respect for his older brother, he hasn't told anyone other than Anastasia, even though we all were close friends. The only thing I've learned about it is that it takes a great toll on his body, and that it effects other Adam's abilities."

"You think he could sense what my Miracle was?" I asked.

She met my eyes. "It's a possible hypothesis."

"He was afraid of effecting my Miracle ..." I suggested.

She nodded. "I bet his miracle involves physical touch. There's still too many possibilities as to what his Miracle could be, but I bet he didn't shake your hand because he was afraid of disrupting your Miracle somehow."

I frowned. "That doesn't seem right. At first, he reached out to shake my hand, but then stopped half way, as if he realized something."

"Hmm. Maybe he sensed that your Miracle was different somehow, so he played it safe and didn't touch you?"

I sighed. "I'm not sure."

"In any case, I bet that's the reason behind Ana and Ben's reaction at learning you don't know your Miracle. Maybe they were afraid of it being unstable or powerful."

I frowned again. I knew too little about this entire situation to be comfortable. How should I proceed from this point on? This unknown power inside me could be dangerous to those around me. At least Miranda would be immune to it, but still ... it made me uneasy.

Miranda noticed my discomfort. "Just take it one day at a time. I'll be with you from now on, and if something happens I have the skill to stop it, okay?"

I didn't reply, though I knew she was right. This was who I was and I couldn't change that, so I would just have to be careful and mindful of my surroundings moving forward.

She gave me a warm smile of encouragement. "Let's start getting ready. Our plane leaves in three hours. Don't forget to pick up the autoinjector from the Recovery Center."

I sighed and followed her back inside the apartment. We spent a couple hours at the apartment, getting some breakfast and showering, then I left to go get the autoinjector—something that I was dreading all morning.

Or so I tried to.

Elizabeth met me in the lobby after a receptionist there contacted her for me. She was wearing another t-shirt—this one all black with 'I don't have to like you to save your life' written in red letters. She also had on a white lab coat and a pair of blue jeans. Her hair was up in a ponytail like it was when I first met her.

"Hiya, John," She greeted me cheerfully, seemingly in a good mood.

"Elizabeth, hi," I greeted back.

"Liz, please," she said, "I'm guessing you're here for your autoinjector ...."

"That's right," I replied, trying to keep myself from frowning.

"Well I'm afraid I don't have it," she confessed.

"What?" Part of me took this as good news.

"Sorry. We've had the compound complete for over a week, but the day that it was finished, Paladin Samson came and collected it. He said to tell you to come meet with him first."

"Oh, great," I responded. All of me took this as very bad news.

"Um," I started, "is that normal? For Samson to collect it like that."

She shook her head, "No, not that I've ever seen, but Miranda's a particularly strong Eve. Maybe he wants to caution you about how dangerous she'll be after she Breaks."

"Right. I'm sure that's it," I said, sarcastically.

She gave me a humored smile. "Relax. He's not that scary once you get used to him."

"Uh-huh. Well thanks for letting me know yourself," I told her, turning slightly as I prepared to leave.

"No problem. You and Miranda should come visit me sometime—fully healthy, I mean. I don't want to see you if your half-dead," she said, correcting herself.

She bit her lip for a brief moment, then continued, "I mean, I'll still fix you two up of course ..." she sighed, "just be careful okay?"

I chuckled at her, "we will. See you later."

She raised her hand and gave me a quick wave, "bye."

I turned and walked out, feeling uncomfortable about this new development of Paladin Samson. I went to his office, jogging at a brisk pace, trying to make up some of the time I lost at the Recovery Center. I entered and approached the receptionist, which I recognized as the same man who I spoke with the first day I arrived here. He looked up expectantly at me as I approached.

"I need to speak with Paladin Samson, but I don't have an appointment or anything ..." I explained.

"Okay, I'll send up a notification to his secretary to notify him. What's your name?" the man asked.

I told him, and he told me to wait until he heard back. I did, but it was only a few moments before the man told me that Paladin Samson would be right down.

This made me even more uneasy. I would have felt more comfortable meeting him in his office. A minute passed before I heard the elevator doors open, and Samson stepped out of it, approaching me confidently. I instinctively stood up straighter and met his eyes politely. Samson had that sort of presence that you can't help but show him respect. In his left hand was a Velcro pouch that looked like something you could attach onto your belt, but it also had a strap of its own, neatly folded up and tucked into a side pouch. It wasn't very big, obviously designed to hold an autoinjector and nothing more. I also saw what was obviously a Seal in his hand as well, complete with a leather covering, just like Miranda's Seal had.

"John, walk with me," he said, not-quite-ordering me.

I matched his pace as he headed out of the building, "sir, I'm here for the autoinjector. Elizabeth said that to see you about it."

"Yes, I wanted to talk with you first before you accepted this role," he answered.

We walked down a stone path at a moderate pace, putting more and more distance from the building.

"What about, sir?" I asked.

"Miranda, of course. I'm about to tell you something that besides Miranda and myself, only the Prophet knows. Miranda is my daughter."

I stopped in my tracks from surprise before I recovered quickly and took a couple long strides to catch up to him.

"Oh. I had my suspicions, but your names are different," I stated.

"Yes. When Miranda was born and tested positive as an Eve, I was already being groomed for the position of Paladin. The Prophet at that time changed my last name in the Church records upon my request. I didn't want her peers—or mine, for that matter—to think that I would show favoritism," he explained quickly.

The was rather surprising information, but the fact that he was just bluntly explaining it all was even more so.

"I see," was all I could respond with.

"You are now officially her Adam. Trying to reverse the connection between you two is now too dangerous, and she'd likely not survive the process. So, I'm telling you now so that you don't get surprised when you meet the rest of the family later on."

Yeah, that would have been a shock, but I doubt he's explaining all this just for my sake. "Is that really all there is to explaining that to me, sir?"

He stopped walking forward and turned toward me. I did the same, cautiously.

"No. I explained it so that you know what position I am in, and why I care so much about Miranda's wellbeing," he said, holding up the autoinjector.

I looked at the autoinjector before looking back at him.

"You love her?" he asked simply.

I didn't have to hesitate, "I don't know. There hasn't been much time—I hardly know her."

He nodded once, "I'm glad your honest. Miranda cares for you, and she's going to place hope in you using this autoinjector if she Breaks."

I swallowed and braced myself for the death threat I was about to receive if I didn't use it on her.

"John, do not let Miranda Break." His voice was so stern; the importance of his commandment was not lost on me.

"What?" I asked in my confusion.

"Do not allow her to enter the Break Phenomenon. It's dangerous."

I narrowed my eyes, "the rumors about what that autoinjector does is true, isn't it?"

He ignored my question, "if she breaks, she will be *extremely* dangerous. Your Miracle isn't known, and you have no experience with what the real capabilities of a Miracle Child are. She will overwhelm you. Promise me you will not let her go that far."

I paused for a moment from his intensity, and then nodded once.

He placed his large right hand on my shoulder, "say it."

"I promise," I responded.

He searched my eyes, making sure I meant it, then he nodded once and handed me the autoinjector.

I took it from him a little awkwardly, and then he held up my Seal.

"This is undisputable proof that you are a Miracle Child. It's an essential tool to your work—especially as a Law Adam. It's also dangerous for someone else to get their hands on, since it excuses you from any consequences for breaking any laws. Consider it apart of your own body—in other words, it would be painful for you to lose it."

He held it out to me, and I took it. I flipped the leather cover over and took a look inside, seeing my own reflection in the polished silver and gold Seal. I hadn't earned a Title yet, so there was no engraving on the side like Miranda's had.

I looked up and met Samson's eyes.

"Take care of her," he told me.

I nodded, "I will. I'll protect her with my life."

He gave a small hint of a smile as the corners, "good."

He immediately turned around and started walking back to his office.

"If you don't hurry, you'll miss your plane," he said, not turning around.

14

The plane had been in the air for less than ten minutes, but I could tell that Miranda was already uncomfortable. Although her face was calm and composed, her shoulders were tense, betraying her attempt to it hide from me. She really didn't like flying.

The plane was the same design as the one we took on the way here, but instead of sitting at the love seat like we did last time, we sat across from one another at the small table. She was wearing the same outfit she wore when we first met: black jeans, brown belt, white blouse. It was a look that suited her well. She wasn't looking at me, but to her left out the window. I knew she was waiting for me to start the conversation.

For a moment, I simply watched her, taking in her natural beauty. Her outfit brought back the memory of how we first met, and it made me realize what that moment and this one had in common. This was the first time since that meeting that I had looked at her without any guard over my thoughts. I had been afraid of having my emotions get in the way of logical decisions.

So much for that, I thought.

I could tell that she knew I was watching her, but she sat still, unbothered by my gaze. Her eyes flashed from the window to meet mine, and her lips gently curved into a small smile.

Her eye contact made me feel pressure to speak. "So, explain this investigation of yours?"

She leaned forward and put her elbows on the table without hesitation, suddenly focused on me. I was right to think that she was waiting for me to ask.

She took a deep breath and began, "I arrived in Chicago the day before we met. I was sent there to investigate the Guards organization and disband their activities if I deemed it appropriate. The Church has left them alone all this time because they keep more ruthless gangs in line, and it was concluded that more dangerous groups would rise in their place if we removed them. I didn't know this at the time, but now I'm sure I was sent here under the assumption that I would disband them. The new policy that the Prophet announced about having a Blessed Pair as a constant presence in the cities would mean that we no longer need the Guards as a deterrent."

I nodded in understanding. "That explains it. I was wondering why you would only now investigate a gang that has been around this long."

"Yes. Well, I'm not sure I can consider them a mere 'gang' now. It'd be more fitting to label them a terrorist group at this point."

"Mm," I said, nodding again. Then my distracted mind realized what she had just said. "Wait, what?"

She smiled at my reaction. "Let me continue. As soon as I arrived, I set my sources to work as I poured through the files that the Church already had on them, which didn't help much. However, I did learn later that night that recently the Guards are much more active, and that bothered me a great deal. For one thing, the files the Church claimed that they only had access to old revolvers and other similarly outdated weaponry, however I discovered that they're now carrying weapons much more dangerous. Additionally, I found out that this was a change that they only initiated sometime this year. So, what does that tell you?"

Her questions took me by surprise, as I just expected an explanation, not a quiz. Though, I realized that this was probably beneficial to me. I needed to learn how to think as an investigator.

"That they're preparing for something?" I asked.

"Yes, but there's something more to it than that. If they could acquire more powerful weapons, why hadn't they before?" she asked back.

"Maybe they couldn't," I replied.

She smiled mischievously. "And that leads us to the million-dollar question: why can they now?"

"Did they increase on their 'protection tax'?" I asked.

"That was one of the first things I checked into, and the answer is no. They neither increased or decreased their protection costs. It seems that they didn't want anyone to take a closer look at them," she said.

"Where are they getting their funding from then?" I asked.

"Another important question, and that question lead me to the building that exploded when we first met," she said.

"You blew up their building?" I asked.

"Hardly. I made a blunder and didn't realize that the building was rigged. I originally broke in there because it was the most heavily guarded building that was under the Guards protection. I assumed it was the building where they stored their valuables or arsenal, and would be a good place to look for clues."

"You wanted to find who was funding them."

She nodded. "I triggered some alarm as I was shifting through the place, so I left in a hurry. I had no idea that the building would explode."

"Was anyone besides us caught in the blast?" I asked.

She shook her head. "No, thank the Supreme. The building was deserted when I infiltrated it, and the blast was so well controlled that the only damage done to the surrounding buildings were a few shattered windows."

"Did you manage to discover anything before it blew?" I asked.

"Only that the building wasn't what I thought it was. It was storage for old hard-copies of various records never claimed by their owners. This included things like birth certificates, personal financial records, and so forth," she explained.

"Well that doesn't make sense. Why would they go to such extremes as to protect that?" I asked.

"Exactly. After it exploded, I knew that I had missed something.

I would've gone back for a second look, but by then I had discovered something more important," she replied, giving me a flirtatious look that made it clear she was talking about me.

I felt a smile tug at the corners of my mouth, and I took a moment to pounder what she had explained so far. That building definitely seemed like the key to figuring out what the Guards were up to. What had happened in the past thirteen years? I looked out the window next to us and narrowed my eyes as I started thinking about how much time had passed. I shouldn't care about what that organization did. It was no longer part of who I was, and by all rights it shouldn't matter to me anymore. However, it was my father's organization, and I didn't want them to change it into something twisted and warped. Thirteen years ... I could hardly remember what the Guards were like back then.

Looked back at Miranda again, who was watching me patiently. "What did you find when you went back there?"

"Nothing. There was little possibility of finding anything, but it still annoyed me that I ended up with nothing. I looked into the building and found proof of what I had guessed earlier: they were definitely hiding something. The energy consumption of that building was off the charts for just being a place to store hard copies."

"What did you do next?" I asked.

"Over the course of the next couple weeks, I investigated as much as I could on my own. I broke into a few of the buildings under their control, but they weren't anything important relevant to the investigation. Our only option is to go knock on their front door and see what we find there. It's the only place that their financial records could be kept."

Upon hearing her suggested course of action, I was reminded again of how insane she was.

"Yeah, there's no way that they're just going to let us walk in the front door," I told her.

"Oh, I know. And as much fun as it sounds to destroy half of their headquarters to gain entry, I think a subtler method would be easier.

I don't really feel like cleaning up afterward anyway," she said, a sly smile on her face.

Yup. Insane, but in a cute way.

"What do you have in mind, exactly?" I asked.

Her smile turned mischievous. "That mark on your shoulder should work nicely, I think."

I was surprised that she knew about my tattoo until I remembered about the Eve's Gaze. It was easy to forget that she knew everything about me. After I recovered from my surprise, I frowned. I didn't like the idea of using it to deceive the Guards. Additionally, my tattoo was slightly different than the one of an average grunt, since I was the son of the founder. It could raise red flags. But Miranda knew all of this, so I'd have to trust her on this, especially considering how much more experience she had in these investigations.

I felt the plane suddenly start slowing down, and I automatically looked out the window, seeing only the tops of trees.

"We're approaching Chicago, but we still have ten minutes or so," Miranda explained, her eyes looking out the window as well.

"Already? That was quick," I said.

She nodded and met my eyes. "Well once we get some distance from the cities, we can break the sound barrier safely."

"Oh. Right," I replied.

I felt a little stupid. Although it was only my second trip on a plane, the speed of air travel was still common knowledge. I stood up and moved to the love seat, which was more comfortable than sitting at the table. Miranda was still looking out the window, and was momentarily not paying attention to me. I used that privacy to think.

I had no idea what was going to happen when we arrived there, and that made me nervous. If it came to a physical fight, could I hold my own? I didn't ask for the specifics, but from how Miranda was making it sound, we could be fighting against people with automatic rifles. I had to go against that? Sure, I was a lot stronger and faster than them, but not fast enough to dodge a freaking bullet. If Miranda gave me a pistol, I might be able to do something, but not on my own. No matter what way I looked at it, I wasn't strong enough to protect

Miranda from them. If I had my Miracle, it might make a difference, but I felt powerless as I reviewed my abilities.

I looked down at my right hand, staring at my palm. I felt a desire to know what power lurked within me. I knew that desire stemmed from wanting to keep Miranda safe, yet I also rebelled against that desire. Wishing for something like that came with its own risks and uncertainties. Miranda's words came back to me from earlier.

You will have to be under a large mental pressure and in a life or death situation before you will be able to draw it out.

I saw what she meant by that now. I wasn't going to attempt to use it unless I had no other option. But hell, I wasn't even sure how to try to use it. I didn't even know what "it" was, since my Miracle could be absolutely anything. I frowned at that thought, realizing that since it could be anything, it might turn out to be more dangerous for Miranda if I used it. She might be immune to my power, but what if my power brings down the building we were in?

I realized that Miranda was watching me from the corner of my eye, but I didn't look up, still wrapped up in my thoughts. What if using my Miracle meant hurting, or even killing others? I would have to be very careful with when that moment came.

Miranda stood up, unintentionally drawing my attention to her. She walked over and sat down on my left. She sat sideways, so that her body was facing me, and grabbed my left hand, slipping her fingers between mine.

She met my gaze with a gentle, kind one of her own. "You think too much."

I exhaled sharply through my nose in amusement at her comment. She was observant. She raised her left hand and placed it on my left arm, then traced it upward and slowly gripped my shoulder. She leaned forward, closing the space between us and gracefully kissed me.

Her movement held no hesitation, and her forwardness was immediately pleasing. The kiss was slow, sensual and careful, lacking any lust while still being arousing in its own way. I reached up with my free hand and cupped the back of her neck, feeling her smooth skin with my thumb and her silky hair with my fingers. Her hand that gripped mine tightened as I tasted her. The kiss started to build, gently losing the innocence it started with and filled with a smoldering desire for more. In a single moment, she slowed the kiss down and our lips parted. She exhaled gently through her nose, and I felt the warmth of her breath on my neck, then she opened her eyes and looked at me, without retreating.

Again, I wanted more of her. Again, I felt a desire to continue where we left off, and take it even further. I wanted her, but I let these feelings be merely feelings.

"You're always so forward," I told her, but my tone wasn't one of a complaint.

"I don't need or want to be anything different. You are my Adam. You belong to me, and I have the right to do whatever I want to you."

"Oh really?" I challenged, raising an eyebrow.

She gave a smile. "We belong to each other. You needn't be so cautious."

"I'm not," I argued.

It was her turn to raise an eyebrow. "Oh really? What would you call it then?"

"Savoring the moment," I replied.

She laughed gently and leaned away from me, reverting to her more comfortable position before our kiss. I let my hand that was on her neck fall to my lap as she moved beyond my reach. Her hand still rested on mine as she met my eyes, looking past a lock of hair that had escaped from behind her ear as we kissed.

"While I do the same, I also don't plan on leaving your side anytime soon. There's no need to rush, but there's no need to wait either," she stated.

"Then it's best to let us get closer naturally," I replied, understanding her meaning.

She gave me a smile. "Looks like we're of the same mindset. Sorry I mistook your movements as hesitation."

"Hmm," was all I said in response.

Silence surrounded us for half a minute before she spoke once more. "Don't let your Miracle stress you, Johnathon."

I swallowed and looked out the window on the far side of the plane. "Easier said than done."

"I told you before, I'll be here to keep you from hurting anyone if something goes wrong," her voice was one of encouragement.

I hesitated, then nodded.

I suddenly noticed the skyscrapers outside the window that were rising through the layers of clouds. We were at the city, but it seemed like we were circling it. I mentioned this to Miranda.

"That is strange. Press that button next to you," she said.

I obliged, activating the speaker so we could reach the pilot.

"Yes sir?" answered a voice from the speaker.

"Is something wrong? Why haven't we landed yet?" Miranda asked.

Her tone was authoritative but wasn't one of rebuke.

"I apologize, but it seems landing protocol is strict right now because of the Prophet's speech in Chicago later today. Extra security measures are being taken. We should receive the green light to land any minute now," answered the pilot.

"Ah, okay. No need to apologize. It's out of your control," Miranda replied.

"Actually, it looks like we just received permission to land. We'll be on the ground in a couple of minutes, Ma'am."

"Thank you," Miranda replied simply.

She nodded once to me, signaling me to let go of the button. I did so.

"The Prophet is here?" I asked.

"Apparently," she replied.

"You're not aware of his schedule?" I asked.

"No. It's not really our business. We have our tasks and he has is. They rarely intersect like this. This could make our job easier, but in the same way, it could be harder," she said thoughtfully.

"What do you mean?" I asked.

"With this amount of security force in place because of the Prophet, the Guards will probably lay low in their HQ or whatever they call it. Meaning that there should be a lot of members coming in throughout the day, so it wouldn't surprise me if they didn't look too closely at your tattoo. It would make our infiltration easier."

I nodded. "I see. But then there will be more people inside."

"Yeah. We'll have to be careful," she said distractingly, as if her mind was in deep thought.

I stayed silent, letting her strategize. She had the lead on this anyway. I needed more experience before I could help her.

She stayed silent all through the landing, though I saw her body tense up and then relax when we came to a stop. We exited the plane together, and there was a car waiting for us just a short walk away, with Zachariah Cobalt standing beside it, waiting for us. Before we reached him, I asked Miranda why he was here.

"He's our Crusader. In the Law career, each Blessed Pair has a Crusader to help them with the extra footwork that is involved in investigations. They help with anything that needs attending too, from being our driver to digging up information for us. It's not a coincidence that he was there to take you to the Paladin. It might feel weird, but treat him like you would a subordinate. Trust me, they feel most comfortable with formality," she explained.

I didn't respond as we continued walking. I had to take a moment to remind myself that I was no longer "just a human." I was a Miracle Child, so it was best that I started acting like it.

When we approached the car, he opened the back door for us. "It's good to see you again, sir. Ma'am."

"Likewise," Miranda replied, sliding into the car first.

I nodded to him, "Have you been well, Zach?"

"Yes, sir. Thank you for asking," he replied.

"Good," I responded and then sat next to Miranda.

He closed the door after us.

"Or treat him like a friend, whatever," Miranda teased.

"Sorry, it just happened," I responded quickly before Zach made it to the driver's seat.

He immediately started driving, which told me he already knew where he was heading.

Miranda spoke to Zach, "Did you find out where it is?"

266

"Yes, ma'am. Their headquarters turned out to be the eighth one on the list you gave me," he replied.

"Really?" she said, surprised. "The abandoned building?"

"They seem to utilize an underground area that's not shown on any of the building's schematics," he explained.

"I see. Give us the details," Miranda ordered.

Zach obliged, explaining to us where the entrance is and how to gain access. He even handed us a tablet that had pictures of the alleyway and the entrance. His explanation lasted the enter car ride, which was about thirty minutes.

We arrived at a small, cheap hotel in the middle of the Lowers. It was definitely something I hadn't expected. I wasn't going to complain, but I had thought that the Church would've provided us with a more comfortable hotel. I voiced my question to Miranda as we climbed the stairs toward our room, wording it carefully to make sure she knew I wasn't complaining.

"It's my choice where we stay, and if I had desired to stay at the most luxurious hotel that the Uppers could provide, the Church wouldn't have complained in the slightest," she explained as we entered the room we just rented.

"So why did you pick here?" I asked, locking the door behind us.

"Its location suits our investigation. It'd be a pain going all the way to the Uppers just to return the next day. Additionally, if someone tailed us, the fact that I can enter and exit the Uppers as I please would send up a red flag immediately."

I left it at that, satisfied with that answer. Still, hotels weren't very common in a district as poor as the Lowers, unless you counted the ones that charged you by the hour. If someone tailed us to the hotel, they would certainly be suspicious, though it would definitely not be as bad as us entering the Uppers. We each took a seat at the table in the room, facing each other. I was about to ask what we were going to do next, but it became clear after she handed me the tablet. I took it without question, and turned it on. I raised my eyebrows when I saw that it contained all the files the Church had on the Guards. She walked me through her investigation in more detail, and we spent a good chunk of time looking at pictures of several of the more dangerous members of the Guards. I was flipping through them, ignoring their names but memorizing their faces with the weapons they were known to use. I was a little daunted at the firepower against us. It ranged from automatic rifles to shotguns, and all of them were very expensive to obtain. At least they didn't have any explosive weaponry. The list didn't seem to bother Miranda.

I froze for a long minute when I came across the picture of James the Scruff-face. His full name was James Dorian, and I skimmed through the tiny amount of information they had on him.

Miranda noticed my interest. "You remember him, right?"

I nodded. "It says here that we don't know what his Miracle is, even though we both saw it?"

She frowned slightly. "We did, but that doesn't mean we automatically know what it is."

"So, it's not telekinesis?" I asked, thinking of the time when he forced his subordinate down to the ground.

"Telekinesis can't teleport you. I don't really know what he did back there, and that worries me. What else is he capable of?" she asked, rhetorically.

"We will have to deal with him carefully," I stated.

She nodded. "I think he was the one who brought down our plane, but we can't jump to conclusions. Especially because I'm positive the other one with him is also an Adam."

She reached forward and swiped her finger across the screen on the tablet, flipping from James' picture to the picture of the man with the cold, lifeless stare. I remembered him immediately, and again I felt nostalgic at the sight of him, as if I had seen him before. I read his name at the top, and I suddenly realized that I *had* seen him before. I even knew him personally. Devon Grey, was, while technically unrelated to me, considered my older cousin in the Guards.

"He's the current head of the Guards? I didn't recognize him at all," I told her.

Miranda half-shrugged. "Well that's not surprising in the least."

"True, but still … he's another one we have to be careful around,"

I replied. It had been over ten years since I'd seen him. We were only kids back then, so I got what Miranda was saying. "Either way, if one of them has the power to bring down a flying plane, then it's obvious that they're strong," I continued.

She nodded, but that's all. I noticed that she was focused on her thoughts again.

We stayed silent for a long minute before I spoke, "Is it really a smart idea to go into their headquarters with so little information on them?"

She frowned again. "It's definitely risky. Very risky, but I don't plan on fighting them immediately. Our primary objective it to obtain information, both about finances and about their abilities. Our actions afterward will depend on what we discover."

I listened silently, thinking. I was nervous about this, but I didn't let it show. I went to swipe the tablet to jump to the next picture, but it appeared that his picture was the last one on the list.

"When do we leave?" I asked.

She met my eyes. "Are you satisfied with the information?"

"No. I wish we had a lot more," I replied honestly.

She half-smiled. "Sorry, let me rephrase. Are you done reviewing the information we have at our disposal?"

"Yes," I answered.

"Then we leave now. After the Prophet leaves the city, our job could get more difficult. Let's use this distraction while it's here."

CHAPTER 15

Even though it was still early afternoon, the buildings we were walking between cast deep shadows, making the long alleyway dark. Miranda walked one step ahead and off to the side, subtlety leading me. Every step made me more tense. It was an alleyway like the one where Rachel was killed. The slightest movement or noise made me go on the defensive, and my eyes darted all over, taking in details and assessing everything as a potential threat. There was no one else in this alleyway, but knowing that didn't ease my tension at all.

Miranda's confidence was the polar opposite of my nervousness. She walked as if she belonged here and knew exactly where she was going. We both wore long, heavy leather cloaks, which was a common apparel of a degenerate in the Lowers. It was warm under the sun but in the dark, dampness of the alleyway, it felt almost comforting. We wanted to be as forgettable as possible, especially since there was a chance Miranda could be recognized.

"This is it, John. Remember what we discussed?" I heard Miranda say from beneath the shadow of her hood.

"I do," I whispered back, then increased my pace as she stepped back behind me, letting me lead.

We decided that this was the safest way to deceive them. Female members were rare in the Guards, mainly because it was a more aggressive lifestyle that only attracted a few. It would draw attention if it was obvious that she was a woman. I didn't say it, but I also knew that if her face was seen, we'd get a lot more attention because she was beautiful.

It was just a few more feet in front of us when I noticed the entrance to the building. It was just like Zach had described earlier. A very steep set of stairs leading downward were carved into the building on our left. It didn't go very far down, but was deep enough to clearly be an entrance to the basement of the abandoned building. I descended and came to a halt on the last step, with Miranda following suit on the step behind me. The stairs were so steep and we were so close together that I could hear her gentle breath. About four feet in front of me there was a heavy steel door complete with a sliding slot to look through; though that was currently closed.

Miranda gently placed her hand on the middle of my back. It was a simple gesture, but one full of support and encouragement. I was reminded of the words she said to me before we entered the alleyway.

No matter what happens inside—even if it's fatal for us, I'm glad that you're the one by my side.

Her simple touch eased me into being more relaxed, while also giving me a strong determination. I refused to let her come to harm.

I hadn't moved from the last step on the stairs for a reason. Even though I couldn't figure out where it was, there was a camera recording us. It was standard procedure to wait on the last step of the stairs until the panel on the door slid open.

A long minute had passed before it did, making a loud, rough sound as the heavy steel slid open and made a *bang* when it hit the end of its track. I knew someone was looking through it, but it was so dark I couldn't make out a single detail. Not only was it very dark at the bottom of the stairs, but it was obvious that darkness filled the air behind the door as well, completely concealing whoever was looking at us.

I stepped forward confidently. Hesitating here would make him suspicious, which could prove deadly. I grabbed the left sleeve of my heavy cloak and pushed it up on my arm until my tattoo was revealed.

It was different from most of the other Guards tattoos. A Guards tattoo was one of an escutcheon—a decorative shield used as a coat of arms—only a handbreadth in size. It had a red outline and was filled with a pitch-black center. Coming out from the darkness in the center of the shield was a fox, who was hunched low and showed its small but sharp-looking white teeth, as if it was threatening the onlooker. It had one paw extended forward, protectively sweeping in eight flawless, blue jewels.

Mine differed in only a small way; in addition to the eight blue jewels were three ruby red ones, which signified my heritage. It signified that I was high ranking in the Guard, which they called Nobility.

A short moment passed before the panel slid shut with another loud *bang*. I heard some locks being undone, and I let my sleeve fall to cover my arm again. The door finally swung open, and a very short hallway made of stone greeted us. It gave off an almost sinister feeling, since it was lit only by a single candle on the wall. The hallway was barely ten feet long, and it was so narrow that it would be uncomfortable for two people to walk next to each other. At the end of this small hallway was another heavy, steel door, except this one was locked electronically, with what looked like both a hand scanner and a vocal password.

The man that opened the door for me was tall and broad, with a powerfully built body. He had brown hair that was long for a man and left messy, making it obvious how little he cared about his appearance. His face was ordinary; neither handsome nor ugly. His only defining feature was how far apart his eyes were, which made me recognize him from the Church's files. I knew he'd been known to use a shotgun, and I was sure I'd see it somewhere in this room if I looked around. I kept myself from doing so since I was supposed to be his superior, and I wanted to make it seem like I was at ease here. He was slightly taller than me and had large muscles, but I was utterly confident that I could destroy him in a physical confrontation. My strength surpassed any normal human, even without my faster reflexes and my recently honed martial arts prowess. I let the confidence show in my eyes when I met his cloudy blue ones, and his gaze quickly dropped to the floor respectfully.

"Sir. I apologize for the delay," he said, speaking to the floor.

"Close the door," I ordered, my tone one of authority.

He hurried to obey, slipping past me as carefully as he could. Miranda was smaller than both of us, so she was able to stay close on my heels. It was a good neutral position where she could either be protected by me or strike at him without difficulty. Since I was in front of her, she was easily overlooked.

"Would you like me to take care of your cloak, sir?" The man asked, glancing at my eyes before returning his to the floor.

I was thankful that the current leaders of the Guards were so frightening to the lower grunts. It made my job of being intimidating much easier.

"No. I won't be staying long," I replied.

I purposefully said 'I' instead of 'we' to make it seem like Miranda was completely unimportant and just someone in the background. However, it seemed that the Guards hadn't made him a door man for nothing; he hadn't forgotten Miranda's presence.

"And your companion's cloak?" he asked, his eyes jumping up to her.

I took off my hood and stared directly at him, applying a mental pressure to keep him from taking a closer look at her. Removing my hood allowed me to see her out of the corner of my eye, and I found that Miranda was also taking measures against being identified. She had positioned herself so that her head, which was still covered by her hood, was right next to the candle. The light from the candle made it very difficult to see any details of her already hidden face.

I spoke clearly, "I don't have the time for this. Open the door."

"Err—yes sir. Sorry," he said, then hurried past us again and pressed his hand against the scanner.

After that, he spoke clearly into the speaker, "the Guards will serve and bring us freedom."

The door gave a clunk noise, and he leaned against the door and pushed. It slowly opened, making little noise as it did so but it was clearly thick and fortified. It was a sharp reminder that if my tattoo had been a fake, breaking into this place would've been much more dangerous.

He stepped forward and stood to the side in an almost polite way, as if he was holding the door open for us to enter. The door led us to another hallway, but this one was much longer and lit with overhead electrical lighting. The white light against the dark stone felt out of place; it was something new and modern against something that was old and faded. The contrast made the place feel a little unreal. I strode passed him confidently and didn't stop, walking through as if I owned the place.

He spoke after I passed by him, "I'll inform Master Grey that you have arrived immediately."

I didn't want that at all. "No need. I plan on introducing myself momentarily. Watching the entrance takes priority, especially with the Church here."

"Err—right. Yes, sir," he said, then I heard the door slowly shut behind us.

I was halfway down the hall when the echo of the door closing finally eased into silence. Now the only sound was our footsteps walking forward. Although I hadn't seen anything, it had sounded like he returned to the first room, but looking back could prove to be a fatal error. A leader of the Guards wouldn't check behind him; he would assume that his order was obeyed. I was too distracted from my acting to notice, but it was plainly obvious now; the air was different. It was cool and moist, with a lot of water in the air. We were approaching the end of the hallway, and I wasn't sure whether to turn left or right. I wanted Miranda's opinion.

She was close to me, just a bit to my left and one step behind. Even with my stride being longer than hers, she kept pace with me easily.

She must have felt it was safe to speak, because she whispered, "That tattoo worked better than I had expected it too. He assumed you were someone of high importance, and even though it worked in our favor, I'm fearful that it might have worked too well."

I felt my legs stiffen for a moment as I had a sudden realization, but I recovered quickly enough that it didn't affect the rhythm of our steps.

Did she not know my history? Had she not seen that far back? I swallowed. I had assumed she knew all of this, so I trusted her plan when she suggested this route, but if she didn't know who I was as a child, then this could get complicated. Still, right now wasn't the place to discuss such a detail. Any distractions could get us into major trouble. I had to just hope I was mistaken about her lack of knowledge.

"Which way?" I whispered.

"It doesn't matter. We have to explore this place till we find where they store their documents. If we're lucky, we can find Devon Grey's personal room. He's sure to have some interesting information tucked away there," she replied.

I turned right at the end of the hallway, and followed another hallway that was very similar, except that there was a door ten feet down on the left.

"Should we start with this one then?" I asked.

"Might as well. Stay confident when you enter. If you peek in and there's someone in there, it'll look suspicious," she advised.

I nodded and took a deep breath to steady myself, then opened and walked through the door. I entered a large, spacious room that was well lit by the same type of white electrical lights that had illuminated the hallways. The square room had wide, heavy tables tracing the walls, each on flush with wall. There was one table, at the far side of the room from the door, which was round and pulled away from the wall so that people could walk around it. The tables were littered with papers, notes and blueprints amongst several different computers and laptops. More importantly, there was three people standing around the large, round table that Miranda and I were facing.

The closest one to us had his back to us when we entered—his attention was on the table in front of him. The other two stood on the opposite side and was facing us, so their faces were recognizable. The one standing on the left was James Dorian, who's blue eyes bore into mine as soon as I entered. The one standing next to him I recognized from the Church's files. He was Devon's right-hand man, but I couldn't remember his name. Compared to James beside him, he didn't seem very intimidating. The man with his back to us was on his cellphone, but after he heard the door open he turned around to face us. Devon Grey's ice-cold gaze swept over me, not showing an ounce of surprise—or any emotion at all, actually.

"Yes. He's here now. Keep up your good work," Devon said before ending the call from the doorman.

"This is rather unfortunate," Miranda whispered to me.

No. Shit.

"Well?" Devon asked. "Aren't you going to introduce yourself, Mr. Uninvited Guest?"

I didn't move immediately, so Miranda whispered, "No choice anymore. We might as well face them here and now."

I felt my jaw clench and my body tense up as I started to walk forward into the center of the room. I stopped when I reached the middle, and then lowered my hood cautiously.

Devon's eyes narrowed the instant he saw my face. "Thomas?"

I swallowed but stayed silent. I hadn't heard that name in so many years, and it surprised me that he had recognized me so easily.

"Devon," I replied in greeting.

His eyes returned to their normal cold, calculating gaze. "I suppose you being alive is more likely than someone being able to fake our tattoo. But I'm rather surprised to see you with the Church. I thought you'd be smarter than to follow that group of oppressors. What your father would say if he saw you now …."

I tried to keep myself in check, but the mention of my father pissed me off. "Don't talk as if you knew him."

"It's apparent that I know what his ideals were better than you do," he replied in a harsh tone, narrowing his eyes at me.

I gave him an aggressive glare as my anger started build.

Miranda stepped forward on my left and lowered her hood. "We came here to request your cooperation in our investigation into your affairs. You can start by surrendering to us all of your financial records, as well as explaining where your newly acquired income has come from."

His cold eyes slowly left mine and looked at Miranda. "What laws have we broken against the Church?"

"Stealing funds from the local businesses and using those funds to purchase illegal weapons, including your firearms, for starters."

"Are we not allowed to accept donations and gifts from locals who wish to offer their support? Additionally, those weapons have only been purchased to use for our own protection against the dangers that lurk inside the walls of this city. Protection that neither the police or the Church attempt to provide," he answered smoothly.

"Those reasons do not change the fact that your actions are in violation of not only the Church's laws, but the laws of the city of Chicago. There's also a matter of your involvement with a terrorist organization that is a danger to the Church and all of its citizens," Miranda responded.

"What evidence do you have of this?" he asked, unsurprised.

"None. Yet. However, as an Eve of the World, I need no warrant, proof, or special permission of any kind. All I need is a hunch and the time to spare," she replied sternly.

"Well, that settles that. They have to die," James said, his voice filled with excitement as he stepped around the table and stood next to Devon.

He stretched his hand forward, as if he was reaching for something, but Devon reached over and grabbed his arm tightly.

"Do not presume that you have the right to act here." Devon's voice was hard and commanding.

James gave him a dark glare, not backing down. "I do not serve you, Devon Grey, but someone much more powerful than you. These two threaten that individual's plans, so it's only natural that I don't hesitate."

"I didn't think I would have to remind you, but that individual placed you under my command. This is a private matter, and I do not need you butting into my business. I know what needs to be done, so rest assured that I will handle it my own way," Devon's grip on James' arm grew tighter, and after a short staring contest, James consented.

"You have this annoying habit of leaving their death to that of chance—and chances shouldn't be taken when we're in theses crucial stages," James said, lowering his arm.

"Even if these two escaped right now, they couldn't stop us," Devon stated, turning his gaze back to me.

"I suppose that's true," James consented as he leaned backward against the table.

Miranda raised her arm and summoned a pistol in her hand, aiming it dead center on Devon. "Are you sure you wish to fight against a fully-trained Eve?"

"Miranda Pierce; I've been warned about you. I know what your abilities are, but you are at a disadvantage."

Miranda didn't show any surprise that he knew her name. "And what advantage do you have over me?"

"The home field advantage," he answered as he started to slowly step towards us. "You didn't think that I'd protect this place with just a muscleman, did you?"

"Get ready," Miranda muttered, and her pistol immediately disappeared. In its place was a long and heavy silver blade that she grasped with both hands. She held it forward defensively, still cautious of him.

"That won't save you," he said, his tone as serious as his eyes.

I felt a chill run down my spine that made my entire body tense. I was afraid of his unknown ability. His confidence worried me, and I felt a need to retreat. I exhaled through my mouth slowly, and forced myself to be calm. My breath came out in a mist in front of me, but I didn't let it distract me as I stared back into Devon's cold eyes.

Then my mind realized the importance of what my eyes had just processed. His confidence and my fear weren't the only reasons behind the chill running down my spine. The air around us was much, much colder than it was when we first entered.

What happened next seemed instantaneous. One moment there was nothing but air between Miranda and I, the next a large sheet of ice had appeared as a barrier between us. I jerked my head to the left as my entire focus was suddenly on Miranda. My entire mind was immediately on figuring out if Miranda had been injured or hurt by this ice. I recovered quickly, but it was too late; the sheet of ice was only a distraction. Thicker ice rapidly formed out from the sheet, and quickly enclosed me in a dome. The ice had moved quickly to trap me, but if I hadn't been distracted by the first sheet of ice, I probably would've been able to escape.

I didn't have much room in this ice prison. If I was standing in the center, I would have about five feet of space around me and three feet of space above me. I quickly assessed my surroundings to see if there was anything else immediately threatening me, or if the ice would make any other movements. After a couple seconds of it being completely still, I refocused on the sheet of ice that separated me from Miranda.

When it first appeared, it wasn't thick, and I could see Miranda on the other side, but after the ice dome had enclosed me, the barrier grew thicker, and it was no longer clear enough for me to make out anything on the other side. I pressed my hand against the ice that separated me from her without thinking, and then immediately pulled it back as the cold instantly sunk down to my bones. I gave a short shout of surprise as my hand suddenly felt like it was being burned.

It was *cold*. Very cold. Ridiculously cold. I had never experienced this degree of cold before; it had burned my skin on contact. But before I felt the pain, I had realized how solid the ice seemed, as if it was utterly still and unmovable. How could I get out of this?

Just as I had that thought, I saw movement from the corner of my eye and turned in time to see Devon smoothly move through the ice, as if it was as thin as water. He rushed to me, his movements controlled and agile, and before I had any time to react, his fist connected hard against my jaw.

I staggered back a step, but recovered quickly as my mind started to go into fight mode. I felt my jaw burn with an intensity that matched the cold of the ice. I had time to notice that his fists were coated with a pure, reflective ice before he landed another blow on the side of my stomach. I managed to tighten my abs and hold my ground this time, but only barely. His strength was immense, and the burning sensation I felt with each blow made it much worse.

I swung my right arm, aiming for his face, but he dodged around it and stepped toward me. Then he followed up with a quick knee to my stomach. The blow was much harder than his punch, and the force of it made me fall to my knees. I hadn't even begun to recover when I saw his foot enter my field of vision. I couldn't dodge in time, and it collided with my face, pushing my entire body back several feet until I smacked into the ice wall behind me. The cold penetrated through my clothes and ate into my skin instantly.

Out of reflex I leaned forward away from it, ending up on my hands and knees in front of Devon. His speed didn't outclass mine under normal circumstances, but the cold that radiated off of the ice seeped straight into my muscles and made me sluggish.

"Is this it? This is all the son of the Captain is capable of?" he asked, his tone was one of disappointment.

I felt irritated at the mention of my father, but I didn't let it show. I slowly stood up and looked him in the eye. My body was stiff, and the parts he struck hurt like hell.

"Why don't you give it another go and find out?" I taunted, bluffing.

I knew his combat capabilities surpassed mine, and the environment he created with his Miracle gave him a very large advantage. The only way I'd win this one was by sheer luck. Even though he never responded to my comment, he knew full well that he was stronger. He took a couple steps backward, putting space between us, but he never let down his guard. His arms were still tensed and he was constantly watching me from the corner of his eye. I knew I needed to plan my next move, but it was difficult to focus. Part of my mind was constantly focused on finding out what happened to Miranda, which merely distracted me from getting out of my current situation. The cold pain from his blows didn't make it any easier to think clearly, but even in my best condition I doubted I would have a way to fight against him.

His voice was filled with contempt, "This is almost comical. I can hardly believe how foolish I was to ever wonder if you would be better suited to lead the Guards. You're lack of strength is appalling."

I couldn't disagree with that last statement. Twenty minutes earlier, I was confident in my strength and combat abilities, but that was merely because I was comparing myself to a regular human being. Thinking it over now, of course my abilities would be subpar to an Adam who has had much more time to hone their abilities and discover their Miracle. I was, in the best-case scenario, three years behind a typical Adam my age. Three weeks of training would prepare me against normal humans, but against an Adam who could use his Miracle? I hardly stood a chance. Still, I couldn't back down. I didn't know where Miranda was or what condition she was in.

"Why would you ever wonder if I was better suited for the Guards?" I asked, buying time.

His eyes hardened as they bore into mine. "Put yourself in my shoes, Thomas. I'm your cousin—even if it's not by blood. Growing up it was always said that my duty to the Guards would be to be your right-hand man, and to follow your lead when you replaced your father. Then your father died before you were ready, and then you vanished. You dropped all of your responsibilities and ran."

I grinded my teeth at his accusation. It felt as if he was blaming me for leaving the Guards.

"Ran? I was banished! The day after the funeral I was exiled, just so your father could make a power grab undisputed."

"He was testing you! Yet you let him have it easily! You didn't even fight what was happening!"

"I was eleven and my parents had just died! You honestly think I was mature enough to make a decision like that?"

I had a pistol Miranda gave me tucked into the back of my jeans, and if I got the right opportunity, I knew it was my best bet to defeating him. My only choice was to maneuver the fight to where I had time to draw the gun and be able to fire without him dodging. But with his reflexes, my only option might be to shoot point-blank.

"A Captain would," he replied simply.

"Well there you have it. I'm no Captain."

His chin rose and he looked down on me. "Obviously not. Don't worry, I'll be sure to fulfill the dreams and expectations of both our fathers'."

I clenched my teeth at his arrogant attitude, but in the back of my mind I knew I had no way to argue against his words. He was right. Perhaps I'm not the son that my father wanted me to be.

It was thirteen years ago, but I still had memories of my life in the Guards. I remember what my father had expected of me; to take his place and further his goals even after his death. My path had seemed so sure, so concrete and immovable. It felt like even if the earth split open or the sky fell around me, my path would still be to the lead the Guards.

Yet, what had happened felt like something much worse than the earth splitting open or the sky falling. My parents died. My mother, who was my support and comforter, and my father, who was my guide and future, vanished completely from my life in one simple, quick explosion. Suddenly, I was on my own, trying to survive in the streets.

I gritted my teeth harder as my anger at my cousin climbed. He stood there, talking as if he knew exactly what I went through and passing judgment on me. Who the hell did he think he was?

Then, part of my mind realized the significance in what he had just said. It picked up on the clue he'd unintentionally let slip. In my anger, I pounced on it like a starving lion. I had no way to hurt him physically, so I instantly resorted to my voice.

"Did your daddy leave you behind too?"

He narrowed his eyes ever so slightly. "What?"

"You said you'd carry on the dreams and expectations of both of them. Obviously, Uncle Grey must've kicked the bucket and left you behind to pick up his mess."

"Quiet. Don't speak as if you know what happened," he replied, his voice sterner then it was previously.

"Oh, my mistake. I didn't mean to come across as if I actually cared. Tell me, o' fearless Captain, how did it feel like to hear about his death? Did it tear you in half? Did it make you cry? Did it make you realize just what I had to go through? Then again, your heart is as cold as your Miracle, isn't it? You probably heard the news and felt nothing; as if you were simply reading it out of the newspaper."

His eyes, which had been cold and unmoving, suddenly turned murderous. I had him, so I pressed my advantage.

"Or maybe you felt like you just got a stroke of luck. After all, the seat of the Captain was all yours now, wasn't it? I wonder how you managed to keep from smiling at his funer—" I was cut off by his movement.

I was expecting it, but I still couldn't defend myself. My eyes had managed to follow his movements, but my response was a full second too late. Devon, who had been standing two feet away from me, suddenly launched forward. His hand jumped straight to my throat and lifted me off the ground as if I was nothing more than a child. His cold grip felt like it was burning my flesh and was so tight I thought he was going to snap my neck. I couldn't breathe, and I stared down at his eyes. Their cold blue burned with anger, and I saw in them his intention to kill me.

His voice was as hostile as his glare. "I've had to shoulder a burden that makes your life look like fun. I wasn't happy about my father dying. Know why? Because I was the one who murdered him, Thomas. I had to choose between my father and the Guards, and I choose the Guards. Don't talk like you even have any idea—"

Bang!

The shot from the pistol seemed twice as loud in this small dome of ice. His grip released immediately and I fell to the ground, barely managing not falling on my ass. I sucked in a breath and coughed a couple times from the pain of the air rush down my bruised throat.

As soon as he had lifted me off the ground, I had reached behind me and drawn Miranda's pistol. I managed to point it directly at his stomach and fire without him noticing, since he was so absorbed in his anger.

He took a step backward after releasing me, but after that he froze in place for a moment. That moment of peace felt unrealistically long, since I was praying that he would fall backward, wounded and no longer able to fight. However, after that moment of peace came to an end, he exhaled, almost as if in relief.

"That was close, Thomas. A good shot, but I'm afraid weapons like those aren't enough to fight against an Adam," his voice was filled with its regular arrogance, and I noticed that his anger had disappeared.

He lifted up his white shirt to reveal his stomach. A layer of ice coated protectively over his abs and chest. The bullet was smashed halfway into the ice, but it never even reached his skin. There were a few small cracks spreading out from the impact point, but those were the only signs of damage done. After a gentle tug, Devon pried the bullet out of the ice. He looked at it for a moment before tossing it to the side, as if it disinterested him. I heard the bullet hit the concrete floor a few times, filling the small dome with sound before it fell back into the cold silence. The ice covering his skin wasn't very thick, but the fact that it could stop a bullet that easily showed how dense it was.

I couldn't beat him. I knew that now. His Miracle was too strong. Additionally, I was sure this wasn't all he could do with his ice. I bet if he wanted to, he could've killed me as soon as I was trapped in this dome.

I swallowed as my concern for Miranda swelled, and that very concern caused my mistake. I glanced at the left wall.

"Oh, don't worry. The girl is unharmed for now," he replied in a cold voice.

He reached out and touched the ice wall with the tips of his fingers, and it immediately became clear, allowing me to see through it and see Miranda. The wall that separated us was more unique than the other walls that surrounded me. Instead of it being thick and strong, it was instead made up of two thinner walls, with about two inches of space between them.

She was relentlessly hacking at the wall that separated us with her sword. I heard no sound as her powerful blows struck the ice, though it didn't seem to affect the integrity of the wall at all.

She took a moment to pause, realizing that her attacks were futile. She was panting hard, her breath coming out in a white mist.

I heard Devon's voice as I studied Miranda. "I don't know why, but it seems your body is resisting the temperatures of the ice. I originally thought it was a result of my rushed job to contain you, but I see that's no longer the case."

"What do you mean?" I asked him aggressively.

"Don't tell me you haven't noticed. Look at Miranda. Her swings are sluggish and crude, and they lack her full strength. I'm sure she's realized it herself, yet keeps swinging away, trying to get to you."

I couldn't tear my eyes away from Miranda as he continued talking, "She wouldn't have even been caught in this dome if she wasn't so focused on saving your ass to begin with. Putting up that barrier between you two was more effective than I planned. You both just stood there, dumbfounded while I took my sweet time wrapping the thicker ice around you."

I tightened my fist. I had to do something to get her out of there. If what he was saying was true, she might be starting to freeze to death. But how? This ice was so incredibly dense that just a thin layer was enough to stop a bullet in its tracks.

"Well, if the god your Church worships comes down to help you, then so be it. Otherwise, you'll die here. I wish this could've ended another way, Thomas," he said, turning to go.

"No, you don't," I shot back.

He hesitated, stopping in his tracks for a short moment before whispering, "Hm. Perhaps I don't."

He left me. Even though I knew he would never allow it, I still had to restrain myself from stopping him and asking him to free Miranda. I swallowed and looked through the clear ice.

I continued to stare at her, who had given up on merely slashing the wall and was clearly trying to think up a way to pierce through it. I searched my own mind again for a solution, but nothing came to me.

Miranda seemed to have come up with an idea, because I saw her eyes sharpen and become more determined. A flash of blue light marked her summoning a weapon—one I had never seen before. It resembled a lance, but it was much shorter and seemed to be wielded with only one hand. It was made of a polished metal and seemed to be thick, but she maneuvered it without any signs of straining, which made me wonder how heavy it was. The most notable part about this lance was the rivets that ran along the side, but it became clear what their purpose was moments later when arcs of electricity sparked between them.

Miranda was channeling her Miracle through the lance and causing the tip of the lance to heat up, glowing a soft red. She set her stance and readied her weapon, looking solid and unmovable. Even through the cold ice distorted her slightly, she took my breath away. I swallowed and had time to take a step back before she moved, flashing in a blink of an eye and thrusting her spear into the ice.

My body tensed and I took an involuntary step forward as a white mist shot out from where her lance had pierced the first layer of ice. Miranda flinched backward as the mist met her hand that was holding the lance. Whatever this mist was, it obviously hurt her, and it was quickly filling up the space.

"Miranda!" I shouted without thinking and stepped forward, placing my hands on the ice.

I flinched back as I felt it burn my skin again and clenched my teeth in frustration. I watched helplessly as I saw her back up until she was right next to the wall of ice behind her. She slowly sank to the floor. I could tell that she was coughing from breathing in the mist. I watched her and silently begged for her to be okay, before I lost sight of her as the mist became too thick.

"Think, John!" I hissed at myself.

I had to get to her, and I had to do it now. Yet determination alone wasn't going to get me anywhere. I breathed deeply for a long few seconds as my mind raced through options I had at my disposal. Again, I came up empty.

"God ... please." I spoke, feeling desperate.

I had never prayed before. Unless you were a Miracle Child or a high official in the Church, you were not permitted to worship or privately pray to the god of the Church. Now was different. I was a Miracle Child, so the god of the Church should be able to hear me. I silently begged for a miracle, but after several seconds of silence I felt foolish and my anger started to build.

I tightened my hands into fists as my thoughts focused into a desperate and reckless idea. I had to use everything at my disposal, no matter what happened. I pulled my arm back and struck without hesitation, twisting my hips and putting my full weight behind the blow. My fist collided with the ice and it felt as if I had just punched solid stone. My skin split at my knuckles and pain swarmed in my mind. Blood landed on the ice, and I heard a *tss* noise as it instantly froze solid.

I gritted my teeth as the pain on my knuckles slowly died down. That wasn't nearly strong enough. I couldn't just put normal muscle behind it, I would have to use my full strength, even if it caused me to break the bones in my hand. I tightened my fist and prepared to strike it again, this time using my full strength as an Adam.

I realized how foolish my previous thinking had been now. It was foolish to think about bystanders or innocents when it came time to use my Miracle, because the only time I would use it was if Miranda's life was in danger. Right then, I didn't care in the slightest what would happen if I used an unknown ability. All I knew is that if I did nothing, Miranda would die, and that was unacceptable.

I struck with my full force, and pain erupted from my hand. I groaned and let my hand hang limply at my side while I struggled against the flow of pain that rushed through my mind. I breathed raggedly through my clenched teeth and waited impatiently to recover enough to try again. Tightening my hand into a fist intensified the pain for several seconds and I struggled to ignore it as I slowly raised it back into a striking position. I knew I only had one more strike left out of my arm, so I had to make it count.

I breathed out a slow breath and calmed my panicked emotions. I let a controlled rage simmer at the back of my mind. Devon did this to her. He hurt her. James was just as guilty, so he will die too. Everything disappeared as I focused intensely on two goals: save Miranda, and kill Devon and James.

I felt pure power radiate from my right hand, and I struck without hesitation.

I saw a strange white light cover my hand as it raced toward the ice, but I was too focused on saving Miranda to care what it was or what was happening. I felt my hand connect with the ice, but it didn't hurt. I saw the ice instantly crack and break apart.

White fire erupted from the impact point, burst through the sheet of ice as if it was as fragile as paper. The fire expanded and burst in every direction, blowing me off my feet. I was knocked backwards. My back hit the ice dome behind me, but I broke through it as if it was thin glass. I flew back another ten feet before crashing into a table. I hit the side of it with my back and felt it start to tip as I tumbled over it awkwardly. I hit my head painfully against the concrete floor and black spots littered my vision. They disappeared after I sucked in a few deep breaths.

I swallowed and shakily stood up in panic as I remembered Miranda. My eyes flashed around the room, looking for Devon or James. But the room was empty, and I knew that they were long gone. I saw what little remained of the ice dome, and beyond a small stump of ice that outlined where the walls of the dome had been was the still form of Miranda's body.

"Miranda!" I called out, quickly climbing over the table and rushing over to her. I went to feel for a pulse, but suddenly froze as I noticed that my right hand was still on fire. I felt no pain, but I didn't have time to investigate it right now; I used my left instead. Her skin was so cold, I immediately thought she was dead. That brief moment passed into sudden relief as I felt a faint pulse of life. Even if she was alive, she wouldn't be for long if I couldn't warm her up.

I looked at my right hand that was coated in the strange white fire. My sleeves had been burnt off, revealing my tanned skin and making me realize that the fire was coming off of my skin. I touched my left arm with my burning right hand, wondering if the fire burnt my clothes, or if it was just from the force of the original strike.

The white fire immediately disintegrated the thick leather upon contact. I had a sudden thought that I didn't want it to burn my clothes, and to my surprise, it stopped doing so. I could control this intuitively. I just had to be clear about what I wanted from it.

I reached down and touched Miranda's arm, being sure to focus what it was I wanted from the flames: produce heat without burning her clothes.

I worked; it let her clothes unharmed, but I could feel them getting warm. I moved my hand onto her stomach. I exhaled in frustration. This wasn't going to be quick enough.

I tilted her head back and put my mouth over hers, but I breathed out warm air from my lungs as I did. I stopped and turned my head over her mouth, feeling the warm air that she exhaled. I repeated the process several times, and I gradually saw color return to her face.

I felt myself relax. She was going to be okay. My fire was extinguished with just a mental command.

I looked around the room again, trying to get a better idea of our situation. The explosion of the white fire was more devastating than I had noticed before. Most of the tables were burnt—so were the papers and electronics that had been on them. There went our information.

The door we entered from was shut, and I was surprised that the sound of that explosion didn't alert anyone in the building. Why weren't we being surrounded right now?

On the other side of the room, behind the large tables that James and Devon were next to, was a shut door. I cautiously went over and peeked behind it. It was a small storage room, used for storing more tables and some cheap chairs. There was space enough to hide in here while I waited for Miranda to recover. I picked her up and carried her into the dark, unlit room. I closed the door behind us and crouched down against the back wall. I held Miranda against me protectively, and waited.

My adrenaline went away as I rested, making my right hand burn with intense pain. I examined my knuckles, and was surprised to see a bit of white bone. I rested my hand at my side in a relaxed position and struggled through the pain as I let my body heal.

Several minutes passed by, and then I felt my phone vibrate in my pocket. With the position, I was in—holding Miranda on my lap—I couldn't pull it out of my pocket with my left hand. I carefully used my right hand, fighting through the pain it caused me.

"Hello?" I answered through clenched teeth.

"John, it's Zachariah."

Damn. I should have called him as soon as I secured Miranda in this small room.

"Status?" I asked, knowing that he was assigned to observe the headquarters while we were inside.

"It seems that they abandoned the building. Devon and James both exited together, but they got into separate vehicles. A few others left the building at the same time, including the doorman. I don't think they plan on returning to this building."

That explains why no one heard the blast.

"Miranda got hurt fighting against Devon. I'm waiting for her to recover before continuing on," I explained.

"I see. Orders?" he requested without missing a beat.

"Follow James. He mentioned that he's serving someone more powerful than Devon …. Sounds like this mystery person is the mastermind of whatever they're planning, and it'd be nice to uncover their identity."

"Understood. I will contact you if I discover anything," he answered.

"Good. Talk to you then," I replied, then hung up.

Then I waited.

CHAPTER 16

I became alert the moment I felt Miranda stir in my arms. I wasn't sure just how much time had passed, but I guessed about an hour. Miranda wasn't fully awake yet, but since she had just shifted I knew it was only going to be a couple moments before she was. I lifted my right hand and examined it, seeing how much had healed in such short time. It was still sore when I tightened my hand into a fist, but the skin had repaired itself almost completely. Miranda shifted again, making my focus center back onto her.

A few more seconds passed, then she sleepily lifted her hand and set it on my chest. She grasped the leather coat in a tight grip.

"John?" she muttered, opening her eyes very slightly before closing them again.

"I'm here," I replied.

She raised her head and opened her eyes, blinking several times before meeting my eyes. A powerful flood of relief washed through me as I gazed into her eyes. I cared for her more than I realized, and I knew now that I would have felt broken if she had died. I reached up and cupped the back of her head, pulling gently so her forehead against mine.

"John? What's wrong?" she asked, noticing my odd behavior.

I shook my head, letting her know that nothing was wrong. "I'm glad you're alive."

She hesitated, then I heard her exhale and her body relaxed in my arms. She reached up and grabbed my wrist affectionately.

A moment passed with us that way, then she looked up and around us. She tensed up, uneasy in this unfamiliar place.

"It's okay. We're safe here," I explained.

"Where are we? And what happened to Devon?" she said, standing up. She moved too quickly, and suddenly became off balanced. She placed a hand on the wall for support.

"Easy, Miranda. You've been unconscious for over an hour," I told her.

"An hour!?" she asked, her voice appalled.

I raised a hand, signaling her to be calm, "we're in a storage room behind the room where we fought Devon."

She took a couple deep breaths before calming down.

I took a step closer to her and grabbed her hand gently, "are you okay?"

She nodded and gave me a small smile, "I feel a little weak still, but I'll recover in a few minutes."

She twisted her hand around and threaded her fingers through mine.

"What happened? I remember trying to break through the ice with my lance, but ... did that really work?"

"Not really," I replied, "after striking the ice, it broke the first layer and a white mist shot out, which I'm guessing was some kind of super cooled gas. It filled up your dome quickly, and you passed out. I used my Miracle to break us free."

She showed surprise, "you're Miracle?"

I nodded.

She smiled. "Can I see?"

"Sure," I said, and held up my right hand.

I frowned then, suddenly realizing that I didn't know how I activated it, but I figured it was probably a lot like using it. I focused on what I wanted it to do, and white fire instantly ignited on my skin, covering my hand in flames. The dark room was suddenly lit up in the white light, and it hurt my eyes. I saw Miranda's face flash to one of fear as she gasped and jumped back away from me.

Surprised by her reaction, I quickly extinguished my fire.

I felt like an idiot. "Sorry. I forgot that you're afraid—"

She cut me off with a shake of her head, and she took a couple of deep breaths. "Don't be. It just surprised me, but I know that it can't hurt me."

She took a deep breath and collected herself. "Show me again."

I carefully complied, and the white flames flickered gently across my palm.

She watched it for a short moment, staying where she was, then she stretched out her hand and slowly stepped forward.

"It's warm," she commented, "even without reaching it, I can feel how warm it is."

The fire washed over her fingers harmlessly, and upon contact with her skin, the fire would change with white to blue.

"Woah. Interesting."

She hummed in agreement, feeling the fire with her fingers for a long moment before she pulled them back. I extinguished my fire immediately afterward.

"Of all the possible miracles you could've had, and it had to be fire," she said, sighing.

"Sorry," I replied, apologizing for no reason.

She shook her head, wearing a small smile. "I was trying to be funny. Besides, this doesn't really feel like fire to me."

I looked at her curiously. "What do you mean?"

She half shrugged. "I don't know how to explain it … it's just, the more I look at it, the less I fear it. It's as if my mind is convinced that it's not fire."

"Could it be because of the color, or because it's my Miracle and you're immune?" I asked.

"No idea," she admitted, then after a pause she continued, "let's get out of here. We need to contact Zachariah and get in pursuit of Devon and James."

"He called while you were unconscious," I said, then explained everything that we talked about.

"Okay, then let's spend a few minutes searching this place. They left a whole room full of clues after all," she said as she started to open the door out of the room.

"Yeah, about that ..." I began, letting her take in the state of the half-burnt room.

She spent a small moment taking in the ruined, half-burnt state of the room. She sighed, then stepped into the room. I followed her.

"You couldn't have at least left one laptop untouched?" she complained.

"Sorry. I was too busy saving your life to think about the laptops," I remarked, teasing her.

She stuck her tongue out at me in response before saying, "well let's search the rest of this building and see what we uncover."

"Should we split up and search it?" I asked, as we walked to the door.

"No, I don't like that idea. Besides, I want to hear about what happened on your side of the ice. You said you could see me, but I couldn't see you at all. What happened exactly?"

I took a deep breath and explained it all to her, starting at when Devon first attacked us up to when I used my Miracle. She listened to everything patiently and only asked a question a couple times. I followed Miranda as I explained it all, watching her open a door and taking a glance into it before shutting the door and moving on.

When I finished she took a deep breath and sighed. "This was my miscalculation. I thought I knew everything about you from the Gaze, but I didn't see any of that. When did you switch from Thomas Glenn to Johnathon Aster?"

"After I was banished from the Guards, Devon's father gave me a new identity, Johnathon Aster. I used it from then on, but after Rachel's murder and the years I spent living Outside, I had to modify it. Vivian was already in a good position in the World Police's Chicago branch, so she was able to help me," I explained.

She stayed silent for a thoughtful moment, then asked, "Is there anything else that I might not know?"

"Well I don't know what you saw and what you didn't. Did you see where I was when I was on the Outside?"

"The monastery?" she asked, glancing at me as she closed another door.

I nodded.

"Yeah. I saw that. I remember you being furious for a long time. You had a lot of dark thoughts, and you kept dreaming of the night Rachel died."

I nodded again. "Then no, I don't think there's anything else important."

We continued on in silence for a brief span, which was interrupted with Miranda sighing. "The Church has never had to deal with rogue Adams before."

"Really? Not once?" I asked, surprised.

She shook her head as she walked toward the door. "It's one of the reasons why the Church is so aggressive about bringing countries under their protection. Right now, those countries lack both the knowledge and the manpower to identify Adams and Eves in their society. We knew that we'd have to fight other Adams and Eves eventually, but to think that there were two in our own backyard is rather concerning."

"Three counting me," I corrected her.

"Sure, but I know of your special circumstances. What I don't know is how these other people managed to pull it off."

I frowned thoughtfully. "Hm, now that I'm thinking about it, isn't sending only one Eve and a half-trained Adam to face two Adams a little arrogant of the Church?"

She didn't answer immediately as she carefully opened another door that we came to, but after giving it a quick survey she shut the door and continued down the hall. "No, not really. It isn't arrogance as much as it is desperation. Manpower is very limited in the Church as far as Adams and Eves are concerned. We die in the field all the time while fighting against the Outside. Considering how much time it takes to train us, it's extremely hard for the Church's strength to increase. The only reason we are alone is lack of manpower, and not because the Church doesn't consider this an important assignment."

"Is that really the only reason?" I asked.

"Well, I didn't want to sound full of myself, but they do trust in my strength as an Eve. I can summon my core without fear of snapping now, because even if I do you're there to stop me."

I stayed silent. I hated that answer.

I shifted the subject. "How come you didn't summon your core when we were stuck in that ice dome?"

She glanced at me before checking another room. "Um, my core isn't well suited for indoor use … it might have brought the building down on us if I summoned it here."

Brought the building down? What the hell was this thing?

"Uh-huh … sounds like not summoning it was the right call then," I replied.

She hummed in agreement and continued searching the rooms of the hallway. We saw another six or so rooms before we finally found it.

"Here we go," she said after poking her head inside a room.

She walked in and left the door open behind her for me to follow. I shut the door behind us out of habit.

The room was large, but because it doubled as a bedroom and an office space it seemed a little cramped. There was a large bed on the far side of the room with a nightstand on one side of it and a dresser on the other. That was the only evidence there was that this was a bedroom; the rest of the room was dominated by studies. Three full-sized bookcases lined one of the walls and were filled with books; they even overflowed onto the ground. In the corner on our left was a table and a chair, which was used as his main workstation. It also had a large stack of books on it, along with several pieces of paper scattered around and a laptop.

"What makes you think this is Devon's room?" I asked, noticing the lack of personal items such as photographs or other markers that would make her arrive at her conclusion.

"This is obviously not the room of a grunt and the only leader here is Devon," she answered.

"James Dorian seemed to have that alpha male personality and even questioned Devon's authority."

"True, but did he seem like the heavy reader type to you?"

"Fair," I consented.

"Plus, from their conversation, it sounded as if James hasn't been working with Devon for very long. He wouldn't have had time to amass such a collection of books."

I sighed. "Where do we start?"

She looked around for a moment. "Check the nightstand for a journal or something he kept personal notes in, and look around the bookcases. I'll see what I can find from the desk and the laptop."

I agreed and headed over to the nightstand. I heard Miranda start to shift through the papers on the desk, while I opened the night stand drawer. Inside was empty except for a single book. It was thin, and I recognized it immediately, though I was surprised to see it in Devon's possession. I pulled it out carefully, wiping off the dust that littered the cover so I could read the title clearly.

The Miracle of the Church

I opened it and raised my eyebrows. It was covered in hand-written notes around the sides of the text, and from the condition of the binding, it'd be a safe bet that Devon had read this book several times. It was the religious text of the Church that stated everything that the Church believed and stood for. I skimmed through the pages and glanced over his notes curiously. They were completely mixed in tone which helped reveal to me which notes were written first, and which notes were written after several reads.

"Did you find anything?" Miranda asked.

I glanced up, but I saw that she had her back to me and was fiddling with the laptop. "Yeah. A copy of *The Miracle of the Church*, believe it or not."

She looked at me over her shoulder, "Really? Wow. He's lucky he's technically an Adam, or he would've been executed for unlawfully having that."

"Mm," I acknowledged and flipped through a few other pages. "He's really studied it."

"You read it in your training, right? I didn't assign it since I assumed they would make you read it."

I nodded. "Yeah."

"What did you think of it?"

I looked up and met her eyes again. I tried to gain some sort of insight as to how I should answer that question, but I came up empty. All I could sense from her was a guarded curiosity.

I took a deep breath and looked down at the thin book in my hands. "To be honest, I'm not exactly sure what to think. I noticed that there were a few contradictions in the text, but they weren't necessarily a mistake. It was as if some content was just missing from it. For instance, in the earlier parts there's several subtle prophecies, but only the more notable ones are explained to have actually come to pass. The last few parts also seem way too convenient for the Church, and although I don't want to say it, it makes me wonder the credibility of their religion."

A moment of silence passed before Miranda spoke, "John."

Her voice was cautious. "Be careful with that line of thought. The Church doesn't force the Miracle Children to be believers of their religion, but they won't take kindly to a Miracle Child discrediting them."

I nodded. "I know. Even though that's how I feel when I read the text, one thing is abundantly clear and indisputable about this entire thing."

"What's that?" she asked, her tone returning to its natural state.

I held up my hand a used my Miracle, watching the white fire dance along my skin. "This. Miracles."

I shrugged and paused a moment before continuing, "Even if the text makes it seem oddly convenient for the Church, it's clear that what Miracle Children can do is beyond what we understand of physics and genetics. The fact that I can even do this is outside human understanding, and I can see it reaching into the realm of the Supreme Being. Whether I believe that or not, I haven't decided yet."

"I see," she said, then turned back toward the laptop.

I heard her resume her typing, and after a short time of silence I asked, "What do you believe, Miranda?"

Her typing came to a halt, and after a moment of hesitation, she peeked at me from the corner of her eye. "What you said about the text has merit. I agree that when reading the text, it seems to lack something, and I didn't overlook those apparent contradictions either."

She turned back to the laptop before adding, "I've decided that it's more comforting to believe in the Supreme than to believe in nothing."

I hummed in response and flipped to the end of the book I was holding. I wanted to see what Devon's conclusion on all of these notes were. The last page of the book was typically blank, but when I turned to it I wasn't surprised to find it riddled with notes. The words he wrote here were as expected; he didn't believe in the Church's god.

Devon's parting words came back into my mind, *if the god your Church worships comes down to help you, then so be it. Otherwise, you'll die here.*

I understood what he meant after seeing his notes. He tested the Supreme because he wanted to believe in him, but couldn't find a logical reason.

"Holy hell ...." Miranda muttered, snatching my attention immediately.

I stood up and walked over to her, looking at the laptop from over her shoulder. "What'd you find?"

She didn't reply and instead let me read the screen. There were lines of text with pictures and diagrams of God's Wall. I read a few lines in silence, shocked by what my cousin was planning on doing.

"Are they insane?" I muttered.

"If this is true ..." she said in a hushed tone.

"I know," I answered. "If this is true, the Prophet will be executed on national television while he gives his speech about how having Adams and Eves in the cities will make them safer. When's he due to go on the air?"

She glanced down at the corner of the laptop where it displayed the time. "In five minutes."

I swore. "We can't get across the entire town in five minutes!"

Miranda stood up. "Let's go, John. I have an idea. It'll be risky and for it to work, we have to move *now*."

I followed her out of the room as she ran down the hall to the building's stairwell. She pulled out her cellphone and started making a call while she bolted up the stairs. We had managed to climb three stories already before Miranda had gotten through to whoever she was calling.

Miranda's voice was filled with urgency. "Vivian? We need your help."

CHAPTER 17

I stood on the edge of the superhighway that ran around the edge of the Lowers and connected into the Uppers. It was constructed so that the important executives who resided in the Uppers could quickly gain access to their factories in the Lowers. It was also five hundred feet in the air, towering over most buildings in the lowers. I was panting and bent over, struggling to regain my stamina after following Miranda. She was panting too, but she was recovering faster than I was. I felt my calf muscles burn slightly from over use, but I knew that they'd repair themselves in less than a minute.

I straightened up and looked back at the way we had come. We'd ran along and jumped from rooftop to rooftop for almost a mile before vertically jumping the last thirty feet up to reach the superhighway. We'd left the Guards' building three minutes earlier.

"Is there no other way?" I asked between pants.

Miranda took a deep breath to regain control over her breathing before answering me. "No. If we inform the Police it would only result in them being killed by Devon or James and forcing the assassination ahead of their schedule. If we play our cards right, we can get to the Prophet ourselves before Devon makes a move."

"No, I mean is there no other way for us to get there?" I clarified.

She looked at me, confused. "What's wrong with this?"

I sighed. "You'll see for yourself soon enough, but Vivian is a terrifying driver."

"How can she a bad driver on the superhighway? The magnetic strips keep you on a single line, so she can go as fast as she wants—"

I interrupted her, "she drives manual."

Miranda blinked at me, finally understanding my hesitation. "Oh."

It wasn't even thirty seconds later when we heard a car's engine and saw a police cruiser race toward us, going well over one hundred miles per hour. Even from this distance, I could tell that it was an all-white car built low to the ground, specially designed for speed on the superhighway. She was driving on the far-right lane, and it wasn't long before the car slammed on the brakes, sliding past us by about ten feet before finally coming to a stop. Miranda walked forward and opened the backseat door and slid in, leaving the door open for me. I followed and closed the door behind me.

Vivian adjusted the rearview mirror until I saw her blue eyes, "Why hello, John. Long time no see."

"Hey, Viv," I replied, feeling a little awkward.

"Sorry to skip the greetings, but we are short on time, Vivian," Miranda cut in.

"That's what I figured, seeing as John doesn't have time to text his best friend," she accused.

I thought about all of her texts that I had been ignoring this past week due to my training. I sighed, "When will I hear the end of this?"

She gave an evil chuckle, "Probably not until death. So where am I going?" Vivian asked as she returned the mirror to its correct position.

"God's Wall, and we need to be there immediately," Miranda answered.

"Rodger," she replied, and I heard the tires squeal as the car suddenly shot forward like a rocket. "Care to fill me in on the emergency?"

"This information is confidential and under no circumstances are you to report this to anyone without direct permission from the Church, understood?" Miranda said.

"Yeah, yeah, I know how that game is played," Vivian responded in a carefree way, but I knew that she would take it seriously.

"We have evidence that the Guards have recruited two rouge

Adams and plan on using them to assassinate the Prophet," Miranda explained.

"Assassinate him? Are they out of their mind?!" Vivian exclaimed, outraged.

"It seems so. We do not know their motives, but the threat is real."

"Why didn't you say so over the phone? I could've tightened security immediately!" Vivian hissed, grabbing her radio on the seat next to her.

"Stop, Viv! Does the police have the ability to stop an Adam?" I retorted.

Her hand froze on the radio, then she pressed a button on the side. "Officers, report in."

The officers responded, each one sounding off their position and that everything was fine.

Vivian's voice sounded over the noise of the radio. "Doesn't the Prophet have Miracle Children to guard him?"

Miranda answered her, "No. Anyone who kills the Prophet would bring the wrath of the Church down upon them. It would mean the end of the Church's protection. Anytime the wall is breached, they would be stuck batting the Outside on their own. No one would be crazy enough to bring that down upon themselves. He has some Miracle Child assistants whose Miracles specialize in non-combative tasks, but they're no match for those two Adams."

"Maybe that's exactly why Devon doesn't think this is such a crazy plan," I stated. "Chicago is one of the few cities that has a stable wall. It's never been breached."

"It's possible."

Vivian cursed suddenly.

"What is it?" I asked, urgency in my voice.

"Every team checked in except for the ones guarding a back stairwell. The rogue Adams must be making their move," Vivian replied.

She reached forward and flipped a switch on her dashboard, activating automatic control. The magnetic coils activated in the tires and we were jerked sharply to the right as the car aligned with the magnetic strips on the highway. I felt the car rapidly increase in speed as Vivian drove faster. She had both hands on the radio, adjusting its frequency.

Finding the frequency she was searching for, she pressed the button the side. "Teo, Mark, what's your status?"

Silence responded.

Vivian swore again and tossed the radio onto the seat next to her. "They were protecting the entrance to the building next to God's Wall."

I looked out the window, taking in my surroundings and trying to get my bearings. I could see the two buildings that were on the side of God's Wall, and at the speed we were going, we'd be close enough to get off the highway in half a minute.

"We'll have to run, John. Building hop like we did before." Miranda said to me.

"The closest building to the superhighway is a hundred feet down. We can't survive that fall," I replied.

"We can, just not uninjured. If we're lucky, we'll still be able to run afterward," she replied.

She was crazy. A hundred-foot drop? We'd have to land flawlessly, distributing the impact throughout our entire body just to avoid death, but she's hoping to still be able to run to God's Wall afterward?

"I'll get you down there," Vivian spoke up.

"How?" Miranda asked.

"Put your seatbelt on."

"Whatever you're planning—" I started.

"Just shut up and do it, John," Vivian ordered.

Miranda buckled on her seatbelt. "It'd be safer to make the descent in a car like this than it would be on our own, John."

Shit. They were both crazy. I was outnumbered, so I put on my seatbelt.

"Ready?" Vivian asked, flipping the switch back down to manual drive.

A shock ran through the car as the magnetics disengaged, and Vivian was pressing hard on the breaks, dropping the car's speed rapidly.

"Ready," Miranda replied strongly, bracing herself.

"Ready," I said, unconfident in this plan.

"Okay," Vivian muttered.

Silence lasted in the car for a couple seconds as Vivian concentrated on her timing. Then she jerked the steering wheel right, and we flew off the edge of the superhighway.

There was a long second where the car seemed to float in the air. The only sound I heard was the engine of the car reviving up as the resistance of the pavement had vanished from underneath it. I managed to suck in two rapid breaths before gravity managed to get its firm grip on the car, and we suddenly lurched downward.

I closed my eyes as we fell and waited for the brutal impact. I heard the car's computer system start beeping as it detected that we were falling and would crash. Airbags suddenly burst out from the side door to my right and from the back of the passenger seat in front of me. I opened my eyes in surprise, trying to get a handle on what was happening. Another activated, springing up from the vacant middle seat between Miranda and I, filling the space between us.

I got a glimpse through the windshield before the airbags completely blocked my vision and guessed that we were only halfway down the descent. A little panicked, I sucked in some deep breaths and felt the muscles in my body tense up as I waited for the inevitable.

We impacted, and my torso was forced forward and down, straight into the airbag in front of me. The airbag absorbed the impact incredibly well considering how far we fell, but I still felt my forehead hit the seat in front of me hard. It gave me an instant headache, and I immediately saw black spots swarm my vision. Even though we landed, we still had the momentum pushing us forward. After bouncing on the roof of one of the buildings and Vivian slamming on the breaks, the car started to slide along the gravel on the roof and into a spin. It didn't last very long before we slammed into the lip of the roof, coming to a halt. I was thrown to my right and my head hit the glass of the window through the airbag.

There was a moment of stillness in the car as I recovered, groaning slightly and touching the spot where my head hit the window. I felt blood, but pulling my hand back and examining it, I saw that I wasn't bleeding that bad. I'd heal in just a few minutes.

"Miranda? Vivian?" I called out, the airbags blocking my vision.

I heard a small *pop* noise, then a hissing sound as the airbag rapidly deflated. Miranda met my eyes, her face showing concern, and I gave her a nod that I was alright in answer to her unspoken question. My eyes drifted over her face and head, searching for any signs that she was hurt. I felt relief when I found none. Now that the airbag was out of my way, I could also see into the driver's seat.

There was blood all over the steering wheel's airbag, and Vivian was clutching her nose. She hadn't made a sound of pain, but her body was tense and I could tell that she was holding back a complaint.

"Vivian?!" I said, worried.

She gave a long groan and shook her head slightly. "It's just a broken nose."

Her voice was slightly muffled from her hands.

"Let me see," I said, shifting forward to get a better look.

"Hang on," she said, stopping me.

She flexed her hands back and forth, setting her broken nose. She gave a loud groan again, then I saw her body slowly become less tense.

She turned to me and removed her hands. "Does it look straight?"

Her face was practically covered in blood. "Yeah. You won't win any beauty pageants for a few weeks, but it'll heal. Are you hurt anywhere else?"

She shook her head, and I saw a small smile start to form on her face. There it was; Vivian had a daredevil side in her.

"That was pretty sweet, wasn't it?" she said, excitement in her voice.

I let out a quick laugh, relieved. If she could make a comment like that, then she was definitely okay.

"John, we need to go," Miranda said as she opened her door.

I looked at Vivian one more time, then followed, scooting over the deflated airbag. Exiting the car, I found Miranda waiting for me.

She took a deep breath and her face slowly turned serious. "This is going to be dangerous, so follow close behind me and mimic my speed and movements. We're high up, so if we judge this wrong we could fall to our deaths."

I nodded and looked toward God's wall, letting the gravity of our situation sink in. There were four buildings between us, and we were four hundred feet from the street. I knew from memory that there was a lot of space between the end of the building and the base of God's Wall. That usually open space was undoubtedly jam packed with people today. The trip would have to be made by cutting through the crowd of people, which could be difficult.

"Let's go," she said, then started running toward God's wall.

I followed behind her as precisely as I could, unsure of how we were going to descend from such a height but trusting that she had a plan. Miranda had increased her speed to the point that I was almost sprinting to keep up with her. The heavy leather cloak I was wearing was slowing me down considerably, but Miranda had the same problem, so why hadn't she removed hers yet?

I saw her jump, leaping toward the other building, but she was easily ten feet from the edge of the building. I didn't have time to figure out why she was doing this before I jumped in the same spot she did, copying the force she used as best as I could.

After I jumped, I knew immediately that we weren't going to make the distance that spanned between the two buildings. I took a panicked breath as I began to fall, following Miranda almost perfectly. I looked down at the four hundred feet of space between me and solid concrete, my mind completely filled with the thought *I am going to die.*

Then I realized that we would collide with the building. I saw a flash of blue light below me as Miranda summoned a pistol to her hand. Three shots rang out in quick succession followed by glass shattering, right before the momentum carried her perfectly into the broken window. She landed in a roll, dispersing the heavy impact into forward momentum. I copied her, feeling the glass crunch harmlessly underneath my thick leather cloak. I only needed to keep my arms tucked into my chest to keep them safe. If I had misjudged that jump by even a fraction, I would've died. No question about it.

The room I was in now was a small office space that had a large desk, a couple of chairs and little else. Miranda had already crossed the room and was wiggling the locked door handle. She took a step back and gave it a solid kick, smashing it open. I followed behind her as we raced down the hallway, feeling adrenaline rush through my veins. I wondered if this was what my life would consist of from now on; jumping through buildings as we rushed to prevent the murder of the most powerful man in the entire world.

I caught my reflection in one of the windows as we turned a corner, and was surprised to see that I had a small smile on my face. Apparently, Vivian wasn't the only one with a daredevil side.

We turned the corner, and I saw that at the end of the hallway was a window through which I could see the next building we would hop into. Miranda sped up to a sprint like she did before. I hesitated barely a moment before matching her pace, making sure that I was at the right distance from her. If I was too close to her when we jumped, I would crash into her when we landed, and if I was too far away from her, I would have a hard time guessing when to jump or how much force to use. Miranda was much better at knowing what a Miracle Child could do; all I had to do was match her.

Two more shots rang out before the glass shattered. She jumped, launching herself out of the window. Again, I mimicked her.

We breached the next building the same way as the first, rolling harmlessly over the glass to disperse the impact of our landing. It was another office building, but the window we'd entered through was one that led us directly into a hallway. I quickly stood up, but Miranda was already starting to run down the hallway and toward the third building. I panted but didn't hesitate to follow after her. On the third leap, we ran into trouble.

Miranda shot out the window, same as she had with the others, but some moron had his desk directly against the glass of the window, so we had to land on his desk and roll off of it. Miranda hadn't managed to move out of the way before I came flying in, so I landed on her when I crashed to the floor in a heap.

"Sorry," I muttered, standing up and helping her to her feet.

She shook her head. "There was no helping it. Let's move. We're out of time."

She rushed forward and kicked the door open, this time not even bothering to check to see if it was locked. We exited the office and started down the hallway, traversing through the building. These three buildings were empty as expected, but I knew the next building, which was the last one before God's Wall, wouldn't be. People often watched the Prophet's speeches from the buildings, that meant that on the far side of the building there would be a large number of people standing between us and the windows.

Miranda and I ran down the hallway, but to my surprise, Miranda led us past the hallway that would've lead us to the opposite side of the building. Instead, I followed her to a door that led into the stairwell.

She didn't hesitate before vaulting over the railings, falling two flights down before catching herself on the railing.

She looked up and shouted over to me, "John, don't fall behind! For all we know they're about to kill him!"

I swallowed and gave her a nod, then backed up and prepared to jump. We were still well over 10 floors up. If I missed, I'd die. I took two more breaths, then vaulted over the edge.

Wind rushed past me and blew my leather coat up above my head, which slowed my descent a little. Hardly a moment passed before I reached out and grabbed the railing. My landing was rougher than I expected, but with my strength it was within my capabilities. Still, it felt like my arms were going to be yanked out of their sockets, and the way my body swung forward and hit the railing was far from Miranda's graceful landing.

I looked down, trying to get an idea of where to go from here, and saw Miranda leaping across the stairwell some five stories below me. She was descending a lot faster than I was, barely hesitating after landing before leaping again. I swallowed, then leaped, pushing hard off the railing and twisting in the air, preparing to catch myself again after descending a couple of floors.

After a couple more tries, I managed to get the hang of catching myself smoothly, timing it so that I'd get my feet in front of me to help absorb the impact. It wasn't exactly easy on my muscles, but I did my best avoid thinking about that. I knew they would be completely healed soon enough.

It only took a few more leaps after that before I could just drop straight down and land next to Miranda, who was shrugging out of her leather cloak. My eyes darted over her figure, enjoying how she looked while also double checking for any injuries that she might've been hiding from me. A second passed before I realized that I was more just checking her out more than I was checking on her health. I forced my eyes off of her as I rebuked myself.

I followed her lead, shrugging out of mine and leaving it on the floor. The only sound in the stairwell was our heavy breathing. It was obvious that I was more out of breath than she was, but I tried to not let my pride be effected by that fact.

She looked over her shoulder at me. "Good?"

"Good," I replied.

"Then let's go," she answered, rushing forward through the door that led into the building.

We ran through the lobby and exited the building, ignoring the looks of the few dozen people that we passed. There were people everywhere on the street crowding toward God's Wall.

"How the hell are we going to get through that?" I panted.

Miranda didn't reply, but I saw her eyes dart over the surroundings as she searched for a plan. I let her think as I scanned our surroundings as well.

God's Wall was a miniature version of the Walls that surrounded the city. While the main Walls were easily a thousand feet tall, this replica was only fifty feet tall, with a sloped base that stretched another twenty feet high. The wall stretched two hundred feet wide between two tall buildings. The left building housed the Chicago Police headquarters, and the building on the right belonged to the Church. The area in front of God's Wall was only ever used for citizens in the Lowers to hear the Prophet's speech. It looked like there was at least three hundred feet of space between us and the base of God's Wall.

On the buildings surrounding God's Wall were a dozen or so huge television screens, displaying the Prophet from several angles. He was dressed all in pure white ropes and spoke in front of a polished wood podium. His voice boomed over the audience, echoing down the streets that connected into this plaza. My eyes darted all around, searching for a route through this mess of people. Then I saw something on one of the televisions that immediately caught my attention.

"Over there!" I exclaimed, pointing at the television that showed the Prophet from his side, revealing the top of God's Wall and the part where it connected into the left building.

It was covered in dark shadow, but I could see movement. Movement that shouldn't be there according to Vivian.

Miranda noticed what I was showing her. "We have to get up there immediately."

"How?" I asked, feeling desperate.

I saw no path that would take us up there in a timely matter.

"We jump up there. I'll boost you, but you can't hold back with the jump, John," she said, her emerald eyes meeting mine with conviction.

I quickly understood what she meant. "Miranda, if I use my full strength ... it could break your arms."

"Do I really look that weak to you?" she asked.

I stayed silent. Not because I was afraid of saying *yes*. It was the opposite. If I said the truth, that I thought she was strong, then I'd have no argument against this plan. I didn't want to hurt her.

A moment passed in silence before she turned toward the Wall. "I'll be fine, John. Let's go."

She took off, and after a second of hesitation, I followed.

There was a line of cars between us and the crowd of people in the plaza, and I saw Miranda hop up onto one of them before crouching down, gathering her strength. I landed on the one next to her and looked at her, wondering what her plan was. She launched, springing forward at a supernatural speed. Her arc was perfect for maximizing distance, and right before she descended into the crowd I saw her twist and straighten out her body, landing between the group of people without landing on anyone. I saw a small commotion as she probably bumped into people after she landed from her momentum, but the grace of her entire performance made the differences between her and I utterly clear. It showed how much experience she had controlling her muscles.

I swallowed and crouched, focusing on the muscles in my legs as I prepared to use as much muscle I could. If I removed all of my metal limits, my muscles would tear themselves from the effort, and there was even a chance that my bones would crack. I also quickly ran through a mental simulation of what I was planning to do. I sucked in several deep breaths, pumping my veins with oxygen and preparing to launch. Then I opened my eyes, and jumped.

I heard the car's windshield crack from my left foot, but it didn't affect the outcome. I twirled my arms around in the air for a quick, panicky moment as I struggled to maintain my aerial balance. I saw rows and rows of people standing in the plaza underneath me as I flew over them. I shouted out to the people below me to move, but they didn't even have time to look up before I came crashing down.

I fell onto several people, who collapsed into a pile on the concrete.

"Sorry!" I shouted as I got to my feet and rushed forward into the crowd.

My leg muscles hurt with every step I took, but I had planned well; they would still have plenty of strength left for the jump up the Wall.

My sense of accomplishment diminished rapidly as I discovered how difficult it was to force my way through this dense crowd. I clenched my teeth and tried harder, using above-human strength to shove my way through the crowd as fast as I could.

"MOVE!" I commanded, startling and upsetting several people, but I was never there long enough for them to do anything about it.

I shouted again, frustrated at my slow progress. I finally got a glimpse of the empty space that spanned between the crowd of people and God's Wall through a small gap in the crowd, and I felt my pace increase out of my anxiety to get through.

It was just a few more seconds of pushing before I made it clear of the crowd. I didn't know how she managed it when I had jumped farther than her, but Miranda was sprinting toward the wall ahead of me. I bolted after her.

God's Wall loomed ahead of me as I got closer and closer; I was terrified that we weren't going to make it.

I reached the base of God's Wall, which turned out to be steeper than it seemed a few hundred feet away, but with my speed and momentum it wasn't difficult to quickly scale up it.

Miranda reached the top of the base right before the Wall actually started, and she immediately turned around and lowered her stance as she got ready to boost me up the wall. She was going to practically throw me up the fifty-foot wall. Even when I accounted for part of my current momentum being redirected into the actual jump, I wasn't sure if I was going to make it.

I steeled myself and speed up, my doubts disappearing as I saw how determined Miranda was. She was confident that I'd make it. I felt my jaw tighten as I prepared to use all of my muscle to launch myself.

I gave a small leap and aimed my foot to land right in the threaded hands of Miranda. My aim was perfect, my pacing was exact, but when it came time to jump, a vivid image of the consequence my jump would have on Miranda disturbed me. I immediately lost my resolve to use that much force against Miranda's brace.

I heard Miranda grunt as her arms absorbed my momentum and she struggled to redirect it upward, but a moment later was catapulted up and away from her. I saw the steel wall race past me as I stared at the top of the Wall—my destination.

I watched the edge of the wall as it got ever closer to be, but I noticed how my momentum was rapidly coming to a crawl. I stretched, feeling a sharp tension on my shoulder as I pushed it to its limit to get a hold of that ledge. I felt my fingertips just get over the smooth edge before gravity started to pull me down.

Pain crushed down on my fingers as they supported my entire weight. I quickly threw my other arm up, and with momentum, I managed to get a better hold.

I sucked in a quick breath as I heard the crowd below me shout out in surprise at my actions. I swung my body to the left and vaulted over the wall. I landed securely and rested my hand against the railing of the top of the Wall, taking in a few deep breaths. I looked to my right at the Prophet, who looked at me with surprised eyes, then moved and refocused on something beyond me. I knew immediately that the assassin was charging at me from the fearful expression that flashed across the Prophet's face.

I could only tell that it was a human in shape, and from its size I guessed that it was a man, but he was completely concealed behind a black, shadow-like fire that danced all over his body. I couldn't see any details about the person it enveloped. The only other detail that I could make out was a long sword, which was also covered in that dark flame. The figure was only a few paces away from us, his sword raised threateningly. I set my feet and held out my hand before using my Miracle.

I willed forth a burst of white fire that launched from my right palm and rushed toward the dark figure.

He reacted by immediately lowering the blade to block my unexpected attack. The flames contacted the solid blade of shadow, but the figure dodged to his left, avoiding the flames. I eyed the figure cautiously as I waited to see what he would do. My flames had eaten away his black shadows and revealed that the sword he wielded wasn't actually made out of that strange darkness as I had thought. The metal blade was now a soft red color from the heat of my flames.

I sensed that the figure was watching me too, carefully anticipating what I was going to do next. Another Adam? How many of these rogue Adam's had Devon managed to find and unite? I took a deep breath and focused my mind on the situation before me, leaving the thinking for later.

The crowd was raising a commotion and I could hear various shots of surprise, but I couldn't afford to take a glance at them. My full focus needed to be on the Adam in front of me.

I knew that if it came down to a fight, I was the inexperienced one. That was explicitly clear during my fight with Devon, but now something was different. I had my Miracle, and I could feel its power giving me strength. I needed to beat this unknown Adam and protect the Prophet, who was a couple of feet behind me. I didn't know what this Adam's Miracle was capable of, but I did know that my flames could eat it away.

I lowered my stance a couple inches and raised my fists, all the while letting my white flames grow. It traveled from my legs up to my torso, and I felt my shoulders start to give off flames of their own. I was covered in white fire, but it wasn't so bright that it blocked my vision. Through the flames, I could see the figure standing still, cautiously observing me. If my flames could eat away his Miracle, then having the flames cover me would be the best protection I could have.

He turned around and bolted away from me. I hesitated a brief moment, surprised. He was running? I took a step forward, about to follow, but then I forced myself to halt and looked back at the Prophet.

If I left him alone, who knows what could happen. What if another attempt was made while I left in pursuit? The Prophet was looking at me in almost wonder. I was surprised for a moment, shocked at why he would make such an expression. Sure, I was on fire, but still.

If he was a normal civilian, I would expect his face to be clouded in fear, not this expression of wonder. He was the Prophet, and must have seen hundreds of different Miracles, why feel wonder at seeing just another Miracle?

His blue eyes stared into mine, and I got overwhelmed with a sense of ... kinship. It was a look of kindness that someone would only use toward a member of their own family. It was intimate in a way. The depth his gaze was the cause of my surprise.

"Chase him, Child," he said, his voice layered with gentle patience, but I detected something odd in his voice ... excitement?

I didn't spend any more time pondering it; there was a more important task at hand.

I turned around and launched myself into pursuit, bringing myself up to sprint in just a few strides. The moment with the Prophet hadn't lasted long, but that was long enough for the figure to have already made it half way along the top of the Wall.

I pushed myself harder, speeding up to gain ground. My strained muscles complained painfully, but I gritted my teeth and ignored it as

I forced my mind to focus completely on my target. As I ran, I realized that my flames had extinguished as my concentration shifted.

He had reached the entrance to the side building, and burst through the double doors that separated the building interior from the top of God's Wall. I was almost on his heels, crashing through the doors just as they were about to close again.

A hallway stretched out in front of me, and I could see the figure still running of me. There was a door to my left that was open, and I glanced inside as I passed. It was a stairwell, and there were two men dressed in police uniforms on the floor. They were laying in a pool of blood, obviously dead. I surged forward, feeling my desire to catch the guy deepen.

I saw the black figure in front of me vanish from sight, and was momentarily surprised, until I felt a gentle pull forward. I recognized this feeling from when I was Outside at the plane crash. This was a part of James' Miracle; a way to teleport people.

I continued forward, not hesitating. I felt the pull on me strengthen as I got closer and closer to this portal—or whatever it was. Then suddenly the pull turned against me as I reached the source. The feeling shifted into a strange crushing feeling, as if an invisible force was pushing on me from all sides. It wasn't especially painful, but it was enough to make the ride uncomfortable. It only lasted a moment before I saw my surroundings morph from the steel hallway to a large, open room.

I only had a second to take in my surroundings, but from the large painted glass windows and the old, cold stone it was easy to tell that I was in an old church. I suddenly noticed three figures were standing in front of me, obviously anticipating that I would be right behind the figure cloaked in that black darkness.

The first was James, who was on the far left of the three. The middle was the unidentified figure I had pursued, but I got the feeling that he wasn't facing me. Though, I couldn't be sure due to him being covered in that darkness. Lastly, on the far right, was a woman I had never seen before.

She was blonde and somewhat cute, with freckles that littered her pale face; it was her brown eyes bothered me. I only had time for a glance, but that was enough to take in her bored, lifeless stare. Even when next to the figure coated in darkness, and James' strange Miracle happening right in front of her, she remained uninterested. My gut was telling me that she was dangerous. I didn't have time to pounder it, for my short moment of peace was over.

His scruffy face broke into a cruel smile as he watched me come out of his portal, and he held up his hand with his palm facing me, as if telling me to stop.

"I don't think so, weakling," I heard him say, then I was suddenly pushed backward into the portal again.

The crushing feeling returned briefly, and then I was catapulted out from the portal, and flew twenty feet down the steel hallway before landing roughly on the floor.

The pull from the portal was gone, and I could only assume that it was closed. I sat up but otherwise remained motionless as my body recovered from my all-out sprint. I was familiar with the physical exertion that sprinting took on my body thanks to my training, but I had pushed myself more than normal, and the result was my calf muscles burning painfully from overexertion. I was panting, but my heart rate was recovering quickly and within just a few moments I was breathing regularly. I was close enough to the stairwell to hear footsteps rushing up them. It sounded as if the person was skipping entire flights of stairs. Only one I knew could do that was Miranda, or some other Miracle Child.

I only hesitated a moment longer before I forced myself to my feet. I didn't want Miranda to see me sitting down when she arrived. I felt a little silly and rebuked myself, but I didn't want her to see me weak or defeated. I felt relieved that my legs weren't shaking as they supported my weight, and I was a little surprised that they were able to recover so much in just a short amount of time. Too bad they still hurt like hell.

I heard Miranda hesitate when she reached my floor, probably in shock at finding the bodies of the police laying there. Then she dashed out into the hallway. She met my eyes briefly before looking around the hallway.

"You okay?" she asked through her light panting.

"I'll live," I responded.

She walked down the hall, approaching me, and I saw her swallow as her breathing slowed down to a regular pace.

"Did he get away?"

At her question, I automatically glanced down the hallway, to where the portal was. For some reason, I felt as if I had failed, and I had trouble looking Miranda in the eye.

"Unfortunately. He escaped through one of James' portals, like the one we saw in the Outside by the plane crash. I followed him, and I saw where they went, but James pushed me back through the portal," I said, summarizing.

She started pacing back and forth, as if she was suddenly irritated.

"Shit," I heard her say, and I had thought she was cursing at the fact that they had gotten away, but then her next action made me think otherwise.

She had turned and walked toward me, and I sensed hostility from her. Instinctively, I took half a step backward, but then I forced my legs to stop retreating as I reassured myself that I had been mistaken; this was Miranda after all. I was still in a state of confusion when Miranda reached me.

Her hands came up and pushed my chest, forcing me backward about six inches before my back hit the steel wall. It didn't actually cause me pain, but I got the very clear message; she was pissed at me.

Her voice was firm, but she wasn't yelling. "Dammit, John!"

"What?" I asked, my mind still trying to make sense of what was happening.

Her expression was one of anger except for her eyebrows, which were furrowed out of concern.

"That's exactly what I'm wondering! What the hell were you thinking!?" she hissed, and she pushed on my chest again, forcing my back to hit the wall again.

"Thinking about what?!" I asked, my voice rising to match hers defensively.

She took a step backward and put her hands on her hips. She looked up to the ceiling and took a few deep breaths to calm herself. I saw her shoulders relax before she looked back at me, meeting my eyes. She took a few steps forward, but I saw gentleness in her movements now. Her anger had vanished. When she reached me, she raised her hands and cupped the back of my head with a soft touch.

"John, you cannot put me before the mission," she stated.

"What are you talking about?" I asked her, suddenly confused.

"You didn't jump with all of your strength back there."

"If I had, your arms would've been broken. I reached the top, didn't I?" I argued.

"Barely!" she stated firmly. "John, let's face it, it was a miracle in and of itself that you managed to get a grip on the top of the Wall. If you hadn't, not only would you have fallen fifty feet, but the Prophet would also be dead."

"But that didn't happen," I stated back.

"No, John, that's not the point. You should've used all your strength. Broken arms are nothing compared to saving the Prophet's life, especially with how fast we can regenerate."

"That's not fair, Miranda. You know me, right? Then you know that I can't stand to see you in pain." Or any girl for that matter. Every time I did, I vividly remembered that rainy night in the ally, and heard Rachel's screams. Though lately, when I was tormented by it, Rachel's screams have been replaced with Miranda's.

"I know, but you need to get over it. If you don't, and we have another situation like this one come up ..." she sighed, "good luck won't always be there for you."

"I don't know if I'll ever be able to 'get over it,' Miranda."

She sighed again, but this time in frustration. "Well you're still an idiot for chasing him through James' portal. Didn't you think about what would happen when you got on the other side? You'd be staring down James, the black figure, and likely Devon. Honestly, when I saw you chase after that figure ... I thought you were going to die."

A brief moment of time lapsed as I processed what she said, and then I asked, "Did I worry you?"

She gave me a look that made it clear she thought I had just asked a stupid question. "That's an understatement. Look, you can't die on me, John. I need you to stay alive. You're my future. Don't pull any more stupid stunts like diving into a portal okay?"

Part of me liked that she was worried for my safety. "It was thanks to my stupid stunt that I know where they teleported to ... but you're right; I didn't think about it like I should've. Any one of them could've been on the other side, just waiting to—"

I cut myself as I realized something, and Miranda noticed my reaction. "What is it?"

"I didn't see Devon anywhere," I stated.

"Grey wasn't there?" she asked.

I shook my head, confused. "No, he wasn't. The only ones were the man in shadow, Dorian, and a girl I hadn't seen before. Could Devon be the one coated in shadow?"

"No, Adam's only have a single Miracle. Besides, why put all that effort into hiding who he is? We already knew he's involved," she argued.

"Not necessarily. He probably thought we were dead," I countered.

She shook her head. "No, if he was truly concerned about us knowing about him, he would've made sure that we were dead. He wouldn't have left us with a chance of survival. He's smarter than that."

I couldn't argue with that. I saw how careful he was with his planning, so something still didn't add up.

"Why leave us with a chance for survival anyway? Even if he wasn't concerned with us knowing he's involved, why wasn't he concerned about us stopping him?" I asked.

Miranda parted from me, taking a step backward and crossing her arms thoughtfully.

I thought over my conversation with Devon, and his words replayed in my mind.

Even if these two escaped right now, they would not be able to prevent what is to come.

"He had faith that we had no power to stop the Prophet's assassination," I stated.

"But why? What did he think was so powerful that our presence did not matter?" she asked.

I thought about it again, and this time I remembered what James had said to Devon.

I do not serve you, Devon Grey, but someone much more powerful than you.

"What if he had his faith placed in a person?" I asked, "James had mentioned that he served someone stronger than Devon."

"I remember that, but to whom was he referring?"

I shrugged. "The figure in black?"

She frowned a little, as if she wasn't convinced. "It's possible, but … I don't know, he seemed a little underwhelming to be someone that could keep a person like James in line."

"This also doesn't fully explain why Devon would be so confident. If his faith really was in the shadowy person, why would Devon think he's unstoppable?" I questioned.

"It could be that he is; unless he's up against fire," she suggested.

I frowned, not liking that conclusion. It seemed too convenient for us.

"Where did you see them go?" she asked.

"I don't know the exact location, but it was definitely in an old church. There were painted windows and old stone," I explained.

"Well, there's a few places that could be. Luckily for us, you had Zachariah follow him. Let's touch base with him and see what we can figure out."

CHAPTER 18

My phone rang just as I was getting in the car. I saw that it was Vivian, so I answered it without hesitating.

"Viv?" I said in greeting.

"Thank GOD! Are you okay?! I saw what you just did—chasing after him was incredibly dangerous—are you stupid?!" her tone changed after each sentence, morphing from worry to relief, and then from relief to anger.

"Yeah, I'm fine," I replied after holding the phone a little way from my ear.

I vaguely took in the details of the car's interior, noticing that it was different from the other car that Zachariah drove earlier. He must've switched before picking us up, because this one had much more space in the back. It held two rows of seats, and one of them was backward so that they faced each other. There was a sheet of glass separating the back from the front, and it was slightly tinted. I glanced up at the rear-view mirror to confirm my suspicions; the window was only one way, which prevented Zachariah from seeing us. Miranda had taken a seat on the front row. I just took a seat across from her automatically, since my attention was focused on Vivian.

Miranda was also on her phone, but she was talking to Paladin Samson. She had just finished updating him with our situation, and now she was quiet, obviously listening to his instructions on how we should proceed.

"Oh. Good," Vivian replied, then I heard her give a sigh of relief. "How about Miranda?"

"The same," I answered her. "How about you? You got checked out after that car crash, right?"

I heard her make a *tsk* noise with her tongue, obviously annoyed. "They made me ... I told them I was fine but they're convinced I might have a concussion. I'm imprisoned here until they run a test."

"I know you hate hospitals, but that crash wasn't anything you should just brush off," I told her, my tone serious.

Miranda cleared her throat gently, getting my distracted attention. She was still on the phone, but she patted the leather seat next to her, signaling me to sit with her.

I met her eyes curiously, trying to discern her intentions. Her invitation made me curious; if she wanted to sit next to me she was the type who would get up and sit next to me, invited or not. Her green eyes were not as they normally were, and that completely captured my attention. Miranda was normally calm, confident, and undaunted by almost anything, but she'd have moments of insecurity. In those moments of shyness, she's not sure how I'll respond to her actions, but it's obvious to me what wants. In those short, rare moments, I was utterly drawn to her. She was always beautiful, and I did like her confidence, but the way her eyes were looking at me now was exquisite.

The mystery I was always struck with, however, was what brought on these moments of, well, pure beauty. What goes through her head that makes her look at me the way she does now? If I knew what was behind these brief but beautiful moments, I was sure I would trigger them as often as I could.

"Hello?" Vivian said, and I realized that she just asked me something.

"Sorry, what?" I replied.

I moved forward and sat next to Miranda, so that she was on my right. I switched the phone to my left ear automatically, so Miranda wouldn't feel cut off.

"I asked you what you were going to do now," she repeated.

"Oh. We're going after them," I replied simply.

I felt Miranda's touch as she grasped my hand and threaded her fingers between my own. I looked over at her, meeting her eyes and seeing her small smile. She was no longer on the phone, which surprised me for a moment since I hadn't heard her end it. She leaned forward and rested her forehead against my shoulder. I felt her silky hair brush against my arm. Her thumb rubbed gently against my hand.

"John!" Vivian said, this time slightly annoyed that I wasn't paying attention.

"Uh, sorry, Viv. Miranda's distracting me," I replied, pushing the blame onto Miranda.

Vivian sighed. "Look, I know you got crazy fire superpowers now and superhuman strength and everything, but you're still only human, okay? Basically, be careful."

I took a deep breath. "Okay. I will. Thanks, Viv."

Part of me wondered if what she said was true. Was I still human?

"Sure. I got to go now, but call me later? I'd feel better knowing everything went well."

"I will. Bye, Vivian."

"Talk to you later, John," she answered, then hung up.

I lowered my phone as Miranda spoke, "Are you sure you two are nothing more than friends?"

I was surprised at her question, but I tried to conceal it as I answered, "Sometimes I think we're more than that."

Miranda looked up at me, meeting my eyes with a surprised expression. There was another emotion there as well, but it was hard to identify. Worry? Concern? I couldn't be sure.

"Sometimes I think she's the older sister I never had," I clarified with a small smile.

Her surprise expression flickered into annoyance. "You tease."

I chuckled. "Jealous, are we?"

"What if I was? I believe it's a natural emotion when I hear you speak affectionately to a woman other than me," she replied.

I raised an eyebrow. "I didn't say anything affectionate."

"It wasn't the words you choose but the tone that you said them in," she replied in an accusing voice.

"Well, I can't help that. You know what she means to me," I replied.

She hummed in agreement. "I do. For the past few years, she's been your only friend and confidant. And the only other person in this world who had a connection to Rachel. I understand your feelings toward her perfectly."

"And you still feel jealous?" I asked.

"Of course. Wouldn't you if our roles were reversed?"

I thought about it, and immediately frowned. She was right, I probably would.

Miranda noticed my frown, "See?"

I did. "Still, you don't have to be worried. There's nothing between Vivian and I."

"Worried? Why would I be worried?" she said in a sudden, almost bewildered tone.

I blinked, a little taken-aback by her reaction, "Well—you know …."

Her face relaxed into a smile and she leaned forward. Her expression was utterly charming. "I believe I've told you before, but I have no problem repeating this; you are mine. You are my Adam, and have been ever since your blood entered mine—accident or not. That's something no other woman has, so what should I be worried about? Or is this your way of telling me you're planning on joining with another Eve?"

Her strong eyes flickered into a mischievous gaze as she teased me, but I found myself so drawn in by her that it took a few seconds before I could respond.

Eventually, I was able to think again. "It's possible for an Adam to have more than one Eve?"

"Possible, yes, but it's forbidden by the Church," she answered.

"Moral reasons?"

She shook her head, "As Miracle Children, we're not bound by the Church's laws, since we are forgiven by the Supreme."

Damn, I knew that. I momentarily felt like an idiot.

"So then why is it forbidden?" I asked.

"If an Adam has two Eves, those Eves are immune to his Miracle, and he immune to theirs, but the Eves are not immune to each other. Additionally, it's very likely that drama and conflict would result in the group—which would be detrimental to the combat effectiveness of the team. So, the Church feels that it's too risky for an Adam to have more than one Eve."

"So basically, I'm stuck with you," I summarized.

She raised an eyebrow. "Is it really so horrible?"

I put on a show of thinking deeply. "Well ... that's debatable."

She laughed challengingly. "Oh really?"

I nodded. "Yeah. See, you put me through three weeks of physical torture, and I have to deal with the Break Phenomenon—like talk about high maintenance."

She broke eye contact and looked down, showing guilt, but her small smile didn't leave her face, so I knew she understood that I was joking.

"But then again, you're gorgeous and a great kisser, so that's a positive."

She replied in a playful tone, "Is that all I am to you, a pair of lips to kiss?"

I knew she hadn't meant to, but her question sobered our playful atmosphere. To be more accurate, her question turned my mind from flirtatious to serious reflection. I was in deep. I knew this, especially when she had almost died right in front of me. It wasn't love, but at this rate it wouldn't long. How many hours had I actually spent with Miranda? A week's worth?

No, it was less than that. She was practically a stranger, but I knew I was willing to die trying to protect her life. She had my loyalty and had captivated my interest in a remarkably short time. I felt that something was wrong; it was as if this was too good to be true. I was falling for her, but I knew nothing about her.

"No," I replied after a moment's hesitation.

Her gaze suddenly felt too strong for my eyes to bear, so I looked away out the window. I saw the superhighway, but I didn't process any of it. My mind felt torn, as if I was trying to think in several directions at once, and in the end thought of nothing at all. The only thing that I could concentrate on was a single question I kept asking myself; *what did Miranda mean to me?*

I could sense Miranda close the gap between us, but I couldn't muster the courage to look at her. I felt her soft lips press against my neck once, then she whispered to me, close enough that I felt her warm breath on my skin.

"I'm sorry."

My surprise shook me out of my dazed state, and I met her eyes in confusion. She was so close to me that it was almost difficult to focus on her eyes.

She continued, "I know that we're in two different places. I feel as if I've known you for years, but to you I am unfamiliar. It's an easy thing for me to forget, so sometimes I overstep ... I know you're not ready yet, so I shouldn't have said something like that."

No. She was wrong, and that was rare for Miranda. I wasn't acting this way because I wasn't ready to feel romantic feelings toward her. I was acting this way because I was more than ready—almost anxious even—to love her, but that feeling was what made me hesitate. Those feelings ... it was too fast, wasn't it? Shouldn't it be built up with trust over time?

Miranda leaned away from me after giving small smile. "I'll be patient."

I only hesitated for a moment before I leaned toward her, returning to how we were moments earlier and staring into her eyes. "Maybe you don't have to be."

Her green eyes changed as her caution melted into what I could only describe as desire. She advanced slowly, but every inch that her face moved toward mine was an inch that I pulled back, a little surprised by the change in her. Her strong gaze never wavered as they looked into mine, and she only stopped advancing when I had nowhere else to retreat to. I was cornered, but I wasn't against where this was leading.

"If I don't have to be patient, then I won't be," she whispered sensually, and her tone was one I hadn't heard her speak before. It was soft, confident, and excited, but also smooth and controlled. Her tone alone made my blood quicken as it raced through my veins.

She tilted her head as her eyes started to close, and she resumed her advance, making it clear that she was about to kiss me.

I was suddenly hyper aware of Miranda, and only aware of Miranda.

Where I was? I had no idea. Where I was going? Didn't matter. What had happened earlier that day—all of it was pushed aside as my mind focused solely on Miranda's presence.

I inhaled her scent as I noted that, while it was normally a subtle and gentle scent, was now intoxicating. Her crimson hair had been let down from her pony tail before we got in the car, but her hair stayed out of her face, for once being in obedience. She had her hand on the seat next to my waist, which was supporting her as she leaned into me. In my daze, I grabbed her elbow and couldn't ignore the smooth skin and the warmth of it. My other hand was already on her neck, threading my fingers through her hair on the back of her head as I slowly pulled her toward me.

Our moment, however, was suddenly broken with a sudden appearance of two people in the seats across from us. I didn't have time to recognize who they were before I acted out of reflex, raising my hand and readying myself to release a wave of white fire at the intruders. Miranda's hand grabbed my arm and pulled it down, stopping me from acting. Only then did I realize that these invaders weren't hostile.

"Uh … sorry," Anastasia said, her eyes darting to the side.

They were in an odd position. It was as if Benjamin was carrying Anastasia princess-style before taking a seat across from us. Anastasia carefully slid off Ben and sat next to him on his left. At the same time, Miranda suddenly retreated from me. This I had expected, but not her reaction afterward. She was still sitting just a couple inches away from me, but she put her hands in her lap and had her eyes glued to the floor. Her cheeks were tinted red from embarrassment. I couldn't help but find her entire reaction incredibly adorable.

I watched her with a small smile on my face before I noticed

Ben watching me from the corner of my eye. I turned, and he gave me a nod of approval, as if he agreed with my response to Miranda's adorableness.

"We have horrible timing ..." Anastasia said, her tone apologetic. Even though she had spoken aloud to the entire group, I had a feeling that she was mostly apologizing to Miranda.

"Really?" Ben said in disagreement. "I think if we were any later it'd only have been worse."

"Well ..." Ana replied, not disagreeing.

Miranda cleared her throat, recovering from her moment of embarrassment. "I hadn't expected you two to teleport directly into the car. It was my understanding that the plan was to pick you up a little farther along the highway."

"Yeah, well, I thought I would just skip a step," Ben said, this time his words were slightly apologetic.

I felt the car decrease in speed then, slowing down even though we weren't across town near the old church yet. Miranda knocked on the window behind us, and a moment later the window rolled down half way.

"Yes, ma'am?" Zachariah asked.

"We have already picked up the others, no need to stop. Continue to the Church," Miranda instructed.

A moment of confusion crossed his face, but he recovered quickly and replied, "Will do."

Before the window was closed again, Miranda asked him to hand her something that was on the front passenger seat. When she had turned back around to face the rest of us, she was holding a tablet.

Still confused as to what was going on, I looked from Ben to Ana and asked, "So where did you two come from exactly?"

Ben shot me a grin and pointed a finger up. Not understanding, I looked to Ana for clarification.

"We skydived over the city, using Ben's Miracle to teleport us safely down here. It saved us the time it takes to land, as well as having to be picked up from the airport. It's one of the reasons why we were selected to assist you on this mission."

"That, and because these two are considered a powerhouse," Miranda added.

I raised an eyebrow, silently wondering how dangerous that made them. The power of Miracle Children was already outrageous ...

"So, you knew that they were joining us?" I asked Miranda, keeping my tone free from accusation. I merely wondered why she hadn't told me.

"Yeah, I was going to brief you but ..." she trailed off, and I got the picture.

A short moment of silence followed before Ben turned to Ana and asked, "How come our briefing sessions aren't that fun?"

Ana shot him an annoyed look from the corner of her eye as Miranda cleared her throat, a failed attempt to hide her slight embarrassment.

I found myself suddenly captivated by Miranda; I had just found out something new about her. She had always been forward and unashamed about the physical aspect of our relationship. I realized that she was only that way when we were alone. I supposed it was the natural reaction; she had told me that she wasn't used to physical contact.

"Anyway, we should get right to it. We'll be there in just a few minutes," Miranda stated before reaching up and slipping the tablet snugly into a horizontal holder on the ceiling of the car that I hadn't noticed before now. The camera on the back of the tablet was pointed toward the floor, and after a slight delay, it lite up and displayed blueprints onto the car floor between the two seats.

"You both have been brought up to speed on the situation, right?" Miranda asked as they studied the blueprints.

Ana nodded while Ben replied, "Yeah, we saw the clip. You guys did great trying to stop it, especially with Miracles that didn't suit the situation."

"Well, we can't all have such a convenient Miracle as you," Miranda replied.

He gave her a smirk before looking back at the blueprints.

"Hmm ... is this all we have to work with?" he asked aloud.

"This is the entirety of the building," Miranda answered. "This is the front, with only a small hallway separating the entrance from the main sanctuary. These are the back rooms here, and there's no back exit."

Ana eyed the blueprints carefully. "I'm surprised that this building hadn't been demolished when Chicago joined the Church. The Church doesn't allow any other religious practices or symbols."

"It's the Lowers," I answered. "Do you really think the city would spend their limited budget on demolishing some building no one cares about when the building will decay and fall apart in time?"

"Fair point," Ben stated.

Miranda looked to me. "What part of the building did you see them in?"

I pointed to the sanctuary. "Here. I'm positive. No other room is big enough to be it."

"How long ago?" Ana asked.

I looked at my phone for the current time before answering, "Roughly twenty minutes ago."

"Damn, they could be long gone by now," Ben said.

"But if an enemy Adam has a Miracle of teleportation, then it could be an entire city altogether," Ana surmised.

"That is a possibility, yes," Miranda agreed.

"Okay, so what's the plan?" Ben asked.

Miranda took a deep breath. "Even though you both have the most combat experience and undoubtedly have better teamwork than us, I think it's best for us to go up against the man in shadow."

"What's your reasoning?" Ana asked.

"It's a hunch of mine, but I think John's Miracle is highly suited to fight him," Miranda answered, confidence in her voice.

I felt unease wash through me. I tried to not let it show, but I wasn't sure if I had succeeded. Miranda was betting on me, and now I had to step up. I couldn't just follow behind her this time.

"Okay, then we'll handle the other two," Ben stated as Ana gave a firm nod.

"There could be a fourth," I stated, assuming that the two they were counting were James and the other girl I saw earlier.

"You saw only two besides the man in shadow, right?" Ana asked me.

"He's thinking of another Adam we fought against earlier today. He's the leader of the Guards, Devon Grey, and his Miracle seems to be able to summon and control ice. He's definitely a part of this group and also seemed to be the one who planned the attack on the Prophet, but it isn't confirmed that he's present at the church," Miranda explained.

I leaned back in my seat, having memorized the simple blueprints. "He also coats his skin in ice, and it's strong enough to stop a bullet at point blank range. His ice is also cold enough to burn you on contact."

Ana leaned back in her seat as I had, and started twirling a strand of her blond hair around two of her fingers, clearly thinking.

"How has the Church missed these Miracle Children? Everyone is tested at birth, and tested again when they reach adulthood," Ana pondered.

"That's exactly what I'll be looking into after this is over," Miranda stated.

There were a few knocks on the glass window behind Miranda and me, capturing all of our attention. Zach held his hand in front of the window with three fingers raised, signaling the three-minute mark.

Ben rested his ankle on his knee, while Ana crossed her legs. They both seemed relaxed and at ease, but after a second look I realized I was mistaken. Ben's right index finger was twitching as he rapidly tapped his thigh, and Ana was subtly biting her cheek. Were they actually worried about what was to come?

"Tell us about James Dorian," Ben's voice was natural and clear, but his finger hadn't stopped twitching.

Miranda cleared her throat. "His Miracle is unidentified. As you know, he possesses some form of telekinesis and teleportation ability, but we have no theory as to what it actually is."

I could feel the tension in the car start to rise every second that we got closer to the church.

"Well, I have been thinking about that, I have a theory," I spoke up.

All three of them looked at me as I continued. "I think he can manipulate gravity."

"I considered that, but it doesn't explain his teleportation Miracle," Miranda responded.

"What if it's not teleporting?" I suggested.

She gave me a curious look.

"What if he's using intense gravity to forcibly connect two points of space?" I suggested.

"Like a wormhole? Damn, that'd be an incredibly powerful Miracle," Ben said.

"It's a bad theory though, since gravity doesn't really work like that," I confessed.

"No, but that's only because of our limited understanding of the universe," Ana explained. "For instance, my Minor is the manipulation of air, or to create wind, basically. However, I can do things with this wind that doesn't make since according to what we have attempted to explain through science. I can pressurize air to the point that it is able to cut through a variety of materials that shouldn't be possible—such as steel or other metals. What I'm trying to explain is that for Miracle Children, the general rules of the sciences do not apply to us, because we end up breaking them."

"I see," I responded.

Ben spoke up next, "if he really does have the Miracle of gravity, it would probably take both of us to take him out."

Ana nodded in agreement.

"Okay, then you two handle him, and I will handle whatever else appears in our way—whether it's the unknown Eve or Devon. John, you focus on getting to the man in shadow," Miranda said.

I took a deep breath, "Okay."

I looked down at my open hand that rested on my lap as I contemplated the task that was ahead of us. I was being asked to fight against the man in shadow, who's abilities were unknown and who wouldn't hesitate to kill me. Did I have the strength to protect Miranda from that? I knew Miranda was stronger than me, and that she could take care of herself, but it was impossible for me not to feel as if I should be her shield.

I felt Miranda's shoulder bump into mine as she leaned against me, and I looked up into her gentle eyes. I was reminded of what she said to me after I had foolishly chased the man in shadow through James' portal.

You can't die on me, John.

"I won't," I muttered softly to her.

She blinked, momentarily surprised, then her face melted into a small, yet enchanting smile as she rested her head on my shoulder.

"I won't if you won't," I stated, again softly.

"Deal," she whispered back.

I felt the car slow, coming to a stop. I frowned as a feeling of nervousness washed over me. Those three minutes went by practically instantaneously. Miranda raised her head from my shoulder and looked at the two sitting across from us, who were staring into each other's eyes.

"Ready?" Miranda asked, her voice serious.

They gave her a quick nod in response.

"Good. Let's go," she said, and we exited the car, each of us prepared for the worst.

CHAPTER 19

It was a lot darker than it should have been for this time of day. The sun was setting, sure, but the dark grey clouds that covered the sky also dampened the last of the sunlight. The street we were walking down was old and neglected, with wide cracks and deep pot holes in the cement. We moved forward at a steady pace. No one had said a single word since we left the car a few moments ago. Tension thick in the air between us as we steadily advanced closer and closer to the old church, which loomed some fifty yards ahead of us. Ben was on the far left, walking forward with his hands in his pockets, seemingly relaxed, but I could see that the muscles in his shoulders were tensed.

Ana walked next to him, but she didn't bother trying to play it causal as she walked with a pistol in each hand. Her eyes focused completely on the church in front of her. Miranda and I walked a few feet behind them and on the opposite side of the street. Miranda was walking so close to me that my hand would sometimes bump against hers. She had her twin silver swords grasped tightly in her hands, and I could tell without even looking at her that she was as focused.

Part of me wondered what the hell I was doing here. A month ago, I was a nobody—a face amongst a million others within the Lowers. Now I'm calmly walking toward a fight against Miracle Children that wouldn't hesitate to kill me. I wasn't sure if my life had improved or if it had all gone downhill.

I was very calm, but I knew that I shouldn't be. I didn't feel fear, or anxiousness, or any emotion really. I was a pool of water that lay completely still, and nothing was going to disturb that peace. It was an illogical feeling, but I couldn't shake it. Even the thought of death didn't so much as ripple my emotional balance. I didn't have time to ponder the reason I felt this way, and shifted my mental focus into observing my surroundings for any sign of our enemies.

The old church was a large building, probably stretching three stories high if you included the height of its odd pyramid towers that marked the corners of the building. It had a single entrance, with a large entry way where a set of double doors once were, but had been torn off their hinges. It was probably made of wood and someone tore them off long ago to sell. The stone was very dark, especially in the low light from the overcast sky. I could see old traces of etchings and designs that were carved into the stone decoratively, but time had eroded them down into an ugly misrepresentation. The holes that riddled the stained-glass windows and the missing chunks of stone added to the eerie feeling that it gave. The entire building was surrounded with a wrought iron fence that ended at two stone pillars, which marked the entrance. The sight of the building made me uneasy. I was sure that this building looked elegant and beautiful at one time, but now, I got a sober feeling from it—as if I was walking into a graveyard. It was like the building itself was dying.

I expected us to stop and survey the surroundings before stealthily or cautiously entering the fenced area, but the other three didn't even hesitate before walking between the two stone pillars. I knew that they were on full alert, but it still surprised me to see them being so rash. Perhaps this was the confidence of a Miracle Child raised in the Church.

The fenced area was pretty much just a courtyard of stone, which was riddled with cracks from age. There was about fifty feet between the entrance to the courtyard and the church.

The wrought iron fence continued around the church, leaving about fifteen feet of space between it and the side of the church.

I suddenly felt a shiver run down my spine as my body unconsciously reacted to a danger. I came to an immediate halt as my body locked up. The other three had stopped just as I had, obviously experiencing a similar feeling. My gaze darted around the courtyard, searching for danger.

I suddenly felt a huge pull on my body, forcing it immediately to the ground, as if gravity had suddenly turned vicious. My mind was blank for as I struggled to understand what was happening to me, but I recovered quickly and took stock of my surroundings. I was being pinned down on my stomach painfully, and I could see that Ana and Ben were sharing a similar fate. But with my head turned to my right, I couldn't tell if Miranda was affected. I tried to twist my head over to look at her, but the force was too strong for me to move.

I saw James Dorian step out from behind the corner of the church, wearing the only type of smile I could ever picture on him; a cruel one.

"Hm, there more of you then I was expecting. No matter."

I gritted my teeth as I struggled to think of a way to get free. I knew I could probably move if I used my strength as an Adam, but I knew that if I did I wouldn't be in top form to fight against the man in shadow. This was Ana and Ben's battle, I needed to let them handle it, but what could they do?

I saw Ben attempt to get up, using purely raw muscle, but James didn't let that go unnoticed.

"No, please, don't get up," he said, poorly restraining a malicious chuckle as he increased the force that was keeping us down.

Now it was so strong that it was difficult for me to even draw in a breath of air. Ben had immediately returned to the ground, not being able to fight against the strength of this push. I saw a flash of blue light from Ana, and then she slowly stretched her arm toward Ben. I only caught a glimpse of something small and green in her hand before Ben touched it, and it immediately vanished.

Now I understood why Ben had tried to push himself up when he could've just teleported away; it was to get his arm in a better position to reach Ana.

My eyes flashed at James and saw the small green object, which I now recognized to be a grenade, drop to the ground just a few feet behind him. The grenade made an audible clunk as it landed on the hard, stone ground, and James noticed.

The pressure holding us down vanished as quickly as it had appeared. In its sudden absence, I sucked in a breath too quickly and choked on air. I coughed and closed my eyes, preparing for the blast of the grenade, but not before seeing James turning to face it.

The grenade went off with an incredible boom that immediately dulled my hearing and made my ears ring. I felt my bones vibrate from the sound wave, and even though it only lasted for a moment, the effects it had on my body were surprising. I forced my eyes open to get an understanding of my surroundings, but it took several moments before they could focus on anything. I saw smoke and a cloud of dust where the grenade had detonated, but I couldn't see James at all.

Ana had already stood up, with her pistols aimed at the last place James had been. She started to unload, firing the heavy pistols at a rapid rate. She ceased firing with the one in her right hand. With a series of flashes of blue light, her pistol was replaced with what could only be a rocket launcher. Ben reached over and touched it before teleporting away. As soon as he had gone, Ana had her other pistol back in action.

I felt Miranda grab my wrist and pull me to my feet. My reflexes were good enough that it didn't affect my movement, but still I felt off balance and even a little dizzy. Miranda half pulled me away from Ana and toward the entrance to the old church.

My hearing returned in time to hear her say, "We have our own fight to get to, so stay with me."

I took a breath and shook my head, clearing the shell-shocked feeling I was experiencing and forced myself to focus on the situation at hand. I increased my pace so that I was no longer being pulled behind her. I looked over when I saw the dust suddenly forced down to reveal James; he was unhurt and wearing an excited smile. The bullets that Ana was shooting at him didn't seem to connect, but there was no way that she was simply missing him.

I heard a small explosion above us that I knew must have been from the rocket launcher, but my eyes still jumped up to see Ben free falling some eighty feet up, aiming the launcher down at James. I reacted instinctively, turning and grabbing Miranda before crouching down, shielding her with my body.

Another explosion detonated even louder than the first. I felt my ears ring in a high pitch and my body vibrate from the sound wave, but the dazed effect didn't happen again, probably because adrenaline was now pumping vigorously through my veins.

Miranda didn't hesitate to stand back up, and I didn't either. We made it to the entrance way, and we took several strides inside before coming to a halt. I noticed as we passed that the doorway was curiously coated with water, but I didn't have time to ponder it.

The room we were standing in now was a small entrance hall, more wide than deep. The room was lit by a couple of lightbulbs that were dangling from the ceiling, but they weren't bright enough to illuminate the room. The room was empty, and there was only a single doorway in the middle of the side wall that led into the sanctuary, but it was currently covered with a slab of ice.

Standing in front of this door was Devon Grey, patiently waiting for us. I heard a strange sound behind us, and glancing behind me I saw ice slowly climbing its way over the doorway, blocking our exit.

Grey took a steady breath. "I had not expected to see either of you alive again. I assume it was John's Miracle that allowed you to escape."

I crouched slightly, preparing my leg muscles to move at a moment's notice. Miranda was currently taking several paces to my left, putting space between us and almost cornering Grey.

"That's right," I replied simply. Do we strike him immediately, or try to acquire some information from him first?

He didn't respond right away, but instead gave me a very cold stare.

Then he said, "John, you are to proceed alone. Someone wants a second meeting with you. Miranda, you shall be my opponent."

"What's stopping us from fighting you together?" Miranda asked sternly.

"This is your only chance to reach the man who attempted to take the life of the Prophet. In comparison, I am hardly a prize, and I'm sure that's how the Church will view it. We did not loiter around here after our location had been discovered to be put at a disadvantage with numbers."

I glared at him. "Then why not escape while you had the time?"

"Who says we need to escape from anything?" he shot back. "We will test our strength against the Church, and we will prove our dominance."

"I'm not splitting from John," Miranda spoke immediately, and I restrained my surprise at her words.

It was originally our plan to separate—for me to take on the man in shadow. Why was she protesting?

"Then you shall gain no insight to the identity of the one who tried to kill the Prophet," Devon replied.

Miranda exhaled angrily from her nose, glaring at Devon murderously. She looked over at me then, her expression one of worry. I gave her a slow nod in response.

"Fine," she responded, speaking to Devon without looking at him, "I'll just make short work of you, and then join John afterward."

"No," Devon answered, a small smile spreading on his lips, "you won't go join them until you're called."

Miranda's gaze left my own and met his, surprised.

He walked to his left slowly, no longer blocking the path, and stopped a couple paces away.

"John," he said, signaling me with his hand that I should approach the frozen doorway.

I gave Miranda a questioning look, and she answered with a confident nod. I cautiously walked up to the frozen wall, keeping a careful eye on Devon. The ice began to part, as if it was being melted away, except that there was no water left behind. It left an opening wide enough for me to fit through, but it didn't go all the way to the other side, so I couldn't see what was behind. I took a deep breath, then walked forward.

The ice kept parting as I approached it, and after a few paces I glanced back behind me to confirm a suspicion. The ice was reforming after I had passed it—I was going to be trapped once I got through this small tunnel of ice.

The entire tunnel wasn't very long—less than ten feet even—and on the other side was the massive sanctuary. It was barely lit, making it very difficult for me to make out many details, and that only further put me on edge. The man in darkness would blend into the long shadows perfectly. I took a deep breath and prepared myself for the fight against this mystery Adam.

CHAPTER 20

Something was wrong. I had no idea what it was, but as soon as I had entered I had an unmistakable feeling of danger. Yet, I couldn't make out anything that would make me feel endangered. The room was large, longer than it was wide. Unlike the last room, this one was lit by very dim candle-light. There were only a few candles long the walls, and a couple on stands along the pathway from the doors to the pulpit. There were no pews, undoubtedly looted along with the doors.

The stained-glass windows that littered the ceiling where missing large chunks, undoubtedly from vandals, and revealed some of the cloudy night sky. The only strong source of light was the pulpit at the end of the sanctuary. There were several dozens of them, lining the stairs up to the pulpit and covered a statue at the back of pulpit. The statue was made of a white marble and depicted a man in a robe, spreading his arms out in a welcoming gesture. The lack of pews and furniture gave the place an empty feeling. A lonely atmosphere coated the thick air, and was emphasized by the dim, scentless candles.

I was about to take a step down the main isle toward the pulpit when I had finally noticed him. He was standing a few paces in front of the marble statue, and even though he was clothed in that deep, dark shadow, I could tell he had his back to me.

I could tell that there was something different about him then the last time I chased him along the wall. The darkness he wore had a different texture. Instead of being a black fire, it was more solid, and it clung to him as if it was his own skin. Looking at it strained my eyes. I couldn't see his skin, but it was obvious how built he was from the outline of the black shadow. He was broad, muscular, and powerful. Perhaps it was the atmosphere of this place, but facing him this time was utterly different then atop the wall. On the wall, I was cautious, wary of his unknown Miracle, but this time, the feeling he gave me was far from merely cautiousness. It was fear.

All I could do was stare at him for several seconds as I wondered if confronting such a being was the right move. I swallowed, and forced my legs to move forward, walking cautiously toward him. I had no choice; Ana, Ben, and Miranda all were fighting their own battles, so I had to do the same.

I got half way down the sanctuary before he titled his head, reacting to my footsteps. My feet locked up, and I had a sudden feeling of absolute, ice-cold dread wash through me. If I fought against this man I would lose, and I would die. I stood there, staring at him with wide eyes.

He spoke a single word, but his voice was so distorted that it made my gut twist, sickened. I felt a cold shiver slide down my back.

"Johnathon ...."

His voice was deep, and it almost came out in a growl, but I could hear the emotion in it; the impatience, the excitement ... it was as if he had been waiting a lifetime to meet me.

"Who are you?" I asked automatically, shocked that he knew my name.

"I am Vice. You may call me that."

"How do you know my name?" I asked.

He turned to face me, and I suddenly felt a flash of fear. I couldn't see his face fully, but the slithering shadows left a gap big enough to see his mouth, which was spread wide with a grin of excitement.

"Johnathon, we are connected by a fate you haven't even begun to comprehend. We are destined to fight, destined to clash and destined to kill one another. Now, show me."

Connected how? I had no idea what he was trying to say, but I was getting a feeling that something was extremely wrong here.

"Show you?" I muttered; I couldn't look away from his twisted smile.

"Show me, John! Show me a Miracle!"

His voice had risen to an excited, commanding shout. He raised his hand out to me, his palm up and his hand tensed, gesturing me to obey. I didn't respond. I had taken a step back, as if my body was prepared to turn and run. I forced myself to stand in place as my mind sluggishly tried to plan what I should do.

Why? Why was he so excited to face me? Why did he know my name? Why was I overwhelmed with this paralyzing fear?

"Fine. I shall force it out of you," he stated, and I could hear a disappointed tone, even though his voice was distorted.

His hand twisted around so that his palm faced me, and out of it leapt a massive stream of black shadow. It was thick, pure black, and made no sound as it rushed toward me. I clenched my teeth as I forced myself to find a way to protect myself. I needed a wall. A wall to protect me—a wall to consume this darkness that was heading straight toward me.

I summoned my white fire, and it did as I willed, streaming out from my skin all over my body and forming into a large wall that towered over me. The black shadow clashed against my white flames, resulting in a screeching noise so loud it pierced my ears. I felt my legs shudder as the instinct to cover my ears overwhelmed me. It was over in just a second, and I wondered what the hell had happened. It sounded as if reality itself was tearing apart.

The white wall of flames that had protected me was now dangerously blocking my view of Vice. I dispersed it, revealing Vice and his smile that seemed to be filled with utter joy. My heart pounded rapidly from a mix of adrenaline and fear.

"Magnificent, John! To think someone was out there with a Miracle as powerful as my own!"

I felt my gut twist again as I heard the excitement in his voice. I held my palm out to him, and imagined a ball of fire launching at him. I summoned my fire, and it did just as I imagined. Vice laughed, with excitement and happiness coating every sound. He took a step forward, as if he was going to charge at the white ball of consuming fire head on, but he dodged at the last second.

It was *fast*—almost instant even. He was eighty feet away one second, and right in front of me the next, a sword of pure black shadow already in mid-swing. Adams can already move superhumanly fast, but this was on a completely different level.

I had no time to contemplate it as I raised my arms up in a defensive guard, coating my arms with white flames to help. It absorbed the blade edge, but not the force of the impact. He was *strong*. Inhumanly so. Another earsplitting screech sounded, and I was blown off my feet. I flew fifteen feet through the air before landing painfully on the stone floor. It hurt, but I used the leftover momentum to roll backward and get my feet underneath me. I raised to a crouched stance, ready to dodge at a moment's notice.

The pure power of his strike had demolished my willpower. I held motionless as fear raged through me. I felt powerless. I was going to be killed. I was defenseless against that kind of strength. I looked up at him, then froze when I realized that he had vanished. I felt a slight breeze from behind me—*I'm going to be killed.*

I instinctively ducked down. I felt a *whoosh* of air over my head, and the candle stand that was next me was instantly, soundlessly, cut through. Actually, it was more accurate to say that the shadow sword had *erased* part of the stand.

I vaguely noticed that the floor was covered in Vice's darkness, but I didn't have the time to spare to think about it. I managed to spin around, facing him and prepared to blast a stream of white fire at him, but he was faster. I put up a guard and transferred my fire attack into another defensive shield, and braced myself for his kick that I barely saw coming.

A screech sounded painfully in my ear, and the force made my arms crash straight into my face before I felt my body thrown off my feet and into the air. I opened my eyes to watch the ground rushed under me, and prepared for my landing. I managed to somehow land on my feet and slowed myself down considerably, but I was going too fast. I lost my balance and fell backward. I hit the ground hard on my back before rolling backward with my momentum and returning to my feet like I had before.

I saw Vice lean forward a little, and I immediately felt like he was going to charge toward me again. Without delay, I quickly raised my hand and pushed forth a large blast of white fire. It was a wave of flame, stretching from the floor to a few feet over my head. It was wide too, easily six feet. It rushed forward, causing a painful screeching sound as it ate away the darkness on the floor. Vice moved, dodging the white flames. I didn't see him *actually* move, but he had suddenly appeared on my left side, some distance away from me.

"Holy hell..." I muttered to myself, finally realizing how Vice had been moving around so fast.

He was using the darkness on the floor to teleport himself. I wouldn't stand a chance against him if I didn't get rid of this black shadow on the ground, but how was I supposed to be able to clear all of that away without leaving myself open to his attacks? I couldn't shoot waves of fire out like I was before. I needed something bigger— something that shot out all around me. I needed and explosion.

How the hell could I make it explode? I clenched my hands into fists and summoned my white fire, coating my entire body with flames. I concentrated for a long second, visualizing what I wanted it to do. White fire burst from me, rushing outward in every direction, as if my body had exploded. It shot out in a dome, quickly erasing a large section of the darkness on the floor. This gave me enough space to fight, but it didn't clear away the entirety of the darkness. I had to make sure I stayed in this area.

I hesitated for a moment, then decided to diminish the fire that was coating my body. I still had no idea what the limitations of my Miracle were, and in the past few moments, I'd learned that without its protection, that pure darkness Vice could wield would devour me. I couldn't afford to exhaust my Miracle.

Vice moved to the edge of the darkness that was covering the floor. His joyous smile, ever present on his face thus far, was absent.

"John, are you not taking me seriously?"

I blinked, surprised. What the hell was he talking about? I was being pushed back—he had me on the defensive from the beginning. He was the most dangerous person I'd faced, and I was at a disadvantage since I had no experience using my Miracle. If I didn't fight him seriously, I was going to be killed.

Still, there hasn't been a single moment thus far that I wasn't fighting him seriously—but I was being timid. I was being too cautious against him. I needed confidence. I needed to be aggressive. I needed to live.

I set my shoulders and glared at him, determined to go on the offensive.

His smile immediately returned, giving me another shiver. I had no idea what was making him so happy and it was disturbing me. What did he know that I did not? I had foiled his plans at killing the Prophet, so why was he so disturbingly joyful to be fighting me? I didn't detect anger or rage, just an overwhelming feeling of happiness and excitement.

"That's much better. Show me what you're capable of!"

He spread his arms outward with his palms facing the sky, inviting an attack by lowering his guard.

I spent a long second to take a deep breath, summoning fire to coat my entire body. If I was going to fight him, I couldn't afford to hold back. I had no plan, but there were a couple things I kept in mind. First, as I fought him, I had to make sure to stay away from the darkness that was covering the floor, otherwise, I wouldn't be able to keep up with his speed. My first burst of white fire was a good start, but it only eliminated a little less than half of this room. As for his strength, I was sure I was outmatched, so I needed to either focus on evading his strikes or block them with my Miracle until I saw an opening. Everything else I would have to come up with on the fly.

I leaned forward and bolted, sprinting straight at him. His smile widened with excitement, but he made no move to defend himself. White fire started to build over my right fist and forearm as I prepared to strike him. I stopped a few feet away from him as I struck, releasing my pent up white flames. It shot out from my fist like a cannon, immediately engulfing Vice.

Or so I thought. He surprised me as he appeared to the left of my flames, easily dodging them. He sprinted toward me, closing the short distance between us extremely quickly. I took a step back from him, preparing to defend myself. I wasn't confident about a close-quarters fight after feeling how powerful his blows were, but at least he had stepped out of the darkness on the ground.

He struck, aiming at my face. I deflected it with my right arm while simultaneously striking with my left, aiming for his right side. A moment of excitement raced through me at the thought of landing a solid hit, but a wave of darkness pushed my arm out and away. My curse couldn't be heard over the screeching sound that filled the air around us. He must've shot a blast of his darkness from his left hand to deflect my strike.

I leapt backward quickly but he advanced along with me, preventing me from putting any distance between us. He swung downward with both arms, a blow that had more power than speed. I dodged to the left, violently overexerting my calf muscle to make the dodge in time. I came out of my roll and felt my calf twitch a couple times and protest painfully, but luckily the muscle hadn't torn. I gritted my teeth and pushed forward, not giving him a moment of rest. I couldn't afford to let him dictate the pace of this fight.

His blow had erased part of the stone flooring, causing a dent in the ground. If I got hit by that, I knew I wouldn't be able to recover. As I was rushing toward him, he whipped his right arm up and away in a back-handed swinging motion, even though there was still ten feet of distance between us. Darkness burst forth from his swing and charged toward me. The stream of darkness that he brought forth was big enough that it blocked my view of him. I felt frustrated; how was I supposed to attack him when it took everything I had just to defend myself?

I made my white flames protect me by forming a V-shaped shield in front of me, only blocking the darkness that would hit me and ignoring the rest of it. The painful screeching noise sounded again, and I saw darkness blow past me on both sides, but my shield held and kept me safe. Only a moment had passed before from the corner of my eye I saw movement on my left, and realized my mistake. He could move freely within his darkness, and that darkness was now surrounding me. I gritted my teeth and turned to face him as he advanced out of the shadows.

He was too quick, and I knew I wouldn't have time to fully block his strike. I was going to be blown backward again. He was right on me, and I only had a second to act, so I jumped back away from him. It wasn't enough to move out of his striking distance, but it was enough that the blow coming toward me wouldn't hit as hard. I coated my body in white fire as I brought my arms up in a guard, preparing for his strike. I barely made it in time before his foot connected against my guard.

The moment his foot hit me I felt pitch-black darkness burst forward, and the force behind his strike hit me like a cannon. I shot backward like a rocket, blasting through the darkness behind me with a deafening screech and flying dozens of feet before smashing into the floor. I clenched my jaw tight to keep myself from yelling out in pain. My arms weren't broken, but they hurt like hell. At least I had learned something from that; his monstrous strength did not all come from his physical muscle, but also from his Miracle. He used it to increase the force of his blows by expanding his Miracle outward immediately upon impact. The timing and control that took was incredible, especially considering the speed of his strikes.

Figuring out the secrete behind his strength hardly mattered. His kick had blown me far back, almost to the entrance to this sanctuary, and back onto the darkness that layered the floor. I didn't even get a chance to recover before he appeared above me, staring down with a disappointed scowl.

"Why?" he hissed, anger was clear even in his distorted voice.

I didn't answer; I had no idea what he was going on about. He was mentally insane—to attack the Prophet and bring down the only protection humanity has against the outside is insane enough, but how he was acting towards me was psychotic. Instead, I raised my hand and a burst of white, burning flames rushed out of my palm. I heard the screeching noise again, which meant that I was hitting him and he hadn't been able to dodge in time. I took the opportunity to increase the intensity of the flames that I was throwing against him. It was gushing out of my palm with enough force to reach the ceiling. It vaporized the glass and stone instantly, but from the high-pitched shriek, I knew he was still alive.

I saw his dark hand spring out from my fire and grasp my wrist. His contact with my bare skin created an even higher pitched screech, giving off a louder and more violent sound. I didn't know what had happened, but I was suddenly on my stomach and I felt his foot pressing down on my back. My arm was bent backward and up behind me, and with a sudden jerk I felt my shoulder explode in pain as it was forcibly dislocated. The pain immediately cut into my concentration, and the flames that were pouring out of my hand ceased. I somehow managed to keep myself from screaming in pain as he let go of my wrist and my arm feel limply to my side.

"Why, John?" he growled at me again.

"Why ... what?" I hissed out between breaths, desperately trying to buy time.

He stomped on me once, then he kicked me in the side, moving me several feet through the air before he kicked me again in the opposite direction, teleporting in front of me each time and landing another kick before I was even able to land.

With every kick, he spoke a word. "Why ... are ... you ... so ... weak?!"

He finished with a final kick, and I lay still on my stomach as the fresh pain paralyzed my body. I could taste blood. I had a broken nose and cracked ribs on both sides, but the pain from those injuries was minuscule compared to the pain pulsating from my dislocated shoulder.

He reached down and grabbed a fistful of my hair, dragging me upward. My body automatically moved, getting up so that it would take some pain and pressure off my hair. I was on my knees, my left arm grasping desperately at his hand that held my hair. My right arm hung useless at my side. My hand felt the solid darkness that was coating his arm. It was cold and lacked any texture. It was just a force—a solid, indescribable substance. Grasping it let off more of the piercing sound, but I also noticed that holding it gave a vibrating sensation. Surprisingly, contact with the darkness didn't hurt me. I glared upward at Vice and hatred toward him flamed up in my mind from the pain he was causing me.

He was looking down at me with a smile, but it was lifeless and his quiet chuckle no longer held its earlier joy.

"I *finally* find someone whose Miracle can equal my own, but he's still so weak it's pathetic. Is the universe mocking me?" his voice was gentle, as if he was asking this to himself, rhetorically.

I shot him a sneer. "Life can really be a bitch sometimes."

I couldn't see it, but I could feel his gaze focus on me in anger. I didn't want to die. My comment had just been my pride talking, but after I said it I couldn't help but laugh inside. Even if it cost me my life, I had gotten to him. I felt as if I had managed to throw the best punch yet. That feeling didn't last long.

"No. I'm not about to let life do whatever it wants to my future. Vice walks his own path and forges his own future. I'll make a hero out of you yet." I heard anger momentarily coat his words, but that tone had hardened into determination by the end of his sentence.

"Yeah?" I challenged, "and how are you going to do that?"

He tilted his head, as if surprised. "I'm going to utterly break you."

He drew his right fist back, preparing a punch that was aimed at my face. I felt my sneer vanish from my face as a thought ran through my mind; shit.

The impact of his punch forced me to the ground. I tasted blood, and pain flared in my shoulder as if someone had shoved a red-hot pike directly into my shoulder joint. I shivered as it took all my concentration not to scream. I wasn't going to give him that satisfaction.

I vaguely felt him grab my ankle and pull me, but I wasn't sure on the direction.

"John, I'm going to break you, so that when you recover, the only thing left in your soul is utter hatred for me."

Just as the pain had dropped to the level below overwhelming, he swung my body around from behind him and throw me forward. I was lifted off the ground and slammed into a wall. My back hit the wall and the impact knocked the air out of my lungs. My cracked ribs protested with extreme pain, and another red-hot pike was shoved into my shoulder, but then that pain vanished immediately. Somehow, the impact against the wall had popped my shoulder back into joint. The wall I landed against was the stone wall that separated the sanctuary and the entrance hall, where Grey and Miranda were.

He reached me before I slide down the wall, and grabbed the base of my throat with his left hand, pinning me against the wall with a single arm. He wasn't strangling me, but if I resisted he could easily do so.

A moment passed before I could suck in a shaky, painful breath. "You really think you'll be able to break me by hurting me?"

I had to speak loud enough to be heard over noise that was coming from his hand against my skin.

"No, I do not. The only thing you've shown me today is how good you are at getting your ass kicked."

I reached up and grabbed his arm with my right hand, even though moving it was still painful. I had to act or he was going to kill me. At this point it was obvious that I was no match for him. I needed to find a way to escape from him, and then attempt to regroup with Miranda, Ben and Ana.

"But then I had a sudden thought," he continued, his smile steadily returning across his face, "I bet you'd break if I started hurting *Miranda*."

I felt dread skin into my bones as my worst fear was suddenly a very real possibility. My mind was overcome with panic, and I suddenly abandoned any plans that I had to escape from his grasp.

Even over the screeching noise, I could hear impatient excitement coating his every word, "And I have the perfect calling card to get her attention."

No. I had to move, or Miranda was going to be forced to fight this monster. It was different now; it didn't only affect me anymore. I had to prevent him from getting her.

Instinctively, I twisted and aimed a kick at his stomach, but he didn't even bother blocking it. He didn't budge even an inch from the blow. I, however, was throbbing in pain from my cracked ribs, which didn't like my sudden, explosive movement. He reached back with his right hand, and I saw him forming a thin rod of darkness.

He thrust it forward, and it penetrated through my skin as if it was made of butter. I felt it pierce through my shoulder and exit the back, penetrating directly into the stone behind me. Screeching noise sounded, but I could barely hear it as pain had swarmed my mind. My willpower snapped, and I let out an uncontrollable scream.

I thrashed around, and my left arm went instinctively to grab whatever it was that caused me this much pain and remove it. But I couldn't pull it out. It was a hundred times worse than my dislocated shoulder. The part of the rod that was imbedded into my shoulder started to grow spikes outward, digging further into my flesh. It was by far the most painful thing I had ever experienced, and for several, extremely long seconds screaming in pain was all I could do.

About fifteen feet away from me, the wall I was pierced against suddenly exploded outward in a flash of blue electricity. I saw a of her crimson hair, and I felt the scream die in my throat. I was used as bait, and it had worked perfectly.

Vice slowly turned his attention from me to the green-eyed beauty staring at us with determined, strong expression. She looked to me, and her eyes widened slightly and her mouth parted a sliver as she registered the sorry state I was in. It only lasted a moment before her features hardened into fury as her deadly gaze focused on Vice.

She lunged toward us with a flash of blue light, moving as fast as lightning. One moment she was fifteen feet away from me, the next she was making a slice upward, wielding it with two hands. I saw the sword fly past me with such speed that it was a blur. Her target dodged, using that darkness on the floor to teleport halfway across the sanctuary.

"John, hold on, I'll remove this—" her voice was pained as she reached toward the rod of solid darkness.

"Don't touch it!" I ordered in my panic, grabbing her slender wrist with my free hand.

She froze, probably due to the intense panic in my voice. I tightened my grip on the rod, using as much muscle as I could, and with a shout I ripped out the rod. My Miracle was the only reason that I could touch this darkness. I had no idea what it would do to Miranda, but I wasn't going to find out. The spikes that had grown outward from the spike came with it, tearing through my flesh. I tossed it away from me, and it landed in the darkness on the floor and disappeared. The pain clouded my vision and I fell to my knees before Miranda caught me. Hot blood started flowing out of my wound. Luckily, the rod he impaled me with was thin, including the spikes. If I wasn't a Miracle Child, I would definitely have been in risk of bleeding out, but a wound like this was only debilitating.

Actually, I doubted that luck had anything to do with it. He could've killed me at any time since I had stepped foot in the sanctuary.

"What the hell happened, John?" she asked, but I couldn't answer her.

I smelled her shampoo, and felt her small frame against me. I couldn't let her be dragged into this. I couldn't let her be toyed with like I was.

"Miranda, go," I spoke.

She looked at me questioningly.

"Please. Run. He is going to hurt you just to get to me," I begged of her.

She stared into my eyes for a moment longer before standing up and looking down at me with gentle anger. "John, do not ask such a selfish thing of me. I can't leave you behind any more than you could leave me."

"I know it's selfish, but please. I can't let you be hurt," I told her.

Her anger turned into determination. "Don't worry, I'll kill him for what he's done to you."

All I wanted was her to be safe, and if she faced this monster, I wasn't confident that she'd win.

"Welcome, Miranda Pierce. Now that all the players have assembled, we can finally begin the main event," he spread his arms and gave a short, mocking bow when he welcomed Miranda.

We remained silent, but I did glance back to where Miranda had come from, wondering what had happened to Grey. I saw nothing that would help me answer that question, so I looked back at Vice.

"Oh? With a look like that, Miranda, I'd wager that you don't like the way I entertained John before you got here. You're practically oozing bloodlust."

Miranda squared her shoulders. "Our orders stated that taking you alive was preferred rather than killing you, but I don't think I'll restrain myself."

His smile grew and he laughed a for a couple moments before he raised his hand. "Before we get into that, let's have a talk."

I saw Miranda's movements hesitate with surprise, and I saw his head turn toward me.

"John, did you know that Miranda doesn't really care about you?" he asked, his smile turning sadistic.

Miranda and I stood there in silence for a second, confused by his sudden question.

"Hmm, perhaps I should put it a different way: it's not that Miranda doesn't care about you, it's just that she has no romantic feelings toward you. She values you as one would value a key to something important, nothing more. She's using you, my foolish hero."

"Bullshit," Miranda replied harshly, readying herself to attack.

"Is it?" he asked rhetorically after a short laugh. "John, do you actually think a woman would care for you after she's seen the things you've done? After she's seen the people you've killed? She fell for you practically overnight, even knowing the awful things you've done—didn't that strike you as odd?"

I felt shock rush through my body as I registered what he was saying. How the hell did he know so much about me?

"I don't judge John for making that choice," Miranda stated firmly.

I remembered exactly what she had said about it when we first met, *I would've done the same if I was in your shoes.*

"How noble of you," he replied with a sneer, "but what if there was actually another motive with your sudden acceptance?"

"There was none," Miranda answered, even more firmly than before.

It was obvious that she was getting irritated.

"John, what she hasn't told you yet is that Miranda actually needed to pair with an Adam—" he started but was interrupted by Miranda.

"Shut up," Miranda hissed.

He paused, his smile widening. "Those limiters don't last forever, do they Miranda? The microchip keeping you from summoning your core and snapping was almost completely dissolved. They only last, at most, until you're twenty-sixth birthday, and you were getting very close to being removed from active duty. And then, miraculously, Johnathon appears before you. John, who has no idea what you're really like and has no experience with the Church. To make matters perfect, you even Gazed upon him. All that was left was a little manipulation and a tug or two at his hormones and you got yourself your very own Adam to keep you from being benched."

My mind was racing. He was making accusations that matched up with what I was taught but hadn't been put together before. The microchips that they surgically implant when Eves are born are slowly eaten away and dissolved over time until they either disappear or the Eve pairs with an Adam. I had just assumed that Miranda's chip only dissolved because I had joined with her. When her blood reacted to mine and underwent a change, the process would destroy the microchip within a week.

Yet Miranda could summon her core the very first day we paired. The chip had to have already been eroded before we joined, and the pairing process must've damaged it enough to allow her to do so. But honestly, none of that mattered to me. Even though it could be true that Miranda had manipulated me to remain in active duty, it could just as easily be a giant coincidence. But what bothered me was that Miranda hadn't just explained that to me. Instead, she had told me a completely different reason.

Eve's Miracles are closely tied in with our emotions, so the limiter isn't an exact science. Using it this time was on accident.

Why? What was her reason for saying that? She had to have known better but instead she hid it from me. What was I missing?

I could see Miranda was about to lunge at him, so I argued back, hoping to keep her at bay. I didn't want Miranda to face Vice alone. If we could delay long enough, Ana and Ben would come to help.

"If Miranda was manipulating me, then why would she bother continuing to do so after the three-week mark? She was in the clear by that point. I would be stuck as her Adam."

He smiled. "Wrong. As Miranda knows, the three-week guideline is merely a safety measure. It can happen at any time, but the longer the wait the more dangerous the process becomes. Doesn't it seem a little strange that your training was only three weeks? Surely you don't think that's just a coincidence, John. She was keeping you distracted! Keeping you busy until it was past the safety threshold!"

I stayed silent in my surprise. I hadn't thought of it that way.

He continued a moment later, "Besides, there's an even more important reason for her to keep you hooked on her."

I could tell that he was baiting me to ask, but I'd die before I gave him that satisfaction. Waiting for Ana and Ben wasn't the only benefit for delaying. I was getting stronger every second that passed as my body recovered from my numerous wounds.

He continued when he noticed I wasn't going to respond, "With an Adam as traumatized as you, how else is she going to be sure that you'll use the autoinjector if she Breaks? If she has anything less than your utter loyalty, there's a possibility that you'll fail when it comes time to act."

Again, I was chilled down to my bones from the knowledge he had about me. I knew that his theory was plausible, but I didn't want to even consider it.

"Rumors are a powerful thing, my naïve hero."

Miranda? Manipulating me all along? Impossible.

But didn't this make more sense?

His distorted voice floated over to me, "Come on, John! Think! Hasn't she done something that made you wonder if she was rushing things?"

She'd kissed me on the cheek the second night we knew each other, and by the third night she tried to kiss me, and when I remembered how I felt that night, I knew that I wanted to kiss her as well. She'd even asked me to stay with her that night. She never had any hesitation when it came to physical contact, but couldn't that mean that it didn't mean anything to her?

I could hear the joyful tone in his voice as he continued, "has she ever said something that seemed possessive?"

Look, you can't die on me John. I need you alive. You're my future.

What if she wasn't talking about our relationship? What if she actually meant that she couldn't be an Eve without me? That without me, she'd be stationed at a place like the Academy, stuck in a stasis like that doctor, Elizabeth?

Dammit.

My eyes moved from Vice to Miranda, who was a couple paces ahead of me. Fear started leaking into my mind as I had a thought; what if this was true? What if the woman I was falling for didn't give a shit about me? What if everything she had been telling me was merely to string me along? I had felt that way when I first talked with her, hadn't I? I called her a manipulator. So, didn't this fit? Didn't this make the most sense?

"Enough!" Miranda said to him as she turned her head to me, "John won't belie—"

Miranda's words died in her throat as she met my eyes, and I knew what she was seeing. In the moment that truly mattered—in the moment where my belief in her was essential, she saw doubt. I doubted her feelings toward me. I realized my mistake as soon as her solid, clear green eyes broke into a surprised pain.

I'm yours, John. I'm your Eve. Isn't it a better question to ask why you're hesitating to trust me back?

I believe I've told you before, but I have no problem repeating this; you are mine.

No. I wasn't going to doubt her.

I remembered what it was like to be around her. What it was like to hold her, to hear her whispers and to touch her smooth skin. I was being an imbecile. There was no proof that she was manipulating me. Throughout our private conversations and intimate moments, I felt that there was more evidence of her love than of her being a manipulator. Even if there wasn't, I wasn't going to let some random Adam stand there and tell me what Miranda was or wasn't. It was my choice, and to me, she was real. She was genuine.

Her hurt eyes closed and she stood still for a moment, then she turned back to Vice. She said nothing in response to my moment of doubt. I felt guilty from hurting her, but this wasn't the time to reconcile.

Miranda tightened her grip on her sword and crouched, readying herself to attack. Vice was laughing joyfully, as if seeing that moment between Miranda and I brought him complete fulfillment. I heard nothing but genuine happiness from his laughter, and I couldn't help but feel sick to my stomach.

Miranda lunged, moving with a grace and speed that I couldn't even hope to mimic. She reached him in three strides and gave a quick but powerful slice downward. Miranda's sword swung through the air and landed heavily upon the stone floor where Vice had stood a tenth of a second ago. He had teleported behind her, still utilizing the darkness on the ground. I hadn't warned Miranda of that trick yet, and for a moment I felt afraid that she was going to be killed, but she ducked below his strike as if she had been expecting it.

She twisted around at the same time, swinging her sword agilely, but he dodged again, this time moving several yards away. Miranda didn't hesitate and pressed forward, reaching him in two quick strides and slashing diagonally down again. He dodged without teleporting this time, and aimed another right punch at her. She couldn't get her sword up in time, so she brought up her arm to block it.

"No!" I shouted, not wanting her to get hurt by his darkness, but it was in vain.

His fist contacted her skin, but instead of it tearing through her arm, it made a screeching noise and Miranda retreated, jumping back several times to put a lot of distance between them. I got a glance at her arm, and to my relief it was still intact, but was red, as if it had gotten burned. A small sigh of relief escaped from me when I saw her minor injury. I had thought that she was going to lose her entire arm.

"Intriguing," Vice stated, giving her a wicked smile, "I suppose I should have predicted it since you are paired, but you are resistant to my Miracle, though not nearly to the same extent that John is. Be thankful, young Eve, that John is your Adam. If not, you would've been killed."

Miranda didn't reply, and I noticed her studying the darkness that covered the floor. It seemed she had figured out that the darkness was how he was teleporting around.

He laughed excitedly before adding, "And appreciate it while it lasts. After today I doubt he'll still want to be paired with someone like you."

"Bastard," she hissed, and started running toward him to fight again.

I couldn't just sit here and watch, I had to help her somehow. I tried to stand up, but pain flooded my mind and I didn't even make it halfway up before falling back down to my knees. Miranda had reached him and swung her sword again, but he teleported away and shot a wide burst of darkness at her. She dodged by rolling out of the way and advanced to him. There was only one way I could support her while in this state.

It took a short second to concentrate on what I wanted to do, but when I was ready I raised my hand, palm facing away from me. A white wave of fire erupted from my hand and surged forward. I didn't make it thick, but instead made it tall and wide—wide enough to cover the entire sanctuary. The noise was deafening, but it was effective and it ate away the darkness on the ground. It devoured everything, not just the darkness. It ate away the candle stands that were along the main isle leading to the pulpit, disintegrating everything but what I told it to ignore; the stone that made up the sanctuary, and the candles that lined the walls.

Miranda didn't need to do anything; it washed over her harmlessly. Vice easily put up a small shield of darkness to protect himself. I noticed that the farther the white fire got from me, the harder it was to concentrate on keeping it up, but I managed to hold out until it had reached the end of the sanctuary.

Taking away his ability to teleport, Miranda should have the upper hand when it came to speed. I hoped that was the case. After a moment of hesitation, Miranda launched herself at Vice. A slim sword appeared in his hand, but it didn't have a hilt or a guard; just a blade of darkness. He held it up to block Miranda's heavy strike, but his sword sliced through hers as if it was merely paper, instead of hardened steel.

Miranda retreated immediately and looked down at her broken sword in surprise.

"John's blood may protect you from my Miracle, but that same protection doesn't extend to your weapons. You cannot win against me with those kinds of toys," he sneered.

"We'll see about that," Miranda replied, and with a flash of light she replaced her broken broadsword with her twin swords.

For the fourth time, she charged at him and attacked with a flurry of swings, each one honed with precision and speed. He would evade most of her attacks, but there were a couple of moments when he was forced to use that sword of darkness. Each time he did, it easily sliced through her own swords. She never missed a moment, and every time he broke one of her weapons she replaced it with an identical short sword. After the third one was cut in half, he landed a backhanded blow to her face. It was a strike powerful enough to move her entire body several feet to the left, but she recovered almost immediately and resumed her attack.

It steadily went downhill from there; Miranda received more and more blows. It seemed as if she was slowing down. I cursed my uselessness and forced my body to stand. My wound had mostly clotted up already, but it still hurt like hell to move. I watched them battle, and I knew I couldn't keep up with their speed. It was appallingly apparent to me just how much Vice was holding back when he'd fought against me. Pathetic indeed.

Their exchange had paused for a moment after Miranda backed off. Her back was to me, but I could tell that she was panting heavily and I could see that her right calf muscle was twitching. That didn't surprise me; she had damaged her muscles by moving at those speeds. The fact that they hadn't torn yet just showed how much control she had over her body.

"I'm surprised by you, Miranda," Vice stated. "I would've thought you would be a little more upset with John. He dumped you, didn't he?"

"Shut up," Miranda hissed.

"I mean, if you truly cared about him, wouldn't you, at least, be more furious with me? Furious at the fact that, with just a few words, I tore apart all the trust you worked so hard to build. That is assuming you cared for him as much as you claimed. Looks like I was right—"

Her swords vanished and was replaced with two pistols. She didn't hesitate to interrupt him as the sanctuary was filled with the sound of rapid gunfire. She emptied her clips, but he hadn't even bothered to dodge. The bullets harmlessly hit the darkness that was coating his body and vanished, as if erased. I knew he was goading her, but I didn't know why. What was he trying to accomplish? It was clear he overpowered both of us, so why didn't he just kill us? What was he waiting for?

"I can see that my words are frustrating you, but still ... I expected some stronger emotions than mere frustration, Miranda. I mean... I ripped John away from you." his voice was dripping with glee.

I knew something had changed in Miranda, but I couldn't make sense of just *what* it was. My senses had suddenly gone on alert of her, as if I sensed some sort of danger from her. It was a foreign feeling and just pure *wrong*.

Her posture changed; she straightened her back slightly and breathed out a calming breath. It was obvious to me; she was no longer lost to her emotions—no longer filled with an uncontrollable anger toward Vice. In a sense, she was the opposite. She was empty of emotions.

I knew in my gut what this was—even before I had the chance to prove it.

Miranda Broke.

CHAPTER 21

She extended an arm upward with her fingers spread, as if she was reaching for something. Her gaze, however, didn't stray at all from Vice. I looked up wondering what she was reaching for. It only took half a second to survey the sanctuary ceiling, and even less to take a glance at the sky that was now covered by storm clouds. I didn't notice anything significant.

I saw the sky split open with blinding lightning above us, lighting up the sky with brilliant flashes of blue-white light. Deafening thunder roared and made the air tremble with the tremendous sound that was produced. In the flashes of light, I could see something black falling. Another flash of lightning violently illuminated the sky, and my eyes lost the dark object until it came crashing through the ceiling of the church. Miranda caught the object, but it's momentum was too great for her to fully absorb. Her arm swung down and behind her at a high velocity. The long object cut into the ground as it did, which slowed it down enough to allow her to fully stop it.

The dark object in her hand was undeniably a sword, but it was so massive that I had to second guess myself. It exceeded eight feet in length and had a guard that was two feet wide. It was doubled edged, with its blade wavy on both sides and had a sharp tip at the end. It was a dark color, but it had a blue hue to it, reminding me of the night sky, and it was as smooth as ice. Along the blade were flashes of silent lightning that seemed trapped inside whatever material it was that made up the sword. Miranda held the gargantuan sword behind her with one hand, as if the entire thing was weightless to her.

I saw her grip tighten on the hilt of the sword, and I felt the air suddenly charge with electricity that made the hair on my skin stand up. The blade transformed, folding in on itself as it flawlessly turned into a smaller, more agile-looking blade. The change only took a second to finish, and now it was a blade four feet long, thin as glass and looking light. It was now a single-edged blade with a straight edge and back, and another edge formed between the edge and the back of the blade at a 45-degree angle that made up the tip of the sword. It had a guard and a handle, and both were made from the same material as the blade.

I heard Vice's excited laughter, as if he had just received exactly what he had been wishing for, but my eyes were glued on Miranda as I tried to comprehend what I was seeing. This was her Core? It was beautiful, but terrifying at the same time. The flashes of blue-white lightning along the blade made the sword almost seem alive.

Miranda moved, stepping toward him with grace, fluidity, and *speed*. I had thought Miranda could move fast before, but this was on a monstrous level. She reached him almost instantly and swung her sword down in a heavy two-handed strike. Unlike earlier, she was too fast for him to evade her blows, so he brought up his sword and parried her slice. He held his black sword up at an angle so that Miranda's Core—Skyfall—was deflected to his side.

He lunged to the side away from Skyfall, putting several feet between Miranda and himself. At least, that was his intention, but Miranda's reflexes and speed were too great for him to escape. She was on top of him before he had even taken two strides away from her, and she attacked again, this time trying for a slice to his side. He parried again, and then they started fighting for real. They exchanged strikes, but none of them connected with their target. Although neither of them had managed to land a hit, it was obvious that Miranda had the advantage and initiative in this fight. She was attacking at lot more and was forcing Vice to focus on defense. This frightening display of expert swordsmanship only lasted for a few seconds before Vice unleashed a wave of darkness.

Miranda flashed to the right, avoiding the wave entirely before dashing in at him again. Skyfall clashed against Vice's sword of darkness, and upon contact it seemed as if one of the trapped lightning within Skyfall broke free. The entire room was violently illuminated and shook with the sound of thunder as the lighting flashed out onto Vice. It connected with the darkness, but even raw lightning was absorbed by him harmlessly. The lightening that escaped from Skyfall had spread apart, and some of them had missed Vice and connected with the ground. The lightning gorged out deep cracks in the stone floor and sent small, heated chunks of stone flying in random directions.

Another furious clash of swords passed between the two of them, and with each blow Skyfall released more lightning. Each flash left blinding lines in my vision, and the sound was so loud I could feel it vibrate within my chest. Miranda was swinging Skyfall more and more aggressively, and Vice was being pushed back by her intensity.

The entire fight immediately changed with a powerful downward cut. Vice had his sword raised over his head horizontally, ready to parry her blow, but Miranda's Skyfall had cut clean through the dark sword. Her strike continued downward, cutting through his dark armor and into his body. Vice's smile had vanished, and for the first time since I had laid eyes on him, I saw him get serious.

Darkness exploded out from him in three massive waves, forcing Miranda to leap backward and away, but these bursts of darkness followed her movements as she tried to retreat. I saw Skyfall morph from a sword into a large shield, and she stopped evading and took the relentless darkness head-on. The bursts were thick enough to cover her completely as they rushed by her, and momentarily blocked my sight of her. I barely had time to mentally plead that she was alright before Vice shouted, getting my attention.

"YOU DARE WOUND ME?!" his voice echoed off of the stone walls.

He was glaring at his feet, where a small splatter of blood lay on the stone. Even though I could only see his mouth, I could tell that he was scowling in rage. He lifted his leg and smashed his foot into the stone, erasing the blood and a good chunk of the floor underneath, as if the blood's very presence had offended him. He recovered from his moment of rage a second later, and relaxed his composure. His face then turned from the stone floor to me.

"Shouldn't you consider stopping her soon, John?" he asked, his smile slowly returning.

Stop her? I turned my eyes over to her as I wondered why he would suggest such a thing. She was finally fighting against him on equal terms. If we kept this up, we could win—

The sight of Miranda instantly halted my thoughts of victory.

She managed to survive the blasts of darkness by using Skyfall as a shield, but it had only protected her from the knees up. The darkness had eaten away her jeans, but since she had my blood in her, her legs looked the same as her arm had, red as if mildly burned. I saw blood on her legs around her calf muscles, and at first glance I thought it was a result of the darkness, but then I took notice of her arms, which were in a similar condition but were unburnt. These wounds weren't caused by darkness, so what the hell had happened?

Blood gushed out of her wounds after each violent beat of her heart. Her muscles were twitching, but she kept it under tight control and stayed steady on her feet. I realized what had caused her wounds; her own muscle had not only torn itself, but also the skin that covered it. She was pushing her body well beyond the limit, and that was taking its toll on her. She was breaking. The very sight of her was heart-stopping. It looked like she had crawled her way up from hell itself just to fight. A Holy Demon suddenly seemed like an accurate description of her.

How had I not noticed earlier? How had I let her fight this long and let her body get this damaged? Even if I didn't know about her wounds, I did know that any of her heart beats could be her last. If her skin looked like this, how the hell did she look on the inside? How many of her bones were cracked, or even crushed? How much longer did I have until her heart burst?

Fear filled me, and I started rushing to Miranda as her shield morphed back into her single-edged sword. I had to fix this, or she was going to die. I felt pain flare up from my cracked ribs with every step I took, but I forced it out of my mind. This was nothing compared to what Miranda was going through. When I was fifteen feet away from her, Miranda turned, reacting to my advancement. I met her eyes, and I saw exactly what I expected to see in them—an empty shell.

I expected it, but it still made my body lock up. Her green eyes weren't supposed to look like this. They were emotionless and ridged, a world of unmoving, passionless green ice. Worst of all, they held no recognition of me. There was no change in expression on her face when she looked at me like there usually was. She might as well have been staring at a wall than at me. I had to free her from this.

She dashed forward and thrust Skyfall toward me, and her speed was well beyond something I could evade. The weapon hit my stomach, but it was nullified immediately. Her Core was completely her own power, so there wasn't a single thing about it that could hurt me. I was even immune to Skyfall's momentum and weight. Miranda knew this, but not in her current state of mind.

I grabbed Skyfall with my bare hands and a surge of electricity rushed into my body. It was harmless to me, but it still made my hair stand on end. Skyfall was smooth to the touch, as if it was glass. I still didn't have a plan of attack, but I was a quick study, and just from her one attack I already learned that I had no chance at catching her if this became a contest of speed.

She reacted by jumping up and rotating her body to deliver a kick aimed at my face. I held up my arm and prepared to block her kick without breaking my arm. I adsorbed the impact from her kick more easily than I had expected, and realized that this was probably due to the damage she had already inflicted upon her muscles. I knew that she couldn't use her full strength by this point, and that she was only going to get weaker the longer she fought.

Realizing my advantage, I grabbed her by the ankle before she had time to recover. Miranda wasted no time in pulling Skyfall out of my grasp, which was easy for her to do since I was only holding onto it by one hand.

As she began to fall, she twisted in mid-air to kick me with her free leg, trying to get me to release my hold on her ankle. I blocked by grabbing her calf, but I almost lost my grip on her as I did so. Her skin was slippery from the warm blood that pulsed out from the tears in her skin. I recovered from the shock of feeling her blood-soaked skin and tightened my grip so that I wouldn't lose hold of her. I fell with her to the ground, but she landed hard on her back while I managed keep my feet underneath me in a crouched position.

I pulled her under me and straddled her hips to keep her pinned on the ground. I was too close for her to attempt to attack me with Skyfall, so she abandoned it and resorted to using her own fists. When I was moving to get her under me, she punched me twice in my face, but once I had her pinned, I was able to protect myself easier. I managed to block her strikes and eventually grab her by the wrists. She started arching her back and forcing her hips upward, trying to buck me off. I tightened my grip on her with my knees, keeping myself from being thrown off balance.

My grip on her wrists was tight, and I felt her blood pumping wildly under her skin. How long did I have before her heart couldn't take it anymore? The thought horrified me. Even for an Eve, a heart beating this harshly couldn't last very long. I was horrified at myself for not noticing earlier. It felt as if her entire body was trying to kill itself from the inside out.

I felt a presence behind me, and my gut was telling me that I was in danger. I had momentarily forgotten about Vice.

Out of a sudden, protective instinct, white fire suddenly erupted out of me, spreading out thick flames all around me to shield me from an unconfirmed threat. It had been instinctual to summon the white-hot barrier of fire that now protected me, but I kept it up even after reason told me that Vice had no intention of killing me like this.

I knew what task I had to do, but I hadn't yet convinced myself to do it. Miranda needed to come back to reality, and my hand was already gently touching the handle on the autoinjector that was strapped to my thigh. My arm started shaking as I was overcome with self-hatred and as an internal conflict ensued.

I was being weak—a coward. I didn't know for sure what effect this autoinjector would have on her. Miranda was suffering right in front of me, yet I was hesitating to fix it. Miranda was going to die if I did nothing—how selfish could I be? It was this moment that she needed me the most. The longer I delay, the more likely it is that her heart bursts. Even Eves can't survive an imploded heart.

I knew all of that, but was this truly the only way? What if the rumors were true? What if this caused her such intense physical pain that it would break her mind? Did I have no choice but to risk that? Did I have no other choice but to cause her to scream in utter agony to save her life?

A piece of me died as I slowly pulled out the autoinjector. I knew it didn't matter. I couldn't let her die even if it meant ultimately losing her. I wanted to cry. I wanted to flee. I wanted to wake up from this nightmare that was happening in front of me. I was going to hear the screams of someone I cared about. A woman who had somehow entranced me to care for her to this extent in a mere three weeks. A woman whose beauty and grace had no equal in my eyes.

"I'm—" I started, but my voice lost its strength.

I didn't even have the courage to apologize to her for what I was about to do. I closed my eyes for a moment as I gathered my willpower, then I opened them and met her eyes one more time, even though I knew I would see nothing in them but emptiness. Yet when I had met her eyes I saw something in them that made my entire body freeze.

Her eyes, which weren't looking at me at all but was glancing around us at the white fire, were filled with fear. No, it wasn't fear that filled them, but terror. Now that I noticed it, her movements at trying to get away from me were much more frantic and disparate than before.

An idea—more like a figment of an idea—had suddenly wormed its way into my mind. What if it could work? What if I didn't need to kill myself, to take part of myself away from Miranda to save her? What if I could still be who Miranda cared about and still protect her from her own power? I had to try. It was my responsibility as her Adam, and the one she cared for.

But what if this was my own excuse? My own cowardice? What if this theory was merely a fictional invention of my mind to save itself?

I shook my head. No. I couldn't think that way. The fear in her eyes was plain as day, and if she could feel fear, then there had to be a way to get her out of the fight instinct and into the flight instinct without so much as a scratch.

I knew what I had to do, and any more hesitation beyond this point was dangerous for Miranda. I gritted my teeth and concentrated, forcing more white flames to spew forth into this sphere of fire that I had up for protection. I purposefully kept the sphere from growing, so instead the flames inside the sphere were intensified. The white flames swirled around us, beating against our clothes and whipping Miranda's hair around as if she was in the middle of a gust of wind. The heat from my flames made the stone crack loudly and split apart, leaving inch-wide gaps in the flooring here and there.

I knew immediately that this wasn't enough. Miranda had incredible courage. She was practically drowning in her worst fear, but she hadn't snapped out of it yet. The incognita chemical was still pumping through her. Worse still, I could feel the toll that the fire I was summoning was starting on put on me. I didn't know exactly how much time I had left before my fire would vanish, but I knew it wasn't long.

I opened my mouth and exhaled flames, letting them spill forth as if my mouth was the gate to hell. The flames rushed over Miranda's face harmlessly, but she closed her eyes and whipped her head to the side in an automatic defensive reaction.

After a very long minute, I finally saw what I had been begging to see. A single tear shed from her closed eye and fell down her cheek, leaving a wet trail that was immune to my heat and flames.

Instantly, I released my hold on the flames, and they burst outward from the sphere I had them condensed in, generating loud bang and releasing a shock wave of heat and force. It made a spider web effect in the flooring several feet long as the stone cracked from the force, and the noise made my ears ring for several moments.

I had scared her into a flight instinct, and it broke her out of the phenomenon that had trapped her. I released her wrists and exhaustedly shifted off her, barely managing to stay upright. She stayed where she was, panting heavily as she recovered. A few long seconds passed, then she sat up and met my eyes. Her emerald eyes shimmered at me, and I suddenly felt guilt for putting her through that. While it had saved her body from undergoing extreme physical pain, did I not just torture her mind?

Her body was shaking from a mixture of the left-over adrenaline in her system and from her badly-damaged muscles. She still somehow managed to close the distance between us and buried her head in my chest. In my extreme exhaustion, it took a lot of effort to keep myself from losing balance.

She wept in my arms, her body shaking more intensely now from her tears. I froze, momentarily surprised by her actions. She didn't hate me? I was happy to hold her again, but it was me who put her in this state. Did I have the right to hold her?

"I was so scared. I thought I was going to die," she said between sobs.

I felt my shirt beginning to get damp from her tears, but she seemed to be calming down.

"I'm sorry," I admitted.

I didn't know those words could make me feel physical pain.

She shook her head against my chest. "Stop it. I'd be dead if you weren't here."

"I'll always be here," I whispered.

I could promise her that, at least. What I just did was risky, and if it hadn't worked, Miranda would probably be dead. The exhaustion I was experiencing was proof of that. I knew that if I had failed, I wouldn't have the physical strength left to keep Miranda restrained long enough to use the autoinjector.

I saw movement from the corner of my eye as a shadow raced toward me, and I knew that our moment of peace was over. I lacked the physical strength to block the blow I knew I was about to receive, so all I could do was tighten my jaw and close my eyes as the uppercut connected to my face. The blow sent me flying, and Miranda was ripped from my arms. I hit the stone floor hard on my back, but my momentum was strong, and I ended up rolling over once before hitting the stone floor again on my stomach. I slid to a halt, and felt my body shake from pain.

"THAT'S CHEATING JOHN!" he roared, his rage from earlier resurfacing.

In my pain-induced confusion, I didn't know what he was talking about. I sucked in air and breathed out a groan, slowly recovering from his abuse. I opened my eyes for a moment to glance back at Miranda, and I saw her laying on the ground. She was supporting herself with shaking arms and staring at me with a worried expression. Vice was walking toward me at a steady pace, but I could tell from his posture that he was still furious. I closed my eyes and battled against the pain, trying to get it down to a level that wasn't overwhelming.

"Don't hurt him!" Miranda said, somehow making her voice strong enough to contain a threat even in her current state.

He ignored her and kept advancing toward me. I only managed to get up on my hands and knees before he reached me.

"You were supposed to TORTURE HER!" he shouted down at me.

He kicked me in the side, but he held back his strength. The force only made me flip over on my back, but the strike was directly on my already-cracked ribs and made me give a short shout of pain. His words gave me a strange sensation of relief, even amongst my pain. I made the right choice.

"I need you to break, John," he stated, but his tone of voice was far from calm.

"Go to hell," I breathed out, voicing my anger.

"I wasn't going to do this, but since you are being so stubborn, I'm left with no other choice," he said as he bent down and grabbed a fistful of my hair.

He pulled me up and forced my head to look toward Miranda. I clenched my teeth as a bad feeling washed over me. I didn't even get a chance to think before he raised his free hand and released a blast of darkness at her.

"NO!" I shouted out and struggled in vain as I watched the darkness hurl toward her.

Miranda was too injured to dodge, and it was everything she had just to bring up her arm defensively. I held my breath as the darkness momentarily blocked my view of Miranda. Then relief flooded into me as I saw it connect with the ground right in front of her.

At first, I thought he had simply missed, but a second later proved that was only wishful thinking. The darkness that hit the ground shot forward, slithering from the point of impact to underneath Miranda and stopping. Immediately, Miranda started sinking into the dark circle that she was laying on.

She struggled, trying to pull up her arm that was submerged in the darkness to the elbow, but it wouldn't budge. She wasn't sinking very fast, and I knew that if I escaped Vice's grasp, I'd be able to reach her before she was submerged. I fought against his hold on me, but it was futile in my condition. I heard him chuckle at my pathetic struggle, but unlike his previous laughter, this lacked the genuine happiness. He was still furious.

Somehow, even in my exhausted state, I managed to summon a short burst of white fire, sending it exploding upward from my body. I felt his grip on my hair release immediately, and took the opportunity to rush forward. My entire body protested with every step, but it wasn't even a distraction to me at this point; my entire focus was getting to Miranda. At the speed that I knew Vice could move, he could have easily stopped me at any time. He was letting me get to her. I didn't care. I had to reach her and do whatever it took to save her life.

I finally arrived at her side and reached forward to start pulling her out. It was useless; no matter how we pulled, her sinking didn't even slow.

I slid forward toward her to get a better position to pull her out, but to no avail. Whatever this darkness was, it refused to let her leave. She had sunk all the way to her stomach now, and I was starting to feel helplessness.

I tightened my grip around her back and prepared to pull again, even though I had accepted that it wasn't going to work.

Miranda stopped me. "John."

I heard desperation in her voice, but not fear. I met her emerald eyes, which seemed to be begging me to listen. She reached up with her one free hand and touched my cheek, then moved it to the back of my head. She pulled me toward her and met my lips with hers. The kiss was unlike any other that we had before. It was impatient and desperate, as if she was trying to tell me something.

We parted a moment later. I brushed her crimson hair out of her eyes so I could see into them.

"My feelings for you are anything but fake," she told me.

I stared at her, surprised. She was still worried about that? I knew better by now. She was genuine. She cared for me, and I for her. She was mine, and I couldn't let her think that anything had changed. I opened my mouth to tell her, but at that exact moment, she was pulled sharply downward, and vanished beneath the darkness.

"NO!" I screamed at the darkness, feeling my stomach plummet into despair.

I hit the darkness with the sides of my fist, as if I was trying to break into it and pull her out. I hit it three times before I coated my fist in white fire, hoping it would affect it somehow. I didn't get the chance to strike, for Vice grabbed my forearm and threw me as if I was no heavier than a child.

I flew a couple dozen feet before tumbling over the ground. The physical pain of my body was practically nothing compared to the pain of seeing Miranda vanish.

"She's gone, John. Stop being so pathetic and accept the reality in front of you," he said, fury no longer in his voice as his old gleeful tone returned.

Gone? Miranda's gone?

I replayed the sight of her disappearing beneath the darkness that greedily devoured her.

She's dead?

I thought of the moments I'd spent with her. I remembered her scent and the way her green eyes contrasted against her bright crimson hair. Miranda Peirce, my Eve, dead?

I felt fury—real fury. A murderous rage filled me. It burned away all rational thought except a simple goal; revenge. My blood boiled, eating away my fatigue and drowning out any complaints of pain. I stood up slowly but smoothly, and stared at him with pure conviction. If Miranda was dead, then I was going to use everything I had to avenge her. I didn't care who got in my way. I didn't care if this man was supposed to answer for his attempt at killing the Prophet. None of that mattered; all that mattered was that he still breathed, and that was something I planned on correcting.

White fire exploded out from me as my emotions took on a tangible form, and they swirled around me like a tornado. I was invincible in this, but that didn't matter. What I needed was a weapon, a tool I could use to annihilate my foe. I bent the flames that were circling me down into the palm of my hand. I condensed them, forcing them into a small rod that steadily grew outward and sharper. I used it all; forsaking my defense for offense. I closed my hand and grasped the thin sword tightly, the heat that it was producing was extreme, but it was harmless to me.

I walked forward as I slowly removed every mental restraint on my muscles, preparing to strike him down with everything I had. His joyous smile had returned, and his laughter was exhilarated.

"You're giving me chills, John!" he said, but I ignored him.

I only had enough in me for a single strike, but that was all it was going to take. I moved, lunging forward at a speed I hadn't thought possible. I reached him in two strides and swung down with both hands. He raised his sword to block it, but my sword sliced through it without even losing momentum. It raced down and connected with the coat of darkness that was covering his head, but even that was devoured easily by my sword of white fire. It produced that strange screeching noise all the while. It cut down into him, and my eyes widened with surprise when I felt no resistance. There was nothing inside the shell, no brain to cut into. It took me only a half second to realize what had happened. He must've teleported away, but in his hurry, he'd left his shell behind.

I looked around, wondering where he could possibly teleport to.

I had already destroyed all the darkness on the ground. I felt a shock run through me as my instinct screamed at me to look up, so I did. I saw him falling down on me, covered in a new coat of darkness and with a sword of darkness ready to cut into me. He must've had darkness covering the ceiling too, but due to the poor lighting it blended in with the shadows.

I gritted my teeth and held my sword up to defend myself as I realized that our positions had suddenly reversed. His sword connected with my own, but this time his sword was the one to pierce into mine. It wasn't deep, hardly even a centimeter, but it was enough to break my concentration. The condensed fire suddenly exploded outward, covering both of us in fire and heat. I was immune to the flames, but the shock wave produced hit me like a train. I was thrown back and I tumbled over the stone floor like a rock skipping over a pool of water. I was disoriented, but I was vaguely aware that I had passed into the hole that Miranda had made in the stone wall. I connected harshly with another wall that halted my momentum. I shouted in pain, and my vision immediately turned black for a long moment.

I blinked several times and gasped for air, trying to recover enough to be able to take in my surroundings. I was in the entrance hall of the church, where Grey and Miranda had been earlier. I could feel my arms and legs twitching, but I was too exhausted to move. A couple more seconds passed before I realized that my ears were ringing from the sound of the explosion. I was so disoriented that I didn't even see Vice approach me until he was standing directly in front of me.

"You are weak, but I'm glad to see that you have potential," he said to me.

I coughed in response, and pain drowned my mind.

"I have plans for you, Johnathon Aster, so even though it would be easy for me, I will not kill you just yet."

He reached down and grabbed my forearm, and I felt a burning sensation along the inside of my forearm. I shouted in pain, but it was gone a moment later when he released my arm. I looked down at it as my confused mind attempted to take in what had happened. I saw, burnt into my skin, a set of numbers.

"These are the coordinates to a facility in Europe. Go, and discover the truth about your Church."

"Fuck you," I replied, speaking my mind.

"Now, now, if you ever want to see Miranda again, I suggest you play along," he said, smiling down at me.

I felt my body lock up as his words registered in my mind.

"Yes, she's alive. I have plans for her too. After all, she's your Eve. It's time for me to depart, so goodbye, John. I'm sure it won't be long before I see you again."

I felt anger, but I had no time to respond before he disappeared, teleporting away again. He was gone, and so was my only way to get Miranda back. As soon as he left, the willpower that was keeping me conscious evaporated, and my vision turned black.

I don't know how much time passed, but I was suddenly being woken up by a male voice. Ben's voice.

"John? Wake up. Damn, what the hell happened to you?" he said, his voice worried.

I blinked as I looked up, my mind confused. The first thing I noticed was the pain that was flooding from every part of my body. For a moment, it completely consumed me, and I closed my eyes again and groaned through clenched teeth. I shifted in place, rubbing my back against the wall I was sitting against. It was an involuntary movement, and one that I severally regretted.

"Easy, now," I heard Ana say, her voice coming from my right. "You have some broken ribs, and your muscles are in horrible shape ... where's Miranda?"

The sound of her name made my eyes fly open. I sat up fully, ignoring the pain as best as I could. I tried to stand, but Ben put his hand on my shoulder to stop me.

I met his eyes and pleaded, "Help me."

He hesitated, then consented. He put my arm around his shoulders and hauled me to my feet.

"Ben, moving him will only make it worse," Ana said, but he didn't respond.

"Where?" he asked me, as if he knew what I needed to do.

I pointed forward, through the hole in the stone wall and into the sanctuary of the church. He helped me forward, but in my pitiful state he was practically carrying me. I led them to the spot were Miranda had vanished into the darkness, and I felt the ground. I stayed there on my hands and knees, my body shaking with frustration at myself for not being able to protect her.

"Is she ... Miranda's not dead, is she?" Ana asked, her voice worried.

I shook my head. "He took her ... but I'll get her back."

Movement from the corner of my eye caught my attention, and I looked up to see a dark-skinned beauty standing a few dozen paces away from us. Ana and Ben both straightened as they looked at Ari.

Ari spoke, her voice sharp and almost loud in the silent room, "Ben, Ana, Boss says to come in."

There were a few seconds of silence as I tried to groggily process what she was saying.

Ben kneeled next to me and looked me in the eye. "John, I need you to listen to me. Ana and I are with Deliverance. The Church is too powerful—too controlling. It's not—"

"Your spies?" I accused.

There was another moment of uncomfortable silence, then Ana crossed her arms.

"Yes, John, and we want you to come with us."

I managed to keep myself from scoffing. Join the group that killed my parents?

I shook my head, "no."

"John," Ari said in an almost cutesy tone, "come with us and I promise you'll be reunited with Miranda. I'll personally help you."

Her confidence made me hold my breath as I considered it, but after that brief moment I exhaled sharply.

"The Church has far more resources available than any resistance group could possibly have," I replied, my tone cold.

Ari narrowed her eyes at me, "as if that's your only reason."

I looked at her in surprise, wondering if she knew about my parents. Her gaze shifted away from me to Ben and Ana.

"Hurry up, you two. We can't waste time here."

Ben reached down and grasped my shoulder tightly. "Good luck to you, friend."

I met his eyes and gave him a nod. "You too."

I didn't look up to see them leave, but heard their footsteps hit the stone floor as they ran out of the church. My body couldn't support my weight anymore, and I slowly collapsed onto the stone floor. I closed my eyes as exhaustion claimed my mind. I had a single thought as I sank into unconsciousness; I will find you.

AFTERWORD

Hello, Taylor Stutesman here, author of The Genesis Project Part One. To start things off, I want to say thanks to you, humble (or not so humble) reader for reading my small work of creation. I hope my work has entertained you in some way or another. I'll even be so bold as to hope that you are eager to read Part Two of my story. To the ones who can't wait until they get their hands on Part Two, my website, TaylorStutesman.com, has more stories about John and Miranda that are available to read for free.

Some of you may recognize the saying *born too late to explore the world; born too early to explore the universe*. I felt this resonate with me from the first time I read it, and I'm sure I'm not alone. I was young when I realized this: I am an explorer—an adventurer. With nothing real available for me to explore, I decided to explore my own imagination. I submersed myself into fictional worlds and the adventures that took place in them, filling my need to discover, explore and live with them. I haven't changed much, as I still don't hesitate to obsess over an exciting universe that I haven't yet explored.

Something has changed, however. See, I used to throw myself into a story with reckless abandon. More specifically, it hardly mattered to me what medium a story was portrayed in. Novels, graphic novels, comics, manga, anime, movies, television series—even video games were fair game to me. A story was a story, and if it entertained me, I didn't care from where it came. My perspective was one of an average consumer. That is, until I found one.

A masterpiece found its way into my hands.

Some may claim that there's no such thing. That all stories are situational to the reader. That since a book impacts no two people the same way, there can be no such thing as a masterpiece—a story formed with such brilliance that other, normal books pale in comparison. When I hear such a claim, a feeling similar to pity wells up within me. Those who make such a silly claim can only do so because they have yet to discover such a powerful creation. A creation that was presented in the best possible medium, with impeccable pacing and brilliant storytelling.

Now, I am not claiming that a masterpiece is a story that everyone loves. In fact, a masterpiece may even be a book that has very negative reviews. It's the cold hard truth that the way a book impacts you as a reader will not impact anyone else the same way. I cannot argue against such a logically sound fact. However, the point of a masterpiece isn't to be accepted by every single reader unanimously. It's to be accepted by *you*. When someone finds a masterpiece, they do not think to themselves that everyone else also loves this book. That would be irrational and even borderline narcissistic. What they do think, however, is that everyone else *should* love this book. That is the true strength and value of a masterpiece—a reader truly loves it.

I write because I wish to create my own masterpiece. I wish to create a book that—even if it's only one single person—someone out there thinks is utterly brilliant. A book that immersed a reader into my world and filling them with a sense of adventure before returning them to reality. I will continue to create, ever-heading toward my goal of a masterpiece.

The Genesis Project Part One is my first step into the massive world of literature. It all started with a single thought when I was daydreaming one afternoon: *what if someone could see your entire memories just by meeting your eyes? What would they think, having seen all your pain, hardships, and struggles? Every sin and mistake, every act of forgiveness and kindness? Any emotional response stemming from such an experience would result in a pure feeling—one without any assumptions or lies. It would be a contempt so strong that no action would alleviate it. But ... just maybe, it would result in an unbreakable love. A unique love. A love without trust.*

And so, The Genesis Project was born. I've always been fascinated with supernatural elements and pushing the human body past its own limitations, so those naturally found their way into my world, and the rest I steadily built up from observing our own world and history.

I wish to extend a deep gratitude toward my family for supporting me in my pursuit to become an author, as well as my editor A., who spent more time working on my book than my pride as an author wishes to admit. Of course, I thank you again, my readers, for reading my creation and I hope to meet you again in Part Two or another one of my works.

Taylor James Stutesman

www.ingramcontent.com/pod-product-compliance
Lightning Source LLC
Chambersburg PA
CBHW020931020726
47495CB00002B/438